GLORY

GLORY

A NOVEL

NoViolet Bulawayo

VIKING

VIKING

An imprint of Penguin Random House LLC

penguinrandomhouse.com

LIBRARY OF CONGRESS CATALOGING-IN-PUBLICATION DATA

Names: Bulawayo, NoViolet, author.
Title: Glory : a novel / NoViolet Bulawayo.
Description: New York : Viking, 2022.
Identifiers: LCCN 2021027998 (print) | LCCN 2021027999 (ebook) |
ISBN 9780525561132 (hardcover) | ISBN 9780525561149 (ebook) |
ISBN 9780593492499 (international edition)
Subjects: LCSH: Revolutions—Fiction. |
Africa—Politics and government—Fiction. | LCGFT: Animal fiction.
Classification: LCC PR9390.9.B85 G55 2022 (print) |
LCC PR9390.9.B85 (ebook) | DDC 823.92—dc23
LC record available at https://lccn.loc.gov/2021027998
LC ebook record available at https://lccn.loc.gov/2021027999

Printed in the United States of America
1   3   5   7   9   10   8   6   4   2

DESIGNED BY MEIGHAN CAVANAUGH

For all Jidadas, everywhere

And in loving memory of
Comrade Pier Paolo Frassinelli

⧑ CONTENTS ⧐

GLORY

INDEPENDENCE

RALLY

When at last the Father of the Nation arrived for the Independence Day celebrations, no earlier than 3:28 in the afternoon, the citizens, congregated at the Jidada Square since morning, had had it with waiting; they could've razed the whole of Jidada with their frustration alone, that is, if Jidada had been any other place. But the land of farm animals wasn't any other place, it was Jidada, yes, tholukuthi Jidada with a -da and another -da, and just remembering this simple fact was enough to make most of the animals keep their feelings inside like intestines. The fierce sun, said by those who know about things to have been part of His Excellency's cheerleading squad by decree, had been up glaring since midmorning, doling out forceful rays fit for a ruler whose reign was nearing all of—not one, not two, not three, but four solid decades.

The Jidada Party regalia worn by most of the animals for the occasion—jackets and shirts and skirts and hats and scarves in various colors of the flag of the nation, many of the articles embossed with the face of His Excellency—trapped the sun's terrible heat and made the wait even more

unbearable. But not all of the animals were going to stand for the torturous wait—some indeed started to leave, grumbling about having work and things to do, about places to go to, about the leaders of other lands who arrived at things right on time like God's infallible machete. These disgruntled animals started as just a smattering—two pigs, a cat, and a goose—but the faction very quickly grew to a respectable mass, and, emboldened by both their number and the sound of their own voices, the dissidents headed for the exit.

At the gate the group found themselves face-to-face with the Jidada Defenders, tholukuthi the dogs appropriately armed with batons, ropes, clubs, tear-gas canisters, shields, guns, and such typical weapons of defending. It was a known fact all over the nation and beyond its borders that Jidada Defenders were by nature violent, morbid beasts, but it was especially the presence of the notorious Commander Jambanja, distinguishable in his signature white bandanna, that made the dissenters promptly turn around and retrace their steps, miserable tails between their legs.

ENTER THE FATHER OF THE NATION: THE RULER WHOSE REIGN IS LONGER THAN THE NINE LIFE SPANS OF A HUNDRED CATS. ALSO THE LONGEST-SERVING LEADER IN A CONTINENT OF LONG-SERVING LEADERS, AND INDEED IN THE WHOLE WIDE WORLD.

Now His Excellency's car wove its way through the throngs with the slowness of a hearse, and the animals fell over themselves like intoxicated frogs, hoping to catch a glimpse of the legendary Father of the Nation. At this point the sun, upon seeing arrive the leader who was decreed by God himself to rule and rule and keep ruling, a leader who'd in turn decreed the very sun to head his cheerleading squad, took a deep, deep breath and thoroughly blazed to impress. A select group of dignitaries—all mals, most of them old—accompanied His Excellency on hind legs. Accompa-

nying the accompanying dignitaries were decorated Defender leaders in military gear, colorful embroidered ropes cinched at the waist, caps pulled low, shiny constellations of medals glinting on solid chests, star insignias bouncing off the shoulders, white gloves on front paws; these were the generals, tholukuthi the true lynchpin of His Excellency's rule. Throughout the square, animals whipped out their phones and gadgets to take pictures and videos of the procession of power.

BEHOLD, HIM. YES, THOLUKUTHI HIM AND ONLY HIM HIMSELF. THE ANOINTED ONE. THE ONLY ONE. THE SUPREME ONE. THE MOST MAGNIFICENT ONE.

With the arrival of His Excellency, Jidada Square came alive. Tholukuthi the Father of the Nation had such an aura his mere presence in any space automatically rearranged the atoms in the air and shifted any given mood—no matter how hostile or dismal or foul—to a positive and electric one. Those who know about things say this quality had especially been a dozenfold more potent a long, long, long time ago, during the first years of His Excellency's rule when his appearance alone made unripe things instantly ripen to the point of rotting, cured the sick of whatever ailments molested them, turned rocks to mush, deactivated storms and heat waves, rerouted floods, wildfires, and plagues of locusts, cured fatal viruses before they even thought of attacking, made dry rivers overflow with water, yes, tholukuthi the Father of the Nation's appearance alone had once upon a time started engines, bent steel beams, and in separate documented occasions, made scores and scores of virgins pregnant so that long before he married the donkey and sired children with her, streams of His Excellency's blood were already flowing throughout Jidada. And now, here was the Father of the Nation lighting up Jidada Square by merely happening, by simply being there. The place ignited in flaming

applause, and even the animals who not too long before had been trying to leave were now part of the uproar, standing on hind legs and cheering His Excellency, not just with their voices and bodies, no, but also with their hearts and minds and souls. Cows mooed, cats meowed, sheep bleated, bulls bellowed, ducks quacked, donkeys brayed, goats bleated, horses neighed, pigs grunted, chickens clucked, peacocks screamed, and geese cackled—the cacophony reaching deafening levels as the entourage of power came to a final stop in front of a raised platform.

THE POOR AND THE RICH DO NOT PLAY TOGETHER

Under a sprawling white tent sat the Seat of Power Inner Circle of the Jidada Party, which of course was the ruling party, otherwise known as the Party of Power, of which His Excellency was president. With them were some of His Excellency's family members, friends, and honored guests. Tholukuthi the group of elites were, in all honesty and jealous down, a magnificent sight—the most exquisite cloth, expensive jewelry, and precious accessories of adornment, together with beautiful, well-groomed, and healthy bodies, told of wealth and good living. These animals represented some of Jidada's Chosen Ones, and were indeed proof of the Father of the Nation's benevolence, for most of them had been made rich by His Excellency, if not directly, then through some kind of connection to him. They were proud recipients of gifts of land, businesses, tenders, government loans that didn't need repaying, inheritors of confiscated farms, grantees of mines, industries, and all kinds of riches.

With not much to occupy them being that the celebrations hadn't started, the miserable animals in the sun feasted on the Chosen with coveting eyes, and at moments actually forgot the heat cooking their bodies, the hunger gnawing at their bellies, the thirst parching their throats, yes, tholukuthi besotted with the pretty picture of their shaded betters sitting

in comfortable chairs and sipping cold beverages. The hot, salivating animals lapped at the sight with their eyes like it were a cool glass of honey-wine, and when they licked their dry, cracked lips, they were pleasantly surprised to taste faint traces of actual sweetness.

THOLUKUTHI HUH???

The car doors opened to a bloodred carpet, and the Father of the Nation emerged. As if on cue, Jidada Square gave a collective gasp. Tholukuthi Jidada Square gave a collective gasp because they'd seen emerge from the car a long horse so frail it looked like the slightest breath of breeze would send him teetering and crashing unto earth. It was a good thing then that it was just hot and there was no breeze. The animals watched agape as the Father of the Nation—older now than the last time they'd seen him, when he'd in fact been older than the last time they'd seen him prior to that—walked toward the platform, one careful, careful, foot after the other, his thin body weighted down by a huge green shirt on which were numerous black-and-white prints of his own face, though a much younger and handsome version. The Old Horse crawled and crawled on the very same hooves with which he'd once upon a time galloped up and down the length and breadth of Jidada at the speed of lightning. When he finally got to the platform, after what felt to the animals in the sun like it were two and a half years later, he leaned on a stand for support, hung his oblong head, and stood swishing his tail as if he were counting the minutes with it.

"What is this place? Who are all these animals? And why are they looking at me like maybe they know me?" the Old Horse said to no one in particular.

"Ah-ah, but what kind of question is that, Your Excellency?! They're your subjects ka, every one of them! Don't you know you rule this land, all of this Jidada, and that what your subjects want is to hear you speak?

Today is Independence Day, Baba; we're here all of us celebrating our freedom, the freedom you sacrificed your life for in the long War of Liberation that you your very self pioneered and prosecuted to its victorious end those many years ago, which means, in essence, we're really here to celebrate you!" the donkey gushed with great glee. She reached to adjust the horse's shirt and smooth out his pitch-black but thinning mane.

Tholukuthi the donkey wasn't just any regular jenny but the wife of His Excellency, which may have been implied by how she looked and moved and spoke and generally carried herself with the unquestionable swagger of power. The Old Horse let her lead him to his seat. The animals closest to the pair promptly got up to make way—some straightened His Excellency's chair, some kissed his face, some fondled his tail, some caressed his ass, some adjusted his clothing, and some swatted flies that were not there.

"What I really want is a nap," the Old Horse said, carefully putting himself down like his backside was made of expensive porcelain. The Father of the Nation wasn't lying. He was at an age when what was most important to him was to be left alone, and besides, those who know about things said the state of affairs inside his head wasn't unlike a tumultuous country without a clear leader.

THOLUKUTHI AHA!

It happened that around the perimeter of the platform were mounted poles bearing the flag of the nation. The brilliant colors of black-red-green-yellow and white caught the eye of the Old Horse. He concentrated on the flags until the colors magically pulled him out of the mist clogging his head. Tholukuthi memory began to return to him. He recognized the flag; it flew in his heart and head and dreams. He didn't at that moment understand what the colors themselves meant, but they were indeed supposed to stand for something, that much he was very sure of. He focused

on them and thought and thought—could it be the white perhaps stood for the teeth of his ferocious dogs, the Defenders? And the red for the blood they could very easily spill? "Perhaps," he said to himself, and his eyes moved on.

He recognized the tall, beautiful donkey by his side—smelling like fresh flowers and decked out in bright colors and flashy jewelry; it was Marvelous, Jidada's First Femal herself, otherwise called Sweet Mother for being his wife and for being sweet, and now generally referred to as Dr. Sweet Mother after earning her famous PhD. He saw too his beloved friends and family, and their presence filled him with joy. He also recognized his Comrades, and swiveled his head this way, that way, scrutinizing them to make sure those who were supposed to be there were there. Tholukuthi they were. Some nodded. Some waved. Some pumped their limbs in the Party of Power salute.

Next, the Old Horse surveyed the packed throngs in the square. They weren't just his subjects, they were bona fide supporters who'd stood with him and by him over the decades, with many of them going as far back as during the struggle for Jidada's Independence. They'd been loyal then and had stayed loyal and were still loyal and would always and forever be loyal. They died loyal and took that loyalty to the grave so that even their ghosts, too, were loyal. They left behind offspring who were born already loyal. The Father of the Nation then caught a glimpse of himself on a mirrored panel, and he didn't start in confusion because he at that moment happened to know exactly who he was and without needing Dr. Sweet Mother to remind him whatsoever. Now—fully in charge of his memory, he sat back and stretched his limbs in front of him and nodded to the sun directly overhead. He adjusted his glasses, made himself comfortable, and tholukuthi, with the seasoned serenity of a very old baby, promptly fell asleep.

LAND OF MILK AND HONEY

He dreamt of the days of glory when Jidada was such an earthly paradise animals left their own miserable lands and flocked to it in search of a better life, found it, and not only just found it, no, but found it in utter abundance and sent word back for kin and friends to come and see it for themselves—this promised land, this stunning Eldorado called Jidada, a proper jewel of Africa, yes, tholukuthi a land not only indescribably wealthy but so peaceful they could've made it up. His Excellency also saw himself in his dream as he'd been back then—beautiful and brimming with unquestioned majesty, a horse that stepped on the ground and the earth agreed and the heavens above agreed and even hell itself also agreed because how could it disagree? Tholukuthi lost now in Jidada's past glory, the Old Horse nestled deeper in his seat and began to snore a sonorous tune that the Comrades around him identified as Jidada's old revolutionary anthem from the Liberation War days.

DEFENDERS, DEFENDERS, DEFENDERS

Being that His Excellency was arrived, the Jidada Army Band started playing. Blood-stirring music accompanied the procession as it poured onto the main part of the square. The Jidada army, just like the rest of the security forces, was made up entirely of dogs. And now, dogs, dogs, dogs, and more dogs marched toward the tent, shimmering black boots lifting and landing with stunning synchronicity. Tholukuthi there were pure breeds and mixed breeds and cross breeds and mysterious breeds of no certain classification. Tholukuthi there were dogs in green tunics, dogs in khaki tunics, dogs in blue tunics. Tholukuthi there were dogs playing musical instruments, dogs flying the flag of Jidada, dogs flying the military flags, and dogs toting long, glinting guns.

It is often easy to forget the beauty and grace of a dog—a creature that can rip flesh into chunks, spill blood out of sheer impulse, crush bone like it were fragile China, hump anything from a human leg to a car tire to a tree trunk to a sofa, all without a single grain of shame, shit all over the place as if it excretes unadulterated gold, be faithful to its master even if that master were a known brute, murderer, sorcerer, tyrant, or devil, viciously attack without apparent provocation, devour human excrement no matter how well fed it is. But at that moment in Jidada Square on the occasion of the nation's Independence celebration, tholukuthi the dogs were simply magnificent. You wouldn't have known they were in fact sweating and drowning in the hot, heavy tunics that also covered tattered underwear that barely held together what needed holding. You wouldn't have known the soles of their boots were worn, or that the majority of them were actually famished being that they hadn't been paid their salaries for at least the previous three months.

I WILL RAISE UP FOR THEM A PROPHET LIKE YOU AMONG THEIR BROTHERS. AND I WILL PUT MY WORDS IN HIS MOUTH, AND HE SHALL SPEAK TO THEM ALL THAT I COMMAND HIM.

Much later, after the dogs had concluded their display and marched off the field, and after speeches from the Minister of the Revolution, the Minister of Corruption, the Minister of Order, the Minister of Things, the Minister of Nothing, the Minister of Propaganda, the Minister of Homophobic Affairs, the Minister of Disinformation, and the Minister of Looting, and after performances by various entertainers, the donkey nudged His Excellency awake. The Father of the Nation opened his eyes and woke from his dream of Jidada's days of glory but found he couldn't at all remember it. He was struggling with his memory thus when his eyes settled on a fancy-looking pig hinding to the platform with the stride of an ostrich. The

Old Horse didn't recognize him and wondered who he was. He fell asleep again, analyzing the pig's long legs.

The long, lean pig was none other than the one and only Prophet Dr. O. G. Moses, founding leader of the famed Soldiers of Christ Prophetic Church of Churches. Most things in Jidada naturally included a prayer—that's how come the charismatic Prophet, who was also Dr. Sweet Mother's spiritual adviser, was on the program. Those who know about things said the pig's church was the top evangelical sect in Jidada and boasted the largest following of congregants, not just in the nation but in the whole entire region—yes, tholukuthi a congregation that, according to those who know about things, wasn't only inspired by the word of God but also by desperation, disillusionment, idiocy, frustration, and a search for a lifeline—something, anything, to help the animals cope with the business of surviving a life that was daily becoming unlivable as Jidada's economy struggled.

Prophet Dr. O. G. Moses did indeed provide that something, that anything—through his gospel of hope and prosperity, through his famous line of miracle products that included anointing oils, and anointing water, anointing purses, anointing wallets, anointing underwear, anointing bricks, tholukuthi through prayer, through his rumored awesome power to cast out the demon of poverty, through his blessed healing touch. By the sheer force that was Jehovah-Jireh alone, the Prophet promised to transform the miserable lives of the government-forsaken Jidadans, and so the desperate masses flocked to the Soldiers of Christ Prophetic Church of Churches like flies to dung. When those who know about things said the Prophet's followers loved the pig to hell and back, tholukuthi they meant the Prophet's followers loved the pig to hell and back. As it is he'd attended the celebrations in a private jet bought by the tithes from his flock so that you may have been forgiven to think his was a church full

of the wealthy in a land of gold-paved streets and homes packed with diamond-dust-speckled toilet paper.

GOD SPEAKS

Prophet Dr. O. G. Moses leaned into the microphone and cleared his throat. Given his popularity, it was the case that any gathering on Jidada soil was bound to have a significant number of his followers in attendance, so that it was no surprise the throngs went berserk on seeing him. They were no longer patriots of the nation at a patriotic celebration, no, but believers in the redeeming and healing presence of God's beloved son. The pig was certainly used to applause, but he'd never heard anything like the applause of that moment outside of his church; tholukuthi it surpassed the applause His Excellency himself had received not too long before. It rang and rang and would have continued had he not held up a white hanky for pause.

"Before I pray, may I take this golden opportunity to thank the most God-fearing femal I know, our very own Dr. Sweet Mother, for the honor of leading this great nation of ours in prayer on such a momentous occasion. I've said it before, and I'll say it again: Good leaders are not born. Good leaders are not made. Good leaders, like the Father of the Nation, like our honorable First Femal and Dr. Sweet Mother—come from none other than God himself. Who also tells us in his very own words in Romans thirteen, verse one, and I need you to hear me properly O Precious Jidadans; God, my Father, says: Let everyone be subject to the governing authorities, for there is no authority except that which God has established. The authorities that exist have been established by God. Consequently, whoever rebels against the authority is rebelling against what God has instituted, and those who do so will bring judgment on themselves. For rulers hold no terror for those who do right, but for those who do wrong. Do you want to be free

from fear of the one in authority? Then do what is right and you will be commended. For the one in authority is God's servant for your good. But if you do wrong, be afraid, for rulers do not bear the sword for no reason. They are God's servants, agents of wrath to bring punishment on the wrong-doer. Therefore, it is necessary to submit to the authorities, not only because of possible punishment but also as a matter of conscience. And now, with that precious word, most beloved Jidada, let us please bow our heads in Jesus's name and thank the Almighty for the matchless gift of freedom for which we're here gathered today, for the Liberators who delivered us from the colonizing devils, as well as for our God-given leaders who indeed make sure that we continue to live free every day and for all time. Let us pray!"

THE UNDYING ONE

Tholukuthi at the very point the Prophet concluded his prayer with an Amen, the Old Horse, awake again, and at the instruction of Dr. Sweet Mother, stood and carefully ambled to the podium. He was still trying to remember the dream but to no avail.

"Forward with the Party of Power!" His Excellency said.

"Forward!!!" the animals yelled.

"Forward with winning elections!"

"Forward!!!"

"Forward with the one-party state!"

"Forward!!!"

"Forward with Dr. Sweet Mother!"

"Forward!!!"

"Down with the Opposition!"

"Down!!!"

"Down with the West!"

"Down!!!"

"To begin with, I know there are some among you who are thoroughly shocked once again to see me and as such may be wondering what I'm doing up here because as you all heard, I died once more last week!" His Excellency tilted his head skyward, swished his tail at the sun, and roared with laughter. Tholukuthi the sun twerked in the lewdest fashion and sent out such an epic blaze a few animals passed out at different points in the stadium while a hen, thoroughly overwhelmed by the heat, laid a fried egg. The throng took their leader's cue and broke into laughter; hooves and paws and feet went up in the air, flags were waved, and His Excellency's totem, along with screams of "Long live!!!," was sung.

The very week before, Jidada's social media had been abuzz with the trending rumor the Old Horse had died of a heart attack at a hospital in Dubai. It certainly wasn't the first of its kind; as His Excellency's age progressed with the passing seasons, Jidada lived with the periodic news of his death—which would turn out to be what the Inner Circle called fake news, of course. The latest rumor, however, was certainly the first to be stoked to the extent that it started to sound like a truth.

"As you know, I have indeed died many times. That's where I have beaten Christ. Christ died once, and resurrected just once. But me I have died and resurrected and I don't know how many times I will die and resurrect but I know I will keep resurrecting and resurrecting and resurrecting—in fact, I promise you my dearly beloved Jidadans that I'll attend each and every one of your funerals because you will all die and leave me here ruling in this beautiful land of the Fathers!" the Old Horse said, to more applause. He paused and reveled in it.

PORTRAIT OF A PROTEST: THE SISTERS OF THE DISAPPEARED

Those who were there said just as the Father of the Nation was feeling his way into his speech, a squad of about twelve stark-naked femals stormed

the podium, seemingly from nowhere. Tholukuthi everywhere udders and breasts and teats and thighs and bellies and backsides and undertails and hips and flanks, everywhere unsightly pubic hairs, everywhere unmentionable femal parts of all sorts of shapes and sizes. And just as Jidada Square, caught off guard by this never-been-seen curse, taboo of unbridled femal nudity, gaped in disbelief, wondering if what they were seeing was indeed what they were seeing, two donkeys raised up a white banner that said, in letters the color of bright blood: "Sisters of the Disappeared." The rest of the squad carried placards bearing photographs and names—according to those who know about things—of Jidadans who'd disappeared throughout the Father of the Nation and the Seat of Power's reign.

The naked femals hinded up and down the stage, straight-backed, tholukuthi faces hard and defiant, tholukuthi eyes ablaze, tholukuthi throats roaring in hot, belligerent voices: "Bring back Jidada's Disappeared! Bring back Jidada's Disappeared! Bring back Jidada's Disappeared!" Despite their obvious discomfort over femal nudity, the animals in the square heard the roaring right in their intestines, where lived the memories of disappeared friends and relatives or relatives of friends and also known and unknown Jidadans they'd read about in newspapers and on social media, yes, tholukuthi heard the chants deep in their hearts, where also lived the unanswered prayers, the bleeding wounds, the nightmares, the ceaseless anguish, the questions over loved ones, over known and unknown Jidadans who'd dared dissent against the Seat of Power only to vanish like smoke, never to be seen again. So that there were some among the animals in the square who in fact found themselves also chanting, "Bring Back Jidada's Disappeared! Bring back Jidada's Disappeared! Bring back Jidada's Disappeared!"—but softly, softly, ever so softly so the sound would not leave their teeth, because their fear was greater than their voices.

Tholukuthi the Sisters of the Disappeared did not stop roaring even as the Defenders, having recovered from their momentary confusion in the face of taboo, having remembered they were in fact famed dogs with a Revolution to defend, accordingly pounced with batons and teeth and whips and became Defenders again. And the Sisters of the Disappeared did not stop roaring even as they felt the mad dance of batons and whips and teeth on their flesh. And the Sisters of the Disappeared did not stop roaring even as they were dragged off the stage. And the Sisters of the Disappeared did not stop roaring even as they were crammed into waiting jeeps and carted off to prison.

A PROPER DISGRACE

"My children, my dear children of the nation. I, like every single one of you, am thoroughly disappointed by the utter, utter shame that just happened on this respected stage! There is no other word for it, even that sun over there didn't know where to look!" the Father of the Nation said, bobbing his head at the sun. And the sun, pleased to be singled out yet again, smiled with all her thousand teeth.

"It is a disgrace any day, but is made doubly so on this honorable occasion of the celebration of our Independence. It is an affront to me, and it is an insult to the Liberators, some of whom, as we all know, paid with their dear and precious lives for the very freedom those shameless femals just disrespected with their ugly nakedness," the Old Horse said. The animals in the tent applauded their agreement.

"And to that end, I wish to remind all and any femals with ears that a true Jidadan femal, the kind of femal we love and honor and celebrate, is one who respects herself and respects her body. Which is why the Bible even tells us the body is a temple. I don't know about you, but it definitely didn't look to me like temples on this stage just a moment ago, it looked

like some public toilets!" the Father of the Nation said, to laughter and whistles.

"But do not ever be fooled, my dear children, to think that those shameless, ugly femals you just saw come alone. They are being used, they are part and parcel of the unending tactics by the West whose main agenda, as I'm always telling you, is to destabilize us by, among other things, attacking our core values, beliefs, lifestyles, our culture. But of course you and I know that is not all. That very West, together with the Opposition, wish to see me gone, they want me removed in an illegal regime change!" Tholukuthi the square roared.

"But I'm not going anywhere! Because me, I was Jidada's leader almost forty years ago, and I was Jidada's leader thirty years ago, and twenty years ago, and ten years ago! Because I was Jidada's leader yesterday, and I am Jidada's leader today, and I will be Jidada's leader when?" the Father of the Nation invited, ears now cocked at the square.

"Tomorrow and Forever!!!" Jidada Square thundered in celebration of the Old Horse's endless rule. Animals stomped their hooves and feet until they couldn't see themselves from the dust. Animals leapt in the air. Animals slapped and embraced each other. Animals butted butts. Animals who could fly flew into the air. Animals reared. Animals ululated. Animals whistled. Animals cried and yelled and sang. And the Old Horse felt himself born again in the heart of the tumult, yes, tholukuthi felt like he'd felt on the day of his very first inauguration those many, many, many, many, many years ago.

THE ANTI-IMPERIAL CRUSADER

"Yes, that is the situation, my dear children of the nation. And not only that, but only God, who appointed me, can remove me, and not the West, who have no moral authority whatsoever to open their mouths to say a

regime change is needed in Jidada! Because what, because who are they under the two-cents shade of a blade of grass? Where, and who would they be right now had they not committed the odious sin of colonizing us? What would that USA be without the stolen land it now has the audacity to cordon off with a violent border? What, indeed, would that country be without the looted sons and daughters of Africa it now keeps in abject poverty when they themselves birthed the country's wealth? And who would the West be without Africa's resources? Africa's gold? Africa's diamonds? Africa's platinum? Africa's copper? Africa's tin? Africa's oil? Africa's ivory? Africa's rubber? Africa's timber? Africa's cocoa? Africa's tea? Africa's coffee? Africa's sugar? Africa's tobacco? Without Africa's looted artifacts in their museums? Do you know, my dear children, that up to now, decades after their epic looting, plundering, raping, kidnapping, killing, and oppressing spree, Britain is still yet to bring back the head of Mbuya Nehanda? Yes, after they sentenced the spirit medium of our ancestor, Mbuya Nehanda Nyakasikana—who as you know is the mother of Jidada's Liberation struggle—after they sentenced her to death by hanging, as if that was not enough, they decapitated her sacred head and sent it to that Britain as a trophy for the crown! And that is where it still remains along with about two dozen heads of other Jidada resistance fighters! Maybe the Queen can tell us what she is doing with our incarcerated dead because I myself cannot tell you since I do not know. But what I can tell you is that before that West can dictate to us about democracy and change, it must first bring back every single one of our looted things. I want them back! I need them back! Africa wants and needs them back! Every! Single! One! Bring back!" the Father of the Nation shrieked with such a fire the stadium ignited in a blazing chorus of: "Bring back! Bring back! Bring Back!"

Yes, tholukuthi the children of the nation, indeed reminded of the sins of their former oppressors, chanted and filled the square with all sorts of

angers, including those inherited from ancestors who'd lived through the terrible time. And the Father of the Nation, in his signature fashion, accordingly and incisively went on to denounce the West for neocolonialism, for capitalism, for racism, for economic sanctions, for ugly trade practices, for aid addiction, for the shutting down of factories and businesses in Jidada, for the absence of jobs, for the poor performance of farms, for the brain drain, for the homosexuals, for the power cuts and water cuts, for the miserable state of Jidada's public schools and government hospitals and bridges and public toilets and public libraries, for the loose morals among the youth, for the potholes on the roads and the unpicked trash on the streets, for the black market, for the fluctuating crime rates, for the atrocious pass rate in national examinations, for the defeat of the Jidada national soccer team at the recent continental finals, for the drought, for the strange phenomenon of married men having second families on the side called small houses, for the rise in sorcery, for the dearth of production of exciting works by local poets and writers.

THE LIBERATOR

"Still, today, as you all know, is a very important day, so important that I cannot think of any other day that is more important, except maybe my birthday, which, for those who don't know, is the day that I happened, and without it we would not otherwise be here celebrating because I would not have been there to lead the Liberation struggle so that Jidada would never be a colony again!" the Father of the Nation said, punching the air with all his might when he said "again!"

At that precise moment the forgotten dream came to him as clear as air, and he was so excited he let go of the platform and did what his doctors abroad didn't recommend he do anymore, which was to stand on his hind legs. The Jidada of the days of glory was suddenly alive and real

in his head so that he could actually smell it, taste its thick milk and rich honey on his tongue.

"My dear, my most faithful Jidadans, no matter what our devious enemies—from the Opposition to the West to these shameless femals you just saw with your own eyes—may wish upon us, I am very pleased and honored to say these indeed are the days of glory, days in which we are fully in charge of our destiny. For don't we own every inch of this rich land? Are we not enjoying the precious fruits, both on and underneath, this blessed piece of earth? Are we not living in prosperity? Are we not the envy of less fortunate nations? Is anyone among you hungry? Or unfree? Or suffering? Or dissatisfied? Or poor? Or oppressed? Are we not set to leave future generations the kind of glowing legacy to make them stand tall among the nations of the world?" The quadruped of the animals in the sun, upon hearing these words, had unhinded and now stood on all fours, pondering in the dizzying heat.

THOLUKUTHI MULLING A LEGACY

—We love the Father of the Nation, nobody loves him like we do, it's just in our blood! And is there a greater legacy than love?—nossir, there's none! But I'll say the one thing that'd make me love him even better would be a job. Just a small job is okay, it doesn't need to be a big thing at all because who am I to want big things? That way I can pay for the one room I'm renting and maybe afford proper clothes instead of these rags. Buy good food for my children every once in a while so they too can know just a little bit of dignity—not a whole lot. Maybe also send them to school. Small, basic things like that.

—Ha—no, it's an excellent legacy 100 percent! It's almost hard to explain, given where this country's coming from, the sheer joy of seeing

a Black president just ruling-ruling-ruling, along with a whole entire Black government! As opposed to what, as opposed to seeing a racist colonial government like before Independence. Only thing is I wish they could also make the country work exactly like when those racists were running things! Then ha, I'm telling you, they figure that out, then we'd have a fierce legacy no questions asked, 100 percent!

—Loyalty is legacy if I must say, and that's the truth itself. Today some idiots will actually laugh at you for wearing the Father of the Nation's regalia, taunt you, saying, All these years of Independence, what have you to show for it besides the regalia, isn't it time for real Change? Trying to manipulate an animal into switching sides. And I just beat my wings and say, Tsk-tsk-tsk! Because, have you woken up one day and looked at your parent and said, You're old, you're useless, you're this and that and so I'm getting another parent, it's time for Change? No, you don't! Never! It's the Father of the Nation for Life! Party of Power for Life!

—Well, me myself I don't mind that Dr. Sweet Mother actually kicked us off our land to make way for her farm! I really don't mind at all, not a bit, kana, ngitsho, I mean it made us homeless, but otherwise where was she going to farm? In the air? On a tree? Inside her mansion? And futhi it's not at all like a white colonizer kicking you off your land! Which, that one is a whole 'nother matter for sure, a matter of war, which is exactly what we did to liberate our land. But why on earth would I ever think to war against Dr. Sweet Mother?

—Even the dung beetles will tell you there is no Father of the Nation, not a single one, in this whole entire Africa, with the balls to tell the West to hump off, to tell the West what time it is like our very own and only

him himself. No one else can claim that for a legacy. And which is exactly why we need him here ruling. Because who will tell them otherwise?

—Jidada is actually one of the best-educated nations in Africa! That's a proper legacy! Everyone, everywhere, they know it. And our constitution is also one of the best in the world. I don't care what haters say, talking about we're not even following our own constitution, at least it's our constitution we're not following. And the day we actually decide to follow it, everyone will see why they call it one of the best in the world. This is all legacy!

—Who'll ever forget that time we kicked white farmers off our land? Ha! I feel like levitating just thinking about it. We showed them who Africa really belongs to! You didn't come with land on a ship when you colonized us and you have the audacity to call yourself a farmer kukuru—kukuru! Ha! And now we have our land back. Well, when I say "we," I don't necessarily include me myself per se, since I persomally don't own any land. It's mostly those ones under that tent over there, but they're still Black like me, so, there's that. Of course the enemies of the regime will come with their propaganda, talking about the Chosen don't actually know how to farm that land, talking about the agriculture sector and therefore the economy has suffered from the land seizures. But so what, when the big picture is that Blacks have the land?! And that's a legacy! Never a colony again!

—They don't call us the jewel of Africa for nothing, no ma'am. What is it we don't have in this Jidada? Land, minerals, water, good climate, everything. And why are the Chinese and these multinational companies swarming all over this country like flies?! It's because they know a

jewel when they see it! Don't even be fooled by how things may appear right now——I mean the terrible roads that kill people, the potholes, the broken sewer systems, the decrepit hospitals, the decrepit schools, the decrepit industrial sector, the decrepit rail system, or should I say a generally decrepit infrastructure. Then of course there's the poor standard of living, the millions who've crossed and still cross borders in search of better, the misery and such things that may look depressing at first glance, that'll make you think you're maybe looking at a ruin. All these things happen to countries, it's a fact of countryness, but rest assured we were in top form once. Plus, the point is not to judge a book by its cover. Because what remains is that Jidada is still a jewel, Africa's jewel. And that right there is the Father of the Nation's God-given legacy, reigning over a real gem. And moreover, he liberated and has protected that jewel so that Jidada will never be a colony again!

A RALLYING CALL

"And the answer to my very own question, my dear children, is that we are on track to leave an illustrious legacy to coming generations. Otherwise, if that legacy were anything less, do you know what it means?" His Excellency paused to keenly observe the crowds.

"It means the revolution has been betrayed! It means there's need for another war of Independence, yes, a new Liberation War, because that's what your ancestors would have done and would want you to do because who is it that said, Every generation must discover its mission and fulfill it or betray it!?" The Old Horse searched the square for an answer. And then, "Aha! I know who said it, I think that was me myself who said it that's why I'm remembering it, and so, having said that whenever I did, today I will add that I, as your leader, will not stand in your way or stop

you from fulfilling your mission! You have my blessing! And I'll tell you all right now that the one thing, if I've learned one useful thing in ruling and ruling and ruling, is that nowhere else does the power of any regime, no matter how tyrannical, lie than in the fear of the multitudes! I promise you once the governed lose their fear, then it's absolutely game over for the regime! If you want to see for yourself, go and try it, not tomorrow, but right now, and then come and thank me! Down with fear!" the Old Horse sloganeered, his eyes blazing with the unmistakable fire of resistance.

The Seat of Power and Chosen exchanged disconcerted looks, asking themselves if what they were hearing was indeed what they were hearing. Tholukuthi the deep silence that had by now descended on the square was so total, so true, you could pick it like a fat tick. As for the animals in the sun, they fidgeted and looked at each other in disbelief. It was, of course, now very common for the Old Horse to misspeak. But sometimes these misspeaks, like at this very moment, were in fact honest, astute insights, tholukuthi insights that were shared by the majority of the Jidadans though of course they'd never dream of saying so, or agreeing with them in public.

About then the vice president, Tuvius Delight Shasha, better known to all Jidadans by Tuvy, for short, began applauding, an act that was soon followed by the whole tent and picked up by the rest of the animals, reluctantly at first, because they didn't seem to understand why they were applauding given the nature of the Old Horse's controversial, even dangerous, message.

"What the hell happened to his goddamn speech? Didn't somebody write a speech for His Excellency?" the vice president growled with contempt, pivoting his bus of a head to face the cow seated directly behind him.

"We did, Comrade Vice President, sir. But you know how His Excellency likes to speak from his own head, sir," the cow said.

"But apparently that head's not working properly today, is it?! This can't keep happening, Comrade. Somebody get him off the damn stand before he says things we'll regret!" A sheep and turkey promptly rose and scrambled for the podium. But the donkey, used to her husband's speech gymnastics, was already maneuvering him away.

COMRADE VICE PRESIDENT SPEAKS

Tuvius Delight Shasha was an old horse, though not as old as the Father of the Nation; in fact, some would insist that compared to His Excellency, tholukuthi he was a youngster. Strong and solid, he picked his way toward the stage with the lumbering movements of a hippo. He wore a red coat despite the boiling weather, decorated, like the rest of his attire, with prints of His Excellency's face. At the podium, he stood and swished his tail and carefully considered the best way to pick up where his superior had left off.

Having to follow right after a speaker as natural and talented as the Old Horse, and while the smoke of his poetic eloquence was still wafting in the air, didn't promise to make Tuvy's job easy. But the vice president braved it. He reminded himself he'd fought and spilled real blood in Jidada's Liberation War that was eventually won, a mere stage wasn't going to bring him to his knees.

"Forward with Jidada, Comrades!" the vice president began, raising a hoof. He took care to speak in the self-deprecating tone he never failed to employ, especially in the presence of the First Femal.

"Forward!" the square rang.

As fitting of the occasion, and because the Party of Power had made it an important and ever relevant topic in Jidada, the vice president spoke of the Liberation War and thanked the War Veterans, yessir, the brave and

selfless animals who'd taken up arms to liberate the nation those many years ago, which of course couldn't be said of everyone in Jidada. He spoke of the peace and freedom enjoyed by all, and thanked the dogs of the nation for vigilantly maintaining that precious peace and freedom. And because he had no prepared speech and was generally nervous about speaking English without reading from a paper, he quickly wrapped up, aware, and quite rightly, that the crowds were uninspired by his delivery, that they were, even then, comparing him to the Father of the Nation.

THE LIVING ICON

"And lastly, we are here in Jidada as Jidada because of the leadership and wisdom and dedication of our one and only Founding Father, His Excellency, who was gifted to us by none other than God as the good Prophet said with his own mouth, who as you all know and must each one of you agree, has for close to four decades now, which is also close to half a century, ruled Jidada with a hoof of iron and a heart of love and brains of a thousand geniuses and the vision of God himself, our Liberator and Ruler who has shepherded us all with steadfastness and compassion and fearlessness and brilliance and justice and unwavering opposition to the Opposition, who, we must never, ever, ever forget, are indeed the shameful and criminal agents of regime change, along with their allies, the West. Our future is brighter than the brightest mortar fire, as well as secure because of our Founding Father's exemplary and visionary leadership and resistance, and we very much look forward to that future and we can't wait to get there. We thank him for dedicating his life to this great land, and we wish for him more years filled with all the blessings every day and any day. Onward with Jidada with a -da and another -da, Comrades! Thank you!"

THOLUKUTHI NO SMOKE WITHOUT FIRE

Tuvy strutted back to his seat a happy horse, swishing his tail with the due pomposity of a hero who'd just saved the day. On his way he saluted His Excellency, who promptly turned away, but not fast enough for Tuvy to miss the look on the Old Horse's face. The confounded vice president dizzied at the pointed rebuff. Next to His Excellency, Dr. Sweet Mother looked at him with a face like a baboon's behind, while a couple of seats from the donkey, General Judas Goodness Reza smiled sympathetically. And Tuvius, confused, wounded, sank to his seat. He ate his liver—and not for the first time—contemplating the mystifying rift between himself and the Father of the Nation, a rift that seemed to widen with each new encounter.

It would've been one thing had he just been dealing with the Old Horse alone—he'd been managing him all these years, dating back to the war days. But now, and to complicate matters, there was the damned donkey in the picture, a wild animal, a proper itchtail with no morals whatsoever, and of course, her little faction of minions, the pretentious and delusional so-called Future Circle, who fancied themselves the upcoming leaders of the Seat of Power, who thought their pointless pieces of paper from useless universities, along with far-fetched ramblings and outlandish ideas, counted as party credentials, which of course they didn't, and would never ever count in a million years. Because the Jidada Party wasn't just any other party; it was a Party of Power, a Revolutionary Party, and even the sticks and stones knew that the only credential that'd ever matter for and to the party was the gun. Not a stupid pen, not a useless book, not a miserable education certificate, not any high-sounding queer theories, none of it but the gun, and only the gun, and just the gun, and always the gun, and forever the gun, yessir, the gun, gun, gun, gun, gun. Tholukuthi the gun. And number two—the donkey and her useless followers hadn't fought in the Liberation

War, hadn't in fact done anything for Jidada in the struggle, not even serve the Liberators drinking water, and this made them nobodies, ciphers, absolute nonentities.

DO NOT SAY, "I AM ONLY A CHILD." FOR TO EVERYONE I SEND YOU, YOU MUST GO, AND ALL THAT I COMMAND YOU, YOU MUST SPEAK.

And now, Dr. Sweet Mother took her place on the podium and stood looking into the throngs. Tuvy watched the donkey grab the mic as if she meant to chomp it with her pebble teeth, and imagined himself shoving it down her giraffe throat before giving her a kick to send her flying to the other end of the stadium.

"First of all I cannot, in all good conscience, stand here as a femal, and as your Mother, and as Dr. Sweet Mother, and as a Christian, and not address the depravity we just saw from the so-called Sisters of the Disappeared on such a respectable occasion. There is of course the obvious issue of who really wants to see all those jiggly, ugly bodies with sagging teats and white and gray pubes in this broad daylight?!" the donkey began, punctuating her opening statement with uproarious laughter that was spontaneously picked up by the rest of the square, tholukuthi the sharp howls of mals rising the loudest.

"So I really must apologize to the Father of the Nation and all the Liberators, the mal elders, the honorable Prophet, our invited dignitaries and guests for what they had to unfortunately witness, though when you have plentiful democracy like we do here in Jidada, sometimes it happens that it gets to the heads of animals as you all saw. And to these pitiful so-called Sisters of the Disappeared, I would like to say, first of all, what wretched backsides did you come out of so that you have the morals of hyenas?! Don't you know we have innocent young ones in this audience?! What

lesson are you trying to teach them?! If you have no interest in respecting your bodies like the Father of the Nation said, then just go to a brothel and be proper itchtails and leave us alone!" the donkey said, igniting a raucous round of mocking laughter. Tholukuthi the First Femal was getting into proper form; she knew her audience, and her audience knew her.

"Now, and this is to be honest—you all know I'm all about telling it like it is. Surely isn't this the kind of behavior that is asking for rape, no?" the donkey said. The audience went wild.

"Just mark my words, Jidada, one day, without fail, these very Sisters of whatever will come crying that they've been raped during these naked parades. I tell you we'll all be expected to show sympathy! And Al Jazeera and CNN and BBC and *The New York Times* and all these so-called rights organizations will be here crying foul! Just because a bunch of misguided femals forgot their place! Shame shame shame!" the First Femal shrieked.

"Shame! Shame! Shame!!!" the square echoed back, as if this were a well-known slogan.

"Shame indeed! But enough of the itchtails, they're not who I stood up for. I have more pressing things on my mind today," the donkey said, clearing her throat and hinding to her full height, which was no small height, face no longer laughing.

The animals who knew Dr. Sweet Mother well—and of course this was most of Jidada—read in that particular clearing of the throat that in fact had absolutely nothing to do with the throat needing to be cleared, and read in her face—now a mass of granite, and in that posture, tholukuthi legs braced wide, tail in the air, chest out and heaving, head high, read in that particular signature phrase, "I have more pressing things on my mind today"—an unmistakable declaration of battle. Tholukuthi the donkey may not have fought in the famous and defining Liberation War, but the sticks and stones of Jidada would tell you that even with just her mouth

alone she could do serious battle and slay. The foremost question throughout the square then was, "Who is getting slain today?"

The animals under the sun had calmly gathered themselves with the
order and discipline of heads of cabbage. They delighted in the knowledge
that they were too wretched, tholukuthi too beneath the donkey to be of
any threat to her, yes, tholukuthi too insignificant to warrant her wrath;
their role in this part of the program was to be mere witnesses—all that
was required of them was to serve as an accompanying choir to Dr. Sweet
Mother's laughter and jeers. The animals under the tent, however, and
despite their Chosen status, had altogether different concerns—the donkey's mouth, besides the tendency to vomit instead of speak, had of late
also become a deadly and unpredictable spear, tholukuthi it could be flung
at any point, and there was no telling who it'd fall on and how. If it'd
prick, if it'd stab, if it'd maim, if it'd annihilate.

"I never thought the day would come that I'd see and hear an animal
dare stand in front of this whole gathering with the audacity of a scorpion
on a testicle and eulogize His Excellency, while in actuality he harbors
nothing but sheer ugliness, Tsk-tsk-tsk, you know!" the donkey snorted
with typical haughtiness.

At that point she abruptly jerked her head up, stood stone still, fixed her
gaze on the sun, and made a kind of twirling gesture with a hoof. Tholukuthi to everyone's utter, utter surprise, the sun did a bounce, then a brief
jiggy, then finally stood at attention, upon which the fluffy clouds around
it promptly scattered and disappeared. And then, it happened—the sun's
rays turned a deep gold, visibly broadened, and spread far and wide in a
dazzling display whose intensity made it necessary for each and every eye
to squint. If it'd been hot before, Jidada Square now felt like the depths of
hell, but the animals were too shocked, too confused to be bothered by the
heat. They turned to look at one another with faces that asked one question,

"How?" and, unable to provide one another with any satisfactory answers, they turned back to look at Dr. Sweet Mother as if they'd never seen her before.

The donkey was herself as shocked as her audience, but more than shocked, she was also thoroughly thrilled. She'd only tried the move on a whim, with no expectation whatsoever that she, Marvelous, daughter of Agnes, herself daughter of Chiriga, herself daughter of Tembewa, could command the sun, just like the Father of the Nation. And now, she reveled in the moment; giddy, jittery, so that it wasn't really on her own accord that she circled the stand one time, circled the stand two times, circled the stand three-four times before she managed to finally get hold of herself. And when she opened her mouth to proceed, her voice, no doubt now empowered, came out charged with a lacerating tone.

"So I have it on good intelligence that he, the animal I was telling you about, is here paying fake homage to His Excellency, when in reality he's busy telling his minions that the Father of the Nation is now old, senile, and unable to rule—those being his words and not mine—and busy plotting, planning for the day he'll take over from our dear Ruler whom God himself chose in his infinite wisdom. I'm standing here to address this nonsense right here right now, with Jidada itself and this sun over there as my witnesses, and I'm saying: This is not an animal farm but Jidada with a -da and another -da! So my advice to you is, Stop it, and Stop it right now! Immediately! At once! And if you have any ears at all you'll heed my advice because what you're doing is swallowing all manner of big rocks, and very soon it shall be seen just how wide your asshole is when those very rocks will need to be shat," the donkey puffed. And, done with her warning, she stood and stared down her nose at the square, panting from talking without pause but triumphant. Above her, the sun outdid itself blazing like it'd never blazed before.

YOU DON'T SEIZE A TERMITE BY THE HEAD

A different animal may have hinded and neighed and huffed and roared and vomited insults back. And if not that, then perhaps trembled in fear and maybe begged for forgiveness. But not Tuvius Delight Shasha, who in fact did nothing. He simply sat in his chair with the stillness of a crocodile under water and watched the donkey from the corner of his right eye. You wouldn't know it from looking at him sitting there like some mortician had embalmed him, but a terrible tempest raged inside the horse. The vice president otherwise showed no signs of irritation. Tholukuthi no alarm. No annoyance. No embarrassment. No vexation. No anger. No nothing. To give himself something to focus on while the donkey's tirade went on, he counted his breaths like a meditating monk, and was still counting when she finished her vomiting and sashayed off the stage in undisguised triumph, and was counting when the last of the festivities concluded, and when His Excellency and the donkey and everyone under the white tent rose to leave, and was counting when the very last animal left Jidada Square. Tuvy even went to sleep that night counting.

A LEADER WHO THINKS HE IS LEADING AND HAS NO POWER IS ONLY TAKING A WALK

THOLUKUTHI EVERYWHERE

A whole three, four hours past her bedtime, and Dr. Sweet Mother still can't stop playing and replaying the YouTube clip of herself dishing it out, yes, tholukuthi telling it like it is in front of the whole entire nation at the Independence celebrations a few days before. It rarely ever happens nowadays that she speaks anywhere, goes anywhere, does anything without ending up on social media like this. And rightly so, for she's by no means an ordinary First Femal—Dr. Sweet Mother, Marvelous, daughter of Agnes, herself daughter of Chiriga, herself daughter of Tembewa, has absolutely no fear—anytime, any day, anywhere, anyhow, she'll reduce a whole animal to size, shred it, squash it under her Gucci heels. It's all there on YouTube, the whole entire world can see it for she's gone viral— Twitter, Facebook, Instagram, you name it, tholukuthi everywhere, she's there, everywhere, she's trending, everywhere, ruling.

She watches on her screen as spellbound animals, both under the tent and in the sun, follow her every move, riveted. She simply can't get enough of it; the unwavering attention, the looks of awe, reverence, admiration—all of it fills the donkey with a thrill that makes equanimity impossible regardless of how many days it's been, no matter how many times she's viewed the video. Now, Dr. Sweet Mother is on her feet once again, pacing and reciting, along with the clip, the famous lines she's said so much in her speeches they have become recognized slogans in their own right: *"This is not an animal farm but Jidada with a -da and another -da! . . . And if you have any ears at all you'll heed my advice because what you're doing is swallowing all manner of big rocks, and very soon it shall be seen just how wide your asshole is when those very rocks will need to be shat!"* And here the donkey howls with morbid laughter, convulses so hard she has to sit on her bed, heaving and out of breath because the image also happens to be the funniest thing under the sun.

TONGUES OF POWER

Part of the brilliance in her speeches, Dr. Sweet Mother knows, comes from her choice of language—indeed, she's discovered she's at her crushingest, her most potent, her lacerating best, when she expresses herself in her mother tongue. It's one contrast between her and His Excellency, who's indeed famed all over Jidada and beyond, including Great Britain itself, tholukuthi by Englishmals themselves, for his eloquence in English. He speaks his first language as a matter of course, but still, in the language of his very own mothers, the Father of the Nation is an emperor in ill-fitting clothes, a miserable cockroach in a spotless white cupboard. Yes, tholukuthi he's uncomfortable in the language and it's similarly uncomfortable in him, he resists it and it resists him, when he stands, it sits, when he pushes, it shoves, when he lunges for it, it slips, bolts between his legs and splits,

and indeed, even when he's talk-sleeping, which happens quite often these days, the Father of the Nation actually does so in an English that is more English than that of the English themselves.

As for the donkey, she shines, flies, soars, leaps, waltzes, sashays, swims, pirouettes, glides, twerks, somersaults—she can pull whatever move, do anything, you name it—only coming short of raising the dead in her mother tongue. Many times she's regretted not having had the option of her first language for instruction throughout her schooling—who knows, she might've altogether had a positive learning experience, yes, tholukuthi in her own language, she may very well have better appreciated those hard subjects she otherwise failed to grasp, let alone enjoy, and so systematically and inevitably failed. And of course as a result she was marked by a humiliating dunderhead career in her primary and secondary school education that earned her all sorts of embarrassing nicknames, altogether an experience that not only left her insecure, her self-esteem in tatters, but continued to haunt her long after leaving school.

She taps the red Play icon again and watches the clip from beginning to end without interrupting it. It's not in Dr. Sweet Mother's nature to toot her own horn, but she has to agree she utterly dazzles in this latest clip, hands down her best performance so far ever since she began speaking at rallies three, four years since—she has simply outdone herself is what it is. The applause at the end of her delivery rings right in her heart all over again, and she increases the volume, feels the sound hit her bones, whip and stir the blood before lifting the intestines, the pancreas, the liver—tholukuthi generally all the innards, and, almost levitating now, flags her tail, raises both her front hooves, pumps them hard and cheers along with her admiring on-screen audience.

"Viva, Dr. Sweet Mother, Viva!!!"

Startled, the donkey turns around to find an animated Father of the Nation sloganeering in his favorite blue pajamas with the white stripes.

She didn't hear him come in and is momentarily flustered to be found in what no doubt appears a ridiculous exercise.

"Baba! Is all well? But how long have you been standing there? You should be sleeping!" The donkey scrutinizes the Old Horse's face, frowning. The clock on the wall says 2:13.

"It is well, Dr. Sweet Mother. I was indeed sleeping like you said I should. But then I was woken up. By the Comrades," he says.

THE SKELETONS IN JIDADA'S CLOSET

He means the famous Liberators—Humphrey Shumba, Eliot Nzira, General Makhalisa Langa, and General Samson Chigaro. According to those who really know about things, the latter, a top Commander of Jidada's Liberators during the war, was the broker responsible for the Father of the Nation's ascent to glory in the closing years of the struggle. After Independence, he'd gone on to serve as General of the Jidada National Army, in addition to being part of the Seat of Power Inner Circle. Besides the General, Dr. Sweet Mother didn't get to meet the other Comrades. They all died around the time of Jidada's Independence; they all died young.

Tholukuthi it took the first decade of the donkey's married life for her, by patiently piecing together fragments of the Father of the Nation's nightmares and sleep talk, sometimes including whole conversations, lectures, debates, arguments, pleas, confessions, musings, by paying special attention to the intimate talk of the Seat of Power and Inner Circle, to understand that the rumors she'd heard throughout her youth, from those who really know about things, were true—that the Father of the Nation in fact lived with ghosts, that the Father of the Nation, and by extension the Seat of Power, the Party of Power, and thus Jidada with a -da and another -da itself, had a complicated history that wasn't necessarily all glory.

THE LIBERATOR VERSUS TIME: A BATTLE OF TWO RULERS

For Dr. Sweet Mother to fully appreciate the scope of Jidada's unglorious past, Time, the ruler of all rulers, had to begin her inevitable siege on the animal of the Father of the Nation. Tholukuthi right as he was basking in the peak of his reign, Time unleashed her loyal foot soldier, Age, who dutifully carried out his slow but sure-footed attack on the ruler's body and mind. The Father of the Nation found himself cornered by an enemy against whom he couldn't set his famed Defenders, yes, tholukuthi an enemy that couldn't be tortured, couldn't be raped, couldn't be disappeared, couldn't be assassinated. He thus faced Age with nothing but anger and his English, lamenting that for all his power and glory he couldn't banish the wretched foe from his life—Look at all the stupid ailments he had to deal with, he seethed, and how they wasted his precious time because now instead of ruling he was always on the wing like some homeless, forsaken bird, he ranted, flying impossible distances for treatment in far-off lands where they couldn't even pronounce his surname properly with the hard *g* as in "God," didn't even greet him appropriately and had no idea to extol him because they didn't know exactly what he was and how much he was in his country that was also his very own, he raged, yes, always in the air because Jidada, he lamented, was so dismal its hospitals were where an animal went to die, raving that Age had taken away his strength, his drive, his libido, goddammit almost his whole entire body because look who he'd been once, an invincible stallion, he fumed, and see how Age had disrespectfully reduced him to a decrepit thing no matter how diligently he'd tried to fight it by having his heart taken out and replaced, by having his liver taken out and replaced, by having his lungs taken out and replaced, by having his pancreas taken out and replaced, by having his kidneys taken out and replaced, by having his corneas taken

out and replaced, by having his trachea taken out and replaced, by having his blood flushed out and replaced, yes, tholukuthi by basically having every imaginable replaceable part of him replaced with the organs of young and healthy stallions, but still Age wouldn't quit. It was common at this time for Dr. Sweet Mother to find the Father of the Nation lashing out in sad, epic tantrums in which he'd spread himself on the ground like a crooked map, the most powerful animal in Jidada reduced to weeping tears of rage and impotence at what he couldn't defeat, couldn't control, not even by decree. Subdued thus, the Father of the Nation succumbed to a mild case of dementia. It broke the lock of his enormous chest of secrets and loosened his tongue so that it was quite natural for him to wake up from nightmares and dream interactions and sleepwalkings with his dead Comrades to promptly and dutifully relate things to Dr. Sweet Mother in candid conversations in which he not only named his ghosts, but relayed to her their fates. And which is how the donkey came to know that every single one of the dead Comrades who now haunted the Father of the Nation had, in one way or the other, threatened his glory, and that they had not in fact died natural deaths.

THE MISEDUCATION OF A DONKEY: WILL THE REAL FATHER OF THE NATION PLEASE STAND UP?

There were other educations for Dr. Sweet Mother, who was simply known as Sweet Mother then, for this was before she got her PhD. Tholukuthi she came to learn that the Father of the Nation may indeed have been celebrated, hailed, for his Liberation War credentials, for his anti-imperial resistance, for his Pan-African politics, for his famed intellectualism, for his self-determination gospel, for his commitment to liberatory and progressive politics, for his endorsement from God to rule and rule

and keep ruling, for his awesome power to emerge winner of any election regardless of how the electorate voted, for his charisma and all of it, yes, tholukuthi what Sweet Mother quickly learned was that the Father of the Nation might've been venerated for all these things and more, but the simple truth was that when it came down to actually practicing, being, those things, he was also none of them.

The donkey learned that the Father of the Nation emerged from the famous Liberation War marked with blood—not just of the enemy but also of his very own brother Comrades, that he simply didn't have the capacity for such a task as leader of a whole nation and that went for the rest of his wretched Comrades on the Seat of Power, who, despite their so-called credentials, despite the stories they told about themselves, she discovered were fathers as much as heaps of dried turds could ever be fathers of anything. She'd learn too that not only were they breathing fiascoes with no love or respect whatsoever for the nation they purported to serve, yes, tholukuthi toads with no leadership, no ethics, no principles, no sense of justice, no compassion, no discipline, no honesty, no idea of what real service to the nation looked like, but they were also no better than the very oppressors they'd replaced.

Still, knowing all these things about the Old Horse and the Seat of Power, was the First Femal worried? Disappointed? Heartbroken? Tholukuthi no: Marvelous had been born with a mediocre plastic spoon in her mouth so that all she'd ever wanted in life was at least a real spoon—it didn't even have to be anything special as long as it was metal. Her marriage to the Father of the Nation then didn't just put a spoon in her mouth, tholukuthi it put a whole fancy golden ladle and she was not spitting it out, whoever, however the Father of the Nation and his miserable Seat of Power happened to be, after all she hadn't married him in order to dictate to a grown animal, a whole few decades older than herself for that matter, how and who to be in his own country that was obviously his, and where he also commanded the sun.

THE SEAT OF POWER SCHOOL OF RULING AND RULING AND RULING, AND A GRADUATE OF DISTINCTION

In those days of serious scholarship, Sweet Mother closely watched the Father of the Nation and Inner Circle with a diligence and attention she'd never given to anything. The sudden life-changing inclusion in the intimate workings of the Seat of Power wasn't unlike enrollment at a prestigious institution. It was indeed an education of a lifetime, and the donkey would appreciate the hands-on structure of the curriculum, which was rigorous but highly relevant, the thoroughly outstanding faculty of celebrated members of the Inner Circle and the Chosen of course, who boasted stellar credentials and years and years of experience. Still haunted by the humbling and not so successful educational career of her youth, Sweet Mother was determined to put that shameful reputation behind her like a tail, open a new chapter, so to speak; tholukuthi she'd show every one of her snobbish former classmates and teachers who'd ever teased and bullied and despised and laughed at her. She'd outshine. She'd impress. She'd be number one. She'd take awards. She'd be first-rate. She'd be ~~sur supre superflr~~ supercalifragilisticexpialidocious.

Tholukuthi just as she intended, Sweet Mother impressed and outshined. She conquered, graduating with distinction—an exceptional authority brilliantly versed in the workings of the Seat of Power and the regime. Even the Father of the Nation himself was shocked; he hadn't expected much from his wife, not because he had anything against femals—he was married to one, after all, and what more, his late mother, whom he'd actually loved very much, was a femal and his sister was a femal and his grandmother was a femal and his daughter was a femal and his granddaughter was a femal—it was simply that he hadn't thought his young wife, a novice and political outsider, had it in her to do well within the rather complex machinations of the Seat of Power.

But, besides excelling at her education, there was also this—which even those who really know about things didn't see coming—the donkey, during the course of her studies, had in fact become radicalized, yes, tholukuthi convinced that if beasts of the degenerate caliber as occupied the Seat of Power could indeed rule, then there was absolutely no reason whatsoever under the Jidada sky why she herself, Marvelous, daughter of Agnes, herself daughter of Chiriga, herself daughter of Tembewa, couldn't rule. This profound revelation occurred to her one day as she lay in the shade of an apple tree touching up on her mathematics by counting apples—32 of them already ripe, 12 of them almost ripe, 21 of them half ripe, and 12 of them unripe for a total of 32 ripe apples in the tree and 45 unripe apples in the tree counting those that could be counted as eatable—yes, tholukuthi it occurred to the donkey that there was in fact nothing special in itself about being married to His Excellency, and that any un-dead femal could've managed the same feat with her eyes closed, a feat that didn't really require any brains, while on the contrary, she her own self had brains, and not only did she have brains, but some serious brains at that, and with those serious brains she could do more, offer more, be more.

Tholukuthi the very first move the donkey made upon coming to her decision was to pick up the phone and call the highest-ranked university in Jidada and say, "Hello, I want to talk to the headmaster? Okay, if there's no headmaster then give me the principal. Okay, if there's no headmaster and no principal then just give me whoever rules the university. Hello, are you the one in charge? Yes, so I'm told by those who know about things that you give degrees over there and I'm surprised you haven't thought to give me one yet like you don't know who I am when everybody else is busy giving me all sorts of things—land, mines, businesses, whatever I want, I get. I'd like the biggest one. Well, by big I mean as in the president of the degrees, the most important one, and about how long will it take to

have it on my wall?" And thus, Marvelous was awarded a PhD in sociology from the University of Jidada before you could say diss, for dissertation. Tholukuthi it was as easy as ordering from a KFC drive-through, or perhaps even easier being that it was cheaper than KFC; it in fact cost her nothing and the degree actually came with a zero-calorie Diet Coke and a purple straw. And just like that, as if by a wave of a sorcerer's whisk, Sweet Mother was no longer just Sweet Mother but Dr. Sweet Mother.

MBUYA NEHANDA AND THE BUTTERFLIES

"Do you know who the Comrades came with today, Dr. Sweet Mother? They came with her." The Old Horse points to the portrait of Mbuya Nehanda, which is right next to the large painting of the donkey's mothers, Agnes, Chiriga, and Tembewa.

"But she didn't have her head, and at the end of her neck, where her head should have been, was an opening, and from out of that opening flew these butterflies, a whole rally of them, Dr. Sweet Mother, I've never seen so many butterflies, you should have been there, it was really something!" the Old Horse gushes, tail swishing. The donkey nods sympathetically; it is obviously one of those nights again, she thinks.

"And the butterflies were red, they were crimson-crimson-crimson," the Old Horse says.

"That sounds pretty!" Dr. Sweet Mother straightens the Old Horse's pajamas. Her voice has the dramatic cheer with which one addresses finicky babies. She starts to lead the Old Horse back to the master bedroom.

"Yes, they were very pretty, Dr. Sweet Mother, they were lovely! And once all of them had come out of Mbuya Nehanda they flew all over the place, like flags, teeny-tiny flags. Only they were red, and it was like, like watching blood dance. And I was following them everywhere. But then

there were many of them and there was only one of me!" The Old Horse is laughing with unbridled pleasure. In the passageway they meet his live-in nurse, Zazu, obviously looking for her lost charge. On seeing them, she halts, anxiously wrings her front paws, perhaps because as they say, those who know about things, Dr. Sweet Mother has a temper worse than a black mamba's.

"I'm sorry. I'd gone to the toilet," Zazu starts to apologize.

"It's fine, cat. Just give the Father of the Nation something to sleep. Did he take anything already?"

"A Xanax, when he went to sleep the first time," the cat says. The donkey sucks her teeth.

"I think he's becoming resistant, give him something stronger," she says, watches misty-eyed as the cat leads the Father of the Nation away. Dr. Sweet Mother accompanies them with her gaze until they disappear in an open door at the end of the passageway.

BEHIND EVERY RULING FEMAL

Back again in her own bedroom, Dr. Sweet Mother resumes her viewing. The Father of the Nation's visit has put her in a reflective mood. She presses the mute button and sits back in her chair. To the donkey's surprise, she finds that watching the clip in the absence of sound allows her to experience it anew. The Old Horse stands out in his green shirt, sandwiched between her empty chair and his nephew, Patson. For the length of the clip, Dr. Sweet Mother marvels at how the Father of the Nation's warm eyes are glued on her, never lifting, never blinking, as if he desperately intends to commit her in that moment to eternal memory. On his face is a look of such devotion she feels overwhelmed by a sweet, tender love; she leans forward to lick the screen with her nose. They said, those who really know about things, that it was this devotion that conquered the

donkey's otherwise growing apprehension and negative feelings once Age came for the Father of the Nation and she suddenly found herself tied to an octogenarian in the afternoon of her youth. They said too, those who really, really know about things, that the Old Horse especially outdid himself with that devotion when he chose to hold open destiny's gates at the critical time that Dr. Sweet Mother came to the realization that she wanted more than simply being wife, that she too wanted her own glory.

The donkey had anticipated resistance, because surely no one born to rule would be so ready to relinquish his seat without ceremony, but then here was the Father of the Nation, a pure picture of devotion with a tail, and without her having to resort to the tactics she'd otherwise prepared in case of resistance. "Go forth, Dr. Sweet Mother, while I take a nap. While I rest my eyes. While I groom my tail. While I count these ants. While I go through these albums from the early days of glory. While I try all my favorite suits to see how they fit now, so many of them! While I pee this pee that's been coming in droplets because of that miserable sorcerer, Age. While I watch YouTube videos of myself during my gone days of glory so I can better prepare for the coming ones. While I continue to write my memoirs in my own head so that one day my enemies don't try to soil my legacy. While I revise this formula for ruling and ruling and ruling absolutely. Hold the reins, dear learned Dr. Sweet Mother, because who truly can hold them in this Jidada of corrupt and unfit savages who aren't capable of anything that requires thinking?" the Old Horse would say, and Dr. Sweet Mother went forth like a baboon that'd found a whistle.

THE CRITERIA OF POWER AND THE PATRIARCHAL ORGANISM

Still, in stepping into the light of her own glory, even with the Father of the Nation's support, Dr. Sweet Mother may very well have stepped on a bed of scorpions: the resistance and resentment were immediate, but of

course they didn't surprise the donkey; she had, after all, devoted all those years of rigorous scholarship to understanding that anything and everything that had anything to do with the Seat of Power was governed by what she called Jidada's patriarchal organism. She knew better than anyone that on the Seat of Power were beasts—the deputy president Tuvius Delight Shasha at the fore—who'd literally waited all their miserable lives, who fasted and prayed to God every day and without fail, who consulted sorcerers and made sacrifices to all manner of deities, who threw all their energies toward one goal and just one goal alone: to one day succeed the Father of the Nation.

Yes, tholukuthi Dr. Sweet Mother knew too, that according to that patriarchal organism, a proper ruler, a real Father of the Nation, like the title itself suggested, could only be an animal born in possession of a fine, weighty set of testicles, and not only an animal born in possession of a fine, weighty set of testicles but one also inclined to use those testicles to literally father the nation. She also understood that the patriarchal organism decreed that an animal was only ever worthy of ruling Jidada, only and only if they'd in fact fought in the famous Liberation War, as if the presidency was some kind of killing feat, and that never in a million years would a non-Liberator like herself ever rule the land that was born of what was understood to be the blood of the Fathers. The donkey knew too that having fought in the Liberation War also meant that said animal was an elder, yes tholukuthi a proper dotard who could pass the test of telling from memory the birthdays of all the old trees of Jidada. She was also aware that the organism demanded that the animal on the Seat of Power be of a particular ethnicity, and not just a particular ethnicity, but a particular clan, because Jidada was a nation in which blood—more than brains, more than qualifications or experience or expertise or talent or otherwise any other criteria—was everything.

And so the donkey, who in fact hadn't spent all those years of rigorous

scholarship for nothing, didn't need to be told that not only did she fail to meet all the criteria, but that in daring to dream outside of what she was supposed to dream, she'd become an enemy to the patriarchal organism itself. Still, her intestines told her not to despair because regardless of all that was against her, she had one ultimate weapon on her side—the Father of the Nation and only him himself; in other words, she was beyond any and all miserable diktats of criteria. Yes, tholukuthi she hadn't gone to war, had never held a gun in her life, and she'd rule. She didn't possess even a single testicle, and she'd rule. She was young, and she'd rule. She was of an unimportant ethnicity, and she'd rule, yes, tholukuthi sit, perch, cross both sets of hooves on the Seat of Power till it suited her, till it looked like she'd been born to sit on it. They said too, those who really know about things, that Dr. Sweet Mother's feelings for the Father of the Nation were by now utterly enhanced by the nectar of power so that it in fact became the sweetest season of their marriage.

A POWER STRUGGLE

They said, those who know about things, that not only did the issue of Dr. Sweet Mother's pursuit of glory throw the Seat of Power into a general state of disorder, it also split the Party of Power itself into numerous factions. One of them of course was the donkey's own Inner Circle—young Comrades who, like her, hadn't fought in the Liberation War but who didn't have the patience to wait for the elder Liberators to die out before they could have their own turn at ruling. Another faction included those who supported Dr. Sweet Mother because even the sticks and stones knew that it was common sense, self-preservation, to ally oneself with the Power under any and all circumstances, yes, tholukuthi this faction also supporting the donkey out of duty, out of fear, being that they owed who they were and what they had to the Seat of Power. There were also the or-

dinary citizens, yes, tholukuthi the ones who stood cooking under the boiling sun at rallies, clad in the regalia of power and cheering out of what those who know about things said could easily have been a complicated sense of loyalty, or perhaps even idiocy. Finally there were the few brave Liberators who imagined themselves the Real, True Patriots of the Nation, and who dared resist Dr. Sweet Mother at their own peril, tholukuthi resisting because they knew, felt in their testicles what should've been felt by any self-respecting patriot, which was that the rightful future leader of Jidada with a -da and another -da, of a land born of the blood of the Fathers, had to meet the right criteria and with no exceptions whatsoever.

They said, those who know about things, that Dr. Sweet Mother was not fazed by this later group, that she dealt with these so-called True Patriots of the Nation just like the Seat of Power had always dealt with its enemies—by declaring war. The donkey was in spectacular form as she set on her enemies—real and perceived, and anyone she felt stood in the way of her destiny. Her method was both strange and confusing to many; she didn't employ the usual and predictable brutal, bloody, and murderous tactics long practiced by the Seat of Power, no—she merely used her mouth, yes, her simple mouth with nothing in it besides its thirty-six teeth and average-size tongue and inspired by God, who by force of the word alone had once upon a time been said to have said, Let there be light and there was light, had been said to have said, Let there be a vault to separate the light from the water, and ah-ah, tholukuthi there was a vault to separate the light from the water, had been said to have said, Let there be this and that, and there was this and that.

Yes, with just the force of her voice, Dr. Sweet Mother confronted her enemies in public gatherings and reduced them to size. Tholukuthi her excellence mostly manifested in the act of humiliating with her spear-sharp tongue, in taking down bigheaded beasts from the very apex of

greatness and bringing them down to the level ground. "Get up," she'd command powerful animals during rallies, and they indeed scrambled to their feet like they'd been missed by lightning, and Jidada watched in disbelief as she vomited all over them to her heart's content, for that is what her talk was like, utter vomit, yes, tholukuthi the reduced, humiliated animals standing there, cowering, not uttering a word, not even a pkle.

THE FALLEN MIGHTY

And which is how Tuvy sits in this latest clip. Dr. Sweet Mother taps Play, leans back in her chair. It's actually interesting, she thinks, how the ugly beast seems to shrink the very moment she powers onto the stage, as if something in his blood has already told him what time it is. She can't remember ever seeing him looking this small, this humbled, this pathetic, and relishes his humiliation. Every animal has a first, and she can bet this is the so-called vice president's first, yes, tholukuthi that never has he in his life—a life that'd otherwise be mediocre, had it not been for the Father of the Nation's patronage—been this disgraced, and in front of the whole entire nation, and in the presence of his stupid, holier-than-thou wife, who acts like somebody gave her a Daughter-in-Law of the Year sash already, in front of his useless, geriatric so-called Liberator Comrades still stuck on a miserable war that ended close to four decades ago, and one, Dr. Sweet Mother knows, that wouldn't otherwise have been won without the superior military power of Jidada's first-ever Revolutionary Party that the Seat of Power cruelly turned against upon gaining independence, declared them Dissidents, arrested the leaders, rubbished the party structures before declaring war on the supporters, ultimately coming just short of erasing the party from Jidada's so-called liberation history. The donkey now sees, and with satisfaction, that the so-called Comrades are themselves

sitting shrunken in their own seats, the mighty doing all they can to make themselves small before she reduces them to proper size. And which she will, in due time. Every. Single. One!

THOLUKUTHI PROPHECY

Her cell phone rings. It's Prophet Dr. O. G. Moses, sharing a customized daily motivational reading. She swipes and reads: "Fear not, for I am with you; Be not dismayed, for I am your God. I will strengthen you, Yes, I will help you, I will uphold you with My righteous hand." Isaiah 41:10. She reads the accompanying text: "Inspiring, fearless words at the last rally, Dr. Sweet Mother. Your voice is truly, most definitely, the voice of God itself, and we're thoroughly blessed by it!!!" Dr. Sweet Mother finds herself by the window, where she stands looking out into the vast manicured gardens. She's very much aware that she hasn't moved on her own accord, that something she can't quite put a hoof on—a force, perhaps—has raised her to her feet. And the force has also placed in her heart, in her head, in her blood, in her intestines, a clarity she's been waiting for, tholukuthi which is that the time of her own glory is nigh.

She lifts her eyes to the morning sky, empty because it's still too early for sunrise, focuses on the open expanse until she feels at one with the vastness. And then she does it—lifts a hoof, very, very gently twirls it and watches, with the garden statues and grasses and jacarandas and rocks and flowers and grasshoppers as witnesses, the sun climb out of its mother's arms a whole three hours before it's in fact due to rise, and sweep across the sky until it is directly outside her window. Dr. Sweet Mother, standing on hind legs now, in disbelief, and overwhelmed, has to fight so hard to keep her trembling hind hooves firmly planted on the plush carpet, her front hooves braced against the panes so she stops herself from lifting, yes, tholukuthi from levitating to embrace the sun.

BATTLE FOR JIDADA

WHEN DEATH COMES, THE RICH ANIMAL HAS NO MONEY AND THE POOR ANIMAL HAS NO DEBT BUT SOME ANIMALS HAVE WHAT THEY HAVE

When those who know about things told it, they said on an ordinary morning following an all-night Party of Power rally, Jidada woke to the news Tuvy had been involved in a fatal car accident. The news said the vice president had been on his way home from the rally, where, unfortunately but not surprisingly, he hadn't been spared what was by now Dr. Sweet Mother's routine vomit attacks. The news said the vice president's vehicle had almost cleared the bridge to the great Dula River, just after passing St. Mary's primary school, when it collided head-on with an unidentified object, tholukuthi the force of the impact causing the car to somersault backward several times before plunging into the Dula—filled to near capacity from a week of torrential rains. The news said the car was submerged in the water for the whole night before anyone became aware of the accident. Finally the news went on to say that all the passengers were probably dead at that point unless a miracle happened, tholukuthi a

highly unlikely event, being that Jidada was no place for miracles, certainly not for those at odds with the Seat of Power.

And, sure enough, when the rescue team pulled the car out of the Dula, all the passengers in it—a bull, a goat, and a rooster—were indeed found dead, the bodies still strapped to their seats. But there was no sign whatsoever of the vice president. While the rescuers painstakingly searched for him, those who really know about things ventured to declare it a waste of time; the horse had most probably been saved by his talismans and escaped. They weren't, in fact, too, too far from the truth. By the time the car landed at the bottom of the Dula, Tuvy's hooves were busy eating the road, tholukuthi bearing the vice president to the safety of his sorcerer's homestead.

A BOY MAY CRY, BUT A MAN MUST CONCEAL HIS TEARS

He found Jolijo pacing outside his surgery, expecting him. The sorcerer was dressed for his life's calling in a billowing cloak of cheetah skin, a cloth of black velvet lining the inside. A string of red and black beads mixed with the teeth of a baby lion bundled around the cat's neck, half concealing a Versace chain. The moment Tuvy set eyes on Jolijo, he lost it, yes, tholukuthi stomped the earth and vaulted and reared and bucked. He hopped better than a bunny, spun round and round and round, tail whirling like some kind of propeller blade. By this time the cat, who'd never witnessed a tantrum of that magnitude, had already leapt up a peach tree, then onto the roof of his surgery, where he now stood vigorously crossing himself—yes, he was a sorcerer but his grandmother was a devout Catholic; desperate times called for desperate measures.

Jolijo was thinking what to do when, without warning, the vice president suddenly stopped in his tracks, as if a controller somewhere had hit a Pause button. The horse stood still, his great head resting on his chest. And then, to Jolijo's utter, utter surprise, he began sobbing—a quiet but horrible

sound that sent the puzzled cat quickly hopping back onto the peach tree. He slid down the trunk, gracefully slinked within the horse's line of vision but didn't dare approach. The sorcerer proceeded instead to his surgery, wherein he busied himself with the already prepared mutis and equipment for the upcoming session. He stirred the dirt-colored bathwater in the large tub, poked the separate stashes of roots, dried leaves, and powders spread on the floor. He was pouring a white muti onto the fire, which immediately provoked effusive smoke that bathed the room in a pungent haze, when the vice president lumbered in and sat in his usual spot opposite the door.

"Did something happen, Chief?" Jolijo spoke like he was probing a sleeping cobra.

"This itchtail just won't stop! I thought she'd go no further than vomiting but here she is, trying to kill me! This itchtail is wild!" The horse quivered with rage.

"But you survived, Chief. Again," Jolijo said.

"I don't want to be surviving anything, I'm tired! I just want to live my life in peace like everybody else! Even the Opposition doesn't behave like this itchtail!" Jolijo, who'd been fearing a real crisis—God forbid something he was neither prepared nor qualified for—calmly reached for his pipe, lit it, and took a long, relieved drag.

"Our fathers, and their fathers, just like their fathers before them, lived by the wisdom that a proper mal's tears flowed in the inside, like blood. A real mal can weep all he wants as long as his eyes, his face, never get wet, for it is taboo." The cat tilted his head back to let out a thick ribbon of smoke. Strung on the roof and going round the room were the bleached skulls of mice. The cat narrowed his eyes and watched the smoke curl toward the bones.

"But what if this mad donkey succeeds one day? And what if she somehow ends up on the Seat of Power, now that she actually commands the sun itself!" Tuvy cried.

"A real mal still doesn't speak pitifully, Chief, no matter his predicament, no matter what manner of monster accosts him, and more so a mal of your stature. But as I said before, all this is quite expected given the circumstances and stakes, even the sticks and stones know that the vocation of ruling is a dance with the devil. And from what my dreams and mirrors tell me, the dance is yet to get hot, Chief, in fact, this here is a fly's bite in comparison to what's coming," the cat said, rising and adjusting his cloak.

COVERED BY THE ~~BLOOD OF JESUS~~ MUTI

For the rest of the morning the vice president underwent purification and fortification rites fitting for one who'd both cheated death and who faced even more of it. He was douched in purifying baths infused with sacred flowers and mutis from the crushed bones of elusive and fearsome beasts. He chewed their dried livers and drank their urine. He smoked the dried shit of mermaids. He drank juices from the boiled bark and leaves from the extremely rare tree of life. His body was smeared with magic potions. Jolijo braided talismans into his mane and tail. Sacrifice after sacrifice after sacrifice was made for his protection.

It wasn't until noon that the sorcerer was at last satisfied that yessir, the process hadn't only lifted the dark shadow of the recent attack on the vice president but also rendered him ready to withstand any weapon of flesh or spirit or however in the name of the white devil death may come to accomplish what the car accident had failed to. It was the kind of production whose weightiness not only restored Tuvy's confidence but also made him embarrassed by what he now knew to have been an exaggerated reaction, for the fact of the matter was that he need not have been the least bit afraid in the first place because he simply had the best sorcerer in the whole of Jidada.

"What day is today, Comrade Jolijo?" the vice president said. His body

felt immensely revitalized, fresh, and invincible—as it always did after these sessions.

"Today is the day that follows Monday. Which you wouldn't be seeing if you'd indeed died like you were supposed to." The cat waited for Tuvy to laugh. When the vice president didn't, perhaps because these were true words, the cat shrugged, went to the miniature closet where he kept a few of the horse's clothes for emergencies such as this one, and fished out a black suit and crisply ironed white shirt. Tuvy dressed in front of the cat, and in no time looked like the vice president he was supposed to be.

THOLUKUTHI NO WEAPON FORMED AGAINST THEE SHALL PROSPER

When Jolijo said the vocation of ruling was a dance with the devil, tholukuthi what he meant was that the vocation of ruling was a dance with the devil. Within a span of a week, Tuvy would survive a hailstorm, three more traffic accidents, four kidnapping attempts, four drive-by shootings. But through it all the vice president, like some anointed first cousin of Jesus on the mother's side and unlike most marked enemy to and by the Seat of Power, emerged unscathed, to the bafflement of every Jidadan, to the disappointment of all who wished him utter damnation—and they were many, for the horse wasn't a loved animal by any stretch of the imagination—to the confusion of commentators who'd prophesized his inevitable end, to the sadness of many of the horse's own victims, who at the very least hoped to see karma deliver where justice had failed them, and, ultimately, to the chagrin of Dr. Sweet Mother's supporters.

But the horse received no congratulations or praise for his triumphs over death; after all, even the sticks and stones knew that since the beginning of time, Tuvy himself had been the active tool to the very reckless arm of

power that was now groping for him, and that far too many hadn't had the fortune to escape. All the ordinary Jidadans were prepared to do, being that this wasn't their fire to fan or put out, was to sit comfortably and watch, convinced the vice president's survival was but a matter of chance, that his dawn too would eventually catch up with him like it'd caught up with so many others before him and would go on to catch up with many more after him.

THERE IS NO NIGHT EVER SO LONG IT DOESN'T END WITH DAWN

And that dawn indeed caught up with Tuvius Delight Shasha on an ordinary Monday that was like all Mondays when the Father of the Nation, and with a husband of the century's unwavering love and loyalty, unceremoniously excommunicated the vice president from the Seat of Power, and thus from the Jidada Party, and thus from the throne of Liberators. Yes, he was supposedly next in line to rule; yes, he'd fought in the Liberation War and considered himself a True Patriot to the bone; yes, he'd given his whole life to Jidada without hesitation and would in fact do so over and over again; yes, he'd walked with the Father of the Nation every step of that long, rocky road to liberation and glory; yes, he'd survived enough dramatic brushes with death; yes, he had in his corner a most powerful sorcerer, but in the end none of it was enough to protect Tuvy from the smashing event he didn't otherwise have language for.

THOUGHTS AND FEELINGS

They said, those who really know about things, that the Father of the Nation might as well have speared his deputy right in the heart. The younger horse had never known such pain. Tholukuthi for the very first time in his

life, Tuvius Delight Shasha came undone-undone. He didn't know what
to do with himself. Where to hold, where to touch, and where to let go,
for he was nothing without the Seat of Power and nothing outside of it.
Thoughts of his journey, and indeed relationship—hell, it could even
have been a marriage because otherwise what do you call that kind of intimate union?—to the Father of the Nation, filled his waking and sleeping
hours alike. What had happened to them? What had he done under Jidada's wide skies to deserve such a fate? Had the Old Horse had a more loyal
soldier, a more loyal companion, a more loyal ear, a more loyal weapon, a
more loyal anything and everything at any point in his leadership? Who'd
been there from the very beginning? Who'd taken care of each and every
problem since, without caring what that problem was, if it was as small
as an ant or bigger than Mount Kilimanjaro? Who put out the fires that
threatened the Seat? Who lit them if they needed lighting? And how on
earth was it possible that he, yes, tholukuthi he who'd loved his country
even better than the best of patriots, better than God had loved the world
that he gave not even a son—because, in all earnestness, what's a mere
son compared to one's own life?—yes, he'd selflessly sacrificed his one
and only life in that terrible long Liberation War so that Jidada, including
the itchtail donkey herself, could be free, and not only had he selflessly
sacrificed his one and only life in that terrible long Liberation War so that
Jidada, including the itchtail donkey herself, could be free, but he also
sacrificed himself again each and every day that Jidada was free, only to
end up in this deplorable position? How and where under the heavens had
it happened that a Liberator and defender of the nation and legitimate future leader of his caliber be treated with such indignity, such disrespect,
such contempt, such thanklessness? All stemming from the wretched do-
ings of a vile femal, and an itchtail at that? Why wasn't there an outcry,
why weren't the animals standing up for and with him? Didn't they see
what was happening, and what was going to happen? Where on earth

were the respectable Jidadans? The citizens of honor, the Real, True Patriots of the nation—when this baselessness, this travesty, was happening
to him? Didn't they know that if they didn't stop this injustice today, tomorrow it was their turn? That none of them was safe until they were
all safe?

FOR BEHOLD, I AM SENDING AMONG YOU SERPENTS, ADDERS THAT CANNOT BE CHARMED, AND THEY SHALL BITE YOU

Yes, tholukuthi the beleaguered former vice president's misery was so
devastating not even Jolijo's mutis could afford him relief. He wouldn't
eat, convinced that in every cup of water and drink, in every plate of food,
no matter who prepared it, was deadly poison meant to extinguish him. He
hardly slept, hardly talked, hardly laughed, hardly shat, hardly anythinged.
He turned paranoid, looking at every animal and everything, including
his own shadow, including his very own reflection in the mirror, with
suspicion. He saw eyes and weapons and assassins and traps and evil
everywhere. And indeed the former vice president's fears proved not un-
founded when on his return from a long walk during one night of insomnia
he thought he saw a telltale movement south of the yard, near his car garage. He hid in the shadows, wondering if what he was seeing was indeed
what he was seeing: a white python with a ginormous head unlike any he
had ever seen on a python walk-crawled purposefully toward his sleeping
quarters.

"Goddammit goddammit goddammit!" the stunned horse said to the
stream of pee that'd escaped him without his permission. He did not
wait to see the return of the creature; he took to his heels and entered the
night.

Many times during his flight he did think—based on what he knew to
be true of the Seat of Power—that he probably wasn't alone in the

frowning Jidada dark, that other monsters lurked in the shadows. And if not monsters, that he was possibly being watched by the likes of Commander Jambanja, a most terrible terminator who'd been making enemies of the Seat of Power disappear without a trace for almost two decades now. Still, the horse kept on, being that there was indeed nothing to do but keep on. Once in a while he'd hear the itchtail's demented laughter ringing in his ears, hear too her words, insulting him, mocking him, belittling him, threatening him, and the anger coiled up in his gut would unfurl, sending his hooves digging harder in the dark. Only one name was on his mind—General Judas Goodness Reza. Tuvy didn't need to be told that his friends were few and protectors even fewer in his greatest hour of need, but he knew he could trust the pit bull.

SHELTER

General Judas Goodness Reza met him at the entrance of his house like he'd known he was coming. Inside, Tuvy was surprised to find a small group of Generals sitting tight in a corner of the dimly lit living room. They spoke in the hushed tones of clandestine old femals at the sudden funeral of an age-mate for whom they shared a collective contempt, tholukuthi the air thick with the distinct smell of dog. The horse was relieved he knew them all. General Talent Ndiza, a gentle-faced, stunningly beautiful ridgeback whose famous looks contradicted the dog's savage cruelty, sat next to General Musa Moya, a stout boerboel with enormous eyes that made him look like he was choking on a bone, who was also famed for his business acumen and owned a chain of mines all over Jidada and also spoke fluent Chinese. General Saint Zhou was an arrogant, sturdy German shepherd with a clunky nose who was, like General Judas Goodness Reza and General Musa Moya, a decorated veteran of the Liberation War, and finally there was General Lovemore Shava, a serene-faced pit bull

who was famed for his levelheadedness and his ability to win any argument against anyone whether he was sleeping or awake and without raising a single hair.

Every one of the dogs wore a uniform, and the former vice president, himself dressed in casual khaki pants and a yellow Party of Power T-shirt emblazoned with the face of the Father of the Nation, even with the ugliness of their relationship, felt a twinge of self-consciousness. Tholukuthi it had less to do with his own dress than the undeniable authority of a dog in uniform, and more so, a band of them all at once. The horse couldn't help but feel small; if only he'd known his day would end in this place, with this particular company, and in these particular circumstances, he'd have dressed accordingly. A long mirror ran the entire side of one wall—Tuvy's own disheveled reflection reminded him of a lunatic.

But the vice president need not have worried—the dogs were upon him in proper dog welcome. They growled good-naturedly. They circled him, tails wagging and tongues lolling. They sniffed his hooves, his tail, his ass. General Saint Zhou actually humped his leg with enthusiasm. And, in light of all this dog love, Tuvy stood there sheepishly, grinning like an idiot and not quite knowing what to do with himself.

"Welcome, welcome, Comrade," General Talent Ndiza said after the dance, looking at Tuvy with fervid eyes.

Judging from the pile of crushed cigarettes, from the thick smoke swimming in the air, the empty bottles of drinks, Tuvy, feeling just a tad less heavy from the assuring reception, figured he'd walked into a gathering that'd possibly been going on for a long time. The realization made him somewhat uneasy, and he immediately began to eat his liver, thinking, What exactly is this meeting that is, from the look of it, the great-grandmother of all meetings, about? Thinking, What kind of gathering is it that takes place at such a time of witches and strange monsters? Think-

ing, Have my feet accidentally brought me in the middle of something here? Thinking, Why is it just dogs at this meeting, as if they're the only animals in the Seat?

"You, old friend, have the impeccable timing of great kings, you couldn't have come at a better moment, please sit." General Judas Goodness Reza gestured, making room between himself and the boerboel.

"Gentlemals," Tuvy said, speaking with a false cheer that didn't match the moroseness he actually felt, including them all in a brave smile.

And when he put his behind on the plush sofa, he felt the weight of his painful predicament sit down with him. And right after he settled himself, the Generals, who'd remained standing, saluted, sat. And the horse looked from dog to dog to dog to dog to dog, tholukuthi both touched and stupefied by the gesture because not even the lowest mongrel had saluted him ever since his crisis began, and not many would look at him now.

"A drink, Comrade?" General Lovemore said, already in the act of pouring the horse a vodka. And Tuvy drank, the glass trembling in his grip. He hated vodka and hadn't in fact tasted it in decades because his very first love, Netsai, had left him for a peacock who drank nothing but vodka so that drinking the particular alcohol had always felt to Tuvy like tasting his humiliation all over again, but today, tholukuthi under the circumstances, the drink had never tasted more divine.

"Comrade? You look like you've been to hell," General Saint Zhou said. "I am in hell, what the hell do you think this is?" the vice president thought, but did not express himself out loud. Instead he shook his bus of a head and let out a heavy sigh. The dog's dancing eyes, when he briefly held them, were full of kind concern.

"Eh, you've got some real enemies in this Jidada, but here you're among allies, old friend," General Judas Goodness Reza said, laying a paw on Tuvy's shoulder and smiling a smile that eclipsed his chunky face. The

horse felt the gentle touch right in his intestines and almost wanted to ask the dog to leave the paw right there. In fact, forget the paw, he wanted to ask the dog to hug him, hold him tight and tell him everything would be okay and not let him go. He let his tears bleed on the inside as Jolijo had advised, clenched his jaw, and avoiding the eyes of the dogs, only said, "Yaaaa, Comrade."

"I hear you. But it'll be well, old friend, trust," General Judas Goodness Reza said, pouring himself another drink. And somehow, in the haziness of the dimly lit room, the horse felt, for the first time since things began to fall apart for him, that perhaps it was going to be well after all.

IN DEFENSE OF THE REVOLUTION

"Eh, Comrades. I'm sure every one of us is aware of the situation we're in, no need to go over the shenanigans we all know so well. As we speak the bones of the Liberators are rattling under this very earth, which tells us what time it is. And the time is Defend the Revolution o'clock, of course in the name of Jidada, and by that I mean the real, the same Jidada with a -da and another -da that Comrade Liberators sacrificed and died for, and not this Jidada of a miserable petticoat Seat of Power that an animal can't even recognize anymore," General Judas Goodness Reza said, taking the time to pierce each Comrade with his eyes.

Tuvy almost uttered an "Amen" at the end of the short speech— tholukuthi he'd heard the General as if he were actually hearing a prayer. But then had he heard correctly? Or was he imagining things? He didn't need to look to know the dogs were keenly watching him.

"Yes, I hear you, Comrade. But the problem, to put it quite frankly, is I don't see how you can possibly defend the Revolution from—how to put it—the Revolution," Tuvy said.

It wasn't that he didn't see how this could work—he'd in fact considered it, tholukuthi literally every single day since his excommunication. But his decades-old experience in the Seat of Power had taught him caution on such delicate matters. It was clear the Generals, gathered in the dead of night like sorcerers, had something up their tails.

"Today the President doesn't see how it can be done, Comrades," General Musa Moya said, rising and walking toward the door with the sway of a seasoned drunk. It didn't escape Tuvy that the dog had indeed referred to him as "president." Tholukuthi President!

"The Revolution will be defended like it's always been defended, Comrade. With the gun, and in these. And we will do it with confidence knowing the itchtail isn't standing alone but with her misguided little faction that didn't even see combat. Revolutionaries will not be usurped by nonentities! Forward with the Gun!" General Lovemore Shava said.

"Forward!!!" the dogs barked. Tuvy picked up his glass and emptied its contents.

"Spoken like a Real, True Patriot, Comrade, spoken like a Real, True Patriot," General Musa Moya said. He stood and raised his own glass to General Lovemore Shava. They clinked, and so did everyone else.

Tuvy, who knew, as even the sticks and stones knew, that not only was there general discord about who'd in fact succeed the Father of the Nation, but that there was also discontent within the Inner Circle due to the rising and dangerous and unfeminine influence of the itchtail, still hadn't counted on this kind of solidarity from the Generals. For the very first time since walking in, the horse felt his liver relax. And his stomach settle. And his gizzards and lungs and esophagus and the rest of his innards also settle. And he felt his blood, which no doubt had been flowing the wrong direction ever since the start of his predicament, now change course and right itself to flow the way it was supposed to.

"Right now, in light of the shenanigans facing the nation, every single eye, alive and dead, is looking to no one but us for leadership, and lead we must and lead we will. And as that leadership we'll be taking the kind of action that shows that, number one, the Revolution will not be hijacked, and number two, Jidada's Liberators cannot and will not be fired willy-nilly from the Party of Power, and at the instruction of demented itchtails who don't know their place, who assume that leadership is sexually trans-mitted, who think the country is their kitchen and bedroom and garden and salon all at once, and who moreover can't even tell you what the air smelled like on the war front! If we let that happen, then what will Jidada become? What will the Seat of Power become? What will the Revolution become?!" General Judas Goodness Reza, on his feet now, barked, and every dog woofed and wagged their tail in agreement. Tholukuthi it took Tuvy every ounce of effort not to hind and ululate like a giddy femal.

"And so, Comrade, in preparation of the work ahead, the intelligent General here has made ready files for you to peruse in the oncoming weeks." General Judas Goodness Reza gestured. General Lovemore Shava passed Tuvy a thick folder. He accepted it with solemnity and began perusing.

"Ah ah ah ah ah! General! But this here is a lot of paper, yeyi! Is there any left where they got it from? I tell you I've never seen a stack this size waiting for me to read and finish it since my school days a long, long time ago," Tuvy said, very much awed by the thickness of the stack.

"I noticed. I can't tell you how sincerely glad I am not to be the one reading them papers. Which is why I had to get those youngsters to read and write that P-h-i- that Ph- that—goddammit, what's the name of that motherfucking certificate that's hanging in my office, Comrade? The one with that round stamp thing the color of gold, that one that they gave me at that gathering when I wore that long red dress and queer cap?" General Judas Goodness Reza said, fumbling with a lighter, a cigarette dangling from the corner of his mouth.

"PhD. You have a PhD in ethics, Chief, from the famed University of KwaZulu-Natal. A staggering achievement no doubt, not every animal in Jidada and indeed all the world can say they have a PhD let alone seen it. Even the Tweeting Baboon of the United States doesn't himself know what a PhD smells like," General Lovemore Shava said.

"Yes, it, that one. Every animal has their thing. Reading is simply not my thing, never was, never will be. But guns, on the other paw, are—I'm a guns animal by my very nature as everybody knows," General Judas Goodness Reza said, holding an imaginary gun, eyes shining.

TO EXILE

And so it was that the very next day, at around the same exact hour that Nicodemus had gone to Jesus once upon a time, former vice president Tuvius Delight Shasha snuck out of Jidada in accordance with the plan hatched at the game-changing meeting with the Generals, yes, tholukuthi to lie in wait in exile as the Revolution was successfully defended in preparation of a new dawn. Not only would exile—out of reach of the Seat of Power's relentless tentacles—guarantee the newly Anointed One with safety until it was time for him to return and save the nation, but it'd also allow him to demonstrate to the whole entire world that yessir, indeed, his life was so gravely in peril that he'd had to flee. But first, the vice president had another long, intense session with Jolijo, tholukuthi an understandably arduous process that took a whole half of the day. And when at last the talented sorcerer pronounced the horse to be more than ready, not just for the life-changing long road ahead but also for his very own emergent glory, Tuvy left for exile with the stride of a conquering lion.

THOLUKUTHI FUGITIVE

#TUVY'S "FLIGHT" TO EXILE

The African Voice @TAV
Ousted #Jidada vice president "flees" to South Africa due to death threats; vows to come back to lead.

> **Sister of the Disappeared** @Shami
> Replying to @TAV
> He'll be back. And one way or the other, one day we'll get our Justice, you can run but you cannot hide.

> **FreeJidada** @freeJidada
> Replying to @TAV
> This gives me life! Welcome to the Opposition experience 😇

> **Bull of Bikita** @truthful
> Replying to @TAV
> Coward, hope the long arm of #Jidada catches your ass.

>> **Simba** @simba_simba
>> Replying to @truthful
>> FYI #Jidada was actually WON from exile. Tuvy will come back *and* rule #Tuvyforpresident

Bosscat @bosscat
Replying to @TAV
Woot 😱 #Jidada. But where's the pics/vid??? Evidence!

My Two Cents @mac2cents
Replying to @TAV
Tholukuthi eish! #Tuvy #Jidada. My thoughts and prayers are in my head.

The African Cow @the_Africancow
Replying to @TAV
Too bad to think the leadership of the Old Horse may be over 😿 The region has never had a better statesman.

> **Peacockbae** @peacockbae
> Replying to @the_Africancow
> You're too funny. Why don't you come live in Jidada for just 10 minutes.

The American Voice @TAV_NEWS
Sacked #Jidada leader flees country. All Eyes On #Jidada! Talks of succession amplify!

> **RamoftheSoil** @ros
> Replying to @TAV_NEWS
> #Sitdown #Notyourstory #Jidadaspeaksforitself

The Voice of Jidada @VOJ_NEWS
Dismissed, Disgraced, Dishonored #Jidada vice president flees.

> **MadeinJidada** @MadeinJidada
> Replying to @VOJ_NEWS
> So #Jidada's top terrorist is crying about being terrorized now 💀

> **Godwin** @Goddy
> Replying to @VOJ_NEWS
> Bruh! 💀

Chipo @Chipo
Replying to @Goddy
When the Frankenstein you helped create comes for you!

The World News @TWN
#Jidada's sacked VP flees for his life.

Ronald Moyo @rmoyoz2020
Replying to @TWN
Shit done got hot in #Jidada. Succession dispute ends with Tuvy in Exile!

Dawta of the soil @Mamli
Replying to @TWN
They should close the border; this beast doesn't deserve any sanctuary.

Zuze Zuze @zuzex2
Replying to @TWN
Please be safe dear leader, and come rescue us fast from this unhinged itchtail who'll vomit on us all 🙏

JKD @thathot
Replying to @TWN
Wow, if this isn't fake news then he's a smart horse #onelife

Ducksure @ducksure
Replying to @thathot
He's not a smart horse he's a good for nothing coward.

Light Force @LightF
#Tuvy goes into hiding 👀

Jidada Shakespeare @Jidshakespeare
Replying to @LightF
Ah-ah, tholukuthi the Ides of March are come in November!

Jidada's Bae @homegrown
Replying to @LightF
Run for it, run for it run

Gandanga @Jidwatch
#Tuvy loses VP post, loses JP membership, flees to South Africa.

> **Exiled Jidadan** @Homeless
> Replying to @Jidwatch
> This is awesome, now you in the same boat as the rest of us,
> horse, maybe we can speak the same language.

> **Mwana WaSt'embeni** @MwanawaSt'embeni
> Replying to @Jidwatch
> Chickens come home to roost 😆

Jefunde @childofthestruggle
The old horse's right hand man flees to SA; path clear for the donkey's
presidency! #Jambanja

> **The SA Dpt of Immigration** @bordercontrol
> Replying to @childofthestruggle
> Nah, we don't want him lana, go back and lie in your bed! Also
> we just have too many #Jidadans here!

> **Mike Robinson** @MikeR
> Replying to @childofthestruggle
> May he suffer like he made us suffer. Amen 🙏 #Justice

> **S'bu** @S'bu1
> Replying to @childofthestruggle
> Tholukuthi bamflashile uTuvy.

TheRealNewsNotFakeNews @trlnfn
BREAKING. Tuvy flees #Jidada, vows to return to lead the country.

> **Tanaka** @Taks1
> Replying to @trlnfn
> Lol 😂

Pro Jidada @proJ4lyf
Fired #Jidada VP threatens to unseat His Excellency!

Dr. Know @drknowPhD
Disgraced former VP flees to exile, ending power struggle. Fair at this point to say that #DrSweetMother is poised for president of #Jidada.

> **Jidadan Panther** @Jidadanpanther
> Replying to @drknowPhD
> How the mighty have fallen!

> **Just an Observer** Nje @timmot
> Replying to @drknowPhD
> Why to SA? Why not to China? Or even Afghanistan?

> **Fancysheep Zhou** @fszhou
> Replying to @drknowPhD
> Gaddafi Style!

> **Uzangenzani** @uza_ngenza
> Replying to @drknowPhD
> That's the lamest thing I've heard. No femal will ever rule Jidada, consult the #criteriaforrulingJidada!

> **NikkiJidaj** @nikki_jidaj
> Replying to @drknowPhD
> Hokoyo Marvelous, I wouldn't celebrate yet! They don't call him Crocodile for nothing, be very, very afraid 🐯

EVEN MONKEYS FALL
FROM TREES

THOLUKUTHI DAWN

The morning appeared like any other morning and indeed would've been any other morning had we not woken up to the seismic rumor that the Father of the Nation had been taken hostage by his very own Defenders in the night. The news felt to us like we'd been shot in the gut, tholukuthi so stunned, so shaken were we that at first we didn't know what to do, what to say, what to think, where to hold, where to touch, and where to let go; yes, we'd always understood, even though some of us no longer believed we'd ever see it happen in our lifetime, that the Old Horse's dawn would someday arrive, one way or the other, but none of us thought it'd come the way it did; tholukuthi we didn't expect it from behind our backs like a thief, no, not by night and when we were sleeping, no, not by hands other than our very own, no, not in the absence of witnesses so we couldn't tell with firsthand authority the story of how it'd actually happened, no—in fact there was even a time back there, a brief moment when we thought

since it wasn't happening the way we'd always imagined it'd happen, then maybe what was happening wasn't true at all.

THE WAY IT SHOULD HAVE HAPPENED

The way we'd always imagined it'd happen, us Jidadans would bring the Old Horse down ourselves, yes, tholukuthi we'd descend on the House of Power in the middle of the day, say around noon—not too early and not too late so none could claim it an inconvenient time. The way we'd always pictured it we'd be such an unstoppable hurricane the armed Defenders standing guard would have no choice but to drop their weapons and flee, while most of them would in fact join us, realizing at last we weren't only fighting for our liberation alone but theirs as well because after all they too were hungry like we were, poor just like we were, suffering like we were, oppressed just like we were.

And with the Defenders out of the way or on our side we'd surge into the great House of Power to occupy every space, while those who couldn't find room remained outside singing revolutionary songs. Inside we'd perhaps find the Old Horse at tea, or maybe eating an early lunch of fancy foods we'd never dream of tasting anymore because we'd become poorer than dung beetles. And if for some reason that itchtail donkey, Marvelous, and so-called Dr. did what she was used to doing with that disrespectful, uncultured mouth of hers, a mouth so filthy even flies refused to land on it, tholukuthi we wouldn't hesitate to backslap some sense into her head so fast she'd finally understand what her mother and grandmother had apparently neglected to teach her, which is where exactly her place was in the world. And if it came down to it, though this wouldn't be our preference at all because even the sticks and stones will tell you that us Jidadans are in our very nature peaceful animals, then we'd have no choice but to make

the Old Horse understand we meant business by lighting things up if needed, tearing things up if needed, smashing things up if needed, burning things down if needed.

NON-STARRING IN OUR OWN MOVIE

Yes, that's how we'd imagined it happening, and we'd played the scenes over and over in our heads and hearts till we could recite, even in our deepest dreams, the lines we'd say to him at the time of confrontation. We actually had the things we'd wear on the day picked out, our bodies had memorized the moves and gestures and postures they'd assume. And so, when it didn't happen just like we'd imagined it, like we'd planned for it to happen, we were caught off guard and disappointed that something so seismic as to shape our and Jidada's lives had indeed happened not only without us but while we slept, tholukuthi somewhere deep in us we felt robbed, left out of our own story.

CELEBRATING LEFT RIGHT AND CENTER

But then in the middle of our disappointment we remembered just how long it'd taken for the Old Horse's dawn to come, how all the proper and possible ways with which we'd tried to free ourselves from his tyrannous rule had failed, and, sobered by these realizations, we very quickly put our regret aside because there was one thing and only one thing that was true and mattered—tholukuthi the Old Horse was finally falling at last. And so, families and friends came together and celebrated. Sworn enemies touched heads and celebrated. Complete strangers stood with each other and celebrated. Supporters of both the Opposition and the Party of Power came together and celebrated. The ailing rose healed from sickbeds and

celebrated. The old and the young stood side by side and celebrated. Animals of all faiths came together and celebrated. The poor and the rich broke bread and celebrated.

But it was still a complicated joy—tholukuthi we'd be ululating one moment, then we'd remember the rocky road that was the Old Horse's terrible long reign and fling ourselves onto the ground, roll in the dirt, and weep. We'd be dancing one moment, and then we'd remember what we'd been reduced to over the years, and weep. We'd be laughing one moment, then we'd recall the rigged elections when we'd dreamt of change, prayed for change, cried for change, voted for change, and where some had died for change, and weep. We'd be cheering one moment, and then we'd remember all those the regime had claimed—the tortured, the jailed, the exiled, the disappeared, the dead, the dead, the dead, the dead—and wail.

Then, as if awakening from a terrible trance we'd reach out for each other, grope around for each other, find each other, hold each other, comfort each other, wipe each other's tears with the frayed flag of Jidada. We somehow, and very, very quickly, had to put all of it—tholukuthi the pain, the suffering, the heartbreak, the dreams unfulfilled, the betrayed hopes, the crushed prayers, all our wounds, all our brokenness—in the past because our long night was ending and a new dawn was rising; we couldn't meet the dawn carrying the sad, terrible baggage of that awful past, no; it absolutely had to find us on a brand-new page and proper ready for a fresh start, best foot forward, no less.

VOICES OF CAUTION: BEWARE OF DOG, BHASOPA LO INJA

But not everyone in Jidada was celebrating. Doomsayers emerged who clearly didn't know what they wanted in life; tholukuthi all along, over the endless, terrible years, we'd stood together as one with them, yes, side by

side like a pair of nostrils, together fervently praying for a Jidada free of
the Old Horse. And now that our prayers had been answered, and answered when we weren't even on our knees, the confused beasts turned
around and didn't want the Old Horse gone anymore! He has to go but
not this way because it's not the right way, they said; It has to be done
properly, they said; This is a coup and we can't, in good conscience, support a coup, they said; Have you forgotten how these very same dogs have
oppressed us since day one of this very regime? What about the tens of
thousands massacred? What about the murdered activists and members
of the Opposition? And the Disappeared, the displaced, the tortured—all
so the Old Horse and this ugly regime could stay in power? What about
the economy they've trashed, the failure of governance, and everything
else that's fallen apart? Aren't we where we are because of all of them, and
these very Defenders you're now cheering? Would the Old Horse even
have been possible without them? Do you honestly think, with everything that's happened, and after all these years, that they'd wake up one
day and remove the Old Horse just for your benefit? the confused animals
asked. Do not be blind, fellow Jidadans, these mongrels don't care a bit
about you; not only that, but this military junta you're unwittingly en-
dorsing will be much, much worse than the Old Horse—one day, not too
far, you'll remember him so much you'll cry for him, they said, the confused beasts. We didn't even have time to waste on these soothsayers of
doom, with their inconvenient concerns and questions and cautionings.
Because, quite simply—hadn't we all failed to remove the Old Horse over
and over for all those years, for all those heartbreaking decades? And
hadn't the Opposition itself failed to unseat him in rigged election after
rigged election? And so, if it wasn't the Defenders themselves to remove
him, then who? And if not a coup, then what? If not then, tholukuthi
when?

VOICES OF UNREASON: WE'LL NEVER BE READY

And yet, another cluster of even worse beasts threw themselves on the ground and filled the air with their stupid grief so that they threatened to drown the sweet song of our joyous jubilation. He's gone! They've removed the Father of the Nation! they cried. Now what'll become of us without him?! Will the sun know to rise without him?! Will we truly ever be the same without him?! they wept. Because, honestly, us we just weren't, we aren't prepared for life without him, the only thing we were ever prepared for was for him to rule until we all died and left him ruling, that our children and their own children would grow old and die and leave him ruling; they cried, the stupids, weeping like it was the end of the world, but so determined were we to celebrate and triumph we raised our own voices with everything in us and silenced them with our noise, and if truth be told, tholukuthi we were actually prepared to go all Defender on the miserable wretches ourselves, yes, proper savage on them because how dare they not only sour our joy but also, right in our very faces and with no shame whatsoever, mourn our oppressor, and how dare they forget how we'd all been living in Jidada, unable to breathe in Jidada, under his tyrannical rule?

THOLUKUTHI NIGHTMARE

On the second morning after the dawn we woke in a state of confusion. We'd collectively dreamt, all of us—every single Jidadan and at exactly the same time—an identical dream in which we saw the Old Horse perched on the highest stone tower of the Jidada ruins, our revered national monument from thousands of years ago, tholukuthi gazing down on us and over the land and looking every bit majestic and un-dethroned, looking as invincible as at the height of his days of glory, Medals of Power

crisscrossed over his solid chest, the brilliant flag of Jidada suspended by God himself just above his head, pitch-black hoof raised in signature defiance. And we watched him point his hoof at the cloudy sky and command the sun to rise in his name, and the sun rose in his name and cleared the clouds, then he pointed to it to move somewhere because it was in his eyes, and the sun quickly found somewhere to go, then he raised those piercing eyes toward the flag and began singing the old, revolutionary national anthem of Jidada with a -da and another -da, and we fell over each other to stand at attention and joined him without being commanded, and gave, at the very top of our voices, the finest rendition of any national anthem ever heard anywhere in the world.

In the morning we woke up relieved it was only a dream, but still upset to have dreamt the wretched dream in the first place. It left us anxious and thinking: What if this is all fake news? What if it's nothing but a cruel joke? Not once since the rumors broke had any of us actually seen the Old Horse with our very own eyes. Where was the evidence he was indeed hostage? And where, exactly, was he? What was happening to him? And where was the donkey? Was it really possible for the donkey to even be silenced with that powerful mouth of hers? And the most disturbing thought of all—even if the rumors were true, what if the Old Horse returned? This thought being because there'd been times previous when news of his death had swept Jidada and we'd wept, not with sadness but with private joy—not because we were evil but because there really were no other options of being rid of him except by death and death alone, only to have him blatantly defy that death itself, materializing like an irremovable curse, like a magician, saying, "Me, dying? Whoever told you these lies?" And, unconvinced that he in fact would not, not emerge this time as he had done many times before, we grew restless and demanded to see him with our own eyes in order that we believe.

POWER IS A KIND OF DEW

And when we eventually saw him for the very first time since his dawn—
the Defenders released a picture—we couldn't believe that what we were
seeing was indeed what we were seeing. There he was, His Excellency no
more, dejected and in disbelief at his demise, more aged than the last time
we'd seen him, which wasn't that long ago, tholukuthi a ghost of himself,
tholukuthi a miserable cheap cell phone on the last 2 percent of its power,
tholukuthi an animal version of the ancient Jidada ruins—majestic once
but now devoid of its former glory. There he was, looking like a prisoner
and perhaps a prisoner, Defenders flanking him on all sides. It's true that
power is a kind of armor, and that once it's been stripped, even the most
powerful animal is nothing but an empty tin. It pleased us to see him the
way he'd become—stripped, dethroned, and powerless; helpless, humbled, and harmless.

THOLUKUTHI PITY

But then at the same time because we'd never seen him like that or thought
of him like that or imagined him like that, there were occasional small moments when our hearts somewhat softened at the edges by the terrible
tragedy of it all; yes, it indeed was a very good thing his dawn had come,
a blessing in fact, for how else otherwise would we've been rid of him?—
but then the way it'd actually happened was also a sad thing, and if he
hadn't been the dictator he'd chosen to become then none of this would be
happening in the first place, and if he hadn't treated us the way he'd done
in all those hard, painful years, decades, tholukuthi we also wouldn't be letting what was happening to him happen: he'd dug his hole and now he had
to lie in it.

AN UNBRIDLED WIFE WILL BE YOUR DOWNFALL

The Father of the Nation's misguided supporters, of course heartbroken beyond measure to see what he'd been reduced to, looked around for something to explain the mad moment and realized they didn't have to look far—the donkey was right there. We'd all missed her at first because we'd never seen her so subdued and looking like a sacrifice, looking like she wasn't even anywhere near, her vomiting mouth for once sealed shut. She and she alone is responsible for all this with that mouth of hers, they said. Which goes to show that a femal has no business whatsoever outside her home, specifically outside the kitchen and bedroom, they said, because look now what she's done, what she's put the Father of the Nation in, what she's put us all in, what she's put Jidada in, they said. Ruling forever was in fact His Excellency's destiny, decreed by God himself and written in the stars, and what did this trash of a donkey, this itchtail and daughter of an itchtail and granddaughter of itchtails do? She squandered it all and did him in and he watched her do it. His dawn wouldn't have otherwise come, they said.

The angry supporters spoke of how if they had anything to say about it they'd have made the itchtail donkey pay for her unpardonable sins. They'd have dragged her on her back, up and down rock-strewn paths. They'd have beat her like a drum. They'd have whacked her joints with sticks. They'd have pulled at her tail until they took the itch out of it. But of course they couldn't, just as we also couldn't walk up to the Old Horse and ask him how it felt; hold our terrible scars to his face to remind him what he'd done to us and ask him why he'd done it to us, just as we couldn't throw at his feet all the terrible things he'd made us carry over the long, hard years—the tyranny, the broken dreams, the indignity, the pain, the poverty, the dead, just so many, many terrible things. We couldn't because it wasn't really us in charge of the happenings.

THE ELEVENTH HOUR

The elite squad of Defenders who went for the Old Horse, speaking on condition of anonymity, would say later they found him reclining on a sofa, surrounded by the most splendid portraits from his days of glory, himself even more splendid that it took all their willpower not to prostrate themselves and sing his praises. They said he was drinking English tea and eating scones and listening to the Voice of Jidada like he did every evening at that time and without fail because he was a creature of routine. He was in a state of such Buddha-like repose the Defenders didn't have the heart to interrupt him, and so they most respectfully paused by the doorway so he could finish his tea.

The Defenders would confess that the whole operation had the feel of an ugly sin, of committing some kind of taboo, and that even though they'd spent some time preparing, when it really came down to the moment, tholukuthi they were ill at ease. That it was only the fear of the big Chiefs behind the whole operation that made them persevere. The dogs kept apologizing as they rounded the First Family up and brought them under guard before the Generals came, and the whole time they couldn't meet the Father of the Nation's lacerating gaze that threatened to slit them open and shred their intestines and livers and hearts. That even under the circumstances, tholukuthi he looked so regal, so born to rule, too beautiful to be intimidated, too beautiful to be deposed, and too beautiful to die.

The Father of the Nation hadn't at first understood what was happening because it was simply unfathomable that even in the face of Defenders brandishing guns he was heard to say, "Is it my birthday again, have you come to surprise me—have they come to surprise me?" Until at last, Dr. Sweet Mother, who'd passed out, regained consciousness, and passed out again when the armed dogs stormed the House of Power—fainting partly out of a genuine fear for her life, and partly out of a profound heartbroken-

ness because she'd never in a million years imagined her and the Father of the Nation's glory would ever come to an end and come to an end that way—regained consciousness and made the Old Horse, who of course was at an age where he couldn't process some things without an interpreter, understand what was happening.

THOLUKUTHI REALITY

It was the hardest thing Dr. Sweet Mother had ever had to do, for she found that even with her PhD, even with her famed oratorical skills, she actually had no language for the impossible situation. When the Father of the Nation at last understood, he sat upright on his sofa like he'd been speared. He reached at his side the way one would reach for a weapon because he at that very moment suddenly remembered his dear friend, brother, and Comrade—the ruler of Uganda, who like him had ruled since before the old trees got old—mention that he kept at his side and at all times, no matter where he was and what he was doing, a revolver, because, the Comrade brother and lifelong ruler said, in the complicated vocation of ruling surrounded by dogs, one could never be so sure how and when one's dawn would come but his would find him ready to send it back to its wretched mother.

Of course the Father of the Nation found no weapon, for he never carried a gun, the business of his protection and security utterly left to Defenders from the very beginning of his rule. And he'd felt perfectly safe and secure under their protection that he perpetually ignored Dr. Sweet Mother and her Future Circle's insistence that he form a special Secret Guard made up only of Defenders who were from his clan, yes, tholukuthi an elite squad of dogs whose loyalty sprang first and foremost from blood because in Jidada with a -da and another -da, blood was everything. Or, failing that, they advised, he enlist a Guard made up of zombie cheetahs or

zombie lions with no connections to life except to be of service to him in order that he totally eliminate all and any possibility of disloyalty. The Father of the Nation had never failed to laugh and wave a dismissive hoof at what he considered far-fetched and paranoid suggestions, saying, "This is Jidada, my dogs love me, they'll never do anything to me, in fact they'll die for me." But what do you know—tholukuthi here were the very Defenders, here doing what the Father of the Nation had sworn they'd never ever do.

THE FIRE THAT COOKS YOUR FOOD AND WARMS YOU TODAY IS THE FIRE THAT'LL BURN YOU TOMORROW

"It's not possible, not possible at all, this is an unfortunate mistake. My animals love and need me. This whole Jidada loves and needs me. The entire Africa loves me. And I know even the Queen of England herself loves me deep down. And the rest of the entire world itself loves me. No, this can't be true!" the Old Horse seethed, so incredulous he spoke with a harsh stammer, so bitter if you'd cut and bled him his blood would've tasted like tar.

And then the Generals entered with their flashing insignias, accompanied by a small group of moderators enlisted to convince the Old Horse that what he was facing was indeed his dawn. All heads were bowed, faces downcast—unable to meet the Father of the Nation's murderous eyes because even despite the circumstances, they still revered him. The one General who wore a hat pulled low confirmed in a subdued voice, "Yes, I'm afraid it is true, Your Excellency, sir, it is indeed like that." General Blessing Bibi was a round, lumpy dog with a meek face. He'd been chosen to speak because of all the dogs present, outside his calmness, he had the best command of the English language, which of course was the Old Horse's preferred language of anger.

"Like what?" the Father of the Nation thundered; he wanted to hear it from the traitors' own mouths.

"Like what it is, dear Excellency sir," General Blessing Bibi mumbled, avoiding the Old Horse's eyes.

"Like what it is? Just what the fuck is that which it is, General Blessing Bibi? And since when am I your dear, do I look like some femal to you? And why don't you look me in the eyes and call it what it is—a fatherfucking coup wena nja, mgodoyi msathanyoko!" the Old Horse roared in the General's mother tongue. Every animal in the room started, not because of the Old Horse's anger, but because never in all his years had he been heard to cuss, more so in a language he was known to not speak too well.

"No, Your Excellency, sir! I know how it appears, dear sir, but it's not really exactly what it appears at all, so there's no need to give it labels, please, sir," General Blessing Bibi said. He still avoided the Old Horse's eyes but traded glances with his superior, General Judas Goodness Reza. He wasn't happy to be doing the dirty work while the General, who really should've been doing the talking given his role in all this mess, sat there like a bride. Moreover, General Blessing Bibi, despite his legendary calmness, was getting agitated and anxious and hoped with everything in him for the situation to remain under control. The plan was to placate His Excellency. And more important, not to fire a single shot. And most important, to make the thing not appear what it was.

"So what are you going to do to us now, you imbeciles? You think that you'll get away with this—" Dr. Sweet Mother, livid, offended, in disbelief, didn't finish her sentence because every single dog whipped his head around to glare at her. The donkey shrunk under the lasers in their eyes, tholukuthi those were the only words to come out of her that night and for the next three nights.

"But tell me, why are you doing this to me, Reza? Involving the army in politics like this, iwe? You of all animals, pulling a what? A bloody

coup, really? General? After everything we've been through, after all I've done for you?" the Old Horse growled, his attention now turned to the bulldog. But General Judas Goodness Reza only sat deaf and mute.

"Please, sir, with all due respect may we hereby desist from calling this thing a coup, especially a bloody coup, it can be seen that there actually isn't a drop of blood in this lovely place," General Blessing Bibi said, frantically gesturing around.

"What the hell are you saying, General? Do you even hear yourself?" the Old Horse thundered.

"All I'm saying, Your Excellency, sir, is stating the true fact that what is happening here is most definitely not a coup," the dog said.

"Then if it isn't a coup just what the fuck is it?" the Old Horse roared. He slammed a hoof on the table and his unfinished cup of Earl Grey dropped and shattered.

"Very sorry about the coup, I mean cup, sir. And, to answer your question, I believe what is happening is only an unfortunate situation that will be straightened forthwith, sir," General Blessing Bibi said. It wasn't hot, but he sweated a river.

"And if I may add, Your Excellency, the Seat of Power voted just a few hours ago to, ehm, allow you to retire and rest—"

"I am the fatherfucking Seat of Power, General, so I don't know what the bloody hell you're talking about! And did you ever hear me say anywhere that I'm tired? Let me tell you, only God, who appointed me, will tell me to rest or retire, not you despicable backstabbing sonsofhyenas! And you may think you're clever but I promise you you're in for a surprise! This is Jidada, my very own Jidada with a -da and another -da we're talking about; just wait and see; you think the children of the nation will accept this? You think Africa will accept this? You think the world will accept this? I know, and you know, and God knows and the sun knows and the land knows and the air knows and the ancestors know, that my

animals will never ever stand for this unconstitutional criminality, this travesty, this abomination. Let me tell you, General, you clearly don't know who you're dealing with. You don't know how much Jidada loves me. You don't know my animals, but today you'll know them, just you wait," the Old Horse raved.

CHANGE OF HEARTS

But the Father of the Nation didn't know us either, didn't know that what was happening to him was actually the best thing to ever happen to us. That after the last election he'd in fact rigged, following the previous one he'd also rigged like the other ones before that he'd stolen—yes, after he and his regime had frustrated all the proper and possible ways at our disposal to remove him in a peaceful and constitutional manner, we'd been left with no choice but to become the kinds of animals to welcome his demise and welcome his demise whichever way it came. Because failure of leadership can change the heart of an animal. Because callous governance can change the heart of an animal. Because corruption can change the heart of an animal. Because poverty can change the heart of an animal. Because tyranny can change the heart of an animal. Because rigged elections can change the heart of an animal. Because the hemorrhaging of democracy can change the heart of an animal. Because the massacre of innocents can change the heart of an animal. Because inequality can change the heart of an animal. Because a regime's ethnicism can change the heart of an animal. Because the poor getting poorer and the rich getting richer can change the heart of an animal. Because crushed hopes, betrayed dreams, the broken promise of independence—all of it—had changed our once patient, loyal hearts so that when the Father of the Nation was waiting for us to show the Defenders how much we loved and needed him, to rise up in his name, we instead poured onto the streets to

help them finish what they had started, yes, tholukuthi to put the nail in the coffin.

THE BEGINNING OF THE END

And in the city center we hinded under the giant jacaranda that was always in bloom, some of us raging, some of us praying, some of us roaring, some of us singing revolutionary songs, some of us singing church songs, some of us talking to foreign journalists. Those who really know about things said inside the House of Jidada the proceedings of impeachment by Parliament were already under way owing to the Father of the Nation's refusal to resign. It was a rare show of unity by the Party of Power and its rival, the Opposition, which otherwise had failed to remove the Old Horse through elections and like most of us were now ready to see him gone at whatever cost.

Had he not seen the throngs of animals with his own eyes he certainly wouldn't have agreed to what he called the falsity that Jidada—yes, his beloved Jidada with a -da and another -da itself, tholukuthi the one and only country he loved best out of the rest, was indeed calling for his ouster. Those who know about things said he'd told the assembled party of negotiators that just like he'd refused the humiliation of being forced to resign, and doing so on TV at that and in front of all his enemies, and through an insulting dumb speech written by someone apparently with the brain of a turd, he was accordingly refusing the dishonor of abandoning the children of the nation at a critical time and when they obviously needed him. And when General Blessing Bibi insisted, "But the children of the nation themselves seem to want you to leave, Your Excellency, sir, they are as we speak gathered outside the House of Jidada and calling for your removal," the Father of the Nation laughed a laugh to flutter flaccid flags: "You must be out of your mind to think children can discard their very own father like

they do used toilet paper! If you and I go to that House of Jidada right this very moment and I see happen what you say is indeed happening, then by all means, General, I will fucking resign; like I said, you don't know my children, you don't know my animals!"

Tholukuthi they went out in a beaten Scotch cart in order not to draw attention. Once they got to the heart of the gathering they slipped into the streets, the Father of the Nation dressed incognito so nobody would recognize him. The sheer size of the throngs very nearly split him open—it was bodies, bodies, bodies everywhere and bodies all over. Had it not been for the familiar landscapes, he didn't know if he'd have recognized the city itself because what was happening wasn't the kind of thing to happen in his Jidada with a -da and another -da, and he stood for a moment and wondered if what he was seeing was indeed what he was seeing. Animals wearing the Jidada Party regalia and animals wearing the Opposition Party regalia marched and danced together, and the Father of the Nation stared at the spectacle in shock, feeling sick, feeling faint, feeling betrayed, because his regime had spent all those years creating a Jidada wherein it shouldn't have been possible for animals of the opposing parties to ever stand together in the name of one Jidada. He wasn't alone in these thoughts—above the celebrating animals, a school of vultures flew in circles, confused and wondering, Where the bloody hell was the blood? And where on earth were the bodies? Because tholukuthi in the Jidada they knew, any gatherings against the Seat of Power always ended, and without fail, with carrion, carrion, carrion.

The Old Horse saw pigs flying an enormous yellow balloon that said "Jidada Will Never Be Your Colony Again!" He saw a cat bearing a sign that said "Down With The Despot!" A ram whose sign said "The Old Horse Must Go." A donkey whose sign said "Enough Is Enough!" There was a peacock whose sign said "Time O'clock." A sheep whose sign said "Old Horse Leave Jidada Now!" A cow whose sign said "Free Jidada."

Another whose sign said "#CommandResignation." And another whose sign said "#FreshStart." He saw a duck whose sign said "Go Go Our Generals." A goat whose sign said "For Our Children And Our Future." A horse whose sign said "The Old Horse Must Rest Now." A chicken whose sign said "The Dogs Are The Voice of Jidada." A goose whose sign said "Down With Corruption!" A donkey whose sign said "House of Jidada Just Finish The Job." A goat whose sign said "Leadership Is Not Sexually Transmitted!" A cat whose sign said "Old Horse Dololooo!!!"

He saw so many different signs, illegal signs, unbelievable signs, ungrateful signs, wrong signs, ill-informed signs, and the animals that carried them danced and ran and yelled and shrieked, baying for his illegal ouster. "Down with the tyrant!" they roared. "Goodbye to a dictator!" they thundered. "Down with oppression!" they shrieked. "Viva New Dawn!" the throngs howled, swallowing the streets, and still more of them coming in droves and more droves. Animals whistled. Animals played vuvuzelas. Animals sang songs. Animals laughed. Animals uttered prayers. More animals came in crawling cars. In bicycles. In buses. In Scotch carts. Animals watched from trees. And the droves kept coming and coming and he didn't understand any of it.

THE MIDDLE OF THE END, AND HEARTBREAK NUMBER ONE

At some point he tilted his head to the heavens, perhaps in search of a sign from God, who'd anointed him, who'd decreed that he rule and rule and keep ruling, but all he saw was the dimmed sun. He gave it a silent command for it to blacken—yes, tholukuthi the Father of the Nation wanted for the sun to cast Jidada into a proper pitch-darkness right in the middle of the day and throw the whole treasonous gathering into disarray so as to give himself time to seek his true friends and together find a way out of this mess of a mistake, but tholukuthi the sun didn't flinch, didn't budge,

didn't nothing—for the very first time in his God-decreed rule the sun flat-out refused to obey him.

And he stood there in even more disbelief, shaking but trying not to shake, feeling utterly alone in the midst of the electric throngs and thinking, But what happened? Yes, asking himself, But what had happened and when had it happened and at what point exactly had it happened that these very animals who'd once loved him had apparently stopped loving him, stopped needing him? And he thought what he'd have done for that love. Tholukuthi his heart ached so much it broke, not just once, but thousands and thousands and thousands of times—one for each and every animal out on the streets and wherever the Jidadans were, who wouldn't love him at that very moment. It was in fact his first real heartbreak.

THE END-END

And when General Blessing Bibi asked him in a gentle voice if he wanted to try to move up the street to the House of Jidada itself so they could see more, tholukuthi His Excellency simply shook his dizzy, grizzled head, thinking, But what about the animals who used to pack all my rallies so there'd be no room to stand, where are they? And where are the Patriots of the Nation who came to my events all decked out in clothes emblazoned with my face, where are they? And where are the femals who'd sing and ululate at every one of my gatherings, who'd send me off and meet me chanting and dancing at airports, yes the very femals who'd gyrate their hips and shake their backsides till their clothes, emblazoned with my face, almost fell off, where are they? And where are the young ones who'd prostrate themselves in my presence as if in the presence of a god, where are they, yes, where are they, all those animals who used to love me, who used to need me, where are they with their love???

Tholukuthi he was standing there thinking of all that love when a thin

cow thrust a flag in his face and said, "I never thought I'd live to see the demise of the wretched tyrant, did you, my love? Now I can die better, now we can all die better, just imagine that!" The demented cow gloated, oblivious of who she was addressing, giggling to reveal uneven ugly teeth and nudging him solicitously as she ambled off toward a drift of baying pigs. He watched her take her leave, feeling so bitter he tasted Gamatox in his mouth, thinking, Where is God who decreed that I rule and rule and keep ruling? And where are my Inner Circles? The Seat of Power? And where are the Chosen? And where are my neighbors? And where are my friends? And where is the world when Jidada is falling apart the way it's falling?

And he turned and made his way back the direction they'd come, moving against the tide of bodies who didn't stop to give way, who didn't sing him praises, who didn't see him when he was right there among them and with them. He picked his way, blindly, bitterly, a heaviness in his limbs. He bumped into a lone figure—a sheep—and was getting ready to spew his wrath on her when he saw himself, that is, saw his face on her yellow shirt and again on her black skirt and again on her red scarf and again on her green hat and again on her white bag. The sheep was weeping, not tears of joy like all the other treacherous beasts, no, but weeping torrents of true heartbreak, and, so moved was the Father of the Nation by her tremendous sorrow, he stopped in his tracks.

"He's gone, they've removed the Liberator! Who was my president, and who was also my mother's president, and who was also my grandmother's president; now who will become my children's president?! And their children's president?! And their children's children's president? Now what will become of me, of us, without him?!" the sheep baaed, and the Father of the Nation was so incredibly touched to see himself mourned like that, as if he'd died real death itself, tholukuthi so touched he reached

out for the grief-stricken animal but stopped because he at that very moment saw a gang of morbid young beasts set his beautiful official portrait ablaze. It ignited and burned, and he could've sworn he felt the flames devouring his own flesh. At last, unable to stand any more of the sacrilege, he headed back to the House of Power, looking older than he'd looked when he left just a couple of hours earlier, and when someone gave him a resignation letter he hadn't written but was supposed to have written and asked him to sign it like he'd written it, tholukuthi he signed it.

SELFIES WITH THE SOLDIERS

And there, while we stood outside the House of Power, came the much-awaited news, just at the same time the sun did a strange flip and dimmed a little bit, casting a shadow in the sky—yes, tholukuthi the news being that the Father of the Nation had finally tendered his resignation. And as the news spread like wildfire, Jidada with a -da and another -da ignited. And on our newly liberated streets, in the midst of the fiesta, the Defenders came out in their tanks, brandishing weapons, and for the first time in a long time we didn't flee for our lives at the sight of heavily armed dogs— Jidada was finally free at last! And on the liberated streets we forgot our fear, our painful history with the Defenders and broke bread with them, we said prayers with them, yes, tholukuthi on those liberated streets we posed for selfies with the soldiers. We leapt to the heavens and back to earth, we danced, beat our chests, and stomped the ground along with the soldiers, and in the jungles right outside Jidada we were heard by lions and elephants and buffalo and rhinoceros and leopards and other fierce beasts of the wild, who trembled at the seismic sound of our liberation.

GOD OF JIDADA

THOLUKUTHI GOD OF MULTITUDES, THOLUKUTHI COMMANDER OF REAL RALLIES

On that Sunday morning at seven o'clock sharp, the spirit of God descended full force on the vast Old Jidada Showgrounds, where just the year before he'd instructed Prophet Dr. O. G. Moses to move the Soldiers of Christ Prophetic Church of Churches. Within a few hours, the grounds were packed to bursting; even the sticks and stones could've told you that yes, in the business of gatherings, nobody and no one, tholukuthi no party or politician, tholukuthi no Seat of Power, tholukuthi no performing artist, tholukuthi no celebration, tholukuthi no funeral, tholukuthi no protest, tholukuthi not even a crisis—assembled masses like God assembled masses. The services began, as usual, with fervor. The way the congregants, known as Soldiers for short, explained it to curious outsiders who cared to know, they said this zealzest, contrary to lesser, miserable churches wherein the program began with the ludicrous energy of grandfather tortoises, only to maybe gradually pick up at different points as things moved along, the Soldiers of Christ Prophetic Church of Churches simply oper-

ated on one gear from start to finish, tholukuthi the high gear, also fondly known to the Soldiers as the fire-fire gear. This, they said, was owing to the overwhelming presence of God that was experienced the moment an animal set hoof, paw, or foot on the holy ground.

"You feel it, Duchess, don't you? That particular energy? Us Soldiers here call it fire-fire. No matter your belief, you just can't not feel it, my sister! It's God himself, he's here! Khona nje vele if we were sitting up front, I'm telling you, Duchess, you'd feel it proper-proper. If we were sitting up front me and you wouldn't even be talking like this," an eye-catching sheep in a large red hat that half hid her face said with sheer glee, aggressively nudging the cat next to her. The sheep, who had to shout in order to be heard, was known as Mother of God, tholukuthi so named after her firstborn son, Godknows. She spoke with the brazen pomposity typical of bona fide Soldiers because, among other things, Prophet Dr. O. G. Moses never failed to impress upon his congregants that if they weren't prepared to be proud of their God's glory, to show off and be loud and arrogant for their Messiah, then they definitely weren't worthy of placing their behinds on consecrated ground.

"It's as if these crowds keep growing, dadwethu kababa," responded the Duchess of Lozikeyi, or simply Duchess for short. Ignoring what the cat considered a nonsense statement was in fact the best she could do to avoid hurting her friend's feelings, but she'd ignored the sheep enough already and she suspected the cup of her kindness would run empty sooner rather than later. Like the sheep, the Duchess was old and extremely elegant, but unlike the sheep, her way of constantly rotating her head and gawking, shaking that same head while emitting guttural sounds that could very well have been contempt or disavowal, of slapping her thighs at what she was seeing, betrayed her as both an outsider and a nonbeliever.

"What did I tell you? We're massive! Just massive nje, okok'thi khonapha so vele, no church in this whole entire Jidada can touch us, not even that

arrogant Apostle Ezekiel's church." The sheep bobbed her head and beamed with animated eyes. The two were neighbors in the township of Lozikeyi, where they lived, and had known each other for over five decades now, which also made them sisters.

"The way you're going on you'd think you're referring to a pile of proper money in your own bank account," the Duchess said. But that was the second thing to pop into the cat's head. Tholukuthi the first thing to pop into the cat's head was: "Apparently this fire-fire thing in the air you were talking about also makes you an imbecile." But she obviously chose to take a sip from her cup of kindness yet again. Now it was Mother of God's turn to do the ignoring. In addition to being an outsider, a non-believer, the Duchess was also what Prophet Dr. O. G. Moses referred to and rebuked in his fiery sermons as a "deplorable pagan heathen sorcerer," for the cat—as suggested by the bright beads blazing around her neck and wrists—practiced the indigenous religion she could trace back to her great-great-grandmother Nomkhubulwane Nkala, a healer and spirit medium. Mother of God hoped for the sake of peace that her vocal Prophet wouldn't bring up one of his favorite topics that day.

"And you're saying, Mother of God, that even in these crowds, you were able to spot Simiso?" the cat said, tholukuthi broaching her real reason for being at the church where she otherwise wouldn't have been found.

"That's exactly correct. But only because she was going row after row, dressed in the very same red dress she wore last time we saw her in Lozikeyi, carrying a picture of her and Destiny, and asking, "Have you seen my daughter?" I really should've talked to her properly mani, Duchess. But somehow I was so caught up in the visiting Nigerian Prophet's sermon I only realized this long after Simiso disappeared in the throngs," the sheep said with genuine regret.

"Well, the milk is spilt, Mother of God, no use regretting. And this

Nigerian preacher you speak of, he came all the way from Nigeria just to preach nje?"

"Prophet, Duchess, not preacher, Prophet. The famous one who not only turned water into wine at a wedding but also bread into cake when they ran out, you may remember he was all over the news for it. He was accompanied by, whatshisname, that rich Apostle from Malawi who's based in South Africa."

"Hmmmm," the Duchess said, cocking her head and grooming her whiskers.

"If you think this place is packed, you should've seen it then." Mother of God glowed with pride, as if she and herself alone were responsible for said packing.

"What I personally want to see myself, are whites congregated in New York City, in London, in Paris, in Berlin—in throngs of this size, in the name of an indigenous African religion, and speaking an African language while they're at it. That, Mother of God, is what I want to see, just that nje, nothing more."

Mother of God ignored her friend, but not before thinking a thought that made her bend down and reach beneath her chair, rummage inside her bag for her vial of anointing oil, and dab her forehead. Tholukuthi the thought that made Mother of God bend down and reach beneath her chair, rummage inside her bag for her vial of anointing oil, and dab her forehead was that if indeed practitioners of traditional religions were devil worshippers like the Prophet said, she may have unwittingly invited Satan to hallowed ground, and this she was hearing wasn't just her friend speaking. And when the sheep sat back up she in fact thought she perceived a dark halo over the cat's head that she hadn't noticed before, which made her bend down yet again and reach back beneath her chair, retrieve her vial, and dab her forehead with the anointing oil all over again.

GODLESS

"Dadwethu kababa! Uyazi I didn't know that imigodoyi actually attended church. That much I didn't know," the Duchess said.

She could've been talking to her partner, but the thick thorns in her voice, and the way the pair of dogs seated directly in front of the friends swiveled their heads, tholukuthi as if they'd actually been pricked, said they were very much the intended audience. If the dogs were surprised to see that the animal talking the type of nonsense that earned fools bitings and beatings and even visits to jail was nothing more than a little old cat, then their expressionless hard eyes and closed faces didn't show it. They simply looked her up and down without moving either eyes or heads, then just as suddenly as they'd swiveled to face her, turned back around.

"I mean, the way they terrorize and clobber and spill blood all over Jidada's streets you'd think they actually worship a devil. Did you hear, Mother of God, what they did to the Sisters of the Disappeared at the Jidada Square, how they almost took out MaMlovu's eye with batons? And now nampa la, here they are, making like they have anything to do with God when they can't even spell his name." The Duchess did not hide her indignation, her intent to draw blood. One dog turned around with a menacing grin and said, "God is for everyone, Auntie. And you're talking about our jobs. That in fact have nothing to do with who we are, and just so you know, we follow orders like employees everywhere," the dog growled before turning back around.

And the Duchess of Lozikeyi, despite nearly passing out from the dog's fetid breath, opened her mouth to speak—intending to begin of course by telling the ugly mongrel that she was not his auntie—but what emanated from her mouth instead was a weird cackle that made Mother of God regret bringing her friend along because she knew exactly what'd follow the uncanny laugh, yes, tholukuthi that it'd be nothing less than a litany of

such devastating profanity the dogs, her beloved brothers in Christ, would have to find somewhere else to sit. And the cat was indeed readying to deliver said litany when, in what Mother of God could only think of as divine intervention, Prophet Dr. O. G. Moses hinded onto the raised platform, looking absolutely magnificent in a white suit. Then he was suddenly on the dozens and dozens of large projector screens planted throughout the vast grounds in order that he was seen and heard by every eye and ear. Tholukuthi the service was also at that moment being livestreamed for the benefit of those of the Soldiers who, for one reason or another, couldn't physically attend, and of course for anyone, both in Jidada and the wherevers of the whole wide world, who wanted to experience the famed fire-fire.

THE SAVIOR

And now, on seeing the Prophet, the Soldiers applauded without cessation until the pig waved a white hanky, cutting the applause.

"Before we begin today's service I'd like to take this blessed opportunity to thank my God the creator, my God the redeemer, my God the good shepherd for favoring Jidada in our time of need, Halleluyah!" the pig sang in a passionate, sonorous voice.

"Amen!!!" the Soldiers thundered in the deafening fire-fire gear.

"For God saw our long suffering, let me tell you O Precious Soldiers, for he understood that we desperately needed a change, needed a new way, and thus saw fit to give us exactly what we needed and exactly right when we needed it even as we least expected it because he is the ultimate Father who knows what his children need without them necessarily asking for it! Yeeeeeees, God, my Father, accordingly sent Jidada a Savior because he understood his nation was in desperate need of saving, Halleluuuuuuuuuuuuuuuuuyah!" the pig cried, yes, tholukuthi his "Halleluyah"

picked up and held by Mother of God and the entire mass until the earth quivered.

Here the Prophet turned to look behind him, where his wife, his assistants, dignitaries, among them Jidada's Chosen and the visiting new Seat of Power, sat under a white tent. And because this endorsement by the charismatic, famous leader of the top evangelical sect in Jidada with a -da and another -da was no less than an endorsement by God himself, the Seat of Power was seen to hind, limbs high up in the air in the signature revolutionary party salute. They sat back down at a gesture from the Prophet.

"I am both honored and delighted, O Precious Soldiers, to present to you Jidada's own God-sent Savior to address you with his own mouth. Please welcome our special surprise guest for today, His Excellency and the President of the Republic of Jidada in waiting and Bringer of Change and only him himself—Comrade President Tuvius Delight Shasha, Halleluyah!"

THOLUKUTHI ANGEL OF CHANGE, THOLUKUTHI PROPHET OF THE NEW DISPENSATION

Upon seeing their brand-new president suddenly in their midst without expecting him, tholukuthi the Soldiers went berserk: "Tuvy! Tuvy! Tuvy! Tuvy! Tuvy! Tuvy! Tuvy! Tuvy! Tuvy! Tuvy! Tuvy! Tuvy! Tuvy! Tuvy! Tuvy!" And Tuvy, who was only addressing his second crowd in his new role as President of Jidada in waiting, was incredibly moved by the throngs that far surpassed the Party of Power's welcoming audiences of his initial return from exile. He basked, tholukuthi reveled, in the love, the goodwill, the support communicated by the applause until he feared his heart would burst. When he finally remembered to raise a hoof in the signature revolutionary Party of Power salute, the Soldiers hushed.

Later, the throngs would go on to say that they didn't recognize the

voice that spoke to them. That what they heard that day was a brand-new voice of power, tholukuthi a voice of a true Savior of the Nation.

"My dear Jidadans. Without eating into your service, I came here in the flesh, and in the presence of the Lord, to deliver the tremendous news of a New Dispensation, a New Jidada. To commit to you, to tell you that this country's long, long, long terribly dark night has indeed ended and we now perch on the wings of a brand-new dawn. And under the light of that brand-new dawn, the long-overdue journey to the promised land can finally begin! In fact, if truth be told, we're already in it because Jidada is Open for Business and tremendous things are happening! Forward with a New Jidada!"

"Forward!!!" the exhilarated throngs roared.

"Forward with the Party of Power!"

"Forward!!!"

"Forward with Unity!"

"Forward!!!"

"Forward with God!"

"Forward!!!"

"Down with the Devil!"

"Down!!!"

"Down with the Opposition!"

"Down!!!"

"My fellow Jidadans, you will no doubt see new changes in the coming times. Among them that I myself, Tuvy, will always address you directly, and with my own mouth. And by this I mean you won't see the femal otherwise known as my wife standing in front of the nation purporting to speak for me because unlike some animals I don't need to name, not only am I an animal who has his house in order and under control, but also because as a wife, my femal has her own God-given place, and that place

is definitely not in insulting honorables at rallies, but rather in the home and church, Amen!"

"Amen!!!"

"And finally, I absolutely cannot leave here without testifying how God saved me so that I could come back here to both save the nation as well as serve it, Halleluyah!

"Amen!!!"

"The Dark Forces were doing their best to eliminate me as you all know, and as you all saw, but they failed. Over and over. And the only reason they failed is I had God's own Defenders defending me! Even as I had to flee to exile for my life as you all saw, I had no fear because I knew I was under His protection, Amen!"

"Halleluyah!!!"

"So, my fellow citizens. There is not much to say but Glory be to God! I can't tell you how much it warmed my heart while in exile, while in the wilderness, to watch on TV, you, Jidadans of all walks of life, peacefully and with unparalleled discipline, throng the streets in record numbers on that great day of change to say enough is enough, to say a brand-new leader was needed, to say it was time for a New Jidada. And let me tell you, you were speaking at one with God! Because the voice of the masses, your very voice, is the voice of God, Halleluyah!"

"Amen!!!"

"My fellow Jidadans, in no time, because God has decreed a New Jidada is come, because we are already in a new dawn, a new season, a New Dispensation, Jidada will wake up like a sleeping lion and roar! And all the countries all over the world will hear her and tremble! And Jidada shall rise like a rainbow and become great again! And every living thing walking the earth—be it on two legs or four legs or dozens of legs or slithering on its belly—will behold the beauty of that rainbow! And this our very Jidada will open up like a flower and fill the world with its divine

fragrance! And it shall gallop to great heights never seen! Milk and honey will flow once more on these very streets! Money, real Jidadan money, and not moneys from other lands, will grow in your very gardens! Never, never, never again will you want for anything! Because of how precious it is, this Jidada, you and I will welcome it with Free, Fair, and Credible elections; in fact, in this coming year we will be holding Jidada's historic free and fair elections so that the New Jidada is indeed born with the beautiful birthmark of justice and real freedom! And so I say to you all today with my own mouth, get ready, please get ready for Canaan, the promised land! Thank you, Comrades, and God bless you and Amen!!!" The Savior bowed and left the podium, tholukuthi chest out and tail swooshing with brand-new authority.

The Soldiers went really, really berserk, the New Jidada so near, so very near they in fact felt it breathing on their necks. They yelled. They shrieked. They sang. They danced. They jumped. They hugged each other. They butted heads and they butted butts. They wept. Then they broke into tongues and prayer so earth-moving that leaves and fruit fell from nearby trees. And God was in attendance at the vast Old Jidada Showgrounds, and God was magnificent at the vast Old Jidada Showgrounds and save for the Duchess and about five or six other unsaved and probably unsavable souls, God was felt by all at the vast Old Jidada Showgrounds.

HEATHEN

"Mother of God, but what just happened? Please tell me what I thought I was seeing is not what I was seeing," the Duchess said.

"Well, it's indeed as you saw it, that was the new President himself, Duchess! I had no idea he was coming. But I'm happy to see and hear him for myself ngoba you don't know the sleepless nights I keep, wondering if it's really true the Old Horse is gone. Fearing, you know, like how in the

past they've said he is dead, only to find out he isn't. But I suppose he's gone-gone-gone. I tell you I never thought I'd see a second president in my lifetime, I can barely—"

"You call this fool, this criminal, this genocidist, this perfect idiot, a president, Mother of God?"

"No one is perfect, Duchess, and besides, who am I to judge when God himself tells us not to? It was time the Old Horse leave, and at this point, whoever leads us now, it can't get any worse. Ngoba what haven't we seen in this Jidada? What really is the defense for keeping the Old Horse ruling? What good thing has he been doing that I maybe missed?"

"Mother of God, all I'll say is I'll ask for the food once it's cooked. Because on this one we could talk until our mouths relocated to the tops of our heads and I just don't have the energy. But what I'll say for now, is I'd want you to bring me back here later."

"You don't say, Duchess?!"

"Didn't I just say?"

"Well, well. Praise the Lord, Ebenezer! I never in a million years thought I'd live to see the day the Holy Spirit move the Duchess of Lozikeyi herself! My, my, my, God is good!" The sheep beamed.

"Did I say what for, Mother of God? Did I even say what for?"

"Hawu, Duchess?"

"I want to come back in a year, hell, forget a year, in just a few months. Bring me back after this upcoming election y'all are so excited about."

"But why after the election, Duchess?"

"Because I want to see if you'll still be saying Amen-Amen-Amen once you open your eyes and realize that God has in fact taken you out of the cooking pot and into a proper inferno itself," the cat said with satisfaction. Mother of God opened her mouth to speak, but it was the Prophet's voice that was heard instead:

LORD OF BLESSINGS

"I greet and bless you once again, O Soldiers of the Master, the Ruler of all rulers, the Supreme Leader, the Potentate, the Liberator of Liberators, the Father of all Nations, the Defender of all Defenders," the Prophet sang, having explained to the Soldiers that the Savior of the Nation and his delegation had already moved on to make similar stops at other churches near and far.

"O Precious Soldiers. The things that God my Father has revealed to me! The things that he has decreed to happen to this New Jidada of the New Dispensation are simply tremendous, to quote one famous leader I very much admire and who inspires me, can I hear a tremendous O Soldiers!"

"Tremendous!!!"

"Say tremendous in Jesus's name!"

"Tremendous in Jesus's name!!!"

"No, I meant just tremendous!"

"Tremendous!!!"

"God. Has. Shown. Me. Jidada's. Coming. Tremendous. Glory. Halleluyah!"

"Amen!!!"

"And in the name of God, my Father, I hereby predict the prosperity that Jidada has been praying for. I hereby predict the peace that our mothers have been crying for! I hereby predict the freedom that the children of the nation have been bleeding for! I hereby predict bread falling from heaven and rivers of milk and honey and Coca-Cola that our bellies have been starving for! I hereby predict prosperity so glorious the streets, roads, and skies of the nation will be filled pam-pam with the lost diaspora come back home at long last, Halleluyah!!!"

"Amen! Amen! Amen! Aaaaaaaaaaaaaaaaaaaaaamen!!!"

"Because his word, not mine, O Precious Soldiers—on Philippians four, nineteen—mark that verse in your hearts, I want you to remember this verse for always: "My God will meet all your needs according to the riches of his glory in Christ Jesus." Yes, you've heard it, now speak it to me—My God will meet which needs? How many needs? Tell it to me now, O Precious Soldiers!"

"ALL OUR NEEDS!!!"

"That's right. As you stand here, right now, I tell you my God is busy meeting all your needs left right and center, Halleluyah!"

"WE RECEIVE!!!"

"But!" the pig said, raising a hoof, pacing now, his body jittery with spirit. "But first, God has a special message for the femals today. That's right, my Father wants me to speak specifically to the femals right now. Where are the femals at?" The pig, neck craned, paused and looked dead-pan into the throngs.

GOD'S WORD TO FEMALS

As in most churches in Jidada with a -da and another -da, tholukuthi femals made up the majority of the congregants, and now, on hearing themselves specifically called upon by the Prophet, on hearing that the Prophet had a message directly from their Father, Mother of God, along with each and every femal of every age present, felt filled with a delicious ecstasy. Tholukuthi they ululated and cried and laughed and sang and shrieked. The Duchess, who saw now how her friend's head was thrown back, face as blissful as a bride's, tears of jubilation staining the wide cheeks scarred by creams in the name of the fur-lightening religion of a long-gone youth, shook her head, muttered, "Dadwethu kababa," and folded her paws over her chest.

"Today Jidada is in the midst of seismic shifts, O Precious Females, Halleluyah!" the Prophet said.

"Amen!!!"

"And in these shifts God is showing us, like he showed us with Eve in the Garden of Eden, like he again showed us with Delilah and Samson's hair, and then again showed us with Lot's wife, and also again showed us with that Witch of Endor's shenanigans, like he again showed us with the wicked Queen Jezebel, he has gone on to show us again here in our very own Jidada with a -da and another -da, the disastrousness, the deviousness, the danger of a delusional, Godless femal if left to her own devices, Amen!" the Prophet sang.

"Halleluyah!!!" the Soldiers roared, tholukuthi a Halleluyah noted for its overwhelming baritones and basses and tenors, for the femals had by now gone so silent they could've turned to miserable pillars of salt.

"Yes, and if for any reason whatsoever you don't understand, if somehow you can't read God's revelations, then turn to your neighbor and say, "Tell me, O Precious Soldier, where is the Father of the Nation today? And how come he's not sitting where God intended him to sit?!" The Prophet strutted up and down the stage, unbuttoning his jacket. The baritones and basses and tenors roared in applause.

"Yeeeeeeeeeeeeees! A femal who didn't know her place, a femal with no sense of boundaries, a femal destitute of shushness and shyness and shame, an unbridled femal, a femal who didn't actually understand why God created a mal first and why she was made last and not just made last but made from a mere rib and not even a paramount body part, a femal who didn't heed God's word when he said with his own mouth for femals not to rule—that kind of femal bredren is the one and only reason the Father of the Nation, God bless his heart, which those who know, know was in the right place before a certain femal came into his life like an angel of darkness

to both dim the light of his glory and also derail him from his destiny—yeeeeeeeeeeees, that type, that species, that order of femal is the one and only reason the Father of the Nation is no longer on the Seat of Power like God had intended, Halleluyah!"

The two dogs in front of the friends turned around as if on cue, tholuku-thi long tongues lolling. They pierced the Duchess of Lozikeyi with those hard eyes that so clearly said, "Let she who has ears listen and hear." And, their point made without them uttering a single word, they neatly turned back around. Now the mals hinded and beat their chests and roared and boomed and thundered and stomped the earth to mush. And when they sat back down, after the Prophet quietened them, they settled themselves with the air of haughty giraffe queens, tholukuthi with the straightest spines, the legs splayed, and heads reaching for God's sky, secure in the knowledge that they were unblemished by Eve and her miserable kin's boundless disgrace.

"Dadwethu kababa! Mother of God, tell me this blali swine isn't standing in this hot sun saying Jidada's coup has to do with that poor child, Marvelous! Doesn't he know that's how dictatorships, like a monster devouring itself, end, with coups?" the Duchess cried, incredulous. At these words the hairs on the dogs' necks instantly stood, but the hounds didn't turn around. And neither did Mother of God show any visible reaction—the Duchess might as well have been addressing a rock, for her friend was at that point wallowing in the deep river of the shame of the sins of her biblical mothers and sisters. And wherever the cat's head turned, wherever her eye fell, femals accordingly hung their heads, yes, tholukuthi reduced, small, shrunken, miserable raisins in the sun against their mal counterparts, who appeared ready to levitate off their seats.

"Listen to me, Halleluyah!" the Prophet called.

"Amen!!!"

"You might think this issue of being outside of God's covenant is just

the First Femal's issue alone, but let me tell you, no, it isn't, because it follows that one problem femal by nature generally implies a whole hornet's nest of them whether they are visible to the naked eye or they're hidden to the naked eye, Halleluyah!"

"Amen!!!"

"It's even the same reason why, when one femal is in the way of the moon, for instance, she'll go about triggering other femals to follow suit so that before you know it there's a whole bunch of them in that unclean condition all at once and all over the place you can't even tell what is what and which is which and what exactly they'll do either separately or together, Amen!"

"Amen!!!"

"Yeeeeeeeeeees, you might remember that—and if you can't remember, don't worry, God loves you because he sent me here like he once sent my brother Jesus to save the world. Similarly my Father sent me to carry the cross of reminding you—as I was saying, you may remember that a group of naked femals stormed the stage when the Father of the Nation was in the middle of his last speech. I saw it. Y'all saw it. God saw it. The birds saw it. The sticks and stones saw it. Am I lying?!"

"No you're not lying!!!"

"I mean naked femals, as naked as a tongue. Naked femals, right in the middle of an important occasion! Naked femals, in the presence of the very young! Naked femals, right there with the very old-looking! Naked femals, during a state occasion with esteemed foreign dignitaries in attendance! Naked femals, with thousands of eyes watching! If there was ever an abomination in this Jidada with a -da and another -da, then that, right there, was the abomination. If you've ever wondered what an abomination looks like, O Precious soldiers, wonder no more, for you've seen it," the Prophet said, his voice suddenly close to breaking.

The pig gazed into the throngs with a face now awash in such sadness the whole showgrounds went silent. Those who were there said never had such a silence been heard or would ever be heard again at the Soldiers of Christ Prophetic Church of Churches, and indeed in any kind of gathering in Jidada with a -da and another -da. Tholukuthi it was the kind of silence before a miracle, the kind of silence after death. And, just as the Soldiers were contemplating it, they saw their Prophet's eyes soften. Then they saw their Prophet's eyes well up and get all wet. And then, before they could ask themselves if what they were seeing was indeed what they were seeing, tholukuthi they saw their beloved Prophet burst into tears.

And Prophet Dr. O. G. Moses wept as Jesus had wept, yes, tholukuthi the Prophet weeping for the deviant naked femals of Jidada with a -da and another -da who'd apparently chosen the wretched path of ungodliness. And, seeing their Prophet's tears for the very first time in their lives, the femal Soldiers, suddenly not knowing where to look, shuffled like they were standing on stolen feet whose owners had just entered the building. And then, like a coordinated choir, every single one of them began to bawl.

They weren't the Sisters of the Disappeared, no, they weren't the guilty ones, no, tholukuthi they themselves didn't, would never even dream of participating in such an undertaking, let alone any event of a political nature, as per the Prophet's teachings, but they still somehow felt implicated, bound to the deviant, ungodly Sisters of the Disappeared just as they knew they were bound to their sinning biblical mothers and sisters. And where they'd been previously filled with ecstasy, where they'd felt the weightlessness of incense, they now felt like mountains—filled with a heaviness they couldn't bear.

"What this blali fool needs is the Sisters of the Disappeared up on that stage full force. And for them to dangle him by those little testicles while they're at it," the Duchess seethed.

"What? You said what, Duchess? You said this who? And do what to him by the what?" Mother of God spat, eyes livid.

"You heard me, I said this blali fool, Mother of God, that's what I said. That pig is a proper blali fool." The cat pointed at the screen with her head.

"Duchess, the reason you're here is because you were hoping to find our friend Simiso. That and only that is the reason you're here, Nomadlozi."

"Look, Theresa, if you have something to say why don't you just come out in the open like the buttocks of a baboon? I don't have the time to be divining right now."

"I'm saying you're not here to disrespect me, Duchess, no, just no, hayi, that I refuse! You can't disrespect me like that."

"Dadwethu kababa! When, and how, did I even disrespect you, Mother of Godknows? I'm asking you, when exactly did I disrespect you?"

"You're here insulting my Prophet, Duchess, you're here insulting my Prophet. How on earth is that not disrespecting me?!"

"Dadwethu kababa, he is indeed a fool, not even a small one, and if you as a femal aren't offended by the things this swine is saying, then you really do need deliverance. And, two, okwesibili, were I to decide to insult anyone right here right now, I tell you this service would end faster than it takes God to answer a pope's prayer. Which I don't need to tell you, Mother of God, because you already know!"

"Just stop, Duchess, please just stop," Mother of God said, looking at the cat like she'd at any second now chomp off her tiny nose.

"Stop what, Mother of God? Wasn't I sitting here nicely nje in the first place when you got me started? And now you're telling me stop?" the cat said.

"If you don't stop, Duchess, me I'll go on and find somewhere to sit. Right now, not tomorrow, but right now!" Mother of God glared at her friend. She reached beneath her chair for the third time, rummaged inside

her bag for her vial of anointing oil for the third time, and dabbed her forehead for the third time. When the sheep raised her head, the Duchess was picking her way through the rows of Soldiers, muttering how she had better things to do than sit in the sun and be disrespected by a bigot who actually knew nothing about God.

NEW DISPENSATION

MAGIC SPEAK

Were you to visit Jidada following Tuvius Delight Shasha's inauguration as interim president, the first thing you may have noted was how everywhere the air buzzed with a phrase that was uttered in homes and on the streets, in places of business, in cars and taxis, in towns and city centers and in the rural areas, in schools, in beer halls, in stores and shopping malls, in internet cafés, in restaurants, in churches and brothels, at funerals, in government buildings, at soccer matches, in beauty parlors and pretty much every imaginable space, a phrase carried in the mouths of the old and the young alike, the rich and the poor alike, by those who understood it and those who didn't alike, by believers in the phrase and naysayers alike, yessir, tholukuthi the phrase "N-E-W D-I-S-P-E-N-S-A-T-I-O-N" was all over, like a virus.

And every time Tuvy heard the phrase that his brilliant team had coined to speak to this new chapter of a New Jidada, he felt larger than Jidada's debt to the IMF. The phrase made him realize it was true what those who know about things said about words—which was that they

mattered; you could sell even a cake of soil by simply using the right words, have grown, thinking animals pull out forks and chow it down without the use of force whatsoever, yessir, tholukuthi words not only mattered but they were power. Words were muti. Words were weapons. Words were magic. Words were church. Words were wealth. Words were life.

So inspired was Tuvy by the realization that he rechristened his new pet parrot with the name New Dispensation—tholukuthi the bird having been acquired explicitly for the purposes of tweeting eulogies and accordingly glorifying the Savior throughout the airs and skies of the nation. Tuvy then went on to hire a lecturer in English from the University of Jidada to teach New Dispensation to say the phrase "New Dispensation." And New Dispensation not only mastered the phrase but he learned to sing it with an impeccable American accent that put the Father of the Nation's British accent to shame. And New Dispensation was such a show-bird that very soon other parrots learned the strange new song that now seemed to always be in Jidada's airs. It felt to the birds like another popular fad not to be left out of, and so in no time crows were cawing New Dispensation, owls were hooting New Dispensation, sparrows were chirping New Dispensation, canaries were singing New Dispensation, doves were cooing New Dispensation, hornbills and other birds were calling New Dispensation, and then cicadas were droning New Dispensation, bees were busy buzzing New Dispensation, crickets and grasshoppers and other insects were chirping New Dispensation so that Jidada's hedges and trees and air and skies and even the jungles outside Jidada were all New Dispensation New Dispensation New Dispensation, yes, tholukuthi New Dispensation everywhere and New Dispensation all the time.

CELEBRATION

"A toast, Your Excellency!" These words, by the newly minted General Victor Zuze, a lanky, mean-looking dog with jaws of steel, came out as if the General were barking an angry command. The whole room, including His Excellency himself, instantly hushed. But just before the General made his toast, Jameson, the youngest of the Savior's twin sons, howled with laughter.

"I'm not gonna lie, Baba, with all due respect, every time an animal says, 'Your Excellency,' I expect to see the Old Horse materializing and saying, 'It's not possible, not possible at all, this is an unfortunate mistake. My animals love and need me!'" Jameson said. His performance earned him a few cautious chuckles around the room.

"Bruh! The donkey at his side too, saying—" and here, James quickly hinded to join his twin brother on the floor. The identical stallions, who were also spitting images of their father, pranced around, tails swooshing, and yelled in a brilliant imitation of Dr. Sweet Mother's famous slogan: *"This is not an animal farm but Jidada with a -da and another -da! And if you have any ears at all you'll heed my advice because what you're doing is swallowing all manner of big rocks, and very soon it shall be seen just how wide your asshole is when those very rocks will need to be shat!"* There was an awkward silence, but it only lasted for a few seconds before the entire room exploded with wild laughter.

"Well, pity the donkey can't speak seeing as she's the expert of shitting rocks right now," said Vice President General Judas Goodness Reza, to more laughter.

"I kind of miss her though. Well, not on the Seat, obviously, but the donkey really did give Jidada things to laugh about, a born entertainer, that one," Jameson said, returning to his seat.

"The only time you'll hear of the donkey is when animals are asking where she is. Otherwise I'd be surprised if a pkle comes from the itchtail anytime soon," Vice President Judas Goodness Reza said.

And which, according to those who really know about things, wasn't too far from the truth. Since her spectacular takedown, Jidada's once vocal femal had seemingly become Jidada's quietest femal, so that cruel comedians had quickly updated her once beloved nickname from Sweet Mother to Silent Mother. In addition to the quiet, the former First Femal, along with the Father of the Nation, were never seen around Jidada; they could have been living in another country. Only they weren't—but their existence, according to those who really know about things, wasn't unlike that of prisoners; they lived under armed guard and not for their protection, their activities strictly monitored.

"I think she'll be back in due time. I don't believe such a vomiter like the former First Femal can simply go silent, or disappear just like that. Besides, I know her," James said.

"Well, you best believe it, son. The donkey knows what time it is, and that should she behave like a monkey for whatever reason, we'll fleece her of every single penny, every designer dress, and anything she ever made on the Seat of Power, and reduce her to the miserable beggar she was before she married the Father of the Nation. Trust me, she's not stupid," the Minister of Violence said.

"And on that note, if you may allow me to raise my humble voice to and for the Savior of the Nation, Comrades," General Victor Zuze, whose glass had stayed suspended in the air the whole time, said, taking control of the floor once more.

"To His Excellency. For essentially saving Jidada's Revolution from being captured, for delivering this dearly beloved nation right from the terrible jaws of an unimaginable doom, an astounding feat which will no doubt go down in our history books, and on YouTube, as well as Face-

book and Twitter, as akin to divine intervention. On behalf of this room and the whole entire grateful nation, which is still celebrating up to today, I hereby express our collective and deepest gratitude, Comrade Excellency. May you make Jidada great again over and over, may you shepherd us with the patience and passion of a crocodile, and may your reign last longer than God's reign!" The General's voice choked with emotion.

The smiling Savior, thoroughly moved, and glowing with satisfaction, was the first on his feet. He lifted the General high in the air before putting him down and playfully nibbling his ears. Glasses clinked to endless applause, and Comrades took turns congratulating the Savior all over again. The gathered were some of the Seat of Power's newly appointed Inner Circle and Chosen, tholukuthi the remaining guests at a dinner party thrown by none other than Jidada's brand-new vice president and former General, Judas Goodness Reza. In attendance were the Generals from the night of the game-changing meeting of the defending of Jidada's Revolution just a few weeks ago, now celebrities, their uniforms since traded for suits following new ministerial and ambassadorial appointments. Present too were their replacements, picked by the Savior himself, and then there was Jidada's old Chief Justice, Honorable Kiyakiya Captured Manikiniki, who'd officiated Tuvy's inauguration as interim president, and his colleague Judge Honor Koro, the only femal in the room and soon to be announced Top Chef for the famed Jidada Electoral Cookhouse, responsible for Jidada's elections. Some of the new cabinet picks were there, along with a couple of Chinese businessmals as well as Jidada's most famous Prophet, Prophet Dr. O. G. Moses.

THOLUKUTHI CHINESE BUFFET

"A special toast, Excellency!" said Comrade Chris Lee, raising his glass. And, turning to face the room, the charismatic Chinese businessmal

addressed the party in his measured drawl. "Comrades, please stand with me please as I propose a toast to His Excellency, the new president of Jidada!" The room stood.

"Mr. Comrade President, I thank you for the kindness you and the Party of Power have always shown us and our brothers in our great relations of dynamic friendship. We would not be here in your country otherwise. We especially feel that friendship in your allowing us to come as we want and mine all and any of the minerals as we please, it reminds me very much like an eat-all-you-want Chinese buffet. As my colleagues like to say, it's always Christmas in Jidada with a -da and another -da, and we love Christmas, especially as Jidada is a very, very rich country with too much minerals even to finish! What it shows is that you, Mr. Comrade President, and the Party of Power, out of the many countries in Africa we have carried out our business in—and we've been all over this great big, rich continent—are by far extremely and profoundly generous, and very welcoming indeed, not just with open arms, but with open legs also, and open hearts and open everything, and it pleases us this openness because it's very much a win-win situation for us because we win, and we again win. We fully embrace this partnership and alliance and look forward to it growing even more with this administration, and we do so with no interference in Jidada, with no meddling in the politics because unlike the West, we are your respectful friends who mind our business, and our business is mining business! And so, Mr. Comrade President, this is to continued friendship, to many more Christmases to come, and to Jidada with a -da, and another -da!"

Comrade Chris Lee delivered the last half of his toast in Jidada's language of power, yes, tholukuthi in perfect Shona. He might as well have performed a miracle, for the room broke out in rapturous applause. Tholukuthi thrilled Comrades mobbed and saluted him, the frenzy not stop-

ping until Dick Mampara, the Minister of Disinformation, having raised his own glass but failing to get the attention of his colleagues, banged on the table with an empty bottle of Jameson, tholukuthi the Savior's favorite whiskey, after which his sons were named.

"I bet none of these clowns can go to China right now and start even a trash-picking business," the peacock, an otherwise happy-go-lucky type, said, seething with disgust. A few years ago, before joining the Party of Power and finagling his way to the Seat, a Chinese mining company had unceremoniously evicted Dick Mampara's grandmother's village without notice, without consulting the villagers, without compensation. On confronting the manager on-site, Mampara found himself having to flee for his life, the manager insulting him in Chinese and firing at him with a gun. Later, Defenders had tracked Mampara down and clobbered him so badly he could not get out of bed for two weeks. Tholukuthi his grandmother had died shortly afterward, of trauma and a broken heart. It was not something Dick Mampara would ever forget or forgive, even if the Seat of Power was friendly, too friendly, the Minister thought, to the Chinese, whose activities in the African continent suggested to the Minister a colonizer rather than the so-called friend they were supposed to be.

"Comrades, in the spirit of not forgetting who we're all here for, which is the Savior and only him himself, I wish to make a toast," the peacock said. Mention of the Savior brought the Comrades back to their senses and their seats.

"Your Excellency, like many of the younger Comrades I've had the honor of watching leaders lead, but to especially watch Your Excellency both serve and save the nation in light of the recent events has by far been the unforgettable highlight of my experience. And as such, I extend my heartfelt thank-you, Your Excellency. For the example. For the leadership. For the inspiration," the peacock said with a dramatic bow.

"If you think that is a highlight that is because you weren't there in 1983! Had you been there in 1983, then you'd have seen the Savior in full form, proper saving and serving the nation like no patriot anywhere!" the vice president said, an animated spark in his eye.

THE GUKURAHUNDI: CALLED TO SERVE

"Nineteen eighty-three, sir? Wasn't that the time of the——"

"The Gukurahundi! So named for the early rain that washes away the chaff before the spring rains! Without which this Jidada, as we know it, the Jidada of one party, the great Party of Power, our very own Jidada, would not exist!" said Elegy Mudidi, the Minister of Propaganda, who now turned to the Savior with open admiration.

Mampara glared at the cat, who, on seeing the peacock's murderous look, purred, and promptly turned away. The two animals, both New Dispensation additions to the Seat of Power and thus understandably trying to endear and distinguish themselves to the senior leadership, were also close in age and more or less matched in accomplishments. But those who know about things said their rivalry in fact lay outside the realm of the Seat, outside the Party of Power—tholukuthi both had found out, through an investigative journalist's trending tweet, that they were interested in the same femal, a model and former Miss Jidada, this of course despite both of them being married.

"Yes, but you youngsters didn't see nothing! Why don't you school them and our foreign Comrades, Chief, so they hear it from the Crocodile's own mouth?" the vice president urged. Faces beamed at the Savior, who glowed from the attention. A fresh silence, tholukuthi the kind of silence that precedes the weighty words of the one in charge, eclipsed the room.

"Well, one is called to do these things, you see. As anyone who under-

stands service and saving knows," Tuvy said, grinning. Even the sticks and stones would tell you that Tuvius Delight Shasha had spent the entirety of his career in the Old Horse's shadow—for the most part seen but not heard. Tholukuthi this new dynamic, in which animals hung on his every word, in which every other utterance from their own mouths was accompanied by "Excellency," "Your Excellency," "Chief," "the Savior," "Savior of the Nation," was both strange and sweet. He spread himself on his chair and adjusted his scarf with such attention that every eye in the room momentarily focused on the thing like it was going to clear its throat and address them.

SCARF OF THE NATION

The famous scarf, in the striped colors of the flag of Jidada—and thus its moniker of Scarf of the Nation—had since its debut a few weeks ago, taken Jidada by storm. The whole of the country, it seemed, had nothing else to talk about, either on the ground or on the internets. What exactly did the scarf mean? Why, in the first place, was the Savior wearing it, and why now and not any other time? What statement was he trying to make? How come he didn't take the thing off, even in hot weather? Tholukuthi little did they know.

"This scarf, Chief, provides you with the kind of protection you can safely wear at all times and without calling attention to yourself, being that a talisman that is out in the open is more powerful. And beyond protection, the scarf is a sensor, it feels things. If there's bad energy, it'll pick it up. If there's danger, it'll know it. If things are well, it'll accordingly tell you. Just listen to it, Chief, you'll know, and you'll get better at deciphering its signals with each day, and of course that's only just the small things it can do," Jolijo had said on presenting the Savior with the scarf. Tuvy, who was in the midst of preparing for his first-ever international trip as

Jidada's acting president, had returned home from a long day of last-minute meetings to find the sorcerer sitting as usual in a heavy cloud of smoke, a pipe dangling from the corner of his mouth.

"You mean this thing of wool can do all that, Comrade Jolijo?" Tuvy said, eyeing the scarf with skepticism. Jolijo bobbed his head.

"All of that as I plainly put it, Chief. And, two, this scarf definitely comes with some responsibility. No animal, other than you—and this includes your wife, mistresses, and otherwise femals in general—shall handle it, or else the muti will lose power, which I'm sure you know by now is not pretty. And most importantly, you're not, and I mean under whatever circumstances, Chief, to step out of this home without the scarf, or otherwise be found anywhere and under whatever circumstances without it—I just can't overstate this enough. And similarly you shall not sleep without it. Think of it as part of your hide, an armor to be worn at all times. And as long as you have it on, nothing, and I mean nothing, shall touch you."

THE GUKURAHUNDI: MOST DEFINITELY, ABSOLUTELY NOT A MOMENT OF MADNESS

Now Tuvy patted the scarf, reached for his glass of whiskey, and drained it. A server leaned in and promptly filled it up.

"It is a shame that today some animals, including those who know better, when they talk about that important and defining time they try to reduce it to a pointless orgy of violence, a mere moment of madness, as we've heard it called even by those we won't name, but you know them. Like maybe we weren't thinking right, like we didn't know what we were doing! Let me tell you, nothing could be farther from the truth, which is that we sat down, we deliberated, we calculated, we planned, we organized, and we meticulously orchestrated a campaign guided by clear goals and objectives. I mean, were it a moment of madness, truly, you think we'd have

spent all that time—beginning in '83, then '84, then '85, then '86, then '87? No, Comrades, no moment lasts that long!" the Savior said.

"And that's long enough for a young one to be born, even start running around and talking!" enthused the alcohol inside Jameson. Tuvy ignored both and carried on.

"It was shortly after Independence. In a normal country we should've been celebrating the defeat of the colonizer as well as the birth of a New Jidada, but no. What did we do? We only emerged from one struggle into another! Because you see, there was this other party causing misfortune— I will not dignify it with a name," the Savior said.

"And you won't be wrong, Comrade Excellency. I myself called it a Dissident Party of nonentities! And 'causing misfortune' is to put it mildly, it's His Excellency being very kind! But I beg you to tell it as it is Your Excellency, so that these youngsters can't say they weren't told!" the Minister of Violence encouraged.

"Very well, Comrade. So, this Dissident Party of nonentities, which as you know was also predominantly Ndebele—who as you know are the descendants of that violent, murderous criminal king, who once served at the bloody feet of none other than the famous warmonger and murderous tyrant, Tshaka Zulu, and who invaded and essentially colonized us before the white colonizers, spilling the blood of our ancestors and seizing territory and our femals, yes, those very descendants, were now busy planning mayhem and rebellion, not unlike their savage ancestors! Seeking to carry out a kind of coup! Of course we had, out of necessity, joined forces with them against the common white enemy during the Liberation War, thinking they were our Comrades. But even then they were busy undermining us at every turn, sowing disorder and discord and disunity on the war front so that it became clear among those discerning of us that we had war inside a war!" His Excellency said, tail swishing vigorously, voice now risen to his typical animated pitch. If he was worried about injuring

the very few Ndebele Comrades present he did not show it, and if the very few Ndebele Comrades present were injured, they did not show it.

"And the Dissidents brought out that war full force when after Independence they had the audacity to engage the Jidada army in two dramatic confrontations! But of course they found us ready and prepared, didn't they, Your Excellency?!" the Minister of Things chimed in. The fierce and brutal dog had been the Deputy Commander of the special unit deployed for the Gukurahundi campaign.

"You, of all animals, know it, Comrade. You were on the front lines, in the thick of it!" His Excellency said, looking at the Comrade with adoration.

"In the thick of it? Let me tell you, we were swimming in blood and muck and bodies! Yessir, proper Defending the Revolution!" The dog beamed.

"And Defend it you did. But back to the story. Shortly after Independence, we find out, not surprisingly of course, that the conniving Dissidents didn't disarm after the war, and in fact had their weapons stashed away. And here's the kicker. When our Defenders went to their villages to hunt the mischievous ex-combatants, and that is who we initially thought were the Dissidents, the villagers offered zero cooperation! We at first thought we were just dealing specifically with mischievous ex-combatants, but we discovered, to our horror, that nossir, we were mistaken; the Dissidents we were looking for were in fact not just the military wing but generally the whole entire tribe itself! And naturally, the whole entire party, being that the tribe was apparently the party and the party the tribe! And when I say the whole tribe I mean even the femals, even the little babies, even the grandmothers, had dissident tendencies! These were the fundamental facts that informed our strategy—a proper, thorough, calculated strategy, and most definitely not some miserable 'moment' of mad-

ness!" His Excellency said, looking at the Minister of Order, a star player and Minister of Defending during the Gukurahundi, who now sat bobbing his head at His Excellency's every word. He perked up at the open invitation to carry the baton.

"And in the meantime the Dissident leadership were of course being dissidents. Instead of working with the government to be part of the government, they worked against us, and did their best to escalate tensions toward the inevitable and unsurprising end. But haaaa, they were no match, nossir, not even! By this time we had the prominent Dissident leaders in prison, where they belonged. Or on the run. We had dismantled their infrastructure and destabilized their organization. And most importantly my special unit, trained by none other than our North Korean Comrades, and I don't need to tell most of you about the famous Fifth Brigade, I mean they were first class, outstanding, simply exceptional!" said the Minister of Things, hinding and gesticulating.

"And that exceptional unit defended the Revolution something sweet! If I could have that kind of unit today, right now, Comrade, I'd be the happiest ruler in the whole wide world!" His Excellency said, speaking slowly and looking at the Minister of Things with the fondness of a lover.

"I can't even imagine how that fat Dissident leader escaped the jaws of a crocodile! He must have had the most potent of talismans is all I can say! To elude that famed, most brilliant unit!" the vice president said with savage glee.

"Even today, I salute that unit—1983, 1984, 1985, 1986, 1987, they did the work, I'm talking proper artists of killing! Pure angels of death! True prophets of terror! Those Comrades accordingly painted that anarchic region red-red-red-red-red, I mean, they made blood dance in the air!" the Savior said, hinding now, hooves flying in an imaginary dance of blood, an unearthly light in his eyes.

"There is that song, Comrade—that the Defenders sang while they were defending the Revolution, it really became a kind of anthem, remind me of it," His Excellency said, turning to the ex-Commander of the Fifth Brigade.

THE GUKURAHUNDI SONG: SOUNDTRACK OF TERROR

"Mai va Dhikondo! Mai va Dhikondo! Mai va Dhikondo! Mai va Dhikondo! Mai va Dhikondo! Mai va Di—Dhikondo Dhiiiiiiiiiiiiiiiiiiiiiiii—" Tholuku-thi the answer to His Excellency's question was not spoken, no. It was sung, belted at top voice by Elegy Mudidi, who in fact boasted an illustrious child-hood career in various church and school choirs. And before the gathering could ask themselves if what they were seeing was indeed what they were seeing, the cat's rival, Dick Mampara, still sore from the cat's earlier dis-respect as well as his other disrespects in general, threw himself into the spotlight, wanting to be avenged.

Dick Mampara, who came from a family that was renowned for its gen-erations of dancers, was at that very moment in his element. Tholukuthi he fancifully shook and shimmied his impressive train of feathers, reveal-ing a surprise iridescent display—tholukuthi he'd had his feathers painted in the striped colors of His Excellency's scarf in order to impress the Sav-ior, which indeed had the desired effect because Tuvy now watched the Minister, spellbound, his tail swishing to the rhythm. And taking this for His Excellency's approval, Mampara went all out. He shimmied. He gy-rated. He jiggled.

About then, Prophet Dr. O. G. Moses, who otherwise ranted and raved against secular music and dance in his sermons—devil music and devil dance, he called them—shot to the floor as if propelled by the holy spirit and danced like one possessed by the demon of debauchery. The two Com-rades were so spectacular that Judge Honor Koro utterly failed to maintain

hold of herself. The cow now flung herself onto Mampara, taking care not to trample him. She shimmied and twisted and twerked with such sensuousness that His Excellency, who could not stand seeing a gyrating femal, threw himself onto the dance floor.

And because the Savior had entered the dance floor, it followed then that everyone could not remain seated; they followed suit. Tholukuthi even the rats, lizards, and crickets and other such creatures who'd been surreptitiously watching the gathering from varied nooks and crannies threw caution to the wind and scurried onto the bustling dance floor. The Comrades cavorted without pause until at last Judge Kiyakiya Captured Manikiniki, an old donkey, felt a strange cramping pain in his chest. Suddenly reminded of the limits of his body, the panicked judge crawled to the front of the room, where Elegy Mudidi had claimed a desk as his stage and pulled at the cat's paw. "Comrade Minister, stop, stop this madness, please, you want to kill me? Remember I have the Savior's Real inauguration to officiate soon!"

THE GUKURAHUNDI: THOLUKUTHI UNREPENTANT

"And that was that. The song only ceased when at last the humbled leader of the Dissidents came crawling to us on his belly and begged for peace. And only then did we say, Let there be peace, but it was of course on our terms. And the Jidada as you know it today, Comrades, was born. Yessir, all because when called to serve, and save, I did not hesitate, we did not hesitate!" the Savior said, caressing his keg of a stomach. He was topless now, having lost his jacket, shirt, and tie on the dance floor.

"To the Savior!" the vice president toasted. The room raised glasses, cheered. Toward the end of the table, the newly minted General Precious Juba tried and failed to steady his trembling glass. He was not drunk, but the song, and the whole affair really, reminded him of his best friend and

Comrade from the war front, Butholezwe Henry Vulindlela Khumalo, a fierce fighter who'd also saved his life when they found themselves in an ambush at the close of the war. He was reminded too of many perished innocent friends, family members, neighbors, acquintances. But the General had stuffed all of it deep, deep, deep in the dustbin of the past. Tholukuthi the past. It had been a necessary move, what with his choice to join the Party of Power after Independence when survival was uncertain, what with who he had since become, tholukuthi a bona fide member of the Seat of Power, a Chosen. Only sometimes, like now, the lid of the past flew open and the buried things came unburied. And the unburied things raised the sleeping hurricane inside him. Tholukuthi it reared its head and raged and raged, and he had to summon every ounce of strength to keep it inside.

"And the beauty of it, Comrades, is that we did what we needed to do without interference. Not from Britain. Not from the United States. Not from our neighbors. Not from the United Nations itself. As it should be, I mean, show me a nation that was born without blood. Even God himself governed through blood and devious fury; we are little ants, we are such Saints in comparison! And today they'll call the thing all sorts of queer names, I've even heard it called a genocide. But I myself call it service. And anytime an opportunity to serve comes my way, I will not hesitate. And so, here's to service!" His Excellency raised a glass.

"To service!!!" The room exploded.

A PROBLEM

The sun had come out. About half the room was gone, leaving behind His Excellency, the vice president, and a small number of Inner inner-circle Comrades. If any of them were tired for missed sleep, their bright, engaged faces did not show it. The Minister of the Internet was telling the

Minister of Things about what many in the Seat of Power regarded as a new but significant problem.

". . . I mean these miserable animals somehow think they've found a voice or something, when in reality it's us who're allowing them to speak," he said. He was famous for being a bad-tempered bull, and he spoke now with a hint of irritation.

"Like I said, I wouldn't worry, Comrade, especially as they're doing it on social media. It'd be a different ball game altogether if they were— say—proper protesting, expressing their misguided sentiments here on the ground. In which case I say, let them bring it," the Minister of Things said with a dismissive laugh.

"Well, they can talk on that thing all they want, it doesn't mean they'll do anything. And besides, our team is on social media, telling them what time it is. I'm not worried," Elegy Mudidi said.

"With all due respect that's downright untrue, Comrade. We know that if left to their devices on that internet, these animals can in fact do damage. Do you mean to tell me you've so very quickly forgotten the Free Jidada movement? To begin with, was it or wasn't it born on the internet itself? Didn't it, at some point, garner the support of hundreds of thousands of Jidadans? Didn't the thing spread all over, including the West, making the Party of Power look like fools? Didn't they hail it the most potent democratic movement in this Jidada with a -da and another -da?" Dick Mampara said, not missing the chance to fire at his rival.

Solemn heads nodded, for, tholukuthi yes indeed, the movement that had started as a harmless spark had, before you could say "Tholukuthi!" quickly spread like a mad inferno and galvanized Jidada right in front of the Seat of Power, with animals draping the flags of the nation around their necks in videos in which they voiced their lamentations against the regime. And because it wasn't a political party affair, and because the whole foofaraw for the most part happened on the internets, where you

couldn't properly unleash the Defenders to bite and beat and butcher like they knew how to do best, it was, at first, somewhat difficult to control. The Party of Power had been baffled as to how best to deal with an enemy they didn't have much experience with, tholukuthi an enemy that grew to the point that it got the confidence to take its business off the unreal world of the internets to the real world of Jidada's streets.

At this point Mudidi, upon seeing the Savior nod thoughtfully, upon seeing the seriousness with which the Comrades were digesting the peacock's words, jumped on his feet and hinded, determined to triumph over his rival.

"Well, all that is true, Comrades. But the big question here is, Did it, and does it really matter at the end of the day? Meaning, we are, in just a short while, having our Free, Fair, and Credible elections, and do any of you know of any party called Free Jidada running? And did we not only successfully shut down each and every one of their gatherings on the ground? And did we not identify the leaders, and did we not put them in their place? And where is the whole business today—when was the last time you heard them say pkle? You haven't, Comrades, because, as they say in internet language, we deleted them! And having said that, we mustn't forget the same internet is helping us keep tabs on our enemies. I was with Comrade Luthereck Phiri just two days ago, and he tells me they have a super database, I'm talking everything from faces to names to phone numbers to addresses to families. Not to mention some of our operatives are even undercover as prominent Opposition activists with two, three hundred thousand followers on Twitter, Facebook, WhatsApp. The internet, in the end, if we know how to use it, will make us win. And lastly, and let us not forget that all eyes, in and outside of Jidada, being on us, we have to convince all that the animals genuinely have a real voice for a change. How do we otherwise assure the world of our New Dispensation if we are seen to be curtailing freedom of speech just like old times, and

not too long after announcing that we've brought that very freedom back to Jidada? When we continue doing the same exact things we've been doing? We have a crucial election to win, Comrades, let's keep our eyes on the prize, we cannot be distracted by petty stuff like internet noise!" Mudidi's speech, finished with the cat panting, was met with resounding applause.

TOWARD A NEW DISPENSATION ELECTION

The inconspicuous servers came in and spread a sumptuous breakfast, and Prophet Dr. O. G. Moses stood and blessed the food. The Comrades were heartily digging in when an enormous army of birds took over the sky. It was, of course, New Dispensation—Tuvy's pet parrot—and his massive choir, tholukuthi the sight of birds of every kind and color looking like something biblical. And for a surreal while, the air vibrated with the frenzied chorus of New Dispensation–New Dispensation–New Dispensation.

"Who knew, Comrades, that His Excellency's bird chorale would be on the BBC, that before he even started proper ruling and ruling and ruling, the Savior would be charming the world left right and center?!" The vice president beamed, pointing at the sky after New Dispensation and his comrades had moved on.

"And not too long ago, it was of course the Scarf of the Nation," the Minister of the Internet added, addressing Tuvy, who grinned and beamed, for he naturally reveled in compliments.

"All of which is good press, especially as we need the West on board to jump-start the economy," the Minister of Looting said.

"Indeed. But why are they taking so long to be on board though, these Westerners? I mean, the Old Horse is gone, I'm here and I'm in charge, and I'm flying up and down telling them come and invest, come, I have all sorts of resources and everything you can think of, and they're not falling

over themselves coming—what exactly do they want, what are they waiting for?" Tuvy said.

"I hear you, Your Excellency. And I know you're working hard, even
the Old Horse himself didn't travel in a decade a quarter of what you've
traveled in just a few months. But please don't get discouraged—don't
they say you have to sire it over and over in order to get it pregnant?
You're doing an excellent job of knocking on doors, it'll all pay off soon,"
the Minister of Business said, not looking up from his phone.

"What it feels like, instead of knocking on doors, is I'm prostituting
myself. Like a itchtail, and at least a itchtail is better because she sometimes gets something from it," Tuvy said with irritation.

"Your Excellency, sir. If I may, it should be remembered that we're here
because the Old Horse burned bridges with the West. But I think it matters, and it's definitely registering, that you yourself are not only an entirely different animal but are also committed to reengaging and rebuilding.
I have every confidence that with a little patience, doors will open," Elegy
Mudidi spoke in the voice of one tiptoeing around a hungry lion.

"But when will they open? I need them to open and I need them to
open now-now, I don't have the time, nobody has the time!" the Savior
roared.

"And they will soon enough, Your Excellency! Only, if I may say, sir,
remember as you continue to court them, know who these Westerners are.
Which is that they're the clowns whose monies make them feel entitled to
dictate to us how we should live, eat, mate, sleep, shit, love, worship, and
die," the Minister of Propaganda said, smiling at his own choice of words.

"So, before they tell you, just go ahead and do it for them. Tell them,
without being asked, you'll carry out reforms, major reforms, reforms-
reforms and not just reforms. Guarantee every kind of rights, especially
femal rights; the West loves femals. Allow for press freedoms. Say yes to
national unity, yes to being tolerant to the miserable Opposition and such

like, whatever they say, just yes it, all of it. And of course, promise an even newer cabinet after the election. A full and proper return to democracy. Free and fair elections. Prosperity for all. An end to all forms of violence, all of it. These are things that give the Westerners orgasms," the Minister of Business said. Around the table, animals chuckled.

"And, remember too, Your Excellency, that the upcoming election is a big part of it. Even the sticks and stones know the Westerners are playing it safe where Jidada is concerned, and especially with the recent change of government, they feel that many dynamics aren't so clear, and so they're treading with care. But once you legitimately win the election, Your Excellency, sir, I tell you they'll be swarming you left right and center like dung flies, you won't know what to do with them. And this time next year no one'll recognize this Jidada, because Jidada will become great, so great that we'll show that Tweeting Baboon what Great Again looks like. But for now, the election," the Minister of Propaganda said, almost breathless with excitement.

"But we have already won the election, Comrades, because don't we fix the menu, gather the ingredients, prepare, and cook it? Haven't we already appointed the Head Chef—and the first ever femal chef in the history of Jidada's elections too? And don't we certify the results?" the Minister of Things said.

"Which is true. Only we have to convince Jidada of the exact opposite, which is that this is a New Dispensation election, which is #freefairncredible. And most importantly, that the Opposition has a real shot at winning. Which means, Your Excellency, I'm afraid, has to continue working super hard to, you know, to sell the New Dispensation," the Minister of Corruption said.

"And His Excellency will deliver, Comrades, trust. Because he is a demonstrated Savior who serves. The hard part has been done, this is just the last lap. But in these remaining short weeks before the election we

need everyone's belts tightened because as you know, our enemies are counting on us to slip," Judas Goodness Reza said, to murmurs and nods of agreement.

The mention of enemies by the vice president was enough to bring Tuvy back to form, for it was true—even right when he was carrying Jidada to glory, there were vile beasts who wished him nothing but failure and damnation, who claimed he did not know how to govern, who said he was no leader, who spread the falsity that he was tyranny itself, who made the ugly prediction he'd rubbish democracy and make the Old Horse and the donkey look good in comparison, who lied that he had no love for the nation, no ethics, no integrity, no vision, no honor, not one redeeming quality, who labeled him greedy, lazy, cruel, devious. It was impossible for him, especially with the eyes of the world on Jidada, to do unto them as he would have liked, to wash them away like the chaff that they were, but he would cut their mouths, yes, tholukuthi leave them speechless with his glory. He'd dazzle. He'd triumph.

"A lion does not concern himself with the opinion of a fish, Comrades. We will win and stay winning. We'll give them the election they want to see, and we'll give it to them something plentiful. Comrades, to the New Dispensation!" the Savior said.

"To the New Dispensation!!!"

BUT YOU HAVE BEEN ANOINTED BY THE HOLY ONE, AND YOU ALL HAVE KNOWLEDGE

"God has just now commanded me to offer a blessing, Your Excellency," Prophet Dr. O. G. Moses said, leaving his Seat and hinding for the Savior. The Comrades promptly sat up and dropped their heads.

"And on his behalf I'm very honored to prophesy that big things, tremendous things, are just about to happen right now, Comrades. The spirit

of God and Great Shepherd and Mediator is about to descend on this room right now and anoint His Excellency in the name of Jesus. I see His Light, His Anointing, His Power, His Glory, all come down and bless you and uplift you and protect you and empower you, Your Excellency. May you receive it all, and every blessing that is right at this moment happening to you," the Prophet said before lifting his voice in a fervent prayer uttered in tongues. And when he said Amen, the Comrades stood, applauded.

"I am pleased to let the Comrades know, that as for me and my Soldiers, we will be casting our vote for the Savior. And that God will be commanding the whole of Jidada to accordingly cast their votes for the Savior. And that no vote cast against His Excellency shall be counted. Because God has already called this upcoming election! It has already been won, Halleluyah!" the Prophet said.

"Amen!!!" the Comrades roared.

PROPHET OF A #FREEFAIRNCREDIBLE ELECTION

And being that the Savior had indeed already won and thus had absolutely nothing to lose, he preached the gospel of #freefairncredible elections even as it felt like a ridiculous exercise—tholukuthi he hadn't seen it happen in such a long time in Jidada it was almost absurd to wrap his carcass around it. But the horse was determined because all eyes were on him and the New Dispensation. With coaching from the brilliant young Comrades in the Seat, he in no time could in fact speak of #freefairncredible elections with such heart, there were times he sounded like a bona fide member of the Opposition himself. And the Opposition, tholukuthi a miserable Opposition that'd for the most part never really known the freedom to be, to exist, that'd never known not to be harassed by the Seat of Power, not to be marginalized, not to be persecuted, not to be tortured, jailed, kidnapped, even murdered, bought in and welcomed this alluring, unexpected

gospel and held on to it tight. And how could they not? Tholukuthi when for the very first time since they could remember, Western election observers would be allowed to monitor the process? When they were holding rallies without having to apply for and obtain authorization from the government? When they could have those rallies in peace and without Defenders coming to disrupt them and arresting the speakers? When they could have those rallies from morning to afternoon or till whenever they felt like, when they could say whatever was on their minds at those rallies without fear? When they could prophesize and declare their victory in advance if they wanted? Yessir, tholukuthi the Opposition tasted, like a forbidden fruit, the sweetness of this long-overdue idea of Free and Fair and Credible elections, held the sweetness in their mouths, savored it, and when they finally reluctantly swallowed it, felt it fill their stomachs with the tangible hope of the first-ever truly free Jidada with a -da and another -da, in which it was possible to win the presidency and rule.

TO BE THE CHANGE

Even the sticks and stones will tell you that an animal can't just preach change without embodying it themselves, and that that change has to begin at the top and then trickle down to the rest of the masses. Tuvy, accordingly, understood that as interim president, as the Savior of the Nation, he needed to persomally manifest this New Dispensation in order that he set a compelling example for his animals, and set a compelling example for his animals he did. The Savior of the Nation had always been an early riser, his alarm set for 5:00 a.m. In the spirit of the New Dispensation he changed his waking time to 4:59 a.m.—yessir, tholukuthi his alarm would, for the very first time in almost four decades, ring at a different hour. And he switched sleeping places with his wife, Matilida, so that he now woke up on the right side of the bed instead of the left side of

the bed. And while he hadn't touched a book since his school days unless by accident, he had a whole library set up in his home, where everyone could see it, and every once in a while he'd take the time to count the books. And though he didn't like the idea of the internet, he finally agreed to having it put in his phone, and in that thing on his desk, and every so often he'd have them open it so he could see, follow, monitor, keep tabs on what the nation was doing and saying. And he replaced the soles of every one of his shoes so when he walked, it could literally be said that he was taking brand-new steps. And he stopped using such phrases as "I don't know," "I think," "I'm not sure" and replaced them with their opposite—"I very well know," "I'm positive," "I'm most absolutely certain"—and was in fact pleased to discover that this way, tholukuthi it turned out he knew all there was to know about anything and all things, which again showed that words indeed mattered. And, armed with these persomal changes that allowed him to walk the talk of a new way of being, a new way of doing things, tholukuthi the Savior of the Nation felt ready to lead Jidada into new heights of glory.

THE NEW JIDADA = A CORRUPTION-FREE ZONE

And it was in the spirit of the New Dispensation that Tuvy, with the Scarf of the Nation around his neck, stood in front of a rally at the Jidada Square one Saturday morning to make the grand declaration that he and the Party of Power were waging a war on corruption, and not only that, but they were also going to win the war. And when the animals heard this they stood in silence, slowly wagging their tails, pondering. It wasn't that the citizens didn't desire a corruption-free country; it was just that where Jidada with a -da and another -da was concerned, corruption was like one of the -das; they simply couldn't imagine the country without it, yes, tholukuthi they breathed it, they ate it, they drank it, they slept on it—it was in every aspect of their lives, including in their very own homes.

Tuvy felt the reluctance in the Jidada Square right in his scarf—the thing was, as Jolijo said, a sensor. It accordingly communicated that though the animals were willing to listen, they very much struggled with the picture he was painting for them. But the Savior wasn't at all discouraged. He was going to make them see, like a good leader; he'd change their minds.

"My fellow Jidadans. Who among you passed a roadblock on their way to this here rally, or has otherwise been subject to a pointless stop, along with an unfair spot fine or bribe, ever since the New Dispensation happened to us? Didn't we end every single one of the corrupt roadblocks, yes, or no?" Tuvy challenged the animals, hinding back and gazing into their midst, waiting for the only answer, the no he knew was coming because this wasn't a multiple-choice question. And the no came, yessir, tholukuthi the no came decked out in the most rapturous applause, cheering driven by praise, by joy, and by gratitude, for that was indeed the truth and nothing but the truth.

The roadblocks that had mushroomed all over Jidada for the past five years—or was it eight years? ten?—tholukuthi for the past however many years, bogus roadblocks where Defenders flagged down every other car, bullied, harassed, and terrorized drivers, checking for everything from fire extinguishers and their precise placement, for spare wheels, missing lights and missing mirrors, for the red plastic triangle thingies, radio licenses, tire pressure, the state of the speedometer, tholukuthi if you had the right spanners for wheel changes, the green fluorescent vests, loose bolts, whether number plates were properly secured, the accepted number of passengers in a car, yessir, tholukuthi the dogs never failing to find fault since they changed the traffic laws on the spot and in their heads and according to the whims of their wagging tails, determined to fleece the poor drivers, who were forced to pay cash on the spot, which they did on every trip and every day and every week and every month and every year after every

year, until, on that one ordinary morning that would turn out to be far from ordinary, Jidadans got into their cars and drove to workplaces or businesses or wherever they were going feeling like there was something maybe wrong but unable to pinpoint what it was exactly that was wrong until they mentally retraced their steps and eventually realized what it was that was wrong, tholukuthi which was that they had, for the very first time in years, driven Jidada's potholed roads without ever stopping for a single roadblock, and so in disbelief were they that they in fact got into their cars again, and drove right back to their homes just to see, and they indeed saw, saw that yessir, tholukuthi there was no single police Defender fleecing them of their hard-earned money in the name of Jidada's wretched traffic division.

And, reminded as such, the animals saw the idea of a corruption-free Jidada with new eyes because—if corruption on the roads had not only been removed but had been removed in the blink of an eye, why wouldn't the New Dispensation go on and similarly remove it everywhere else since it apparently knew where and how exactly to remove it?

"Moreover, my fellow Jidadans. You know and I know that the nuisance roadblocks were only just the small of it. The big of it was what? Yessir, go on and say it; you know you're dying to say what it is was the big of it. To give you a clue, we removed it, that specific big of it, also, like corruption, when the very last thing on everyone's mind was that it could in fact be removed because it commanded the sun. Does that help a little? Does that ring a bell?" Tuvy said. The Scarf of the Nation announced a changed, positive mood, and it was indeed right.

The rally attendees couldn't do it anymore. The Savior's words had catapulted them back to that unforgettable, that golden day when everything changed, when a New Jidada rose with the majesty of a rainbow when they least expected it. Now, fueled by the memory of the day of their recent liberation, the animals danced, stomped the earth until it trembled.

They mooed, they meowed, they bleated, they bellowed, they quacked, they brayed, they bleated, they neighed, they grunted, they clucked, they shrieked, they cackled.

THE AWESOME POWER OF REGALIA

And Tuvy watched the moving mass of fur and feathers in colorful Party regalia and lost himself in the joy of seeing his face on the chests and backs and heads of supporters, tholukuthi on the magnificent teats of femals, their sensuous hips and backsides and bellies. It was a time-tested tradition, especially practiced all over the great continent of Africa by Fathers of the Nation who knew how to rule, who understood proper governance, tholukuthi wherein it followed that the face of the one in charge also needed to be on the bodies of animals in rallies like these, and as they went about their day-to-day lives. Wherein animals generally voted according to whose face it was on the clothes they wore, according to whose name, and which party colors it was on the bags of fertilizer, maize, potatoes, on the packets of sugar and other such goodies received in preelection donations.

"My dear Jidadans. I am glad I have jolted your memories, and you are very welcome. I hope I have aptly convinced you that we will indeed get rid of corruption. As I said, we're waging war on it. If we won a war as humongous, as brutal, as the Liberation War, then what in the New Dispensation will stop us from winning this little here war and accordingly liberating Jidada all over again?" Tuvy said.

The convinced animals agreed with their new president with their hearts and intestines. And if Jidada could indeed win the war on corruption like the Savior said, then well, what on earth wouldn't they do, where wouldn't they go, with this New Dispensation? Anything was indeed possible. Prosperity. Equality. Dignity. Justice. Freedom. Everything they'd

fought for, struggled for, prayed for, cried for, yearned for, watched friends and family cross borders for, and sometimes even died for, yessir, tholukuthi glory was possible.

A BASHFUL BEGGAR HAS AN EMPTY BOWL

Only the New Dispensation wouldn't quite happen without the West's money. Even with its monumental natural resources, even as it was among some of the richest countries on the rich continent of Africa, Jidada with a -da and another -da was still no better than a beggar, a miserable derelict of a country struggling to stand on tottering feet, tholukuthi in need of charity from the very countries that'd once and still oppressed it and its kind. And so Tuvy did what many of the continent's Fathers of the Nation had done and would do—he went begging to the West.

But you wouldn't know, just from observing him on his missions, that he was a beggar president. The Savior of the Nation went begging in style. And nothing said style like an expensive private jet and a humongous entourage of animals who could have, through their numbers, made up two opposing football teams. Nothing said style like always being in the air so that those who know about things would tell you the new president of Jidada would more likely be found in the air rather than on the ground, while those who really, really know about things said he'd once been heard to say—tholukuthi his exact words—that if God ruled a whole motherfucking universe from the air, then there was no reason whatsoever why he couldn't rule a country with a surface area of a mere 390,767 square kilometers from the same air every once in a while.

The Savior attended summits, attended conferences, attended meetings, forums, and such functions with the confidence of a honey badger, secure in the knowledge that the time in Jidada was New Dispensation o'clock, and change had come to the country and he was its bringer; there

was absolutely no reason for the West not to support him. On these begging trips, armed with the knowledge that words were power, the Scarf of the Nation around his neck, Tuvy poured his heart out: Jidada is as open for business as a femal's honey jar, he'd say. He who doesn't pick from the once-famed basket of Africa will be forced to pick from a barren desert after others have picked, he'd say. An investor who doesn't invest in Jidada is like a vase without flowers, he'd say. Jidada right now is like a groundnut, come and crack it open to discover the opportunities inside, he'd say. There is no queue at the gate of Jidada, so why wait? he'd say. Jidada is like a hand, and no hand under God's earth has ever successfully washed itself, he'd say.

Meanwhile, back home, Jidadans watched the skies of the nation for the private jets that cost more than it'd have cost to repair some of their roads, send some of their children to school, buy medicines for their run-down hospitals, alleviate shortages of fuel. They counted the times the Savior came back only to leave again and again, fly up and down again and again, his briefcase full of promises from the West again and again. They waited patiently because they knew good things came to those who waited, and furthermore, the reign of the Old Horse had especially taught them the art of waiting. Tholukuthi they were exceptional at it, they were magnificent.

RETURNEE

LONE GOAT LUGGING A PURPLE HARD-SHELL SUITCASE

Those who see the slim goat in the long white tunic dress, a black satchel on her back, tholukuthi dragging an oversize purple hard-shell suitcase along the longest road without a name, stop what they were doing and keenly watch her as if they've known all along she was coming and so have been waiting for days. They've already recognized—because they've become experts at it—that distinctive gait of a newly returned exile, as if she's reminding the earth she's walked it before, yes, tholukuthi that she's very much a child of the soil and not a stranger. They recognize too, from the gait, from her posture, that whatever this returnee's specific reasons for crossing whatever borders she did, they were painful, heavier still than all of her luggage.

But while they've become experts on returnees, the residents of Lozikeyi still can't know everything there's to know. They have no idea, for instance, as they carefully follow the goat's measured progress, that when she landed at the Jidada Regional Airport just a couple of hours ago she hadn't at first known how to move on the very land she'd once sworn to

never set hoof on, how to breathe the very air she'd once denounced because returning is one thing, and arriving is quite another. That once outside the airport she'd stood under the shade of a syringa tree, near that spot where the statue of the Old Horse had been, and wept.

They have no idea that she'd stayed until the airport emptied and it seemed she was the only one left like some last, lone survivor of an apocalypse, yes, tholukuthi standing there under the syringa tree that she hadn't seen in years because it didn't grow in that foreign soil where she'd sought refuge, that tree with its yellow marble-size inedible fruit that reeked in the stunning sun, the tree with those sprawling branches writhing with whole territories of ants and reaching for the face of God, yes, tholukuthi she'd remained there, standing with her luggage and weeping, until at last, a service worker recognized in the goat's tragic posture, in the sound of her harrowing weeping, the specific lament of a returnee broken in specific ways by her country of broken things, went to her and gently, gently, tholukuthi so, so gently she could have been disarming a bomb, took the handle of her suitcase and set the piece on that red earth there, and then next took the backpack and set it down too, and then gently, again gently, so gently the goat almost didn't feel it, took her in her arms and held her until she finished emptying the torrent of return.

And now, a couple or so hours later, the returnee negotiates the pot-holed road without a name and feels the appraising eyes of animals watching her from the street, from their yards, from behind curtains, from idling cars, from under umbrellas, from behind corners. She wonders if she should've just used a private taxi—an idea she'd dismissed because she wanted to take her time getting to the township of Lozikeyi, where she grew up, where her mother still lives, and which also happens to be her namesake, for Lozikeyi is in fact the goat's middle name, tholukuthi both goat and township named for the Ndebele queen of the South Western Jidada of the precolonial days. And you did good, long-lost daughter of

Simiso Khumalo, for taking public transport has indeed allowed you the extra time you needed to prepare, to brace yourself because even as you've had weeks, even as you had the long journey—it still wasn't enough for you to figure out how to begin to show your face to a mother you haven't seen, let alone spoken to, in a whole entire decade.

LOZIKEYI: PORTRAIT OF A TOWNSHIP

To her relief she's left to walk in peace, because, she rightly reasons, she's been gone so long it's likely no one immediately recognizes her. But the township itself refuses to be a passive observer of this return. And so, Lozikeyi stands to her fullest height, drapes her boldest shawl over broad shoulders so this returnee too can appreciate her full glory in case exile, which has been known to sometimes bewitch the memories of her children, has made her forget it. And Lozikeyi whips such a sonic surge the goat feels her head hum: tholukuthi music competes from blaring radios and speakers; a hubbub of voices rises, falls, fades, and rises again; cars stutter, roar, rumble, and raise dust; playing children's shrieks and chants paint the air the color of their unbridled joy; there's a tickled yell of a pleased adult femal; the cries of vendors singing their wares; an airplane flying lowly overhead; from the hedges, a disorderly orchestra of cicadas, bees, crickets, locusts, and grasshoppers, birdsong. Then Lozikeyi throws, rights her shawl, and the air is laden with the aromas of food being prepared for lunch; there's the occasional whiff of herbs and cigarettes; then the smell of ripe guava, peaches, the fragrance of gardenias, the pungent odor of burning debris; the musty exhaust of a coughing car. And of course Lozikeyi will never in a million years pass up the chance to parade her blossoming daughters, who strut in the budding glory of their youth, hinding straight-backed in the sun, their beauty a call to prayer for all sorts of admirers posted all over the township waiting to bask in a splendor so potent it stays with them all day and haunts

their sleeping hours, yes, tholukuthi leaves a devastating aftertaste in their mouths such that they wake up disoriented and utterly undone. Then there are more random bodies of vendors sitting with their wares in corners; the customers who arrive and leave and arrive and leave; the nimble bodies of children chasing balls and flying kites and riding bikes and playing all sorts of games up and down the vast playground that is the street. And the goat, seeing Lozikeyi as she insists on being seen, meanders her suitcase around all the hustle-bustle, through a stunning inferno that cooks the patches of tarred road to softness and scorches her brow for good measure, and feels something that's been crouching inside her for the ten years she's been gone finally straighten itself.

THOLUKUTHI HER MOTHER'S HOUSE

The gate, when she gets to her mother's house, is locked. Puzzled, the goat rattles the thick padlock, above which is painted the house number, 636. The wrought-iron thing itself is a new addition that wasn't there when she left those many years ago, and so too is the white Durawall that now surrounds the entire house. What comes to mind as the goat contemplates these changes fills her with a momentary panic—her mother no longer lives here, the house has somehow changed ownership. But how? She is contemplating the locked gate, wondering what to do, where to go, when all of a sudden the air rings with the terrible tumult of birdsong. And just as the goat is standing there baffled by a noise unlike anything she's heard before, a massive rally of birds of all colors wheels aloft, temporarily darkening the Lozikeyi sky. By now, the goat has understood their strange chant of "New Dispensation—New Dispensation—New Dispensation," tholukuthi its chaotic echo staying in the air long after the massive fleet has swept off and away, leaving the goat wondering if what she's just seen and heard is indeed what she's just seen and heard.

"That's New Dispensation's choir. New Dispensation is the new president's pet parrot. They're singing the New Dispensation song. Me and my friends know how to dance the New Dispensation dance. Do you want us to show you it? Are you coming from far?"

The goat glances down to see a small kitten looking up at her, breathless from her own deluge of questions. The bare-pawed little one is so fantastically filthy it's no longer possible to tell the true color of her dress, whose sides are conveniently tucked into the leg openings of her panty. Lurking nearby are the kitten's friends, equally outstanding in their dirtiness. The goat smiles, remembering, seeing now in her mind's eye a flash of her own childhood career on these same dusty streets many, many years ago.

The kitten, having carefully scrutinized the newcomer's appearance, which has possibly made her feel self-conscious about her own, has rescued the sides of her dress and is making futile attempts to brush the front clean.

"Hello there, what's your name?" the goat says, smiling.

"Gloria! Gloria! Wena! Didn't I tell you to bathe and wash that filthy dress ages ago angutshelanga?!" This new voice comes from the next house over, where a thin old cat, in a flowing yellow dress, colorful beads around the neck and wrists, stands at the entrance, coolly surveying the scene, tholukuthi one paw akimbo, one balancing on a cane. She could be addressing the newcomer and not the said Gloria because her steady eyes are on the goat, yes, tholukuthi scrutinizing the stranger in the open, unabashed way of the elderly because they're at a stage in their lives when they generally understand a lot of things, politeness included, to be a waste of time. And she isn't wrong because she apparently saves herself the needless labor of waiting to find out who this young stranger at her neighbor's gate is, and what she wants, because the goat simply brings herself over without being asked.

HOME IS NOT WHERE WE LIVE, HOME IS WHERE WE BELONG

"Greetings, Grandmother, how are you?" the goat says, approaching.

"Greetings, child. And the name's Duchess. I am fine if you are fine?" The queen focuses on the goat with narrowed, intelligent eyes. She's impressed because unlike the miserable youth of nowadays, who'll shamelessly bombard an animal with questions without proper greetings, tholukuthi here's one who apparently was raised right.

"I too am fine, thank you. And how are the others?" the goat says. Unlike her mother's, the cat's house is surrounded by neither wall nor fence. The goat is surprised by the living riot of plant life. The whole yard, it seems, is a chaos of trees, shrubs, vegetables, and flowers of every color, and the redbrick house itself is almost entirely covered in a carpet of creepers. This is definitely not how it was when she left, when her neighbor, Sis Jo, lived there.

"The others are all fine. Is it well where you're coming from?" The queen's voice brings the goat back from the luxurious garden.

"It was well when I left, thank you. I'm wondering if you could possibly help me. My name is—"

"Ah-ah-ah-ah-ah! But aren't you Destiny, you?! Yes! Yes you are! Simiso's long-lost daughter, dadwethu kababa! Even as I've never set my eyes on you, child, I know you because of Simiso all over that round face, ah-ah-ah-ah-ah! Those ears, Simiso, those straight teeth, Simiso, that smile, even your voice, simply Simiso, she could've birthed herself, dadwethu kababa, ah, yeyi, let me see you properly!" the cat exclaims, hinding for the goat, who's now on all fours so the elder can look her over.

Destiny is so touched by the old one's joy she blinks away unexpected tears. And now that she is real close, the goat can see, from the cat's adornment, from the cane covered from head to tip in colorful beads, that she is also looking at a spirit medium, a diviner. The cat is silent as she circles

and circles the goat before she is content that yes, the animal in front of her is of flesh and bone and not some kind of apparition.

"Ye Lozikeyi! Y'all come and help my eyes see this! Y'all! Lozikeyi! Come and help my eyes see this!" the cat suddenly shrieks at the top of her voice, head thrown back, face turbulent with a palpable joy.

"Yelina, I say come and help me see this, I say come and help me see this, please come and help me see! Lozikeeeeeeeeeeeeeeeyi bo!" Now the cat's voice is all power and pain and prayer all at once, tholukuthi a voice that rises above every single noise on the block. And the goat understands from this drama of welcome, the absolute weight of the time she's been gone, and similarly, the gravity of her return.

OF THE TONGUE, MEMORY, AND THINGS

"Are you sure you've had enough of this here umxhanxa Destiny? Why don't you just polish it off, nje? Phela we made it for you and there's really not much of it left, just finish it," urges a cow, whose face looks familiar but whose name Destiny, try as she does, just can't seem to remember.

Before Destiny can protest, her plate is piled with the remaining scoop of the dish. The goat senses, from the cow's warmth and enthusiasm, from her attentiveness, from the way she bustles around the Duchess's kitchen and has just generally taken charge of her, decreeing which foods to eat and how much and when—that they most likely have a history, either directly or through her mother. Only that history now refuses to rise from wherever it is that histories go to take a nap. It's not the first face she's failed to name and she knows it won't be the last, that the coming days, weeks will be filled with such familiar but strange faces from the past. Tholukuthi the past. And they very well will, Destiny, ah-ah, you didn't know this was the cost of exile? Of return? But the thing to do is to forgive yourself—it could, after all, happen to anyone. And what kind of magical

memory would yours be to actually remember all these faces and names after all these years? Are you a computer? No, you're not a computer. So, just say: "Excuse me, it's been a real long time and I'm afraid my memory fails, could you please remind me your name again?" and they'll remind you, without judgment even, you'll see.

She doesn't ask, no, afraid it might provoke questions in turn, tholukuthi questions she can't or isn't prepared to answer. And so she simply smiles at the elusive faces of strangers from the past with the appropriate level of enthusiasm, and otherwise finds refuge in the plates of food brought to her like offerings. If she were to listen to her stomach she'd have long ceased eating, but then this isn't really an issue of the stomach at all.

And it's not, Destiny. You're also eating for other things too. You're eating for the time you've been gone, no? For the faces you've forgotten, no? For the phone calls you didn't make, no? The letters you didn't write, no? For the grief you've carried, no? For the pain you've carried, no? For the regret you've carried, no? For the anger you've carried, no? For the sadness you've carried, no? For the loss and loneliness you've carried, no? Tholukuthi you're also eating, Destiny, to figure out, from the taste and the texture and the smell of the food, from the glide of it down the throat and into the gut, if it's at all possible to really leave home, as in, all of you, leaving-leaving, or maybe if something, just a little, teeny bit of you is always left waiting in order that when the rest of you returns there's something to anchor you right back.

A QUESTION OF DUTY

"So, child of my sister, how're things in—kanje where is it that you've been living again?" This is Aunt MaKhumalo, kin only by virtue of a shared last name, and one of the multitudes of Simiso's mock relatives,

tholukuthi a side effect of being an only child without surviving family. Destiny, already drained by the cow's energy, musters the face of a long-lost niece and smiles at the hen, who has parked herself against a wall.

"They're fine, Auntie, thank you," Destiny says, very much aware she's being nudged into tricky territory of which if she's not careful, she'll possibly be trending in Lozikeyi's gossip circles before tomorrow's sunrise. And so she disregards the silence that follows—a silence she very well knows is also a trap to have her fill it with details about her life.

"Well, if they're fine wherever it is you're coming from, then all is well and God is good," Aunt MaKhumalo says.

"All the time," NaDumi, a donkey neighbor, quips, flashes a smile that is all teeth.

"Say, child of my sister, you left the young ones behind or what?" Aunt MaKhumalo says. She is preening herself, and her voice, emanating from inside her wing, where she has tucked her head, comes out muffled.

"The young ones?" Destiny says, frowning. The cow meets her gaze, shrugs, and carries a stack of plates to the sink.

"She means Simiso's grandchildren, your children phela," NaDumi nudges.

"Oh. Oh, no, there aren't any," Destiny laughs.

"There aren't any children?" Aunt MaKhumalo says with exaggerated mock horror.

"No," Destiny says, shaking her horns.

"Not even one ngtsho-ngtsho?" NaDumi says, frowning. Destiny thinks, What the hell? but only says, "Not even one."

"Or maybe they're on the way? There's still a little bit of time," Aunt MaKhumalo says. She has paused preening herself, her curved wing suspended in the air.

"Probably none on the way," Destiny says.

"What, wait, you mean there'll be no children at all?" NaDumi says.

"I mean there'll be no children," Destiny says.

"But why, Destiny Khumalo?" Aunt MaKhumalo says with undisguised disappointment. She has left her spot and flown onto the seat next to NaDumi, where she now sits like she's nesting some eggs.

"It's just I've never really wanted them. Motherhood is not for me," Destiny says, careful to keep her irritation out of her voice. She is bothered by the conversation, and wants it to stop.

But are you really surprised, Destiny? You, who grew up in this very Lozikeyi? Where an animal's business was everyone's business? Where your elders had the right to tell you about your life and feel like they were correct? Where you didn't even know the language for space, privacy? Boundaries? Which is true; she is surprised but not surprised. Surprised because in a way the years she's been gone made her forget. Surprised that things are still the same. The elders continue to look at her like she's spoken from her horns.

"My dear, let me tell you, of course you want children, you just don't know it yet. Besides, what kind of femal doesn't want any children when God gave us wombs? It's just not normal," Aunt MaKhumalo says, lowering her voice like she's imparting a secret wisdom only meant for the young goat's ears.

"And if you don't want them now you might just decide, when they arrive, that you want them after all. And you'll see how it's natural as breathing, and you'll be glad," NaDumi laughs a satisfied laugh.

"Well, Witness, my last-born—remember you played and stole fruits all over this block together—is expecting her last as we speak. She's known as NaChoice now—after her first born, Choice, who's in form one. Then after Choice comes Moreblessing, who's in grade six, and then after Moreblessing there's Denzel, in grade three." Aunt MaKhumalo can barely disguise a pride that says her children are very much her wealth.

"Denzel? You're telling me that's in fact Didiza's given name, MaKhumalo?" NaDumi says.

"Yes, kanti you didn't know, NaDumi? Didiza is indeed Denzel," MaKhumalo says.

"But what on earth is a Denzel, MaKhumalo? Did you run out of names to curse that poor child with a name that doesn't even mean anything?" NaDumi says.

"Girl, you're asking me?—ask Witness when you see her. But anyway, you will be surprised, Destiny, by how much a child just changes your world. I promise, you become a totally different being," Aunt MaKhumalo says. She pauses to greet a hen who waddles into the kitchen, tholukuthi dressed all in black.

"MaKhumalo! NaDumi! Are y'all mad? Why don't you leave that child alone?!" the hen chides.

"What are you talking about, Comrade Nevermiss Nzinga?" MaKhumalo and NaDumi speak in unison.

"Have you no shame, in your old age? We can all hear you from the living room bombarding her with your nonsense! And you, Destiny, don't you know how to tell folks to mind their business mani, didn't Simiso teach you anything?" the hen says, chiding Destiny in equal measure.

And Destiny, who has in fact been dying to tell the two elders to stay out of her goddamn business, smiles a grateful smile. Only you cannot do that, Destiny—to tell your elders to mind their business no matter how much they deserve it, at least not in those words. Because it is disrespectful to do so, what with them being your seniors. Because it is not the Jidadan way. She wishes she could; if only she could. If only.

"I mean, who says she has to get married and have children? Phela Destiny, this donkey and hen are the very same femals who, when some of us joined the struggle for Jidada's liberation, were busy judging us, preaching that it was our responsibility to stay at home and conceive, that it was

unfemal to bear arms. Same as some of our mal Comrades on the war front who thought we were there expressly to serve as their wives and itch-tails, and general caretakers! But didn't we fight alongside them, and for the very same reasons? Didn't we liberate Jidada together even though today this wretched ungrateful Seat will make like this Jidada was liber-ated through testicles? And two, okwesibili, in case no one has told you, Destiny, you live your life for you, unless you have another life some-where in which you'll finally live on your own terms, you hear me?" the hen says. Her comb has turned pale, feathers rustled to chaos.

"Yes, I hear you, Comrade Nevermiss Nzinga," Destiny says, aware how the name she always uttered with effortlessness throughout her child-hood now sounds absurd on her adult tongue. But she doesn't know any other name for the hen, who never parted with her nom de guerre even as Jidada's War of Liberation ended. "Because the war may be over but I'm still a soldier. They won't recognize or bury me at their Square of Libera-tors, but as long as I have breath in my lungs my name will remind you I liberated this country, and that I never missed," Comrade Nevermiss Nzinga said once, many, many years ago when a curious young Destiny asked after the hen's strange name. Tholukuthi those who really know about things said she'd been rechristened by her Comrades on the war front for being an unrivaled sharpshooter.

"Hawu, Comrade Nevermiss Nzinga, kanti are we fighting now?! I didn't know we were at war—MaKhumalo and I here were just talking to the child. Destiny, please accept our apologies, apparently we shouldn't have had that conversation, even as it is a very natural conversation," Na-Dumi apologizes in an apology that is not an apology.

PORTRAIT OF A MOTHER'S LOVE

"But is it really you, Destiny?" NaLove says, fixing Destiny, and not for the first time, with a look of disbelief. NaLove, one of Simiso's close friends from Destiny's childhood, wears, despite the time of day, a black rainbow-polka-dot morning gown. Destiny cannot get over seeing the familiar thing; she almost wants to greet it, ask it how it's been. Once upon a time, almost twenty years ago, when Loveness, NaLove's daughter who'd just moved to Toronto—one of the first in the neighborhood to migrate to North America—sent the gown to her mother, NaLove in fact threw a tea party to show it off to her friends and enemies alike. Destiny is almost sure that whenever it is that she last saw the donkey, she was wearing this very same thing. And now, a decade later, NaLove and her rainbow-polka-dot morning gown don't seem to have aged one bit.

"It's me, Auntie. It's really me myself," Destiny says, and not for the first time.

"Yes, I know it's you I'm seeing. But at the same time I also just can't believe it's you-you-you, like you yourself you, I'm seeing," NaLove says, playfully butting heads with Destiny.

"Well, you better believe it, dadwethu kababa, the ancestors are there and the ancestors are real and the ancestors are merciful and the ancestors are great," the Duchess says, softly tapping the floor with her cane.

"God too, we can't forget the Most High," Mother of God says, being that she can't stand hearing the dead being lauded over her living God.

"But if only your mother were here, if only Simiso were here," Na-Dumi says, shaking her head. At the mention of her mother, Destiny feels again the heaviness that earlier threatened to engulf her when the Duchess called her to her bedroom as the food was being prepared. She'd found a row of somber-faced elders sitting in a neat line at the edge of the bed, like they were at a wake, clearly waiting to address her. Destiny had hesitated,

wondering whether to kneel on the floor or sit in the empty chair by the door. The Duchess pointed to the chair.

"Well, we figured, dear daughter, that we'd address the question you've no doubt been carrying ever since you walked up here and found that there gate locked," the Duchess said, pointing with her chin. And Destiny, put out of ease by the sudden weightiness of the cat's tone, by the grave demeanor of the gathered faces, had been struck by a thought that filled her head with fog, and she could not hold back tears. And the elders, knowing what they knew about the weight of returns, made no move to console the goat. The thought that'd made Destiny weep was that her mother was dead, or worse, though she couldn't think of what could be worse than dead.

"But Simiso will be so happy to see you, Destiny. You don't know how she needed this miracle," said Comrade Nevermiss Nzinga.

"Please, Comrade Nevermiss Nzinga, where's my mother?" Destiny said.

"That, child, is not an easy question, and so we can't really answer you directly," Comrade Nevermiss Nzinga said, shifting her weight in that way that said there was both so much to say and not a straightforward way to say it.

And, there, tholukuthi sitting on the bed with a white duvet cover that was all the rage in the Lozikeyi of the first couple of years of the twenty-first century, the elders took turns telling the returned daughter of their sister-friend how Simiso had suffered at the sudden disappearance of her only child almost a decade ago. How it plunged her in a deep, dense dark that still engulfed her these many years later. How, in the better days of that darkness, Simiso would roam the township like an unappeased ghost, knocking on doors. How if she wasn't knocking on doors she was stopping animals on the streets, approaching them in stores, in churches, in beer halls, at funerals, weddings, rallies—wherever it was that animals

congregated. How she'd pull out a faded photograph of herself and her missing daughter and say: "My name is Simiso Khumalo, and I'm looking for my missing daughter, Destiny Lozikeyi Khumalo, have you seen her? I need to find her. Without her I cannot breathe, without her I'll lose my mind." How Simiso was able to somehow keep breathing for all those years, but unfortunately couldn't really hold on to all of her mind. How in her worst days she'd wander all over Lozikeyi—singing, crying, laughing, shrieking, depending on the shape of her madness that day. How she'd sometimes go through each and every dustbin within her reach, digging for Destiny in the trash. How she'd disappear, first for days, then weeks, months—roaming all over Jidada on foot no matter the weather, searching, only returning when her fragile mind happened to remind her who she was.

THOLUKUTHI FAITH

"Yes, it is indeed painful Simiso isn't here on your return, Destiny, but do not look so sad, dear daughter, I just have a feeling. And neither should you lose hope, have faith," Mother of God says. There's a momentary quiet in the Duchess's living room, a grim air, because no matter how much food has been eaten, no matter how good, no matter how the neighborhood has rallied on short notice to give the returnee goat a spontaneous welcome, no matter the laughter, no matter the stories, they all know none of it is enough to sweeten the bitter taste of Simiso's absence.

"I hear you, Mother of God," Destiny says bravely, made self-conscious now by the sympathetic eyes on her, and struggling to summon a hope that doesn't match the despair in her heart. For the first time since the gathering, the goat feels tired, suddenly overwhelmed by the attention. She wishes she could just up and retreat to her mother's house and process the situation in solitude.

"You know not too long ago at church—and the Duchess can attest to this, Destiny, she was there—our Prophet was just prophesying about how Jidada's coming glory will be so spectacular the lost children will return," Mother of God says.

"And here is one of them," NaLove says.

"Here is one of them, praise the Lord, who works in mysterious ways," says Mrs. Phiri, rising from her corner near the door and stepping outside.

Mrs. Phiri had been Destiny's primary school teacher at Langeni, and while she produced excellent results, she was feared by even the most hardcore of the students because of her legendary cruelty so that everyone at the school, including her colleagues, called her the Tyrant. Tholukuthi if she wasn't spewing mind-numbing insults then she was clobbering students with belts, batons, whips, sticks, rulers, canes, pipes, umbrellas, and whatever else she could use, and if not clobbering then she was lifting them in the air by their ears, or making them bite each other, or sending whole classes to run laps on the school grounds, depending on the temperature of her rage on a given day. These many years later, Destiny can't believe how Mrs. Phiri's voice retains the capacity to make her liver quiver.

"Is it true, Mother of God, that the Savior of the Nation actually came to your church?" NaDumi says.

"Indeed, NaDumi, he was there talking about the New Dispensation, kanti didn't I WhatsApp you the pictures and video from our church group the other day? Those who think they know about things can say all they think they know, but Jidada is going to the promised land, and the Savior is taking us there. You should have seen, too, NaDumi, how the horse just oozes kindness and humility nje, a shining example of leadership itself. And most importantly, how he respects this one who rules from above," Mother of God said, pointing to God.

"Well, I don't know, Mother of God, but I myself don't see any change coming from Tuvy or his corrupt, incompetent party who've proved to us

for a whole four decades that all they're good at is running things down, violence, and looting, basically everything but good governance. What suddenly makes them saviors? When they and the Old Horse are basically cut from the same cloth?" says the cow who'd put herself in charge of Destiny's eating.

"And that's the truth, Mrs. Fengu. And exactly why we're voting for real change come elections. And once we have the Opposition in power then we can start talking about having a real Savior," Mrs. Phiri says, re-claiming her seat. When Destiny hears the Tyrant say the name "Mrs. Fengu," she looks at the cow closely. You remember her now, Destiny, you actually know this face, no? She knows the face, remembers how the cow and her husband, Dr. Future Fengu, had relocated from the UK, where they'd studied, just a couple of years before she left. But time, and Jidada, has dulled the cow's once-fresh face, the bright sparkle Destiny remembers from back then.

"But isn't it too soon for elections, though? We remove the Old Horse today, tomorrow we're what, we're hurrying to the polls? What exactly is the rush for? Aren't these things supposed to take time?" NaLove says.

"The rush, NaLove, is because Tuvy is keen to appear legitimate. You would too if you seized power through a coup and were desperate to shake off the stigma. And of course we know he'll win, which is why he's holding them in the first place and so soon—it's all for show," Sis Nomzamo says. She and her companion, Shami, wear matching red T-shirts with "Sisters of the Disappeared" embossed in black letters on the front and back.

"No! I say no! There's just no way that Tuvy is winning! How? When we marched at the fall of the Old Horse you think it was so he could rule us?! We were celebrating the fall of a tyrant we'd tried and failed to re-move, we were celebrating the right to appoint our own president! And I tell you we intend to finish what we started once and for all in these up-coming elections!" Mrs. Phiri has raised her voice in a way that made her

classes sit up straight and hold their breaths those many years ago. The memory makes Destiny want to laugh.

"But, do you truly believe, Mrs. Phiri, based on what we know of the last forty years, that this Tuvy and the Generals did this coup just to give the country to the Opposition?" Sis Nomzamo says. Her voice has a calmness, a quiet of one reasoning with a rock, and Destiny admires the donkey's skill.

"And with their history, that they can suddenly know how to hold #freefairncredible elections? I understand the desperate need to believe that something better is coming after the Old Horse, but I'm afraid it simply won't happen," Shami says.

"Mina, I just find this whole situation depressing, quite frankly. And I won't lie, if I could find a place to go to and leave this madness behind I'd do so in a heartbeat," Mrs. Fengu says.

"Well, let him try stealing this election. There'll be war! I tell you we will rise!" Mrs. Phiri's voice is determined.

"With what guns, Mrs. Phiri? And who exactly will fight?" Shami says.

"Well, animals can always get guns. Doesn't Comrade Nevermiss Nzinga here still have her Killjoy from the war? And we have freedom fighters among us, don't we? Who told you they don't have weapons?" Mrs. Phiri says.

"And that's the truth. We are here. And let me tell you, Mrs. Phiri, if anything starts right now in this Jidada, you know where to find me and my Killjoy," Comrade Nevermiss Nzinga says, pecking up.

"Sis Nomzamo, Shami. If you don't want your voices turning hoarse, leave it alone. Time will always speak for you," the Duchess yells from somewhere inside her kitchen.

"Well, for today we'll leave it alone, but only because we have a meeting to go to, otherwise these conversations must be had," Sis Nomzamo says. She and Shami rise at the same time and say their goodbyes.

"Hawu, dadwethu kababa here I am bringing out the drinks and here you're leaving?!" the Duchess says, appearing with a tray of drinks.

"I'll drink for them, Duchess, not to worry, it's why I'm here. You don't want a cold beer, Destiny?" Comrade Nevermiss Nzinga says, already reaching for a sweaty bottle of Castle Lite.

"I'm so tired I'd probably fall asleep were I to drink, but thank you, I'll take water," Destiny says.

"Another time, Duchess. And welcome home, Destiny. Get some rest," Sis Nomzamo says from the doorway.

"Of course, thank you," Destiny says.

"Yeyi Nomzamo, before you go. Kodwa how is that cousin of yours, really? I mean Marvelous," Mother of God says.

"Futhi you've asked a question that's been on my mind. Is she really well? I ask because her silence is truly uncharacteristic. It's just not the Marvelous we know," Mrs. Fengu says.

"Well, y'all know she's now just Sweet Mother, after the university stripped her of that degree, which she didn't study for! But anyway, don't say you heard it from me, but it seems Marvelous—"

"Please no, NaDumi, please!" Mother of God says.

"Ihn, kanti what is the problem, Theresa?" NaDumi says.

"I specifically asked Sis Nomzamo here, who is Marvelous's relation and can maybe tell us better," Mother of God says.

"Hawu, hanti I was also just sharing what I heard too being that this is not a secret topic, Mother of God, lami I was saying nje," NaDumi says, flinching.

"It's best not to gossip in such situations, Precious, even the Bible warns against it," Mother of God says. NaDumi, visibly stung, takes a swig of her Castle Lite and busies herself with straightening the doily on the nearest side table.

"Well, my auntie, who's recently visited, says the family is trying to

come to terms, which understandably can't be easy. The Father of the Nation is still hurt and devastated by what he considers an unforgivable betrayal, and his health has been on a downward spiral since the coup. Marvelous is holding up and not doing too badly, which doesn't surprise me, she's a survivor, that one," Sis Nomzamo says, addressing the room.

"We're very glad to hear it, Sis Nomzamo, she'll endure this like other things have been endured. We'll be keeping her in our thoughts and prayers," Mother of God says.

"You must have run out of wretches to pray for, Theresa. As for me myself I have no thoughts and prayers whatsoever for that miserable donkey, none. Far as I'm concerned she deserves whatever hell she's in, and more!" Mrs. Phiri explodes with undisguised contempt.

"Hawu, Mrs. Phiri?" NaLove says.

"What, NaLove? It's the truth! And no disrespect to you, Sis Nomzamo, but your aunt's daughter gets zero sympathy from me, zero. For the things she did, or are we expected to forget them now? That Marvelous was downright ugly, and she can't blame it on the Father of the Nation or the Seat of Power, who we all know are black devils, but she had a choice not to unite with evil especially as I'm sure it didn't hold a gun to her head and make her do so. We haven't forgotten, and we'll never forget. And she doesn't get to be a victim today only because her filthy pond has dried up, which serves her right if you ask me!" Mrs. Phiri fumes.

"Dadwethu kababa! But what exactly did Marvelous do though kahle-kahle, Mrs. Phiri, that you and this whole country are up in arms? I know she was a fool, but when was she ever the government? And wasn't this country in the toilet before she even married the Father of the Nation? And do you honestly think this coup wouldn't have happened were she Mother Teresa?" the Duchess says.

"Like I always like to say, Duchess, it's easier to point at an unfavorable femal instead of holding ugly mals to account. We'd rather do that than

unpack the real and whole truth of how we got here, and do the hard work of figuring how we get out. But soon enough, this Jidada will realize Marvelous is in fact the last of our worries, but I'm afraid we'll be in the mouth of a crocodile by then, not that we aren't already in it, it's just a matter of—"

"Okay, okay, okay. Shami, no, not another session, please, we have a meeting to get to. Everyone, keep well!" Sis Nomzamo says, literally dragging Shami off; the Sisters of the Disappeared finally leave, long after the first goodbye.

"And on that note I guess I'll be going too. But at least I won't be needing to make dinner this evening, I'm as stuffed as a wife's relative!" NaDumi says.

"But first, let's take a selfie for Lozikeyi's Facebook page, girls," NaLove urges.

"But we're not even prepared," Mother of God says. It's a halfhearted protest, for the elegant sheep looks like she's the kind of animal who's ever ready for a picture, even in her sleep. And before Destiny—who isn't on social media, and isn't interested in having her picture broadcast on the Lozikeyi page—can protest, she's surrounded by posing elders. It's a scene she can't reconcile with the Lozikeyi of when she left, before technology and social media were to take the township by storm.

A PICTURE IS WORTH A THOUSAND MEMORIES

"There, it's done. I must say these Samsung phones take lovely photos too. Ende do you remember just how much of a production it was to get a picture taken back when we weren't even Destiny's age?" NaLove says.

"Yeyi! You planned for it days in advance. The assembling of outfits. Gathering moneys—money for transport into town. Money back from town. And of course money to pay the photographer. There was figuring out the outfit. Making sure that outfit was in pristine shape. Sewing what

needed sewing. Borrowing earrings. Shoes. Pantyhose. Lipsticks. Makeup. Going through old albums to make sure one didn't replicate a previous pose. Deciding on, and practicing the new pose. And then gathering the courage for striking a pose in front of a stranger. Gathering courage to get into town, for staying intact when you were told to get off the pavements that were for whites, courage for when you were accused, because of your makeup, for being a itchtail on the prowl!"

And, reminded thus of the long-gone days of their youth, the elders, already on their feet, sit back down and reminisce about the past. Tholu-kuthi the past. And it's suddenly forty, fifty years ago in the Duchess's living room. They stretch their memories as far as their minds will allow, and when they can go no further, they channel the memories passed down to them by their mothers, yes, tholukuthi those memories also including those of their mothers' mothers and the mothers of the mothers of those mothers. And with their minds and their mouths, they propel themselves and each other into a past before Jidada was Jidada, and then past that past to the many pasts of their mothers and their mothers, and then past that past to the past-past-past, yes, tholukuthi back when rocks were so soft you could pinch them and draw blood, when mountains were still grow-ing, when gods roamed the earth, yes, tholukuthi that past of long, long, long before greedy colonists came with guns, divided the earth among themselves like there was nobody on it already, flew strange rags in the air called flags and said, Let there be Country-Countries.

#FREEFAIRNCREDIBLEELECTION

**JIDADA VOTES IN FIRST POST–OLD HORSE
HARMONIZED ELECTION**

POTUS @bigbaboonoftheUS
US election observers will be on site for the Jidada upcoming election
because they have a tremendous record of STEALING elections and
DISRESPECTING the WILL of voters over there. And that's SAD! And
very BAD! And NOT democracy! It's DICATORSHIP!

> **GoldenMaseko** @GoldenM
> Replying to @bigbaboonoftheUS
> It's spelled Dictatorship bruh. DICTATORSHIP. I mean, you
> should know the spelling seeing it's on your forehead 🙃

> **SonofBulawayo** @SonofByo
> Replying to @bigbaboonoftheUS
> Says an unqualified pussy grabber, liar, cheat, conmal, racist,
> misogynist, bully, predator, and and and . . .

> > **ComradeLiberator** @CdeLiberator
> > Replying to @SonofByo
> > And tweeting from stolen land, yazi the audacity, nxaaa!

SmallHouse @MsMoyo
Replying to @bigbaboonoftheUS
Thank you Mr. President. Democracy in Jidada is a farce!
#freefairncredibleelection

LionofJidada @LOJ
Replying to @bigbaboonoftheUS
The Savior for Life! Jidada Party for life! We will WIN regardless
of the vote, what will you do @Potus? A tantrum? Impose more
sanctions? #notoregimechangeforlife 💪

Daddybilly @Daddybilly
Replying to @bigbaboonoftheUS
Tell you what, come and post this after you win YOUR next
election, otherwise for now just mind your own business.

JidadaPartyofPower @JPP
Replying to @bigbaboonoftheUS
We don't take orders from the West! And by the way, who
actually observes your elections? #neveracolonyagain 💪

MadeinJidada @MIJ
Replying to @bigbaboonoftheUS
And what exactly gives you the authority Mr. Pussy-grabber in
Chief?

MaiFari @maifari
Replying to @bigbaboonoftheUS
Thank you for speaking the truth, Mr. President! I for one have
never seen a free and fair election out here! And thank you too
for the election observers, we need to guard the process.
#freefairncredibleelection 🙏

The Observer @Observer
Seen and heard: Tuvy on election observers: "They should do their job
but if they get in our affairs they unfortunately will just have to eat the
road." #freefairncredibleelection

Duckdudu @duckdudu
Replying to @Observer
Oh shit! Oh shit! 😼 #freefairncredibleelection?

Loveisnotenough @uthandolwanivele

Replying to @Observer

Reminds me of a certain dictator I used to know!
#freefairncredibleelection

>   **Duckdudu** @duckdudu
>
>   Replying to @uthandolwanivele
>
>   Gurrrrrrl—birds of a feather! BUT—the certain dictator
>   you used to know is in fact a prince in comparison.
>   Watch!

ItaiCB @ItaiCB

Replying to @Observer

But how can Tuvy or any JP member know what observers really
do? 🦤

TheAfrican @TheAfrican

Replying to @Observer

Surprise, surprise! The leopard showing his true spots!
#GodblessJidada

The Source Poll @Source1

Who do you think will win the #Jidadaelections?
    15% Jidada Party
    80% Jidada Opposition Party
    5% Others

>   **Soneni** @Soneni
>
>   Replying to @Source1
>
>   Frankly, the peacock is the best qualified to lead us to a peaceful,
>   prosperous, corruption-free Jidada. Too bad you have to belong
>   to a political party to be elected to public office in this country!
>   We really need a mind shift! #freefairncredibleelection
>
>   >   **Lookout** @Lookout
>   >
>   >   Replying to @Soneni
>   >
>   >   Right? We have a highly qualified candidate, and animals
>   >   be like, no, we don't know him, he's not from our party!
>   >   #freefairncredibleelection

Jojettilover @Jojettilover
Replying to @Lookout
Leave them alone, it's called Freedom of Choice!

Martin @Martin
Replying to @Source1
No brainer. Tuvy will win by overwhelming majority of at least
98% 💪

Daddybull @Daddybull
Replying to @Martin
You have a demon of idiocy!

Maidei @Maidei
Replying to @Source1
Let me just say that if Tuvy wins I'm leaving. No way I'm doing
five more years of this shit, I'm sorry, just can't #Jidada
abusiverelationship 🙀 🙀 🙀

CdeHungwe @CdeHungwe
Replying to @Source1
My $$$ on Goodwill Beta! The future is here, you can't stop it!
Plus #Godisinit

Melizitha @Melz
Replying to @CdeHungwe
For reals. We need new leaders PLEASE. Currently no
jobs, no $$$, no prospects, no future, no quality
education, no healthcare, no justice, no nothing
#change4Jidadanowweretired 🧟

Thahegoat @Daddygoat
Replying to @Source1
Jidada Opposition Party. The youth will speak!
#freefairncredibleelection 💪

Mabhanzi @Mabhanzi
Replying to @Source1
Tuvy for life! Jidada Party for life! #notoregimechangeforlife 💪

Naledi @Naledi
Replying to @Source1
Not a Jidadan but the Opposition has upper hand. Youthful, educated party with ideas vs geriatrics who've tried and failed for decades #notoregimechangeforlife

NaMzi @NaMzi
Replying to @Source1
Rest in Peace Goodwill Beta and the Opposition. We're burying you soon!

JahPeacock @Jahpeacock
Replying to @Source1
President Tuvy will keep ruling. In fact the election is just a formality, y'all know we got this!

Primrose @Primrose
Replying to @Source1
I'm voting for Goodwill Beta #regimechange #freefairncredibleelection

Daddygaga @Daddygaga
Replying to @Source1
Tuvy! Party of Power! Jidada is ours by right, we liberated it. We'll die before we hand it over to puppets of the West! #Jidadabyblood #neveracolonyagain

The Migrant @Themigrant
In the urban country called Jidada, Goodwill Beta will win. In the rural country called Jidada, Tuvy will win. #Ataleoftwojidadas 🤗

ChiefSabelo @ChiefSabelo
Change is coming to Jidada, nobody can stop this train! #Godisinit #freefairncredibleelection

Verona1 @verona1
History in the making! Get ready for a new president! You can't fix idiotic but you can vote it out #PartyofPowermustfall 💪

Disgruntled @Disgruntled
Praying for a peaceful election. May the will of Jidada be done,
Amen 🙏

ExiledJidadan @exiledJidadan
Gud luck our dearest brothaz n sistas. You're also voting for those of
us who can't be there, as well as the future. You can do this! Godbless!
#freefairncredibleelection

> **Ethel SV** @EthelSV
> Replying to @exiledJidadan
> This isn't right or even fair. The diaspora must be allowed to
> vote, it's our right. I'm in pain 😭 #freefairncredibleelection

The Voice of Jidada @VOJ_NEWS
Jidada votes in first post-Old Horse general election. All eyes on Jidada.

> **NaFungai** @Nafungai
> Replying to @VOJ_NEWS
> So were election reforms done in the first place? 💀 I must've
> missed that part.

MovernShaker @movernshaker
#Jidada you ready??? Let's finish what we started in 2017
#JidadaPartyOut 💪

> **Nyasha** @Nyah
> Replying to @movernshaker
> Sit down, you didn't start shit in 2017. Tuvy and the dogs carried
> out a coup, y'all were just used to sanitize it. And now they'll
> finish their thing, WATCH and LEARN.

New Patriot @NewPatriot
Time to demolish the despotism of the Jidada Party once and for all.
Never again in this Jidada with a -da and another -da should one party
be allowed to destroy and hold the nation hostage for decades!
#Regimechangenow #freefairncredibleelection 💪

Trymore @Trymore
Replying to @NewPatriot
Dream on. Party of Power for life, you'll rule Jidada in your dreams!

Freecat @Freecat
The future will win. Change will win. The end.

Jidadan @Jidadan
Replying to @Freecat
Twitter is not a country my friend. Jidada is for the Party of Power forever, we vote on the ground and we win this election on the ground, not on no Twitter #neveracolonyagain 💪

LEGACY TOUR

WISHES FOR VIPERS

Giant billboards greeted the Father of the Nation wherever he looked. He read: "A Savior Is Come." "Vote Tuvy for Robust Development." "The Voice of the Multitude Is the Voice of God." "Tuvy Leading Us to the Promised Land." He read, "Jobs, Jobs, and Jobs for Real This Time." "Clean Fresh Water, Electricity for All." He read, "Tuvy Delivering the Jidada You Want and Need." He read, "Vote Tuvy for Affordable, Quality Healthcare Guaranteed." Tholukuthi everywhere, where his own face had been for decade after decade after decade after decade, now loomed the devious face of the usurper—mocking him, taunting him, insulting him. Raging flames of anger blazed in the Father of the Nation's humiliated heart, and he itched yet again to travel back in time to that last Inner Circle meeting in which the supplanter and his conspirators had sat around him, talking patriotism and extolling him with what he now knew to be false adulation.

He thought how, once back in the past, he'd patiently wait for the Judases to gorge themselves on the food and drink until they were spread on the floor, bloated bellies up like the greedy gluttons they were. And when he felt the time was right he'd hind to the front of the room in opposition to his doctors, front hooves in the air, and roar, "Down with traitors! Death to coup plotters!" and with the utmost pleasure, he'd relish their terror and confusion as his Secret Guard—now that he knew better—magically appeared with guns ablaze to unleash such tremendous firepower, tholukuthi the onslaught raining and pummeling until every single one of the black devils had been crushed to pulp.

THOLUKUTHI HOW?

At each and every traffic light the Father of the Nation barreled his way without pause, without first looking left and then looking right, because while he no longer sat on the Seat of Power, he still had the instincts of one who ruled. Even at such an early hour, the organism that was the capital of Jidada was already awake and long come to life. The Father of the Nation wondered like he did every single day since the coup—How? Yes, tholukuthi how it was that the sun was really blazing with an intensity he hadn't commanded, and without even flickering out to plunge the treacherous nation into the perpetual darkness it deserved. How flowers were in natural bloom and more so without mixing up their colors. How lorries, cars, bicycles, taxis, and trucks flowed without crashing into each other like he'd once imagined would happen were he, for whatever reason, removed from the Seat of Power. How the birds were flying without falling out of the air. How students were in their correct school uniforms and knew which schools to go to. How it was that upbeat, joyful music poured out of rushing cars instead of heart-wrenching songs of sorrow.

How a bull was leaning against a pole and correctly smoking a cigarette without setting himself afire, yes, tholukuthi how on earth it was that without him ruling, life, Jidada was generally going on the way it'd always gone on.

PORTRAIT OF A BUSINESS DISTRICT

In the city center the pavements brimmed with goods, goods, goods. He saw animals spread wares on the bonnets and trunks and rooftops of parked cars. He saw animals hang goods on trees and wherever it seemed possible to spread wares, and in no time tholukuthi everywhere except the air itself was a vast, eclectic market of every imaginable merchandise: Jeans. Gas stoves. Tomatoes. Shoes. Bread. Dresses. Pens and pencils. Soap. Underwear. Cooking oil. Uniforms. Belts. Flowers. Beer. Oranges. Wigs. Phones. Pots and pans and plates. Textbooks. Chips. Portable radios. Fur-lightening creams. Perfumes. Condoms. Brooms. Sweet potatoes. Combs. Car parts. Toothbrushes and toothpastes. Used clothes. CDs. Onions. Bananas. Pantyhose. Apples. Medicines. Maize. Car-seat covers. Wild fruits. Healing herbs. Contraceptives.

While the Father of the Nation stood wondering if what he was seeing was indeed what he was seeing, a cow in a long skirt and white headdress accosted him to say, "What did you bring us today, Auntie?" The cow called him Auntie because to elude the ugly Defenders guarding his home he'd disguised himself in his wife's bonnet and gown, which he'd selected for its length and because it matched the butterflies, before slipping out with the dead Comrades, tholukuthi the butterflies in tow, and making for the city center.

He didn't know what the cow was talking about, and so he turned away from her to face the busy road, but of course it wasn't long before a duck appeared in front of him and said, "What did you bring us this morning,

Auntie?" at which the irritated Father of the Nation yelled, "What is wrong with you uncivilized beasts? Can't one walk these miserable streets in peace and without being molested?"

"I'm sorry, I didn't mean to offend. I'm just looking for business is all," the duck said.

"But why come to me for that business? And why on earth do you have to be a bother instead of doing that business in a proper office? And shouldn't you be in school in the first place? And what is your name, youngster, and who are your parents and where are they from?"

"Me I finished school. I have an MBA from the University of Jidada. My name is Knowledge Jele, son of Soneni Jele and Mpiyezwe Jele of Bulawayo. And this is my work. And all this is my office," the duck said, theatrically gesturing all round him at the open air.

"You have an advanced degree, you?" the Father of the Nation sniffed at the young animal. The duck bobbed his head.

"And that goat unloading blankets from that red Mazda over there actually has a PhD in history. And the cat selling phone chargers right next to him is an engineer. Actually a good number of the animals you see here are graduates—educate a Jidadan, educate a vendor." The duck threw his head back and quack-laughed, tholukuthi a sound that had a lot of pain and anger and broken things in it.

"Well, I've always maintained education is power. But why are you all out here vending like this?" the Father of the Nation said.

"Me, a vendor? Never! I'm a money changer," the duck said, shaking his tail feathers with visible pride.

"But what on earth is a money changer?" the Father of the Nation said.

"I buy and sell currency, which I hunt for from morning till night all over these streets. And I know with that fine dress you're wearing you definitely have some dollars or euros or pounds for me, Auntie," the duck said with a solicitous wink.

"But whatever are you buying and selling currency for?" the Father of Nation said, perplexed. A ram came and sang what now seemed to be the anthem of the streets: "What did you bring us, Auntie?"

"Another one? How many are you, really? Who sent you?" The duck quack-laughed his painful laugh, and the ram, like he were hearing a familiar, loved tune, laughed along as he wandered off.

"Well, there's enough of us, all right, I mean where can an animal go when ninety percent of the population is unemployed?" the duck said, a mischievous grin on his face.

"But when did things get like this?" the Father of the Nation said.

"Like what?" the duck said, looking around.

"Like this, a whole nation vending, a whole nation saying, What did you bring us, what did you bring us—what kind of life is that?" the Father of the Nation said, sweeping the air with a hoof.

"Things got like this in all these years of the damn Party of Power ruling," the duck said.

"But I don't understand!" the Father of the Nation cried, perhaps addressing himself, or perhaps addressing the Comrades, or perhaps the butterflies.

"Where have you been living, Auntie, really?" the duck said, his eyes curiously surveying the Father of the Nation for signs of what part of the world the old animal may have been possibly spat from because surely, even the dead leaves of Jidada wouldn't think to ask such naive questions.

"Me? I've never lived anywhere and never will. We fought for this country so we could live and die in it and not in the wilderness of foreign lands like godforsaken exiles. You can ask them, they know it too," the Father of the Nation urged, gesturing at the Comrades behind him.

"Ask who, Auntie?" the duck said, alarmed.

"Why, I mean my Comrades right there, the real Liberators. Comrades, come and tell this young one what he doesn't know." The Father of

the Nation gestured to his entourage. The duck looked around at the bodies of Jidadans, already bustling so early in the morning, yes, tholukuthi alert and quick because even the sticks and stones knew that the days, the times were such that the pavements, the streets, the city were no places for the languid, that it was the early bird that caught the US dollar. He opened his mouth to speak, thought better of it, and instead waved his goodbye to the old, obviously confused horse and hurried off, perhaps to his office that was also the whole city.

JIDADA HIGH

The procession would have passed the school had it not been for the fading billboard that said "Jidada High School—Knowledge Is Power," an arrow pointing the direction. The institution stood at the edge of a dismal township. The Father of the Nation led the way past sad-eyed ugly vendors selling snacks along the rusted fence, on which hung bright posters of the usurper, through the gates of the school, past the graveled flagpole area, where the faded shreds of the flag of Jidada flew in the gentle breeze, past the blocks of decrepit classrooms, past the empty library with the busted windows and dangling wall shelves, past the vast dry garden where beds of flowers wilted in the sun.

Outside what appeared to be the staff room, the Father of the Nation stood contemplating a squad of about a dozen girls who frolicked around, tholukuthi uniforms hiked up to reveal thighs they obviously intended for the blind not to miss. The young femals, perhaps aware of their devoted audience, put on a performance. They hinded even taller, thrust their chests as far as they could without their backs snapping into two, hiked up their uniforms just a tad higher, twisted and pranced. When they laughed, tholukuthi from lips painted all the colors of the rainbow, the sound was strange for its softness of bird feathers.

And on that softness of bird feathers, tholukuthi the Father of the Nation was borne back to his youth, yes, tholukuthi to those long-dead days of glory when all the femals knew him, when all the femals sought him, when all the femals fought for him, when all the femals loved him and those who didn't love him fell in love with him, when all the femals and their mothers and grandmothers and even the ghosts of their great-grandmothers wanted him, yes, tholukuthi back when he was young and strapping, when he didn't know peace because literally every breathing moment of his life was filled with the brouhaha of shrieking femals stampeding for him, wanting a piece of him, tholukuthi trying to die death for him.

He was basking in this memory when he saw the girls were now on the move, tholukuthi strutting off the way Jesus must have walked the Sea of Galilee knowing his very own father was in charge of the waters. He followed them to a giant noticeboard where every inch was covered in posters of the usurper and his opponent. He watched the girls take turns posing in front of the display to take pictures with their phones and gadgets. They filled the air with banter and laughter and gleeful shrieks, voices mixing in a bright, messy medley.

"Y'all, I heard the Savior made another girl pregnant at the University of Jidada!"

"Yep, heard it too, saw pictures of her on WhatsApp and Twitter. She ain't that cute!"

"I heard the Savior actually has girlfriends in all the universities of Jidada!"

"I heard he travels with femals in his official entourage!"

"I heard he has, like, more than two dozen illegitimate children!"

"His dick must be all wrinkled, though!"

"OMG, you said dick!"

"Cock!"

"Johnson!"

"Dong!"

"Wood!"

"Prick!"

"Phallus!"

"Ding-a-ling!"

"Schlong!"

"Joystick!"

"Baby maker!"

"AIDS dispenser!"

"Anaconda!"

"One-eyed monster!"

"Old wrinkled lizard of the new old Father of the Nation!"

The girls howled and pulled at each other's tails and howled some more. Tholukuthi they straddled imaginary lovers and made obscene gyrating and humping motions with their liquid hips, accompanied the obscene dance with exaggerated moans of ecstasy. The Father of the Nation, who did not expect to hear such talk from children, turned away in disgust, mortified, wondering: But what kind of school was this? Who was teaching the youngsters such lewdness? And where were their teachers? Their headmaster?

THE FUTURE OF THE NATION

He stopped at the very first classroom that showed signs of life. The unsupervised learners didn't pay attention even as the Father of the Nation, shocked by the mayhem, emphatically cleared his throat for attention. The youth kept on with their racket even as he slammed a hoof on a desk and said, "Order! Order! I command you to order right this instant!" Tholukuthi the disorder went on. The madness went on. In a corner, a shirtless kitten stood on a desk and belted an obscenity-filled chant, using

a pen for a microphone, accompanied by a lamb who banged on an over-turned dustbin. Around the duo, gleeful students jumped and gyrated while some held cell phones up, probably filming the chaos. Students sat on desks, limbs dangling. Students chatted in little groups. Students swiped away on gadgets. Students groomed themselves. Students did everything that had nothing to do with learning.

The Father of the Nation stood there and took in the chaos of the broken furniture. The smashed-up windows. The banged-up, peeling blackboards. The paper littering the floor. The crew of lizards smuggling pieces of chalk out the window. The graffiti on the walls. The unmistakable smell of marijuana. The row of ginormous ants building an ambitious anthill right in the middle of the classroom. Three lizards fornicating on the center page of an open book. The Father of the Nation had been a teacher once, yes, tholukuthi before joining the Liberation War he'd been an educator, bringing light into the miserable dark heads of young animals, grooming them to be good beings, good citizens, and the nation's future, and therefore he knew what a school looked and ought to look like, what students looked and ought to look like. Jidada High School looked like bedlam and its students not students but buffoons, nincompoops, wild beasts.

At last, a gosling with a head the size of a pebble looked up from a tattered book and said, "Good afternoon, have you come to teach us?" and, not remembering how and why exactly they'd come to the school and entered the classroom in the first place, the Father of the Nation said, "But where on earth is your teacher?"

"The teachers are on strike again," the gosling said.

"Why in the heavens are the teachers on strike again?" the Father of the Nation said.

The gosling cackled with laughter, as if she'd heard the funniest question in the history of funny questions, but quickly recovered. The Father

of the Nation banged on the desk again, for order, but of course to no avail. And, seeing from his demeanor that here was an animal thoroughly unaccustomed to disorder, and more so to being disobeyed, the gosling, taking pity, flew and landed on a rafter, and shrieked: "Yeyi! Y'all shut the fuck up, we got a new teacher or something!" By the time she came down, every one of the students was at attention and back in their seats.

Tholukuthi the silence had come about so suddenly the Father of the Nation at first stood there at a loss. And while he gathered his thoughts, a beautiful, arrogant-looking billy kid with a magnificent black coat sat up to his full height and yelled from the back of the classroom, "So, why are you here and what have you come to teach us, old one?"

"It seems to me from what I find here that the state of our education is obviously in dire straits," the Father of the Nation began. The juveniles howled with laughter.

"You think I'm fun? Are you not worried about your future?!" said the former president and former teacher, incredulous.

"Our future was plundered and pillaged by the deposed tyrant while we were in our mothers' bellies, old one, so unless you're here to teach us about making real and fast money to get out of the mess his regime put us in, I'm out," the arrogant kid said, getting up from his chair.

"Hey, I'm off to R. G. Mugabe Street, y'all, I hear there's internships for money changing, who's coming?" the kid said to his peers.

The rest of the students cheered, and, perhaps encouraged by the attention, the young goat strutted around the room, singing, "What did you bring us, brother? What did you bring us, sister? What did you bring us, homie? What did you bring us, Your Excellency, sir? What did you bring us, New Dispensation?" The applause grew and threatened to lift the decaying roof. Then the kid broke into a trot, aimed for the door, and galloped off, singing his "What did you bring us?" anthem. And his classmates, not to be

left out, rose like soldiers called to battle, and running, shrieking, singing, laughing, tholukuthi the buffoons, the nincompoops, the wild beasts broke out the door, out the gate, and disappeared down the potholed road.

So dispirited was the Father of the Nation by the encounter, he could barely see the road from nerves, and, perhaps sensing this, the butterflies took over the procession and led the way. He followed in half-languid steps, the Comrades directly behind him. They traveled with the solemnity of a funeral procession down the road that separated the school from the township, past the animals cutting gravestones under the dry acacia trees, past the mountains of uncollected trash, past the new housing developments where little ones skipped over streams of sewage, past the row of grocery stores, past the public taxi rank.

Tholukuthi the Father of the Nation barely registered his surroundings; his head was filled with the disturbing images of the ugly learners, no doubt the offspring of the likes of the ugly animals he'd seen in the city's pavements and who'd obviously grow up to beget ugly children of their own, and like that and like that the wretched cycle would continue. But how was it that this kind of school existed in Jidada in the first place? And how many schools were like this, with such ugly children? he thought. And what did it mean for the future of the nation? And did the ugly schoolchildren even know how hard he and the Liberators had fought for the very education they were now urinating on? That Jidada's education was supposed to be a towering beacon in the whole African continent?

THOLUKUTHI ONCE UPON THESE RAILS

The lines of rail jolted the Father of the Nation from his bitter reverie. They crisscrossed, uncrossed, and stretched from the station—now in disuse—as far as the eye could see, yes, tholukuthi going forward, not into the future but into the past. It seemed to the Father of the Nation a

long time ago now that back then, in the throes of the Liberation War, operating in small coordinated bands, Liberators would launch attacks on this very railway and many others like it throughout the country—blowing up goods trains, disrupting services, often causing shutdowns for days in a bid to cut off the despotic colonial regime. And it seemed an even longer while beyond that when their ancestors were forcibly removed from this very land to make way for the colonist intruders. They weren't just evicted—they also had to endure the violence and indignity of forced labor, cheap labor, yes, tholukuthi made to build the very rail that had displaced them from their land, the land that decades and decades and decades later, their yet-to-be-born descendants would have to go to war in order to liberate.

But it also seemed like yesterday too that a liberated Jidada also thrived on the railway. The trains came from all over the country. Carrying coal. Asbestos. Gold. Iron ore. Platinum. Cement. Fertilizer. Clothes. Cotton. Trains carrying tobacco. Wheat. Coffee. Sugarcane. Maize. Peanuts. Trains headed to Botswana. South Africa. The Democratic Republic of Congo. Zambia. Angola. Mozambique. Yes, tholukuthi trains carrying the bounty of Jidada with a -da and another -da, Jidada, the then breadbasket of Africa, Jidada, a then treasure trove of boundless natural wealth.

Tholukuthi standing on the rails, the Father of the Nation could actually hear it—the tumult of the trains—a frantic vibration shaking the earth. Shrill whistles rending the air. Steam hissing with utter arrogance in the face of God, and everywhere, the chug-chug-chug of the beast of metal sweeping the land. The exhilarating sound transported the Father of the Nation, filled him with such gladness he broke into a trot, and then into a run—tholukuthi he was a galloping train. "What did you bring us, brother?" he sang, hooves pounding the earth. "I brought you platinum and iron ore and coal," he sang. "What did you bring us, Grandmother?" he sang. "I brought you sugar and cotton and tobacco," he sang. "What

did you bring us, Auntie?" he sang. "I brought you wheat and maize and potatoes from Africa's breadbasket," he sang. "What did you bring us, Comrade?" he sang. "I brought you real Jidada money!" he sang, and there he was, an arrow in the wind, lighting across the field and galloping forward, tholukuthi not into the future but into Jidada's past glory.

GUKURAHUNDI

It was the anthem of the Comrades and butterflies that woke him up. His bones ached from the gallop across the open country. He looked about him and started, ambled to his feet. Around him everything was red like the butterflies, like blood—tholukuthi red trees, red grass, red flowers, red earth, red rocks, even the sky was crimson. The Father of the Nation had seen all kinds of things in his long, eventful life, but never anything like this. And because the whole picture somehow struck him as absurd as it was astonishing, he found himself unable to resist the urge to laugh. And he was laughing like that, having temporarily forgotten the pain in his old joints, when he saw the first of the butterflies enter the earth. There was, just to his left, a huge red tree with flat, broad leaves and round fruits. A red anthill grew under the tree and it seemed from where he lay that the anthill was open at the top, which is where the columns of butterflies entered, swarm after swarm after swarm, until the last of them disappeared.

The sudden rain startled him. Because his great-grandmother had been a rainmaker and knew rains like some animals knew who was coming just from the sound of hooves—he knew what kind of rain it was. Gukurahundi—yes, tholukuthi the early rain that washes away the chaff before the spring rains. Only this rain was bloody, like everything else. He rose and made for the tree with the strange fruits, meaning to seek cover, but he found, to his surprise, that despite the mat of thick leaves,

under the tree was raining just as heavy as it was raining outside it. There was no other shelter. Until he saw the anthill before him split open and the dead Comrades begin to enter. He followed them.

To his surprise the world underneath, just like the world above, was a landscape complete with trees and grass and flowers and rocks and mountains. The butterflies and dead Comrades were nowhere in sight. Tholukuthi the silence that greeted him was like the inside of a bullet. He was looking around him, gathering his bearings, when he saw, to his alarm, he was surrounded by blood-drenched bodies, yes, tholukuthi injured bodies, mutilated bodies, chopped bodies. There were burned bodies, beaten bodies, raped bodies, bleeding bodies. He saw bodies of pregnant femals with bellies cut open, fetuses dangling. In open mass graves he saw bullet-riddled bodies. And everywhere—blood, streams and streams of it. The hot air reeked with the stench of rotting flesh, rang with the most awful pleas for help. He heard cries and howls of pure terror, heard desperate prayers and supplications. The noise gathered itself into such a devastating storm of sound he thought his head would split.

THE FIFTH BRIGADE

A hail of gunfire brought the dreadful noise to an end. The Father of the Nation turned his ears backward and listened with rapt attention, heart pounding. He heard more gunfire, followed by the incessant barking of dogs. And then the packs of Defenders in red berets came trotting, got into formation, saluted him. He recognized the special Fifth Brigade Defender unit and instantly relaxed. The dogs were all blood—tholukuthi blood on their uniforms, blood on their boots, blood on their faces, blood on their teeth, blood on their weapons. The red-eyed Commander fired a celebratory shot, and his troops broke into an orgy of song and dance: "Mai

va Dhikondo! Mai va Dhikondo! Mai va Dhikondo! Mai va Dhikondo! Mai va Dhikondo! Mai va Dhi—Dhikondo Dhiiiiiiiiiiiiiiiiiiiiiii—" Yes, tholukuthi the Defenders of the Revolution and the Father of the Nation danced and leapt and howled and shrieked in victorious celebration, danced even as torrents of bloody rain began to pour, danced even as a vast red river rose around them, tholukuthi bringing up more bodies, bodies, and bodies.

INFINITE REDNESS

He woke up aboveground, back once more on land, surrounded by that redness still, by the terrible silence of the inside of a bullet. He felt wet, drenched, and upon examining himself found he was soaked in blood. With a horrified cry he leapt to his feet, only to find that all around him were dead, blabbering babies. "What do you want from me? Go back to where you came from," he said, walking briskly and away from the little ones. The red land stretched endlessly around him, vast, bloody, bloody, vast. The Father of the Nation trotted, then he galloped, fear filling his soul. Tholukuthi the little babies rose in the air and floated in pursuit. He broke into a gallop and bolted faster than a train—faster and faster and faster, faster and faster and faster, faster and faster and faster, faster and faster and faster—but then the bloody land only expanded and kept expanding so it felt to the Father of the Nation he was running into the very terrible heart of redness.

PAST, PRESENT, ~~FUTURE,~~ PAST

THOLUKUTHI WANDERER

When she first begins going on her long walks, which is better than sitting at home and knowing her mother is out there, feeling she's the reason her mother is out there, Destiny leaves the house very early in the morning. At that time, the outside is always deserted but for the bent-double femals mauling their yards or the front of their homes with grass brooms because this is how, among other things, the unemployed housewives and home keepers in the townships prove their femalness and earn the attendant respect—tholukuthi by the kemptness of their yards, by the sparklingness of their verandas and the cleanliness of their homes. When they see the goat they pause the dancing brooms and stand to their full height and offer ritual morning greetings. They do not ask her where she's going because it'd be cruel being that this obviously solitary child of Simiso has, since her arrival, offered absolutely nothing more than the quiet fact of a presence so hushed the goat has escaped answering the usual questions asked of returnees. No one in the township can say they know why she left the way she did those many years ago, simply disappearing, and where and

how she's been living so that even the most bona fide gossips of Lozikeyi, tholukuthi artful creatures known for tongues so potent it's nothing to seduce a corpse into revealing secrets meant for the grave, eventually give up, and leave the quiet goat alone. But the neighbors do wonder, standing still, grass brooms idle against dusty legs as they watch her until she disappears, just how long this walking business will go on, wonder too if it could be related to the mother's madness because don't they say that kind of thing sometimes runs in the blood?

THE PAST THAT'S COMING

There are otherwise no notable new developments in the township, so that no matter how long they've been gone, returnees are more or less assured of finding the place looking pretty much as they left it. Only now, Lozikeyi is dressed to kill in colorful posters and flyers for the upcoming election. The bright faces of the presidential candidates—the Savior of the Nation and the Opposition leader, Goodwill Beta—smile and grin and contemplate the township from the walls of the shopping center, the disused bus stop, the clinic, the housing office, from the trunks of large trees, on church and school fences, from the faces of rocks, yes, tholukuthi the slogans and messages of the famous candidates doing all they can to appeal to voters: "Only the Savior Will Save Jidada!" "Only Young Blood and Fresh Ideas Will Take Jidada to Glory!" "Vote Tuvius Delight Shasha for President!" "Vote Goodwill Beta for President!" "Vote Party of Power for the Seat of Power!" "Vote Opposition for Real Change!" "The Voice of the Masses is the Voice of God, Your Vote is your Voice, Vote Tuvius Delight Shasha, a Savior, THE Savior!" "This is the vote of your life, vote wisely, Vote Goodwill Beta!"

Lozikeyi, just like the rest of the country, has been thrumming with hope and expectation for the said #freefairncredible election. There is,

wherever Destiny looks, the sense that a corner has been turned already, that the promised land will shortly be arrived at. Tholukuthi the all-too-familiar election frenzy daily fills the goat with a gnawing unease, reminds her of the past. Tholukuthi the past. In fact, there are often times she thinks this could very well be the past itself, as if Jidada has somehow careened ten years backward into that time that was full of many things, including a promise so alive Destiny, like many, was completely swept up by it, tholukuthi taken.

THE AX FORGETS, THE TREE REMEMBERS

And how that feeling had been like a potent drug too, Destiny, do you remember? The titillating possibility? The stubborn dream of a free Jidada future that waited just around the corner? She remembers, how can she not remember? How even though the process was far from free and fair, how even when it was mired in all kinds of violence, how even with the Old Horse being decreed by God to rule and rule and keep ruling, the defiant Jidadans still rose against the tyranny of the Seat of Power in record-breaking numbers and thronged the polls, tholukuthi driven by a hope that proved larger, better, than intimidation, than repression, than fear. She remembers how, with their votes—and her very first vote—the citizens demanded change, called for a better Jidada, a New Jidada. And how as a result the Opposition leader defeated the Father of the Nation in a spectacular upset.

She remembers, too, the euphoria that followed, also a euphoria that'd evaporated like urine on hot sand when the Old Horse and the Seat of Power, with Tuvy, then vice president, at the fore, had simply refused to honor the vote. Tholukuthi how, instead of seceding, the Seat of Power had unleashed its Defenders to defend the Revolution—which was done not on any battlefield but on the bodies of the children of the nation, on her very body. She remembers, her body remembers. Tholukuthi the sharp

sear of burning tear gas. Tholukuthi the pummeling of Defender batons. Tholukuthi the stomp of Defender boots. Tholukuthi the thwack of Defender whips. She remembers, her body will always remember the dreadful struggle for breath. Tholukuthi torture, the body breaking, and pain filling it like a deluge suffuses a river to overflowing.

She remembers how, at the end of that terrible war, the hoped-for future lay broken, bloodied. She remembers, her body remembers. So that when she passes the old Salukazi Market and walks along the Lozikeyi Primary School fence she can barely see where she is going for her thoughts, now whirring in turmoil, for the familiar heaviness in her heart, now awakened, now hinding, for the pain now draping itself around her like a shroud. This country, she thinks, with bitterness. This country! This country! But then was it even wise for you to return, Destiny? To the very same country that broke you? And at this particular time that is so steeped in everything that reminds you of the past? Or did you come for Simiso?

UNLIVABLE EARTH

No, she did not come specifically for Simiso, though, given the situation, she is still glad to be back. And neither was it a question of being wise. She returned, quite simply, because the country she'd fled to, just like the one she'd fled from, had proved to be no refuge.

Tholukuthi after years of enduring exile, of telling herself that a king's son was a nobody in other lands, telling herself that when a lion was famished enough it ate grass, she pointed her nose to the very land she'd turned her back on, sworn never to set hoof on. Then it must be really humbling, Destiny, to be back like this, knowing you wouldn't otherwise be here if where you've been were livable? It is what it is, she thinks, stunned, and not for the first time, by the fact that she is actually back in

Jidada, by the thought that she fled this land only to be spit back on its earth.

OLD AGE SPEAKING

She cuts across Uhuru Park, which was the meeting spot for Lozikeyi's young lovers back in the day because of the lush lawn and the flamboyant trees and flowers of every color and the photographers with their clunky cameras who charged ten dollars for a photograph. Now, a decade later, gone is the lush lawn and gone are the colorful flowers and gone are the lovers and gone are the photographers. At the end of the park, she follows the tarred road for a brief spell, proceeds past the housing office next to the youth center. Past the disused bus stop. Past Brethren in Christ Church. Past the blue house with the humongous guava tree, where the hostile grandmother sheep who'd lived there, perhaps bitter for her own tooth-lessness, preferred to watch her guavas ripen untouched until they rotted and dropped, so Lozikeyi's young ones made careers of looting the tree before the fruit had had the chance to ripen.

"Hawu, if it isn't Destiny herself?!" And Destiny, caught unawares by the deep voice that comes out of nowhere like the voice of God, starts, looks around before she reasons it must be coming from behind the dense wintergreen hedge to her left. She's been walking for a few hours, and stopping for conversation in the hot sun is the least of her desires.

"Here, child of Simiso Khumalo, over here!" A few steps ahead, an old ram in faded blue overalls and an Arsenal cap comes out of a narrow gate, closes it behind him, and watches her with a beaming smile. She approaches him with slow steps, raking her memory for who he could be. Tholukuthi she finds nothing.

"It's you indeed, daughter, look how you've grown, yeyi! A whole

nanny now! The last time I saw you you were this high!" The old ram, laughing now, gestures with a hoof. She regards him blankly.

"Are you telling me you've forgotten me?" he says, scrunching his face in mock displeasure. Before she can agree, the old ram rattles the gate and hollers, "NaMaMo! We NaMaMo! Come out and see who is here, yebana!"

It's only upon hearing the ram say "yebana" that Destiny remembers him—he is SaMaMo, yet another old friend of her mother's. Many years ago, the phrase had in fact been his nickname for how often he used it. As if she'd in fact been standing by the door and waiting for this summons, NaMaMo—the wife—promptly emerges. She's a trim, compact sheep who prances with the disorderly walk of a crab, crinkling her nose as if the air itself smells. She is appropriately dressed for morning chores in old clothes and an apron, and faded brown Bata tennis shoes. She parks herself near the gate without attempting to step out of her yard.

"Who is it, Father?" she says, squinting, and Destiny realizes that the crinkling of the nose probably has something to do with poor eyesight.

"Yebana, NaMaMo! You don't tell me that you really don't see who it is?" SaMaMo says.

"Hmmm, no, it doesn't appear like I do," NaMaMo says, squint-frowning.

"Just look again, Mother, surely you don't see her?"

"See with what old eyes, Father? When I tell you we should visit a doctor because of the cutter—the capa—child, what do they call those cloudy things in your eyes?"

"Cataracts?" Destiny offers.

"Yes, that's it, catharahksi, thank you. When I tell you, Father, that we should go see a doctor because of these catharahksi, I mean I'm really going blind." There's an unmistakable hint of complaint in NaMaMo's voice.

"Well, this here is MaKhumalo's child," SaMaMo says.

"MaKhumalo?" NaMaMo searches her mind, lowering her head and tilting it at Destiny.

"Yes, MaKhumalo herself."

"But which MaKhumalo?"

"Simiso."

"Simiso?"

"Yebana, Mother, surely the next thing you'll be telling us you don't hear!"

"Ihm, Simiso—Simiso—Simiso?" NaMaMo broods. Now she looks upward, as if searching for Simiso's face in the blue sky, among the bold white clouds.

"Ah, the mad goat? Of course, yes, yes, yes, now I see her," and, turning to Destiny like she's seeing her for the first time, voice bright with the sparkle of remembering, NaMaMo says: "Ah-ah, yeyi, hello, my child! And how is your poor mother now?"

"I don't know. I mean, she's been gone and I haven't seen her, so I can't quite say." Destiny is not sure what to feel about the sheep calling her mother mad.

"She'll return, my child. One way or the other. As we speak, she knows you're back. The body has its own way of knowing," NaMaMo says.

"But then, what you did, Destiny, was not a good thing. Just disappearing like that nje! And out of nowhere! No wonder Simiso went mad, what parent wouldn't?!" SaMaMo says.

"Hawu, SaMaMo! The child doesn't need to hear such talk, what are you making her feel bad for?" NaMaMo says.

"It's exactly the kind of talk she needs to hear, because how else will she otherwise learn? The truth is that she didn't do the right thing back then, and now she and her mother both are in this predicament because—"

"Ye SaMaMo!"

"No, NaMaMo, let me finish. Now, what was I saying?"

"You were saying the word 'because'—"

"Yes, because of it. And no, I'm not lying, it's the whole entire truth. And I tell you, Destiny, if only you knew where Simiso's been, what you put her through, on top of what she went through raising you, you'd have thought twice. If only these children had any idea!" SaMaMo vents.

Destiny is too stunned by the unexpected diatribe, she can barely hear NaMaMo apologize for her husband and advise her to leave. "He won't stop otherwise, but please don't mind him, it's old age speaking, my child, he's not always himself anymore," NaMaMo says, waving at Destiny, who's already walking away, wounded and doing her best not to let herself cry. At the end of the street she takes a left and heads toward the old Ngubentsha road—the quickest way back to her mother's house. She is too much in pain, too heavy from the weight of Simiso's absence to continue her walk.

COPING MECHANISMS

Later, she throws herself on her mother's house, tholukuthi scours it from top to bottom because cleaning has always been her way of dealing with pain. The box of a house is shrunken now by the years, the once-vibrant paint has faded from the walls, a broken window has been replaced with thick, clear plastic, the kitchen unit is missing a drawer, the kitchen table dances on its feet, the furniture is generally in various stages of wear. But it's a comfort to Destiny that it's still the same house, still the same furniture of her childhood, for it gives the place a tethering familiarity. She's grateful, thus, for the old mahogany six-seater dining table, the glass display stacked with precious china, the low coffee table and side tables, the wardrobe in her room, the double bed with the metal-and-wood-panel headboard, one of the legs now replaced by a stack of bricks, her high school trunk.

She's grateful, too, for the entire gallery wall in the living room that Simiso has covered with faded photographs of her at every stage of her life, the goat thinks, scrutinizing the old photographs with a lump in her throat. This is you, Destiny, as an infant, fast asleep in a pram under the shade of a peach tree. And here you are on your tummy, learning to crawl, smiling with all of two bottom teeth. That's you running after a postman's bicycle. Here you are in your purple crèche uniform, standing on the tire of a white-and-red Dairibord ice cream cart. That's you in your grade one uniform. That's you again playing house, serving horderves in Coca-Cola bottle tops—pieces of guava and peach and mhagawuwe and mpumpul-wane, along with tomatoes and spinach stolen from your neighbor Na-Bongi's garden, while your play husband Ncane and co-wife Destelia sit on the bonnets of his brick cars. And look, that's you a few years later, holding up a package at a prize-giving ceremony—throughout primary you always came first in English and Ndebele class. That's you lying on the floor of MaDawu's living room, watching *Tarzan* on the first TV set in the whole block. This is you and your best friend, Thandekile Moyo— you weren't related but you looked like a pair of buttocks together; it was hard to tell you apart. And here you are a few years later with Thandekile, Tichaeva Mazarire, Shelly Kunene, Nonceba Makeleni, and Sandra Gwa-tidzo on a grade seven trip to Matopo, looking down on Cecil John Rhodes's grave. This is you in a group photo with Princess Diana, on that day she visited your school. Here you are on civvies day, sporting a box cut and smiling a lipstick-stained smile in your favorite viscose shirt and palazzo pants. That's you in the first year of your period—that was the year your friends called you Black Widow because you were always dressed in black because you were convinced that even with the preparations you took it'd still show and embarrass you. And look, this is you dressed up for the high school leavers' party, where Ncane first kissed you. Here you are, a few years later, graduating from university. Here you are at your first political

rally, where you heard the late founding leader of the Opposition Party speak, even though your mother had forbidden you, for reasons you didn't know, to have anything to do with politics.

MABRRRRRR, THOLUKUTHI MEMEZA MAMA

She's cleaning her bedroom when she finds the CD tucked in a birthday card among her books, an ugly, handmade thing decorated with red and white hearts at the front. She laughs, remembering the day she made the card for Simiso's birthday after she'd eaten the money meant to buy it from the store. The CD is unmarked, and she wonders if it has something dubbed on it. She takes it to the living room, grateful for the ancient CD player that still sits proudly on the trolley beneath the window like a prized relic because Simiso is of the generation that will simply not part with things no matter how many deaths they die. She turns the system on, pops open the slot, forcefully blows into it lest there be dust particles trapped inside. She slides the CD in, nudges the thing closed, and hits Play.

She is not prepared for the voice that jets from the relic with the force of a waterfall. It staggers her backward until she lands flat on the sofa, felled by the awesome force of the water, and she sits there, tholukuthi drowning in Brenda Fassie's voice, drowning in the song "Memeza," that is also a lamentation of an absent mother, drowning in the past, drowning in the present that is full of her mother's absence, drowning in the future she knows will very much be a bloodied river of broken hopes, just like the ugly past. Tholukuthi the past. But she doesn't sink, no. Because Brenda Fassie's voice raises her to safety and places her on solid ground, rings and rings and doesn't stop ringing until the goat realizes the voice is not coming from the relic anymore, but from somewhere else, and that somewhere else is actually her own throat.

You're still singing, Destiny, when you open the main door and walk

out—tholukuthi floating, really, because it doesn't seem from your body, from your movements, that you're actually walking, and doing so of your own accord. And your voice—Destiny, tholukuthi anguish so devastating the Duchess and Comrade Nevermiss and Mother of God and NaDumi and Mrs. Phiri and MaNkala and NaLove and NaGugu and Mai Tanaka and Sarudzai and Soneni and those of your mother's neighbors hear it in their intestines and walk out of their houses trancelike, yes, tholukuthi leave whatever it is they were doing whether they want to or not—your voice doesn't give them time or choice or permission.

And they follow that voice all the way to the little walled house at the corner, where they file through the gate and gather in the open yard with tears in their eyes and clutch at their hearts and watch you sing, Destiny, yes, tholukuthi standing there with tears in their eyes and clutching at their hearts and watching you sing, Destiny, standing there with tears in their eyes and clutching at their hearts and watching you sing and sing and sing and sing and sing—tholukuthi singing singing singing singing singing singing singing, until at last, when it looks like the sky will crack from the sound of your voice, you suddenly cease. No one is prepared for the epic torrent that follows the singing—it's as if a massive dam has broken somewhere inside you, Destiny. Tholukuthi the tears gush. They pour. They flood. Still, let them come, yes, tholukuthi cry Destiny you, returned daughter of Simiso you, wronged, broken child of Jidada you, cry, just cry. Tholukuthi cry.

FAITH, AND A MIRACLE IN LOZIKEYI

It's Mother of God who begins the prayer. The sheep braces her body on twiggy hind legs and faces the sky. And she raises her right hoof high up in the air like she's taking its temperature and says, "Dear Father Ebenezer, one and only God of Glory," tholukuthi her voice a ringing echo that

could be coming from deep within the gut of the earth. And Mother of God's praying companions, the Prayer Warriors of Lozikeyi—femals of faith who've lived with each other so long and traveled every kind of road, every kind of beaten path in every kind of weather together so they're in sync in walking and sleeping moments alike—lift their limbs above their heads and join their sister in supplication. And their braided voices ring and ring and soar all the way to heaven. And they are not shy voices, no. They are not humble voices, no. They are not pleading, as is generally characteristic of voices addressed to God, no. Tholukuthi the way the Prayer Warriors of Lozikeyi sound they could very well be God's haughty sister-wives. Which is perhaps why he hears, yes, tholukuthi God hears and God listens and God attends. Accustomed as he is to being audience to all sorts of miserable prayers, yes, tholukuthi to hearing an invocation every second, every minute, every hour, every day, every week, every month and every year and every decade and every century for thousands and thousands of years, he understands somehow that this isn't a prayer-prayer but a prayer-decree. And that it can't be ignored. And that it can't wait for review.

Those who were there would later tell those who weren't there that first the air got really heavy with the overwhelming scent of frangipani. And that they were frantically looking about and all around them, wondering, asking themselves and each other if what they were smelling was indeed what they were smelling—which it was, and which in itself was mysterious being that there was not a single plumeria tree in the yard or anywhere nearby—when Destiny's mother appeared in the midst of the seismic prayer session like she'd walked out of the smell of frangipani, yes, tholukuthi appearing like an apparition, like a miracle, like a direct reply from God, as if Jesus's father had indeed gotten the prayer-decree, hit a Reply tab, attached Simiso, and pressed Send.

They would say too that the way they remembered it the wrought-iron

gate was closed, but that Simiso had simply walked through without needing to open it, yes, tholukuthi effortlessly passing through like her body was made of air. They would say too that gone was her red dress, filthy from living on the road, on the streets, in the nooks and crannies of Jidada and wherever else her long search for her missing daughter had taken her. They would say too that the goat in fact glowed like Moses on top of Mount Sinai, yes, tholukuthi glowed so much it was necessary to squint in order to see her properly.

They would say too that every voice hushed, except for the Prayer Warriors of Lozikeyi, but only because their eyes were either glued to the face of God above or were shut tight in concentration, yes, tholukuthi breaking that concentration only when they felt the air finally give and shift, felt the unmistakable presence of God in the gentlest vibrations. Which was when they looked around them, eyes focused like they'd been blind all their lives and were only then seeing for the very first time. And indeed Mother of God and her fellow Prayer Warriors saw their prayers had been answered, for there, in front of them, stood Simiso, yes, Mother of Destiny herself in the flesh, tholukuthi a living miracle they could touch.

LOZIKEYI VOTES

DAY OF RECKONING

And so at last, as inevitable as dawn after night, Jidada's long-awaited election arrives to find many of us having failed to sleep a wink and passing the time on social media, checking on each other, strengthening one another. On WhatsApp we see pictures of voters who began queueing at first light in the rural areas because they had to walk long distances to the polls, and we thank them for the sacrifice. On Twitter, Facebook, and Instagram we hear from Jidadans in the diaspora who are angry, who are heartbroken at not being allowed to vote even as their remittances have kept Jidada afloat all these years; we tell them not to despair, that we are voting for change on their behalf. Tuvy and the Seat of Power may have indeed removed the Old Horse but today is their own turn to be removed—when we say we want total change, what we mean is we want the whole entire good-for-nothing Party of Power out.

Our choice and Jidada's choice, President Goodwill Beta, reminds us in a tweet that #Godisinitwewillwinit. We feel good; with God in it we will indeed prevail; by this time tomorrow, Tuvy will have been flushed down

history's toilet, and President Goodwill Beta will be president of this Jidada with a -da and another -da as it should be, the real Savior President, the Democratically Elected One, the God-Anointed One. Friends from countries near and far wish us luck, wish us the change we deserve and have waited long decades for, some of us all our lives. Election observers tweet us wishes of a #freefairncredibleelection. Many onlookers wish us a #freefairncredibleelection. Our African siblings in countries near and far wish us a #freefairncredibleelection. Norway's ambassador to Jidada, alongside the ambassadors from Finland, from Canada, from Iceland, Switzerland, Australia, Ireland, Denmark, New Zealand all wish us a #free fairncredibleelection and we feel good knowing the eyes of the world's top democracies are on our Jidada. Today, with the whole entire world watching, we'll demolish Jidada's despotism, usher in a new era once and for all.

Later, when we finally step out, we're delighted to see that every single flower, including those that haven't flowered in years, seem to have bloomed overnight so that Lozikeyi is all kinds of color and fragrance— even the earth itself is out here dressed for the election. Up above, the Lozikeyi sky is the kind of azure you just want to reach for and lick. We're busy admiring the sky, talking about how fitting it is for such a day as this when we see a dark cloud of birds sweep overhead, flying north, and we don't need to be told its Tuvy's parrot, New Dispensation, and his demented chorale. Today though, because even the sticks and stones know what time it is, the birds are as silent as snails. And after today, they'll just have to sing new songs; we're bringing Tuvy his dawn. Knowing this fills us with such joy we laugh louder than the day the Old Horse fell.

The polls don't open for at least another hour, but already the township streets are choked with bodies hinding for various voting centers. Those who don't want anything to do with the election altogether stand in front of their gates and watch us go fulfill our civic duty. If truth be told, these animals right here are a perfect example of part of what's wrong with Jidada;

it's not just the wretched Seat of Power alone because how, under Jidada's skies, knowing what's at stake, are you going to sit out such a crucial event? And how on earth will change ever come when you're not heading to the polls with the rest of us to vote that change in? And how in the first place do you want to live in a better country when you yourself aren't trying to be that betterness, when you're willingly surrendering your right to shape that country?

THE SISTERS OF THE DISAPPEARED

We are so full of hope, so bloated with excitement we cannot quite walk. And so, no, we do not walk, we do what, we levitate all the way to our voting centers. At Lozikeyi High School, our designated station, we find the Sisters of the Disappeared busy staging some kind of protest. Their number has more than trebled in size, and they actually now have some mals in the movement. We see Sis Nomzamo and Shami and Nothando and Dodo and NaMzi and Marcus and MaThebe and Chenzira and Qhawe among the protesters. Even old animals like Gogo Manyathi and Nkiwane and Banda are busy hinding up and down the length of the gate in their signature red T-shirts, raised above their heads the usual placards bearing photos and names of Jidada's Disappeared. We hear their angry chants of "No Reforms, No Free, Fair, Credible Election! No Reforms, No Free, Fair, Credible Election! No Reforms, No Free, Fair, Credible Election!" They look at us like we're not here to vote for change, like we're here to betray Jesus Christ and so we stab them with our eyes because even the sticks and stones know their little protest is a sham.

For the most part we appreciate what the Sisters of the Disappeared are generally trying to do, what they stand for and everything, but then them coming out here on the day of a harmonized election like this is simply uncalled for and out of line, even the Bible tells us there indeed is a season

for everything, a time to be born and a time to die, a time to plant and a time to leave the earth alone. Today is the time to leave the earth alone. Still, we refuse to give the Sisters of the Disappeared the power to provoke us into a confrontation even though they clearly don't know what time it is; we're here for one reason and one reason alone—to vote for a New Jidada in a #freefairncredible election and that's exactly what we'll do. But now we've seen with our own eyes that perhaps what they say about this group is true after all. Perhaps they do need husbands and little ones and homes to keep them from being a nuisance on the streets, after all. As for those with husbands, perhaps those husbands need to do a better job of instilling God's law to keep their femals under control as Prophet Dr. O. G. Moses always says, after all. And perhaps they do need one or two Defenders out here right now to put them in line, to show them their place, after all.

LOZIKEYI HIGH SCHOOL POLLING STATION

Inside Lozikeyi High we're intercepted by smiling election officials so polite, so gracious we could be here to pay an exorbitant bride price for a femal condemned to the last-act clearance rack. Tholukuthi they handle us like something precious; we feel like some Fabergé eggs, like the testicles of great kings. We stand in the queues with pride. We greet other voters, we smile at each other, we bump heads, we sniff each other. We're happy to see animals who weren't queueing with us in the previous election and the one before it. We're pleased to see animals who've laughed at us, taken us for fools when we trudged to polling stations in previous elections. We're excited to see animals who've just turned eighteen line up to cast their vote—this is how we get the change we want, this is how we show that Tuvy and his wretched Seat who really has power in Jidada.

The lines move. We move. And the lines move. And we move. We see

Glory, who sells fruit from a wheelbarrow outside SPAR Supermarket, wheel his mother, who has difficulty walking, to the front of the line. We press against the wall to give them way, and Mother of Glory, who obviously hasn't heard the rules about quiet, is talking at the top of her voice about how she's seen elections come and go in Jidada with a -da and another -da, and she hasn't seen this kind of peaceful election. She tells us at the top of her voice still that she's here to vote tyranny out, and that after she casts the ballot she can go on and die because her job will be done. We forget the rules about quiet and applaud her like she's the one who's the incoming president, like she's already won. We keep applauding until she and her son disappear inside classroom 5B.

When they come out some ten-fifteen minutes later, Mother of Glory is the one pushing the wheelbarrow and Glory is sitting inside. She grins and bobs her head and swishes her tail and laughs all at once, on her forehead a large sticker that says "I Voted." We cheer her all over again. And overwhelmed, unable to hold it together, Mother of Glory starts to oink-cry. We see Glory pick her up and load her on the wheelbarrow like she's the watermelons he sells outside SPAR for five dollars each and wheel her off, smiling apologetically. We watch other exhilarated voters come out levitating after casting their ballots. Among them we see that terrorist devil Defender, Commander Jambanja, apparently returned from gold panning in the Midlands, where those who know about things say machete-wielding criminal gangs and illegal miners are busy butchering each other over gold. Today, for once, the terrorist is not wearing the ugly uniform he wears every day and all the time no matter the circumstance, no matter the weather.

When we see Commander Jambanja the queue goes dead silent—the silence of anger, the silence of previously wounded beasts who, upon laying eyes on their predator, feel their scars awaken and throb. We seethe; if only it were the case that anger was combustible we'd absolutely raze this

whole polling station with our rage, that's just how much we loathe this brute who's terrorized us for years and years on behalf of the Seat of Power. We're standing there simmering inside, fermenting inside, bleeding inside, when Dingi makes a clean leap from his place in line and knocks the terrorist's hat off his square head.

"Yeah. We're 'bout to vote your dictator boss out you sonofahyena so why don't you take that and shove it up your stinking behind?!" Dingi snarls at the Defender before any of us can react, whiskers trembling with fury.

For a brief moment tiny Dingi looks great in his wrath he could be a whole proper lion that can trample and devour. We hind, stand against the wall and watch the killer, wondering what he'll do—this must be the first time in history anyone is speaking to him like this and living to finish a sentence, and we are, quite frankly, terrified. We hear the son of Satan breathe deep and steady, breathe deep and steady, breathe deep and steady, his own smoldering eyes never leaving Dingi, his ears erect, tail like a rod. The monster's face is otherwise an empty plate—nothing on it to say what he'll do but we still imagine blood flying in the air. Then, to our utter, utter relief, he picks his hat with his teeth, tucks it under his armpit, and struts off like he's just remembered he has somewhere important to be.

"That's right. Walk off and keep walking, fatherfucker, ngoba this time tomorrow you'll be out of a job too because we're taking Jidada back!" Dingi gloats. The monster slows down. We don't breathe, imagining him turning around and making Dingi disappear. Then Phumlani walks up to Dingi and tells him to calm down, does he want to get killed. Only this sets the little cat off.

"Calm down for what, wena Phumlani, when this savage right here, and his ilk, have been terrorizing us all our miserable lives?! Don't look at me like that, y'all know it's true! Tell me it wasn't this filthy fiend and his pack who beat us to near death in the 2008 elections, who disappeared

Bornfree back in the 2013 elections! Tell us how you killed him, you murderer, tell us what you did with his body, you monster! Tell us what you did with my cousin so we can at least bury him, so his old mother can at least die in peace!" Dingi shrieks at the retreating Defender. We hold our breath as we watch the dog strut past the last block of classrooms, past the hibiscus hedge, cut across the assembly area with the faded flag of Jidada hanging limp in the air, then out the gate and past the Sisters of the Disappeared until he is out of sight.

The silence persists long after the Defender is gone, and long after Dingi has calmed down. We hate the Defender for daring to show his face and spoiling our joy, and we hate Dingi for reminding us of what we'd rather leave in the past. The levees inside us threaten to give and break but we hold ourselves. We hold. So we can at least go through what we've waited all night, what we've waited all these terrible years, to go through. It's not a moment we can explain, because it's just so hard to describe. We get to the front of the line. The polling agent says, Next please. We hind, we breathe, we enter. The agent says, ID please, we give ID. He verifies our particulars, bobs his head. He points us to our booths, gives us instructions. We enter. We confront the booths. The levees inside us threaten to give again but we hold ourselves again. We hold and vote for change at last. We vote without fear at last, for the New Jidada we want at last.

THE CROCODILE WHO WANTED TO PLAY CAPTURE THE FLAG

Back in Lozikeyi we're met by the squad of neighborhood youngsters running like the wind and filling the streets with such shrill shrieks of terror. We hold their shaking bodies to calm them down, listen to them tell how they were playing in the little patch of bush behind the housing office when they were accosted by a crocodile. When we hear this we howl with laughter. This crocodile you saw, are you sure it was really a crocodile?

we say. He was really a crocodile, they say. And what was the crocodile doing? we say. The crocodile was singing and laughing and dancing and playing with his scarf, they say. Is that so? And what exactly did the crocodile's scarf look like? we say. The crocodile's scarf looked exactly like the Savior of the Nation's scarf, they say. Hmm, but there aren't really crocodiles in Lozikeyi, how did you actually know it was a crocodile? we say. Because we've seen a crocodile on Google, they say. Hmm, and how big was the crocodile? we say. The crocodile was as big as Goliath the Giant, they say. And did he say anything to you, this crocodile? we say, trying not to die with laughter. The crocodile said, Let's play Capture the Flag, they say. And what did you say? we say. We said, We don't know Let's Capture the Flag, they say. And what did he say? we say. The crocodile said, Let's play Country-game, me I'll be Jidada with a -da and another -da, they say. Really? And what did you say? we say. We said no, you're a crocodile and you'll eat us, and just ran and ran and ran—are y'all going to find and kill him? the shaken youngsters ask, faces full of fear. We burst out laughing. We tell them they've been watching too many You-Tube videos. That there are no crocodiles in Lozikeyi, and if in fact it happened he was real and he actually showed his face, the whole township would hunt him down and tear him to bits and pieces of bits. We make faces, the youngsters forget the crocodile, laugh and laugh and fill Lozikeyi with their golden joy.

WAYS OF AWAITING ELECTION RESULTS

That day we learn the hard part of a #freefairncredible election is the waiting for the results afterward. Time moves like a lethargic snail. We check WhatsApp for election updates, we check Twitter, we check Facebook. We're so tense, tholukuthi so restless we don't know what to do with ourselves. We clean our homes, which are already clean, but it's something

to keep us busy. We wash our clothes, dry them, iron them. We create vision boards for the things we want to do, for the beings we want to be in the New Jidada that's waiting just around the corner, we write Post-it notes to our future selves. We check WhatsApp, we check Twitter, we check Facebook. We send messages to friends and relatives, and when we run out of who to send messages to, we send messages to random strangers. We check WhatsApp, we check Twitter, we check Facebook. Check check check check check. Tholukuthi check. We count the trees, then we count the leaves in the trees we've already counted, after which we count the grass. We check WhatsApp, we check Twitter, we check Facebook. We check WhatsApp, we check Twitter, we check Facebook. Nighttime finds us near undone with anxiety; it's Golden Maseko who rescues us by posting on the neighborhood WhatsApp group to come to his house for an election night party.

We congregate at the artist's yard and cradle bottles of Castle Lite and Zambezi and Lion and talk about the approaching Jidada we voted for. We wonder how we'll welcome it, how it'll look at us, how we'll see it. We think about what Tuvy is doing at that exact moment, if he can smell the inevitable dawn that's coming for him. We picture his big teeth chewing his scarf from worry, ask each other what the so-called Savior will do with the supposedly magical scarf after the dawn, and we kill ourselves with laughter, imagining his dejection. We check WhatsApp, we check Twitter, we check Facebook. We wonder how our incoming chosen president— President Goodwill Beta—is at that moment readying for being the true president of the masses, if he knows what to do with himself on the eve of Jidada's coming glory. Tholukuthi somewhere in the street, we hear a bull bellow his frustration; cats meow back, sheep bleat, ducks quack, donkeys bray, goats bleat, horses neigh, pigs grunt, chickens cluck, peacocks scream, cows moo, and geese cackle; for a brief, mad moment, Lozikeyi rings with the agony of waiting for the results.

THOLUKUTHI AMERICAN PRAYER

It's just after midnight when Sotsha-Sotsha lets out a most anguished roar, tholukuthi bringing us on our hinds and yanking us from musings of glory. We watch the ram watch his phone, body shaking, face made terrible, made foreign, made wild, by a palpable horror. "What's the problem, Sotsha, is Tuvy winning or what?" an anxious voice yells. It goes quiet-quiet-quiet in Golden Maseko's yard, all eyes on Sotsha; we want to find out what it is, but we don't want to find out. When he at last responds, it is to drag himself out of the yard like every ounce of energy has been drained out of him, his big eyes empty, tail between his legs. We part to give him way, watch him disappear into the night without uttering a single word.

When we gather the courage to look at our phones, we find the video trending on WhatsApp, Twitter, Facebook—everywhere. We're ill at ease but we press Play. We see a white Defender in blue uniform. We see the Defender's gun. We see the Defender's gun aimed at the back of a fleeing, unarmed, Black brother. We don't need to be told anymore that what we're looking at is America, and we're not even surprised. Before we can confirm with each other if what we're seeing is indeed what we're seeing, we hear a succession of gunshots from the Defender's gun; we count one-two-three-four-five-six-seven-eight shots fired by the Defender at the back of the fleeing, unarmed Black brother. We see the Black brother slow down before he collapses. We see the Black brother lie still. We don't need to be told the Black brother is dead. We see the Defender shout at the Black body he has just murdered to put his limbs behind his back, and we're not even surprised. We see the murdered Black body lie there, unresponsive. We see the Defender tie the murdered Black body up, like a dangerous thing in need of restraint, and we're not even surprised. We see a couple of other Defenders come running to the scene, and we see that

none of them attend to the murdered Black body right away and we're not even surprised. We see them talking, the murdered Black body at their feet like a reaped harvest, like a big black bundle of nothing.

Long after we've seen the video, long after the black of night has faded, and the Lozikeyi skies have begun to lighten, we remain standing in Golden Maseko's yard, standing in silence and unable to move from the heaviness inside us, wondering what to say this time, not knowing what to say this time, until we see Golden Maseko bow his head and slowly raise his limbs to the heavens. We fold. We bow our heads. When language finally finds us, it is the words of the murdered that pour out of our throats and fill the Lozikeyi night, yes, tholukuthi those last three words we've heard said over and over by Black American brothers begging killers for their lives in the simplest, most desperate of prayers—I can't breathe I

can't breathe I can't—

THE RED BUTTERFLIES

Morning finds us on our feet. Day of the announcement of the election results. Day of reckoning. Day of Change. Day of democracy. We look at the time. We pace. We refresh our Twitter and we refresh our Twitter. We see the Black brother's name trending and trending and trending. We pace and pace and pace. Day of President Goodwill Beta. Day of finally finishing what we started when we removed the Old Horse. Day of a New Jidada at last. We refresh our Twitter. We see the Black brother's name trending and trending and trending. We pace and pace and pace and pace and pace. Time saunters, drags, crawls, but it's a way to move, after all, running isn't always arriving. We refresh our Twitter and we refresh our Twitter. We see the Black brother's name trending and trending and trending.

The butterflies arrive with the sun. We gasp we gape we gawk, wonder if what we're seeing is really what we're seeing. Everywhere red butterflies, everywhere crimson wings; we could be watching blood dance in the air. We pour onto the street, where we see every single one of the flowers that were in bloom yesterday, that we admired yesterday, that filled Lozikeyi with beauty and fragrance yesterday—have dried and fallen to the ground, everywhere a sad carpet of dead flowers. Our intestines lurch, leap to our chests. We're standing there wondering if what we're seeing is indeed what we're seeing, when the butterflies begin to fly away. We follow them. They fly away and we follow. Later, we'll talk

about the strangeness of it, how it felt like we were not following of our own accord, like we'd have followed whether we'd wanted to or not.

Where do we find ourselves, where do the butterflies take us? They take us to house number 635, which of course is the home of the Duchess, which is in fact fitting because nowhere else do we go, can we go, for the interpretation of such strange phenomena. At the Duchess's we see the butterflies descend unto Eden—which is what the youngsters call the Duchess's garden for its stunning profusion of vegetation, most of which we've never really seen anywhere else. Even the Duchess's house is covered in some kind of weird creeper plant. We have no idea how anyone can actually keep such a production in a township, what with the small spaces and the water shortages, but then here's Eden, thriving right in the heart of Lozikeyi—a queer garden that is ever green and colorful no matter the season. We see the butterflies float to the Nehanda tree and start to land land land land land land land land land land land land land land land land land land land land land, and for a moment Eden is some kind of strange airport, red wings fluttering all over.

We're surprised, but we're not surprised that of all trees inside Eden, the butterflies choose the Nehanda tree; even the sticks and stones know it is a special tree—the Duchess has told us she planted it from the seeds of the very tree on which Mbuya Nehanda was hung by the British during the struggle for independence, long, long, long before we were born. The tree bears these curious pods—Nehanda's bones, the young ones call them for their strange shapes, for their color of bleached bone, but for now it's impossible to see any part of the tree because of the butterflies. Those among us who are fundamentalist Christians, the ones who believe church leaders like Prophet Dr. O. G. Moses rebuke and condemn the Duchess as a pagan heathen and even a witch who practices devil worship and paganism, promptly leave, not wanting to offend their God and leaders.

Those of us who aren't Christians, or who have one foot in Christianity

and the other in our indigenous religions because we know what we know, remain behind. We don't take the Duchess—whose real name, Nomadlozi, means "with the ancestors"—lightly, we know the cat is a sangoma, a spirit medium, endowed with the gift of divination, healing, and communication with the ancestors. We've seen the medium treat known and unnameable ailments. We've seen her predict the weather. We've seen her use herbs to help wombs conceive. We've seen her pass messages from the departed to the living. We've seen her interpret our most baffling dreams and decipher unnatural phenomena. We've seen her speak to wild beasts and birds and dung beetles and every living organism. We've seen her identify strange plants brought to her by scientists and tell them what they're for. We've seen her summon up whirlwinds and lightning in her rare bouts of true anger. We've seen come out of her Nkunzemnyama, her raging bull ancestor whose spirit has resided inside the Duchess since she accepted her calling, before many of us were born.

THE MEDIUM AND THE BLACK BULL

We see the Duchess emerge from her house, clad from head to foot in ancestral dress. She carries a traditional stick and whisk. Her face is painted white. She looks at everything with the intense eyes of an owl. Right behind the medium are two of her assistants, straddling drums and lashing at them with fat sticks. Then come the next two, carrying a basket between them, followed by the Duchess's grandnieces Zwile and her little sister Gloria. The last to come out is Gogo Moyo, carrying a burning blue candle. We see the procession stop beneath the Nehanda tree, now dressed from head to toe in the red butterflies. We move closer. One of the drummers motions for us to enter Eden. We enter Eden and form a circle.

We watch the Duchess dance, body moving with the litheness of an animal a whole century younger. She sways and shimmies and stomps and

leaps and crouches and flies. Ropes of colorful beads crisscross over her chest; they jump and shake with each of her movements. She dances until her headdress of lion skin, decorated with a horn and cowrie shells, falls off. We see the Duchess pause in front of the candle, tilt her head up and roar, filling the sky with a call to her ancestors. This is where we stomp and clap in order to help her channel the spirits. The drummers go berserk on the drums, fill Eden with a sound we know is heard in all of Lozikeyi. Gogo Moyo starts a traditional song we know and we take it up.

When the drums are near boiling, we see the Duchess fall on the ground and begin to shake shake shake shake shake shake shake shake shake. Shake. She's entering a trance, and any minute now, Nkunzemnyama, her ancestor, will arrive. The Duchess bellows, thrashes, writhes. She groans as if in the midst of birth throes, breathes like she is pulling her breath all the way from heaven. Her face is in turmoil, dungeons form on the forehead, teeth are gritted, eyes constricted.

Nkunzemnyama arrives thundering with such prodigious fury the ground trembles. No matter how many times we've seen him arrive, each appearance makes our intestines lift. We see the bull fly, charge at the Nehanda tree, circle it in a mad frenzy before galloping back to the gathering. We give way. Gogo Moyo, who is also the Duchess's ancestral wife, and therefore also Nkunzemnyama's wife, kneels in front of him and begins singing his welcome song. We sing along. An assistant appears with a calabash of traditional beer, which Nkunzemnyama picks up and disappears in one greedy inhale. Gogo Moyo takes the calabash and ululates. The drums cease.

We've heard Nkunzemnyama speak many times before, but we don't remember this voice that sounds like it has wounds in it. Voice of pure heartbreak. We hear him tell us he and the butterflies have traveled far, from the land of the dead. We know Nkunzemnyama himself is from that land, but since we've never seen or heard of the butterflies till now, we lift

our eyes to the Nehanda tree and keep them glued. We hear Nkunzemnyama tell us the butterflies were once animal beings like us, who once
walked Jidada like us until they were massacred just a couple of years after
Jidada's independence. When we hear this our intestines lurch, leap to our
chests. Many of us know this story, or know of it, but it's too heavy for our
mouths, we've swallowed it so it stays buried inside us, where we keep the
things we don't have language for, we don't know how to face.

We see Simiso collapse onto her daughter like a sack of maize. Golden
Maseko and Mthokozisi help Destiny carry her mother to the edge of Eden
for some air; some stories will mow an animal down. We hear Nkunzemnyama tell us the dead would like to know where justice is, these decades
and decades later. We lower our eyes, we drop our heads. We hear Nkunzemnyama tell us the dead would like to know what has become of their
murderers these decades and decades later. We swallow hard. We hear
Nkunzemnyama tell us the dead would like to know when they will be
appropriately buried. We swallow hard. We hear Nkunzemnyama tell us
the dead would like to know when we shall hold proper ceremonies for
their appeasement. We swallow hard, and we swallow hard. We hear Nkunzemnyama tell us the dead would like to know when their survivors will
be compensated for their pain, their losses. We swallow hard, we swallow
hard. We hear Nkunzemnyama command us to raise our heads and answer for ourselves. We make to raise our heads, we falter, the heads drop.
We hear Nkunzemnyama command us to raise our heads and look at the
dead. We raise our heads, we cannot see for hot tears of shame.

We see Nkunzemnyama leap onto his feet with a hoarse bellow and
soar, tail like a spear in the air. He whirls and whirls and whirls. We shuf-
fle backward. He bellows and bellows and bellows, and Lozikeyi rever-
berates with his pained, monotonous rage. We cower. The drummers lash
and maul and thrash the drums, bang them to barking; we see Nkunzemnyama charge, stop short of goring one of them. We cower. Gogo Moyo

recites the ancestor's praise names, and we chant along with her. Hearing his praise names, a whole genealogy that tracks his ancestry to the very beginning of his clan, calms the bull. We see him retreat backward, slow-slow-slow-slow-slow, his rumbling now subdued to low, guttural tones. We see him sit and rock back and forth, back and forth, back and forth, beating the earth with his tail. Then we see him still, a tempest having spent itself. We exhale.

Nkunzemnyama's departure is sudden and swift and without farewell. We cast our eyes at the Nehanda tree to see the butterflies too have vanished. The drummers beat a calm tempo, to help the Duchess find her way back from the land of the spirits. We see the medium twist and writhe, as if freeing herself from a terrible grasp. We see her focus with unsteady eyes, like she's lost, like she's waking up in the wrong country. We see the Duchess rise on unsteady feet, looking thoroughly exhausted, looking like she's just climbed down the tallest mountain. She doesn't acknowledge us, she could be unaware of her surroundings. The drums taper, softly-softly-softly-softly-softly, like the sound of butterfly wings. We see Gogo Moyo cover the Duchess's shoulders with a white cloth and, with the help of an assistant, lead her back to the house. We're standing there, watching them, when the heavens suddenly darken with the largest congress of birds to ever sweep across Lozikeyi's skies, and then, before we can ask ourselves what it could mean, we're engulfed in the terrible din of Tuvy's New Dispensation victory song.

INTO OYENZAYO, SIYAYIZONDA

Back on the streets we're met with the bitter breaking news of what we step out of Eden already knowing. Around us, the rest of Lozikeyi boils with the unbearable announcement of Tuvy's election victory. In every corner, outraged residents hind and beat their chests and gnash their teeth and

stomp the earth and roar at the air. Even little ones bare their gums and howl. Even the cockroaches and flies and spiders and dung beetles and ants and lizards and mosquitoes and creatures that had nothing to do with voting seethe. And when S'bangilizwe begins singing the popular protest song: "Into Oyenzayo, Siyayizonda," we ignite. Our fury sweeps us onto main roads and hurtles us toward the city center, whipping up and amassing more angry throngs along the way so that by the time we get to the city to defend the vote, we are a mad writhing sea roaring, just as the song says, of our hatred of this thing that Tuvy is doing, this thing that the Seat of Power has always done. Into 'yenzayo, Siyayizonda! Into 'yenzayo, Siyayizonda! Into 'yenzayo, Siyayizonda! Into 'yenzayo, Siyayizonda! Into 'yenzayo, Siyayizonda!

DEFENDING THE REVOLUTION, 2018

In the city, we stand under the giant jacaranda that blooms no matter the season. This is exactly where we stood during that historic march after the fall of the Old Horse. On this very spot is where we paused for selfies with the soldiers. This, right here, is where we dreamt of a New Jidada. And while we're standing, the giant jacaranda, with no wind whatsoever, with no one shaking it whatsoever, with no reason we can point to whatsoever, just ups and lets fall every single one of its pretty purple petals. And before we can ask each other if what we're seeing is really what we're seeing, we're covered in the softest flowers. We hold our breath, we exhale, we hind. We are fabulous in our fury, we look resplendent in our rage.

And still standing under the giant jacaranda, now dressed in purple flowers, we cast unblinking eyes at the House of Jidada, where we can clearly see Tuvy's New Dispensation scarf where the huge flag of Jidada used to be. We also see clearly the new freshly painted symbols of a horse, Defender, and gun where the old, faded symbols of a horse, Defender, and

gun used to be. We see clearly the big portrait of Tuvy the horse where the big portrait of the Old Horse used to be. And we understand that the change that we believed was written on the wall, the change we so desperately hoped and wanted to see we in fact pictured it everywhere until it became real, the change skeptical fellow Jidadans were warning us about, that the Sisters of the Disappeared and others have been questioning since the coup, was all but an illusion. And all it takes is for Notagain to catapult a rock and knock Tuvy's ugly portrait to the ground as we did the Old Horse's portrait just last year. We shriek, we roar, we charge.

We do not have the time to ask each other if what we're really seeing is what we're really seeing because all of a sudden we're surrounded by swarms of armed Defenders Defenders Defenders. Time veers, leaps backward. We trip on our own hopes, we teeter, hurtle into a red past we now know has been here all along, lurking like a crocodile. And before we can ask ourselves if what we're seeing is really what we're seeing—war is upon us. As it was upon us in the last election, just like it was upon us in the one before that, as it was upon us in the election prior to that, yes, tholukuthi as it has always been upon us. There is the all-too-familiar thwack-smash of hard weapon on flesh, gunshots, screams. Stampedes, chaos, the stench of the Revolution being defended, screams. Wounded flesh, blood in the streets, blood in the gutters, screams. Bodies—one, two, three, four, five, six, seven—drop dead, screams. Up in the sky, clouds turn the color of bruises. And the air so hot, so thick with tear gas we cannot see, we cannot breathe.

DEFENDING THE REVOLUTION, 1983

DREAMING HOUR

At about seven minutes before eleven p.m. Simiso, who otherwise usually slept the peaceful slumber of a dolphin, tossed and turned so much in her sleep she woke her daughter, who was fast asleep next to her. Upon finding herself exiled between a cold concrete wall and her mother's restless body, Destiny at first gently prodded Simiso in the ribs. When that didn't work she braced a firm hoof against the wall and pushed the older goat, but just softly, in an effort to nudge her back to her side of the bed. When that too failed, Destiny brought her mouth close to her mother's ear and whispered, "Mama. Mama." This too was of no use being that the specific ear was deaf—a fact the younger goat occasionally forgot.

"Mother!" Destiny tried, again. This time her voice came out harsh, which of course she hadn't intended, and which made her feel a kind of shame. Her efforts fruitless, she sighed in resignation and turned on her back to face the darkness.

When Simiso first returned, Destiny would wake up in the dead of

night to find her standing motionless at the foot of her bed. It had puzzled the daughter at first, until she understood this was Simiso's way of keeping watch, of making sure her child didn't disappear yet again. Tholukuthi sharing a bed eased the mother's anxieties and made certain the older goat got some sleep, only she never failed to traverse from her side in the deep throes of slumber, as if her ability to live to see the coming morning absolutely depended on erasing the distance between her and her daughter's sleeping bodies.

Now, Simiso thrust her behind against her daughter's side, shuffled, tossed, and, in a voice Destiny had never heard before, said, "Ah-ah, but where are you taking me, where are we going?" Destiny thought to rouse her again. She fumbled under her pillow and fished out her Samsung Galaxy S6 Edge. She woke the phone and tapped the flashlight. She was pondering Simiso's knotted face, the body bundled in a heap of tension when the dreaming goat began to weep. Tholukuthi Destiny, who otherwise in all her years of being Simiso's daughter had never ever seen her weep, had no memory whatsoever of Simiso's tears, now saw her mother cry torrents in her sleep; she came undone and began weeping too.

THE PEOPLE WILL DIE, THE NAMES WILL REMAIN

"What happened, whatever are you crying for?" Simiso says, awake now.

"You were weeping in your sleep," Destiny says, visibly relieved by Simiso's wakefulness. She rises and turns on the lights.

"And so? You see an animal cry and you must cry too, uraythekhanda nje?"

"But what were you dreaming, Mother? Because it looked really bad."

"Ihm, I had a dream unlike any dream, wena Destiny," Simiso says, shakes her head. Destiny asks, "About what?" with just her eyes.

"Home. I dreamed I was back in my village home. Bulawayo."

"Bulawayo? I didn't know that part, Mother, since when?" Destiny says, frowning.

"Don't be silly, of course Bulawayo is my home. My father, Butholezwe Henry Vulindlela Khumalo, the same one who gave you your name, is from there. I haven't dreamt of him in all these years, until today, Destiny, not once," Simiso says, troubled.

Destiny looks at her mother like she doesn't know her at all; it is the first time she is hearing Simiso is from Bulawayo. And she is certain she hasn't ever heard her grandfather's full name from her mother's lips.

"My whole family—my mother and siblings—were in the dream too. They were turned into red butterflies," Simiso says, speaking in a voice Destiny doesn't recognize. A voice steeped in sadness.

"What siblings? To be honest I'm just so confused right now, Mother," Destiny says, by which she means that she has always understood, from the story she knows, the story she was told, that Simiso was the only child to her late parents.

"Bring me water, I will tell you everything," Simiso looks everywhere but her daughter's eyes.

THE FAMILY STORY THAT SIMISO KHUMALO NEVER TOLD HER DAUGHTER

1. THE KHUMALOS OF BULAWAYO

You must know that in the past, there was another me, who lived another life. Independence had come after a long struggle as you know, and my father—your grandfather—Butholezwe Henry Vulindlela Khumalo, a freedom fighter, had finally returned from the war to rejoin the family in Bulawayo, where he'd been born, and where we lived. His two brothers,

Dingilizwe Edward Khumalo and Sakhile Bathakathi George Khumalo, were also settled in the area, along with numerous members of the extended family and clan. It was a big, tight-knit group bound by blood and love, everyone's homesteads just scattered around the valley on both sides of Tuli. Tuli is a river. The larger area is also called Bulawayo, like our village.

2. A LIBERATOR RETURNS

At first, with the coming of independence and life somewhat getting back to normal, it was odd for my siblings to get used to the stranger who was our father, especially as we'd been forced to grow up without him. The war, we strongly felt, like most kids at that time, had unfairly taken him away from us so that he was a blur for most of our childhood as a result. The youngest—my sister, your aunt Thandiwe, and the brother she came after, your uncle Nkanyiso—had absolutely no memory of him. Only me and my elder brothers—your uncles Nkosiyabo, Zenzele, and Njube— knew Father, being that we'd been old enough when he went off to fight. Whenever we saw him during the war it was on the rare times his missions were closer to Bulawayo. But the visits were always brief and clandestine. Mostly in the night. Or sometimes he'd come and we'd hear about it much, much later. On those times he'd be in disguise; he was always afraid we'd get excited and blabber—he didn't want to take chances, there'd been many cases where the colonial government had bombed or burned the homes of terrorists, which is what the colonists called freedom fighters.

With Father's return, our family very quickly prospered. But that wasn't an accident—he was such a hard worker. He gave all his energy to the land. And that land rewarded him abundantly, I mean it just loved him—filled his granaries with bounty harvests, more than enough to feed the family and buy a car, the first in the village, as well as tractors and other farm equipment to boost productivity. He made us understand at a

young age the importance of land, how and why it'd been one of the things for which he'd given himself to the revolution. In no time, with his farming success, Father began several business ventures: A transport company of a fleet of three buses—two of them serviced the Bulawayo village–Bulawayo city route, and one the Bulawayo village–Gwanda route. And then there was the grinding mill and grocery and bottle stores, all of the businesses located in the Bulawayo business center.

Everyone in the area knew our father. Even in the places beyond us, the name Butholezwe Henry Vulindlela Khumalo meant something. Villagers loved and appreciated him, I think because his efforts benefited them, being that he provided crucial services as well as employment; I remember they actually nicknamed him Governor. And not only that but he was just, generous, fair, wise. Our homestead was always packed with visitors. Neighbors. Villagers come from near and far with their problems. Requests. To ask Father to settle disputes. Give advice. To borrow money. For food, those kinds of things. Whatever, no matter what it was, nobody ever left our home not taken care of in one way or the other.

3. INDEPENDENCE, A HOMECOMING, AND A BIRTH: THOLUKUTHI APPOINTMENT WITH DESTINY

I've mentioned before that it was your grandfather who gave you your name but I didn't tell you the all of it. Naming you was his very first act upon his return. He came back on the very day you were born, literally found me on the delivery mat, surrounded by my mother, her sister NaS'thembeni, her church friends, and all these anxious midwives. I remember I'd been in labor since the wee hours of the previous day. Someone was thinking of taking me to Ekusileni, Ekusileni being the nearest hospital. But even though it was the closest hospital to us, it was still very far and there was no car. They were deliberating, speaking in hushed tones. I'm telling you I was supremely terrified, I thought I'd die from the pain. And

then all of a sudden this rich smell of frangipani just comes out of nowhere and absolutely overwhelms the room. We look at each other in wonderment. All of us in that room. And for a moment I actually forget my pain, trying to think if what I'm smelling is really what I'm smelling, because we don't have the tree anywhere on the homestead.

And then—what do you know, there he was. My father, your grandfather. Just standing there, casting a shadow in the doorway. Like he'd walked out of the scent of the frangipani. Something happened the moment I saw him, as if whatever had been tying me up released me, and whatever had been holding you back similarly freed you. Out you gushed. Father knelt to receive you, like it was the reason he'd walked into that hut in the first place. And there, holding you against his heart, and before even exchanging greetings with anyone, he named you Destiny Lozikeyi Khumalo, the very first thing to come out of his mouth. Lozikeyi for the brilliant, influential Queen of the Ndebele, a great and brave leader, according to Father. Destiny because he saw in the coincidence of your arrival and his return, a special significance—you, his very first grandchild, were his welcome gift from the ancestors, tied to his future, and, being that the country was finally free at last, he felt you were similarly Jidada's gift; you were both his and the nation's destiny, and similarly, your destiny lay in the New Jidada. Destiny Lozikeyi Khumalo. That is the story of your name I never told you.

Your grandfather didn't shame me for having you out of wedlock. And when I decided I didn't want a life with your father—his name was Cabangani, Cabangani Sikhosana; we were young, he and I, only kids who barely knew each other when you happened to us—it had nothing to do with love or knowing what we were getting into. I suppose our generation was restless with the coming of independence. It hadn't properly arrived but talk of it was all over—we followed the news on the radio and learned it was only a matter of time. And while we waited for it, waited for our

lives to transform, I—we, the young—supposed independence also meant we were free to do with our bodies as we pleased.

Even though there were questions about who'd actually lead the country, we were excited by our leaders, the Promise Horse of Northern Jidada—we nicknamed the Old Horse the Promise Horse at that time because of all the progressive rhetoric that came out of his mouth and promised a great future, and of course our very own Bull of Ndebeleland, nicknamed Father Jidada for his outstanding leadership qualities, his fierce, unshakable love for the nation demonstrated in his long years of service and accomplishments. You wouldn't know now, from the stories the Seat of Power chooses to narrate as the real history, that it was Father Jidada who founded Jidada's resistance movement, long before animals knew the Father of the Nation's name, or that the Old Horse wasn't even the popular choice for president among the high-ranking liberators, some of whom felt he didn't have the qualities of a true, unifying leader. Still, no matter, that's who we got in the end, and we felt the two leaders, who'd fought side by side for our independence, naturally had the whole nation's interest at heart and would take all of us to the promised land anyhow. To Black majority rule and beyond. To glory, we thought.

4. PORTRAIT OF A LIBERATOR AS A FATHER, MOTHERING GRANDFATHER, WRITER, AND HISTORIAN

And your grandfather, unlike what most fathers may have done—that is, punish me or cast me out for bringing shame to the family—instead simply embraced you with all his being. It was just beautiful, how he doted on you. How he loved you. As if the only reason he'd come back from the war was to devote himself to you. As if so many things had gone wrong, had fallen apart during the war and the only way to put them back together was through loving you. He called you the most perfect homecoming present. Sometimes I was jealous. I think your uncles and aunt were

too. Knowing we'd never really been loved like that because Father had been away, and now that we were grown it was too late for him to dote on us like he did you.

As soon as you could walk you followed your grandfather all over. Like a shadow. If you weren't following him he was holding you. His friends would tease him. Ask him how and when and where he'd learned to hold a baby like that. Like a femal, they said. And he'd laugh. And he'd say it was the war that taught him. He'd say because holding an AK-47, a bazooka, a machine gun, holding any weapon in the bush had always felt to him like holding a life—either one that would be taken in battle, or the one to survive. Sometimes I just wonder who you'd have grown up to be with that kind of fierce love all the time, how different your life would have been, all our lives would have been.

And in the middle of it all your grandfather was busy writing his war memoir. I remember that he walked around with these little notebooks in the pockets of his overalls, always a black pen tucked behind his ear. It was very common to find him scribbling between his chores, but he also had a set writing schedule, which was every day, right after lunch, for a couple of hours, and then very early in the morning, before the day began. It was all strange to my young self, because I thought one only held a pen and paper during their schooling days. And besides, I figured, the war was over, the country was free, and he was home so why not look forward into the future instead of at what was already behind us?

But then here was your grandfather, talking about the past never truly passing-passing, talking about the importance of telling one's story if you wanted it told right because otherwise there was no shortage of those who'd take it upon themselves to tell it for you and tell it however they pleased, talking about the importance of keeping records to make sure the truth remained true, talking about—and somehow these words have stayed with me all these years exactly as he said them—"This war was a complicated

thing, Mother of Destiny. If I don't write this book then one day animals calling themselves the Real Liberators and True Patriots will call us ugly names and then erase us from the story of the very country we sacrificed so much for because now that the war is over many will be perceived to be of the wrong ethnic group, the wrong clan, the wrong gender, the wrong clique, the wrong politics, the wrong whatever else they decide constitutes authentic Jidadaness. If I don't write, then who will I blame when I wake up one day to find myself in the belly of a crocodile that calls itself History, that devours the stories of everyone else and goes on to speak for us?"

You obviously won't remember this but while your grandfather wrote, you were there with him, doing as he was doing, doodling in your own notebooks.

5. APRIL 18, 1983

Anyway, on that morning, I'd snuck out in the wee hours like I did every Monday to meet Cephas Tshabangu. Cephas Tshabangu was my lover. A beautiful billy who taught maths at Bulawayo Secondary and lived across Tuli, where he spent the weekends, biking to our side on Mondays for work. We'd only been going for just a couple of months but we knew already we wanted to spend the rest of our lives together. We were just so in love, Destiny, I never knew a love like that was possible. He and his family were readying to come and talk to Father for formal arrangements. But until then, we were meeting in secret. On Mondays, Cephas would leave his home at the crack of dawn so he could spend time with me on his way to work. Our homestead was right on his route, and he usually got to me with about three-four hours to spare before the start of school. There was a cave where youngsters from the neighborhood had played hide-and-seek throughout our childhood—I'd furnished it with a reed mat and old pillows, made it our love spot.

6. THOLUKUTHI WOOD BIRTHS ASH

I don't know what got into me that day. Because I was, as usual, supposed to set off for home right after my little rendezvous, and be back before anyone woke to discover I was missing. Especially Mother. Your grandmother had called me an itchtail throughout my pregnancy—only seeming to accept me after seeing your grandfather embrace me and you unconditionally. But I don't think it was for my sake she did—more for Father's. And herself. To keep the peace in her marriage. Otherwise I could see that the disappointment and shame I'd caused her never left. She'd been a well-known evangelist, a respected member of Brethren in Christ Church, big in our area at the time—almost everyone went there—and she actually sat on a few prestigious committees. So my getting pregnant at an early age definitely reflected poorly on her, broadcasted to the whole world she was a failure of a mother, made it impossible for her to hold her head as high in church as she'd have wanted to. And even with Father's return and our relationship becoming somewhat tolerant, I always felt her judgment, congealed now into a soft kind of resentment. I didn't need to be told Mother was still offended—thoroughly insulted by my morals, who I'd turned out to become despite, as she called it, her example, her teachings. But still, somehow, I was determined to do better this time around.

7. DHIKONDO: THOLUKUTHI SONG OF TERROR

You can imagine my horror then, when on that Monday morning of April 18, 1983, I opened my eyes to find myself on the floor of my love cave just a few minutes before ten a.m., long after I should've begun my chores, way after the whole family would've woken up. I'd drifted off after Cephas's departure, and overslept! My first reaction was to cry my eyes out. In regret, in shame. But of course after spending enough time weeping on that floor there was just nothing to be done; I simply had to pick myself up, go home, and just face your grandmother. Your grandfather too, who

I knew that despite his readiness to defend me from Mother's judgment would, on this occasion, definitely not be pleased with my choices.

And so there I was, on my way home and utterly miserable, clutching a small gift bag from Cephas and rehearsing what I'd say in my defense. I was at the halfway point, skirting the fence along Progress Primary School. I'd probably have passed without noticing anything unusual had it not been for the curious singing—a dissonant affair that felt, I don't know, off, just wrong. The more I listened, the more it became clear the singing voices were panic-stricken, terrified. Apparently the students were trying—struggling in fact—to sing this Shona song; I didn't understand the lyrics but I still recognized it from the radio. The word *Dhikondo*, repeated often, rang the loudest. I didn't know anyone who spoke fluent Shona in the area, quite frankly, so the whole thing was bizarre, made more so by the obvious trauma in the voices.

At this point I was so astounded I completely forgot my dilemma. I got closer to the fence, from where I had a sweeping view of the front of the school. And that was when I saw the Defenders hinding about in camouflage and red berets. They were busy herding petrified students out of their classes and toward the assembly area. Guns and black boots glinted in the sun. I heard harsh commands barked in Shona. In no time, students were gathered there at the assembly area, huddled tight like sardines. Then I saw the Defenders herd a second group, this time teachers and members of staff. My heart was in my throat by now—I just had this awful, awful feeling. I was also thinking that my cousin, Muzomuhle Khumalo, was probably at that assembly—he'd been Senior Master at Progress for about five years at that point. His twins, Thandanani and Nothando, also attended the school.

I saw the staff being made to lie facedown, in a row, in the paved area in front of the flagpole. Above their bodies, the flag of Jidada flapped erratically in the wind. There was more barking of commands, the petrified

voices of the students continued shrilling. And then, just as I was wondering what exactly would happen, the Defenders pounced on the teachers. Boots, sticks, butts of guns rained on the prostrate bodies, I mean rained, just rained.

Even from my hiding place I could see blood fly. Hear shrieks and cries mingled with the hysterical voices of the students. I didn't wait to see the end of the terrible spectacle so I ate the ground with my hooves. I made straight for home, no longer caring what awaited me there. I ran blindly, colliding with trees and rocks, tripping on stones and roots, in the process somehow losing my gift bag packed with goodies from Cephas—I can in fact still remember, even visualize what was in it: a sky-blue Georgette dress, a white bra and matching panties and petticoat, a yellow midsize jar of American girl, a small mirror, a bottle of Black Beauty, an Afro comb.

8. SHELTER

My uncle SaCetshwayo's homestead was a little way behind ours so that to get home one had to pass it. I don't know how my hooves carried me there, maybe somehow I imagined my home was suddenly far and I desperately needed shelter fast—all I can say is I saw myself pouring into that yard like river water, shrieking as if I'd been missed by a leopard. I could see Uncle under the mabrosi tree at the center of the yard, wearing his usual navy blue work overalls and white sun hat. I made straight for him. The rest of the family gathered under the tree. If I'd had time to think I'd have known, from the way they were seated, from the fact that no one ran to meet me in my obvious despair, that something was terribly wrong. Still, by the time I reached the mabrosi, I sensed that I'd thrust myself between the jaws of a crocodile.

9. UNDER THE MABROSI

No one greeted me. I quickly sat next to my cousin Sibonokuhle and felt her body shake. And I mean she was shaking. She shook. Somebody—I

think my aunt NaCetshwayo—was weeping softly. The whole family was there, and I made eight. Uncle SaCetshwayo looked at me quizzically, frowned, glanced at the spare bedroom where a group of Defenders in camouflage and the very same red berets I saw at Progress discussed in clanging voices. The sight of them made my intestines churn, leap to my chest. My uncle's face was a terrible mask of anguish. I'd never in my life seen him, or any mal adult really, look like that—our fathers were forever strong in our eyes, unflappable. I was already afraid, but I got more afraid seeing my uncle like that. And most important I regretted running through that gate, was even mad at myself for it; why on earth hadn't I just carried on home like I'd meant to do? What had I come here for? Then the Defenders were suddenly there under the tree. I was afraid they'd notice me, know there was an extra body that hadn't been there.

10. *D* IS FOR DISSIDENT, *D* IS FOR DEFENDER

"Right, we'll ask you one last time. Where are the Dissidents?" said the big Defender, who looked like he was in charge—maybe he was their commander, or at least I thought so, from how he carried himself, from the crowded medals glinting above his left breast.

"We don't know, we haven't seen any Dissidents here, my sons," Uncle SaCetshwayo said. He spoke in a quivering, threadlike voice that sounded like it'd snap in two. A voice I didn't even know. It stunned me for its frailty, its strangeness. A black boot flew to Uncle's mouth. A throat was cleared by someone in our group. I saw Uncle's jaw flinch. He lowered his head, spit two teeth and a glob of red onto the earth.

"Who are you calling your sons? Do you know our mother's tails?" Were you there when we were born? Do you know us?" the Commander barked.

"My apologies," Uncle said.

"My apologies who?" a Defender in dark glasses barked.

"My apologies, sir," Uncle said. The rest of them howled with laughter.

"Since you claim not to know any Dissidents, where's your Jidada Party card?" the Commander said. Then, turning to us, "Where are your Jidada Party cards? Whoever has a Jidada Party card please stand up and let's see them." We all remained seated, silent. Beneath us, the hard ground numbed our behinds; above us, the sun fried our heads.

"In the meantime, I think I'll go and do a little private interrogation," the Defender in the glasses said. He took them off and circled us now, surveying us like he was looking at fruit at a market stand—appraising, screening, trying to find a ripe one to pick. I could hear him breathe in and out, breathe in and out. It made my blood crawl. He stopped in front of Sibo. I saw him go tap-tap-tap her breast with the tip of a baton.

"You, come here, I want to ask you something, come tell me about the Dissidents," he leered, an ugly playfulness in his voice. His squad howled. Sibonokuhle began to cry. The Defender reached down and dragged her away, kicking and crying and pleading, toward the back of the kitchen. Then my aunt burst into hysterical sobs and screamed her daughter's name.

11. ALL GOD'S CHILDREN, IN THE IMAGE OF GOD

I remember my aunt clinging to the Commander's hind leg and pleading, "I beg you in Jesus's name. We're all God's children, please! Please!" I remember her fervent prayers. One of the Defenders fired into the air, and my horns almost jumped off my head. My aunt collapsed, fainted. None of us flinched.

"So, where was I? Ah yes, if you don't belong to the Party of Power, then which party do you belong to, old goat?" the Commander barked. At that moment, a sharp, bloodcurdling scream rent the air. You could hear the pain in it. The fear. The sadness. The plea. The desperation. Then it died. But Sibonukuhle's broken voice stayed ringing in my ears.

12. A QUESTION OF MEMBERSHIP

"Didn't I ask you a question?" the Commander said. And my uncle, replying with his thread, said, "I belong to the Jidada Union, sir. It has its roots in this whole region as you know so naturally we all belong to it." You could tell Uncle wasn't really all there, that most of him had gone to be with his daughter.

"I belong to the Jidada Union, sir. It has its roots in this whole region as you know so naturally we all belong to it," the Commander said, mimicking Uncle and exaggerating his Ndebele accent. The Defenders roared with laughter.

"And why on earth do you belong to a party of Dissidents? Of terrorists?"

"It's not—we're not Dissidents, we're not terrorists. We're just a party like any other party, and we're Jidadans, sir."

"Just a party? And Jidadans? Who told you you were Jidadans? Was your great-great-grandfather born on this land or he came from somewhere else to seize territory from our ancestors and rubbish their kingdom?" the Commander barked. The Defenders howled and wagged their tails. One of them tossed his beret in the air, flew after it and caught it in his teeth, and, upon landing, danced in circles.

"Yes, our ancestors migrated from Zululand before this Jidada was a country-country as I'm sure you know the history of this region. But my father was born on this very land, and so was everyone you see here. You should know we worked to liberate this Jidada. My own brother fought in the war. My other brother's son never came back from it." But the Commander wasn't listening to Uncle anymore. He was now busy inspecting us. I tried not to meet his yellow eyes, terrified he'd drag me off too.

13. THE DISSIDENT WE'RE ALL LOOKING FOR

"You, there, you, no, not you, you in the black shirt, come here," I heard the Commander bark. When I looked up, my cousin Cetshwayo was hinding

to the front. But he didn't move like one staring at the open mouth of a crocodile, no, not Ce. To begin with, Ce generally didn't walk, he carried himself. Comported himself like he was something precious. And he was just beautiful and proud and unbowed and arrogant and above all had this fine, regal presence. He presented himself like he'd been called up from the sky. I tell you that every single Defender turned to look at him walk. There was a sustained silence after Ce took his place by his father's side, like the Defenders, having called him, suddenly had no idea what they'd called him for.

"Where are the Dissidents, youngmal?" the Commander said. I noticed his voice didn't sound like it'd been sounding all along. There was this small hesitation in it now. Like Ce made him unsure about things and the Defender didn't know anymore who was in charge. It kind of gave me hope to hear the Defender sound like that. And Ce simply looked at him like he was looking at a heap of dung dressed up in a uniform and carrying a gun.

"You're not answering because you're the fucking Dissident, isn't it? Well, today we'll show you what we do with your kind. Comrade, bring me a gun—no, matter of fact, an ax, bring me a goddamned ax, that should be more fun," the Commander said.

14. NO WEAPON FORMED AGAINST YOU SHALL PROSPER

And the ax was brought. And the ax was a gleaming thing, heavy—from the way the Defender carried it. And the ax was passed to the Commander. It already had some red on it, and we didn't need to be told what it was. And the Commander passed the ax to Ce. Cetshwayo glanced at the ax and then looked off into the distance like he was busy and they were bothering him, like the Defenders were beneath him even. Proud Ce. Arrogant Ce. Fearless Ce. Beautiful Ce. A Defender stepped up to him, kicked him in the privates, and said, "Take the goddamn ax, you Dissident." Ce-

tshwayo didn't budge. The Commander dropped the ax onto the ground, turned to Uncle, and said, "Old goat. Do you want to live?"

15. A MATTER OF CHOICE

"I said do you want to live?" the Defender barked. He sounded himself now, like he was back in charge again.

"Yes, sir," my uncle said. His voice—I thought the thread would snap at that moment.

"Good. Today may just be your lucky day. You see this ax?" the Defender said, gesturing. Uncle nodded.

"Pick it up and hack this Dissident right here," the Defender said, pointing to Cetshwayo.

"That I'm afraid I cannot do. And no, my son is not a Dissident," my uncle said. It was the first time his voice sounded steady. Clear. Firm. Resolute. It was the voice I knew.

"Yes you will," a Defender barked.

"I am sorry, that I can't. And I won't hurt my son." Uncle said, raising his voice. The Commander reached into his breast pocket, fished out a Madison cigarette, stuck it into the corner of his mouth. Then he leaned toward the Defender standing next to him, who lit it. At that moment the Defender who'd gone off with Sibonokuhle hinded back, fastening his belt, a smug look on his face. I glanced behind him, but there was no sign of my sister. Something in me keeled over.

"Okay, this is what'll happen. One of you, we don't care who, really, but obviously one of you—will pick up that ax and chop the other. That's what we want to see here right now. And not just chop but chop to pieces, proper pieces, not parts, you understand? Or else we'll finish every one of you today and I'm not sure you want that. Or maybe you do, I don't know, only you know. It's your choice, really, it's a free country," the Commander barked. About then we heard a volley of gunshots. Just

pha-pha-pha-pha-pha-pha-pha! But there was absolutely nothing we could do to process it all. We couldn't even look into each other's eyes, couldn't nothing.

"But you may want at least some of you alive to tell the story of what happened here today because I assure you it'll be worth telling," the Commander said, speaking between puffs.

Then a Defender raised his gun, pointed it at Ce, aimed between the eyes. And that was when—and I'll never forget that moment—that was when my uncle stooped to pick up the ax. I stopped breathing. Then Uncle straightened—his movements were like in slow motion—and faced us, looked at us huddled under that Mabrosi. He just stood there looking at us with his big, kind eyes. For a long, long time, like he was committing our faces to memory. He was trembling. The ax was shaking. Then, very, very carefully, he gave the ax to Cetshwayo. Who shook his head no. Uncle nodded his head yes. Ce shook his head no. Uncle nodded his head yes. Ce shook his head no. Uncle nodded his head yes. Ce shook his head no—no no, no no no no no no no. You'd have thought they were little ones playing some kind of game, looking at them go back and forth like that.

"You must do it, my son, you have to do it, as you can see the situation for yourself," Uncle said almost sweetly. A Defender bark-giggled. Cetshwayo kept shaking his head. He shook it with such force, if it had had screws it'd have come undone.

"There's just no other choice, my son, I'm deeply sorry to ask this of you." Uncle's voice was gentle but urgent. At that point I saw, from the corner of my eye, my aunt begin to stir.

"I'd rather die, my father, so why don't you do it to me? Go right ahead, you have my permission, do it." Ce roared, like he was addressing somebody far away. Ce had a temper, but I'd never heard him address his father like that. In that seething tone.

"Ce, Cetshwayo, listen, just listen to me, please," Uncle said. He was quiet. He was calm. He was loving.

"Hey hey hey! Enough! Enough! We don't have all day! Stop this back-and-forth nonsense, you're not a bunch of femals," the Commander barked.

"You know I've already lived my life, my son. And it's been a generous life, I can't complain, and I thank God every day for it. And for all of you; you're truly my best things. But what use am I, Ce, if you die and I stay? What can I do for anyone here? And for how long? With what health? Listen, if God wills it to be this way, then let it be," Uncle said.

"God, really?! Tell me what kind of sick, demented, ugly God would sanction this evil? Just what kind of wretched God is this, my father?!" Cetshwayo exploded.

"Please, my son, please, you must understand," Uncle pleaded.

I don't think it was Cetshwayo I saw at that very moment. Or maybe it was and I'd just never seen him become that before. I simply didn't recognize him. It was like something else had taken over Ce. His body trembled. But it wasn't fear. His eyes blazed. He breathed fast, heavy. He looked at his father with something like, I don't know—he had this contempt, this disappointment on his face, like Uncle had somehow let him down. Failed him. Insulted him. And then Ce turned to face us huddled under the Mabrosi. And I realized he was seeking his mother's eyes. He found and held them for a while. And then Ce shook his head, spit. His tears just poured, a whole waterfall of them. He turned back to his father. Who also at that moment had his own waterfall cascading down his face. They stood like that, facing each other between torrents.

16. A WET PRAYER

All my life I'd heard said this thing about tears—that they are a language, that they do indeed speak. And that day, under that Mabrosi, I witnessed— I heard, I understood—the clarity, the absolute eloquence of tears. Because

with nothing but tears, Uncle SaCetshwayo somehow told his son, reminded Ce who he was, that his names were Cetshwayo Zwelibanzi Future Khumalo, son of Sakhile Bathakathi George Khumalo, son of Nqabayezwe Mbiko Khumalo, son of Mehlulisiswe Ngqwele Khumalo, son of Mkhulunyelwa Sakhile Khumalo, son of Mpilompi Khumalo, son of Somizi Dlungwane Khumalo, himself son of uNkulunkulu, the most high God. That on his mother's side he was the son of Ntombiyelanga Emily Mlotshwa, daughter of Nonceba Gumede, daughter of Noxolo Hlabangane, daughter of Nkanyezi Gatsheni, daughter of Zanezulu Mlotshwa, daughter of Nomfula Khumalo, herself daughter of uNkulunkulu. That all these ancestors had all come together to gift him, Ce, to bring about the presence of the body that he at that awful moment occupied, as too had the earth and the heavens and the rivers and the trees and the wind and everything that lived and breathed, and that he was the collective prayer of all these prodigious forces. With nothing but tears, Uncle told Ce that he was a most precious, precious gift. That he loved him with a love deeper, vaster than any ocean, a love true and glorious and absolutely divine, and that that love was not only everything, it was also bigger than that most terrible moment under the mabrosi, that it transcended time, transcended space, transcended death, transcended really anything and all things—a love supreme. And for Ce to never ever forget that, to carry the knowledge with him always because despite what the evil fiends in red berets and camouflage were about to do to them, to us all—for Ce to know that they'd always be bound by unbreakable ties, and so to remember that separation was neither erasure nor annihilation, and besides, it would be temporary. For Ce to remember that he was better than the evil in the red berets because he was grace and beauty and dignity, and more important, to never let the Defenders reduce him to their level of baseness or allow them to diminish him. For him to continue loving himself regardless of what was about to happen, despite the coming darkness, because even darkness eventually ran out of dark and would end with light

somehow because there was no night ever so long it did not end with dawn, and when that dawn came, Cetshwayo would need to face himself in its light, and only love of self, and peace with self, would allow him to do so without crumbling. And then, with just tears alone, Uncle, who was a Christian and, like my mother, a member of Brethren in Christ Church, said the Lord's Prayer with his tears, I mean he cried it—Our Father, who art in heaven. We heard every word of that prayer loud and clear from the terrible torrent gushing down Uncle SaCe's face. When he said Amen, Uncle dried his tears. And we all knew that our elder, our father, had said his peace, and had nothing more to say.

17. THOLUKUTHI THOU SHALL NOT KILL

I'd never really know what Cetshwayo thought of all his father said. If he heard it like it was said. But it was like seeing his father wipe his tears did something to him, you could see it in his changed face. About then we heard another round of gunfire, and, as if that were some kind of signal he'd been waiting for, Ce snatched that ax. And then before I could ask myself if what I was seeing was really what I was seeing, I saw him let the ax fall right between Uncle's shoulder and neck. I guess up until that point I think a part of me—and maybe the others too—had been hoping against hope that we were all caught up in some terrible nightmare. And that by some miracle, somehow, that nightmare would end. But with that first strike that hope shattered-shattered-shattered, just shattered. Much, much later, I'd figure that in that first strike Cetshwayo must've probably meant, hoped to deliver a blow so fatal it'd momentarily stun Uncle and finish him instantly, and that way, spare him the pain, spare his mother the pain, spare himself the pain, spare every one of us the pain and quickly bring the terrible nightmare to an end. I'd later figure too, when I had enough of my head to make sense of the situation, that the Defenders made sure it was a blunt ax—in order to prolong our suffering. And so Cetshwayo let

that ax drop. And Cetshwayo let that ax drop. And Cetshwayo let that ax drop again. Again and again and again. Even today, when I listen hard I can hear the sickening thump.

My aunt had fainted again at this point. I really don't know how many times she fainted throughout the whole ordeal; I hadn't known one could just keep fainting and fainting like that. Over and over. The Defenders just looked on, tongues lolling and casually wagging their tails like it was just an ordinary day and they were watching a most ordinary event. And the ax did its terrible job. And Cetshwayo was getting desperate. And also angrier and angrier. You could just feel it in the air. See it in his strikes. Read it in his terrible, tormented face, his gritted teeth, in those eyes, no longer proud but fiendish. He desperately wanted Uncle to go ahead and die so that the nightmare would end, we all did. And I'm sure Uncle, who'd given Cetshwayo permission, forced him even, had the same desire. But then Uncle's spirit somehow just didn't want to be a part of any of it.

The sun had gotten more unbearable. It had turned yellow-yellow-yellow. Cetshwayo seemed suddenly shrunken, so small. Just remains of himself really. And he bawled. It was the saddest sound, it was the saddest sight, it was the saddest feeling. The air was heavy with the smell of blood now. Of gunk and goo. All the while we sat there zombielike. As if we'd stepped out of our bodies and fled for shelter, left empty containers of ourselves behind. And then somewhere, between us fleeing and our containers sitting under that mabrosi tree, my uncle—Sakhile Bathakathi George Khumalo, my uncle, SaCetshwayo—finally died death. Died in pieces. In pieces. Just pieces pieces pieces. Like the Defenders intended to put him in a drum and maybe make some kind of stew they'd actually feast on and enjoy. We were ordered not to weep. Whoever wept, the Defenders said, would be made to follow Uncle. And we knew they meant it too. But I don't really know if we'd have wept anyway, if any of us had any tears.

The Commander hawked a glob of spit and said to make sure we'd

buried Uncle by the time it dried up. Then they leapt into their vehicle, promising to return to check on our progress. We dug my uncle's grave in haste. Most tools were in the fields, where the family had been working, so some of us used sticks, some of us our bare limbs. No one said a word that whole time we dug—not a single utterance, cry, nothing. Only our tools spoke, pounding on the hard, stubborn Bulawayo earth. My aunt at this time was just there, a parcel really, a shell. Cetshwayo was repeatedly head-butting the trunk of the mabrosi. He was never really well after that. My aunt too didn't live to be completely well, along with two of her children, Sinikiwe and Sibonokuhle, but I don't know how anyone could actually be themselves, could be well, could be whole, could fully function after an experience like the Gukurahundi.

We buried Uncle's pieces under the mabrosi. Just a shallow grave nje. Just to be done with it all before the Defenders returned. We were close to finishing covering it up when they did. They hinded around for a while, smoking cigarettes and watching our progress before the Commander announced the spit had long dried, which he said meant we were lazy, disrespectful, and had Dissident tendencies. They'd allow us to finish the burial, but afterward we'd face due punishment. And they did punish us. We were ordered to stand in a row, and then one of them came with this piece of barbed wire and went down the line, just whipping us. With that barbed wire. But I'd feel the pain only later. Because at that point I was beyond feeling, just beyond pain. Like my body wasn't mine anymore. It was while we were being whipped like that when here comes this boiling Puma.

It comes to a screeching stop at the gate and it's crammed full with more red berets. I look at all those Defenders and I think, This is the end, they've come to finish us. One of them jumps out and runs to the Commander, who is already on his way to the car. They talk fast, and of course none of us understand what's being said. Then the Commander barks at

the Defenders who are there under the mabrosi with us, and they all take off running toward their own car. Then the two vehicles thunder off, one after the other, and then they are gone.

I don't know how I got the strength to get started for home. But I did. At the well near the mopane I ran into Bhud' Charlie. He was one of our neighbors. But I was at that point just a shadow and would've passed him if he hadn't cut me off with his bike. We stood for a while, facing each other, not saying anything. I remember him looking at my battered body and his eyes welling with tears. While we were standing there, a horde of students in Progress Primary School uniforms came galloping down the pathway. If you've ever seen terror on legs, flying. Bhud' Charlie had to trip one of them to get him to stop so he could find out what was going on. "The teachers are killed dead, those soldiers killed dead our teachers with guns!" the lamb said, out of breath, before taking off again. Bhud' Charlie got back on his bike. His last words to me, before he tore off toward Progress, were not to go home.

18. HOME SWEET HOME

I went home. And when I got there, there was no home, I mean there was nothing. I thought I was lost. I thought I was dreaming. Then I thought maybe I'd gone confused. As in mad. Every single hut, every structure burned, razed. And in the air, the ugliest smell that was unlike anything I knew. I'm told I was found fainted at dusk, which was when my neighbors finally had the courage to come out and investigate. I remember somebody passed you to me about then. But I had no strength, no desire, to hold you. I didn't even feel anything for you; if they'd given you to me I'd have flung you away. I was just in so much anguish. Pain of the head, pain of the spirit, pain of the heart, pain of the flesh. Just pain everywhere.

And later, Hlangabeza—this piglet from next door—would tell me how he'd escaped with you. He'd been sent by his mother that morning to

borrow a cup of sugar when the Gukurahundi entered the gate. That was the name—I learned then—they used for the particular Defenders who were unleashing unto our region the worst kind of terror under the pretext of looking for Dissidents. Apparently by that they meant us innocent civilians, we were the Dissidents because it's us who died in throngs. Hlanga said that your grandfather, who'd been carrying you when he got home, must've seen the Gukurahundi arrive, sensed that these weren't Defenders he'd call Comrades, because Hlangabeza said he shoved you to him, instructing him to sneak with you behind the kitchen, crawl under the fence, and hide in the bush by the well and wait until he came to find you.

Hlangabeza didn't go directly to the well, fearing he might run into more Gukurahundi along the way. He hid in the hollow of the baobab tree to the north of the homestead, and observed. He saw Father walk up to the group. Hlangabeza didn't understand what was said, only that from the loud angry voices, from your grandfather headbutting one of the Defenders, who landed on his back, it was obvious it was a violent argument. But it didn't last long; in no time Father was on the ground, the Gukurahundi biting, pummeling, pounding, raining on him with boots and the butts of their guns. When they at last stopped, Father lay still, probably unconscious. Then the Gukurahundi rounded everyone up and sat them in the open area in front of the kitchen. Hlangabeza counted all my family members except me, which means everyone was home. He heard cries and pleas for mercy. He heard barks and commands in a language he didn't understand. At this point the Gukurahundi were busy, bodies bent over my family; from where he was, Hlangabeza couldn't clearly see what exactly it was they were doing. It was only a little while later, when the Defenders pulled them up, that he understood what was happening—they'd tied everyone up.

Hlangabeza watched them drag Zenzele by his horns, then Nkosiyabo, then Nkanyiso, then Njube, then Thandiwe, and lastly, my mother into

the kitchen. Then he watched them shut the door. And then he watched them do something to the door—locking or tying it up, he thought. He was convinced they only intended to leave the family tied up like that, and he figured he'd rescue them when it was safe to do so, but then he saw one of the Gukurahundi throw something onto the thatched roof of the kitchen. He watched the roof instantly burst into flames.

After the Gukurahundi had set alight every other structure in the homestead, they stood around smoking cigarettes and watching everything burn. Then Hlangabeza heard on a radio the Dhikondo song—apparently the Gukurahundi played this very same song wherever they went. He said the Defenders suddenly went morbid on Father's frangipani—which of course was all over the place—as if possessed by a new, separate evil that had suddenly sprouted and flowered inside them. They just slashed and stomped and hacked and tore and trampled and uprooted the poor shrubs, while a couple of Defenders even whipped out machine guns, aimed, and opened fire.

Hlangabeza didn't know how much time passed, but it was long enough for the screams inside the kitchen to eventually still. Then he saw my father move—he'd regained consciousness. He saw my father struggle to his feet. He saw my father look around the homestead. He saw my father register the burning structures. He heard my father let out this howl of pain. He saw my father take off running—still howling—toward the burning kitchen, leave the kitchen and run to Mother's burning bedroom. He saw my father scattering himself all over the yard like there were many of him, like he were grain, like he didn't know what to touch, what to hold, and what to let go of.

Hlangabeza heard a gunshot pop, and he saw my father come down, but it mustn't have been a fatal shot because he saw my father somehow manage to crawl. He saw the Gukurahundi pick your grandfather up and drag him to their jeep, which was parked by the gate. He saw them fling

your grandfather inside, fling him like he were a dirty rag. He saw the Gukurahundi hop in and then drive off. And that was the last anyone saw of Butholezwe Henry Vulindlela Khumalo, son of Nqabayezwe Mbiko Khumalo and Zanezulu Hlatshwayo Khumalo, husband of Nomvelo Mary Khumalo and father of Thandiwe Khumalo, Nkanyiso Khumalo, Nkosi-yabo Khumalo, Zenzele Khumalo, Njube Khumalo and myself, grand-father of just one grandchild, you, Destiny Lozikeyi Khumalo.

19. FINISHING TOUCHES

I was told the same fate had befallen many of our neighbors, including your father's family. I don't know what I remained there for, standing in those terrible ruins. Instead of leaving and going off with the neighbors. Hlangabeza's mother was begging me to come with them and get some rest. She was carrying you on her back now, I think you were sleeping. Her older sons, Mandla and Dingane, and then someone else, an elderly femal, I can't remember who now, also came to convince me to leave. But I just couldn't move. Maybe I thought my family would appear. Undead. Maybe I wanted something to ignite and burn me too so I didn't have to face life. I don't know what I thought. But we found ourselves suddenly in the glare of lights. The Gukurahundi were come, demanding to know what we were doing standing there, if we were waiting on Dissidents. I had no idea whether they were the ones who'd murdered my family, whether they were the ones who'd murdered Uncle SaCe and beat us, or whether they were a new group altogether.

They ordered us to lie on our stomachs. It was like reliving a night-mare. I was thoroughly beaten—all over again. We were thoroughly beaten, I mean beaten-beaten-beaten. First they made all the femals take off our clothes. But when I tell you that they beat us, I'm not really tell-ing you anything. Or everything. Because no language can begin to tell you what they did to us on that Monday of April 18, 1983, in Bulawayo,

Bulawayo, in this Jidada, amidst the ruins of my father's homestead. These many years, decades later, I still cannot find the words, Destiny Lozikeyi Khumalo; even as I'm telling you right now, I know I'm not telling it correctly, that I can never tell it right or tell it well. There are no words to tell it—they've never been, and there won't ever be.

That was how I also lost my hearing in this ear. I know I told you before that it was a birth defect but that is what really happened, now you know it. In the coming days, in the coming weeks, our bodies rotted. We didn't have medical care to treat the wounds, how would we even seek or get it when the Gukurahundi were crawling all over and we were afraid of being finished off? There were also rumors they were waiting for us in hospitals in case we sought treatment. And so we carried colonies of maggots on our bodies, you could scratch the creatures off and just watch them writhe. We stank so much we could hardly stand ourselves. We slept on our stomachs for months. Because our bodies were in pain. We rotted. Chunks of flesh fell off my behind, first one buttock, and then the other. Even today I have holes, valleys, ridges in my flesh. But why am I telling you when I know my words can't really show you what I mean?

PORTRAIT OF TWO BODIES

Simiso ambles off the bed and stands in the center of the room. In one fluid motion, she whips her nightdress over her head. She's not wearing any undergarments. She turns around to give her back to her daughter, who gasps, covers her mouth at the terrible scars, the angry lines, furrows that cross and uncross all over the long back, the holes on the older goat's behind. This is the very first time Destiny's seeing her mother's body as naked as truth, she could be looking at clear water, and reflected in that water, her own body. Later, when Destiny rethinks this moment, she'll feel that Simiso's undressing was also her own undressing.

Which is why, how, she'd found herself taking her nightdress off. Then she stood facing Simiso, who did not flinch at her daughter's own devastated body. And the two goats stood there, side by side and face-to-face like they'd never stood before, stood like they'd just given birth to each other, yes, tholukuthi their naked bodies alike, not just because they were femal, no, not because they were mother and daughter and were thus made from the same clay, no, but because those bodies both carried scars from Defenders, as if the Defenders that mangled Destiny's body on July 5, 2008, had taken meticulous directives from the Defenders that mutilated Simiso's body more than twenty-five years before that, on April 18, 1983, yes, tholukuthi as if the Defenders were creating on both bodies an important archive of the Seat of Power's cruelty.

"This is how, why, I disappeared, Mother. I was just so hurt. So broken all I could think of, right after it happened, was to flee, just leave, and never return. I thought forgetting, not looking back, would help me. I thought it'd erase the whole thing. What happened is that in 2008, right after the elections—"

"Shhhhhhhhhhhhhhhhhhhh, my child," Simiso whispers. She doesn't need to be told a story she already knows. Tholukuthi she gathers her child like she is gathering the kind of delicate flowers that fold to the touch. She carefully feels her daughter's scars, one by one, as if she intends to give each one of them a name. And she caresses each one of her daughter's scars. And she kisses each one of her daughter's scars. And then it is the daughter's turn to gather her mother like she's gathering the softest mushrooms. And she touches each of her mother's scars, yes, tholukuthi one by one, as if she intends to learn their names. And she caresses each one of her mother's scars. And she kisses each one of her mother's scars. And they do this over and over, back and forth, over and over, until the ache and pain that have for so long been shut up inside their bodies are the weight of butterfly wings.

OPERATION RESTORE LEGACY

PORTRAIT OF A NATION'S POST-ELECTION THOUGHTS AND FEELINGS

—Haaaa, Comrade! Didn't I tell you? That we can't lose an election we are in charge of! Because why? Just because animals didn't vote for us? Nosssssir! And come the next one, in 2023, we will win it. And the next one, in 2029, we will win it. And the next one in 2034, we will win it. 2039, win it. 2044, win it. 2049, win it. 2054, win it. Because that's all we do, is win win win win win win! Tichingotooooonga!

—Who right now is ready?! Are you ready to enter Canaan with the Savior O Precious Soldiers?! Because I tell you the promised land has arrived! The promised land is here glory glory glooooooooooorrrrrrrr-rrrrrrrrrry!

—Pity at first it looked like a real harmonized election I almost believed it. Then the next minute we were in a war zone. Armed Defenders out

in full force, doing what they've always done. May the dead rest in peace!

—You should've seen us on election day. How we were all over Lozikeyi, just levitating-levitating-levitating. How we were so sure of victory! When my children asked why we were levitating I told them it was for the New Jidada. Now they won't stop asking what happened to it, where it went. And I still don't know how to look at them.

—Congratulations to my Savior, wishing you a prosperous four years. To the New Dispensation!

—For my own sanity I really just want to move on. So on that note I have nothing much to say. I'll just concentrate on me and my family and my relationship with God. These being the things I know for sure I can control.

—But we warned you. Even all up to the election we were there, warning you, telling you, reminding you. You even called it a harmonized election. You called it #freefairncredible. Don't look at us like that, those were your own words.

—What hurts me is that before the coup I'd never go out to march for anything really. I just stayed home and minded my business. What possessed me to go out and march in support of the coup, taking selfies with the soldiers and all of that, I still can't say. Looking back, it's like it was some other animal pretending to be me, going out there in my stead. Because I really can't see how I could've done that, been in that frame of mind. Or maybe it's that when you spend all your life wanting

something, and it finally does happen, and when you don't actually expect it, you just lose perspective. Which I now know is a dangerous thing.

—I'm not gonna lie, I truly believed change was come. I was so sure. And now these results! What was the use of removing the Old Horse then? Where is the change? Even the way this Tuvy won, if you do believe he won, just stinks of the Old Horse's tactics.

—Me the decision I've come to is that elections are just a waste of time in this Jidada. Because the Seat of Power will always win by rigging and violence. Either one, the other, or both.

—Why anyone would think anyone would go carry out a coup only to give the country to the miserable truly baffles me. I wouldn't even do that myself. But I hope, for Jidada's sake, the Savior at least steers the ship in the right direction.

—The Opposition voters are acting like spoiled children. You lost the election, you lost the election, end of story. Grow up and move on mani, hawu, nxxxx!

—I'm dispirited, but I won't let Tuvy run me out of this country, it's my country. I'll stay right here and fight every day until Jidada is truly free! And I won't give up on the election process either because that is exactly what the Seat of Power wants, that we get frustrated and sit out so they can manipulate things. As long as I have breath in me I'll keep fighting.

—Maybe what we should've done was resist the coup. Maybe we'd have gotten somewhere.

—What is the Opposition planning about the way forward? Ngoba we can't be singing the same old song every election. I'm starting to think this Opposition is just useless.

—Don't try to make me feel guilty for celebrating the fall of the Old Horse, if I can go back to that moment I'd actually still celebrate the ugly dictator's downfall. That devil stole my life!

—If you thought Jidada under the Old Horse was shitty, then shit is about to hit the sky proper-proper. When we say these beasts don't know how to govern, we mean these beasts don't know how to govern.

—This is actually the time to put aside our differences and work for one Jidada. All of us. Maybe this New Dispensation can work out if we come together, if we give it time.

—Me, I'm not going anywhere. For the why? My business is doing fine, my family is doing fine, the weather in Jidada is great! One can live well and in peace here as long as they stay in their lane. So I'm in my lane, no politics for me and my house, thank you very much!

—Someone ought to shoot all these goddamn parrots singing the stupid New Dispensation song. I'm just sick of it.

—With all due respect I don't really see what the big problem is. Because it's not like we haven't been here before, because we have. If we survived the Father of the Nation for forty years we'll accordingly survive the Savior for another forty. Then survive the next and the next and the next. Jidadans are resilient.

—What I want to know is where our so-called neighbors are. And where is SADC? The AU? And why is SA quiet when it has millions of Jidadans within its borders? Why is it not invested in Jidada's liberation when what happens here clearly affects what happens over there?

—Now we will get to see the New Dispensation dispense us out of the Old Horse's ruin into a New Jidada! The Savior is the change we've been waiting for!

—What we really need to do is figure out what we're going to do about our predicament. It's just two choices really. If we allow this wretched party to hold us hostage all our lives or we wage war.

—The irony of it! We thought we were marching into freedom, when we were actually marching into more tyranny!

—Don't tell me God is watching. Coz all my wretched life he's been watching; how long, really, does a God need to watch shit burn before he intervenes?

—Well, Jidada is open for looters now. Just mark my words.

SHITHOLE COUNTRY TO YOU, THOLUKUTHI ELDORADO TO THE POWER

When those who know about things said the Seat of Power and the Chosen entered an obscene season of pillaging and plunder, they mean the Seat of Power and the Chosen entered an obscene season of pillaging and plunder. Of course they had for decades been a party of looters, but now, basking in the afterglow of the election win, what with the New Dispensa-

tion, what with Jidada being open for business, what with none other than Tuvius Delight Shasha as Jidada's second president, the taking simply reached never-been-seen, gargantuan levels. They looted with the brazen audacity of intoxicated baboons, without any shame whatsoever. As far as they were concerned, they in fact owned Jidada with a -da and another -da, yes, tholukuthi her immeasurable riches theirs to take. And take they did, just take-

take-take-take-take-take-take-take-take-take-take-take-take-take-take-
take-take-take-take-take-take-take-take-take-take-take-take-take-
take-take-take-take-take-take-take-take-take-take-take-take-take-take-
take-take-take-take-take-take-take-take-take-take-take-take-take-take-
take-take-take-take-take-take-take-take-take-take-take-take-take-take-
take.

Still, no matter how much they pillaged and plundered, the Seat of Power and Chosen found themselves drowning in an ocean of wealth beyond their wildest dreams. Which is perhaps why they gave in to their imaginations, tholukuthi descended on their barely frequented villages and built massive roads for use during village funerals or occasional holidays. They installed generators and the kinds of equipment to make the animals languishing in darkness and lining in water queues throughout the miserable cities of Jidada envious. They funded the makeovers of rivers so that the river bottoms were scooped out and replaced with imported marble, and they completed the makeovers by installing sunbathing decks on the shores so the mermaids and fishes and frogs and worms and snails and insects and all the creatures of the river could come out of the water and take up the sun in style. In forests and jungles in and around their villages they hung hammocks made of organic materials for lions and leopards to lounge and frolic in. They laid out expensive imported carpets underneath fruit trees so that ripe fruit didn't fall on dirt and bruise. They installed elevators on the mountains so that mountain animals could go up at the push of a button. They built slide parks and state-of-the-art jungle gyms so wild animals could stay fit. And because it was the age of the internet, yes, tholukuthi a time in which nothing actually happened, nothing was real and true and compelling until it was posted on Instagram and Twitter and Facebook for the whole world to see it, the owners of Jidada accordingly shared their wealthy lifestyles on social media, showing off,

celebrating the fortune of endless bounty from a Jidada that kept giving and giving.

LIVING THE DREAM

With a Free, Fair, and Credible election victory in his pocket, Tuvius Delight Shasha, son of Zvichapera Shasha, most favorite and most successful son of Buresi Shasha, is acting president no more but His Excellency in his very own right at long last. And he won despite the attempts of the Opposition and its Western sympathizers who, not surprisingly, had pulled all kinds of gimmicks, including spreading fake news of rigging and violence—the malevolent Opposition stopping at nothing, tholukuthi challenging His Excellency's victory all the way to the Highest Court of the land itself, where the esteemed Judge, Chief Justice Honorable Kiyakiya Captured Manikiniki, presided, but there too, the Savior of the Nation won and still emerged the Chosen one.

Now, thirty-eight thousand or so feet aboveground, His Excellency, Comrade President, floats in blissful repose, his great head empty of worry. The quiet, the peace he feels, is absolutely divine. He knows he is dreaming, because this is an old dream from his early years of growing up in the village and so he is reluctant to open his eyes and emerge from it. And when he finally does, it's as if he's woken from the dream only to enter another; tholukuthi this because in reality he is in a luxurious jet that looks just like the jet in his dream.

As a colt growing up in the village, one of the young Tuvy's favorite pastimes was identifying vehicles by their engine sound. At the distant hum of approaching cars, he and his young friends would emerge from the bush, where they played war all day—their game of choice being that the country was at the time embroiled in the bitter Liberation War. The young

Comrades would huddle together, still as flamingos, tilt their heads, ears cocked to take in the distant roar of motors toiling up and down and up and down the hilly road that was also the only main road in the village, yes, tholukuthi a road with two names depending on who was talking— Rhodes Road for white animals, and Independence Road for Black animals. The exercise was a game of divination that filled young Tuvy with an excitement that sometimes made it hard to properly hear the cars for the sound of his own heart beating in his ears. The young animals heard buses. They heard tractors. Jeeps. Range Rovers. Dodge Rams. Peugeots. Datsuns. They howled the makes and models out loud and waited with bated breath for the cars to appear so they could see if they were right.

And when the tired, dust-covered vehicles eventually came into view, the young animals galloped to the edge of the road, and if their guesses were correct—and Tuvy was almost always right—they shrieked and danced in the dust and claimed the cars that were driven by the white animals as theirs. The squad would wave and watch the cars that were now theirs but that they didn't own pass them by, tholukuthi their young hearts aching for something they knew by feel because they'd been born with the feeling that'd been passed on to them by their parents who too had been born with the feeling that'd been passed on to them by their own parents who were infected with the feeling from when the white animals first appeared from faraway lands across faraway seas to not only usurp their lands but to also rule them. And after their cars that they didn't own had moved on without them, disappearing in billowing clouds of dust, the young animals would retreat to the bush to pick up their toy guns fashioned from sticks, bombs and grenades made from rock, and resume their play war over things that were no play matter.

OF DREAMERS OF GREAT DREAMS

Always, the young Tuvy stayed in the fantasy of the cars, yes, tholukuthi nursing it like a fresh wound as he went about his daily chores and the mundane tasks of village life until at night he took the fantasy to his bed like a secret lover, yessir, tholukuthi where he dreamed his recurrent dream of not just a car but of an aeroplane, and not just an aeroplane but a luxurious jet, the kind of which had not been seen over Jidada skies and indeed in the whole wide world because it would only exist in the distant future. A jet so magnificent the young Tuvy imagined the angels would sneak away from heaven and come to frolic around the supreme machine and take what at that time there was no word for but would come to be known, decades and decades later, as selfies.

The first time Tuvy confided his dream to his mates during their usual game of war they'd howled with cruel laughter at the outrageousness of it, the silliness of it, the impossibility of it, yessir, taunting him so much that the hot-tempered colt raised his AK-47 and, seeing red from rage, summarily executed all his friends before galloping away. It was the last time he held a toy gun—not too long after, he'd persuade his uncle, a village war recruiter, to drop him off at a training camp, where he joined the armed struggle for Jidada's Independence. He held too, in his heart, where most of the Comrades held the dream of a free Jidada, another secret dream—his luxurious jet.

"Eh, Comrade," the Savior says, addressing no one in particular. At the sound of His Excellency's voice, a goat and cock promptly appear, Scarves of the Nation around their necks.

"Who is that one who said that 'I Have a Dream' poem?" Tuvy says.

"You mean Dr. Martin Luther King Jr., Your Excellency?" the cock says.

"Yes that one. Tell me again what they said he said," Tuvy says.

"I have a dream that one day even the state of Mississippi, a state

sweltering with the heat of injustice, sweltering with the heat of oppression, will be transformed into an oasis of freedom and justice." The goat, who's interrupted the cock, finishes his recitation with a voice trembling with emotion, eyes tearing, a hoof across his bony chest because it feels like his heart will break from Martin Luther King's haunting freedom song. He doesn't look at the cock, who glares at him for stealing his moment.

"I remember now. Yes that's what he said. He reminds me of my own dream, as if he had a sorcerer's powers to look into the future from back then and hear and know what I'd dream years later, and then fashion his dream from my dream," Tuvy says.

"It is indeed very likely that the great Dr. Martin Luther King was indeed inspired by your dream, Comrade Excellency, through some strange shifts in time," the cock says, seizing the moment to put in a word.

"Yes, a dream that was born out of the injustice of seeing white animals own what we'd never dream of owning in the very land of our Fathers, but of course you can't banish a dream so I did what, I dreamed in defiance. Yessir, I dreamed that one day I too would sit, not at a table, no, because even a miserable dung beetle can find its way onto a table; I instead dreamed of a luxurious jet exactly like this. And now here I am." Tuvy beams with the bright sparkle of achievement.

"And here you are, Your Excellency!" the cock and goat cry in unison, glaring at each other. Tuvy, oblivious to the hostile competition, leans back into his chair, closes his eyes, and gets lost in his living dream.

While the jet is the Savior's private aircraft, it is also his moneymaker—he rents it to the government of Jidada, which in many ways is really him himself; the government then in turn pays him in the neighborhood of a million US dollars for a trip such as this one. Of course it isn't, by any means, his only business—the Savior owns fuel stations, kiosks, mines, brothels, soccer teams, taxis, pay-as-you-enter toilets, supermarkets, hair

salons, restaurants, banks, real estate, illegal cross-border transport, beer halls, colleges, buses, yes, tholukuthi a diverse range of assets because he is not an arrogant investor—as long as it brings money, he's in it.

He smiles, remembering Marygold, his newest mistress, a mare barely a third his age: "What is the best thing about serving, My Excellency?" she'd asked him not too long after his inauguration, nibbling at his ears. "The wealth!" he'd said without skipping a beat. "And the hardest?" she said. "Spending it!"

THOLUKUTHI THE SAVIOR SERVES, THE SORCERER SEES

"Ha! I see you're thinking about your riches again, Chief," Jolijo says, seating himself next to the Savior.

"How do you know, Comrade Jolijo?" Tuvy looks at the cat with a satisfied gleam.

"Isn't it my job to know what His Excellency is thinking? Besides, if that isn't the face of one of the richest African presidents, then I don't know what it is," Jolijo says, chuckling blithely. He makes to cross his legs but fails, yessir, tholukuthi fails because he is getting so big, so enormous he could kick little dogs out of his way like empty tin cans. But there was a time, when he was just a high school divinity teacher, that Jolijo was a skinny cat who could not only cross his legs but also summersault over fences and Durawalls without missing a beat.

Still, you wouldn't necessarily know from looking at the cat now that he's an even bigger cat—yes, tholukuthi that this very Jolijo, full name Jolijo Perfect Maposa, chief sorcerer to the Seat of Power, son of Perseverance and Rebecca Maposa, former teacher thanks to his brilliant identical late twin brother's academic credentials, now ranks among the top fifty richest animals in Jidada with a -da and another -da. Recently, the sorcerer's duties have expanded to include membership on Jidada's Special

Committee that comprises just him and His Excellency; as it were, following Tuvy's election victory, Jolijo has helped review and select appointments to Jidada's pivotal ministries, governorships, judgeships, top army ranks, and such positions as critical to the Seat of Power.

"And is all well, Comrade Jolijo?" Tuvy says.

"Should I start with good news or bad news, Chief?" Jolijo says. The look on the Savior's face makes the cat regret the quip.

"First, on the matter of the sun—"

"Did you fix it? You know I must absolutely command that sun."

"Right, about that, Your Excellency, I'm afraid I don't have good news. It seems the Former First Femal, Dr. Sweet Mother, well, how do I put it—ruined it, Your Excellency."

"What do you mean ruined it, Comrade Jolijo?! How in the New Dispensation can anyone ruin the sun? Doesn't it rise and set every day all over the world?"

"You are very correct, Your Excellency. But it seems Jidada's sun wasn't at all supposed to be commanded by a femal in the first place, just as it isn't supposed to be commanded by miserable, inferior ethnicities. By commanding it, what Dr. Sweet Mother did essentially angered the gods, who have apparently decreed that it will be another hundred years before any Jidadan ruler is able to command the sun again." The sorcerer speaks in a grave voice.

"But I'll be dead in another hundred years, Comrade Jolijo!" Tuvy cries, mortified.

"Well, yes and no, Your Excellency. And by that I mean yes, your body, as with all living bodies, will expire, and yes you will indeed die death, but no, you don't need to stay dead at all. With the right rituals— and I didn't say it will be easy, but it can be done—you can be brought to life and rule all over again."

"Is it a good time, Your Excellency, am I interrupting?" says a compact pig in a black suit, looking first at Tuvy and then at Jolijo.

"It's always a good time, Comrade Doctor. Comrade Jolijo here was just on his way." The Savior signals the cat to leave. Jolijo slinks off without acknowledging the pig.

The Savior chuckles; it is no secret his sorcerer does not like Brilliant Nzinza, the newly minted Minister of Finance. "He has quite the arrogant airs of a sewer rat, he thinks he's better because he was educated in the West and talks like a goddamn book, I tell you he's no Comrade-Comrade, Chief, he'll cause us problems, this blali swine," the sorcerer had protested on the pig's prestigious appointment—one of the very few instances the Special Committee had been sharply opposed. It was of course to no avail, tholukuthi even the sticks and stones know that the pig, with his impressive credentials and solid international career, besides being highly intelligent, is an economics wizard. That if there's anyone to raise Jidada's wasting economy from the deathbed, he's just the animal to do it. Comrade Doctor is Tuvy's nickname for the pig, and one that's very quickly stuck.

A NEW MEMBER OF THE FAMILY

"You know the whole of Jidada, and indeed the world, have been raving nonstop about you, Comrade Doctor. Not to mention the Comrades, who are all excited to have you in the family. And it's a big family as you can see." Tuvy laughs, brings his seat to an upright position. The pig wiggles into the opposite chair.

"Big family. Gotta love it, sir. But—"

"But? And please, call me—"

"My apologies, Your Excellency, this is all rather new to me," the

Minister lies in a meek voice, wincing and adjusting his green glasses. Tholukuthi the truth is that he verily loathes this colonial business of titles.

"I was saying, about the family, sir," the Minister says.

"The family?" Tuvy says, frowning.

"Yes, you were talking about the family, the Comrades—"

"Ah, yes, the Comrades. As you can see, it's a big family, so tight-knit that when you see one of us you see two, three dozen, if not more, be it on land or in the air. And we intend to show the world wherever we go that we're ready to lead Jidada to proper glory. And that is the message we'll communicate at this big party, this gathering, this—mnxxxxm, zviya what do they call this thing where we're going, Comrade Doctor?" Tuvy says, carefully rearranging the scarf around his neck.

"We're going to the World Economic Forum at Davos, sir," the Minister says.

"That is the message we'll communicate at this World Economic what?" Tuvy says.

"Forum, forum, sir, at Davos," the Minister says.

"Yes. That is the message we'll communicate at this World Economic Forum at Davis," Tuvy says. He doesn't see the barely perceptible shake of the minister's head.

"Exactly, and that's fantastic, Your Excellency. While we're here, I've been meaning to make a suggestion."

"Go ahead, Comrade Doctor. Isn't that what you're here for?"

"Thank you, sir. The thing is, I think the, well, family is just—a tad too big, for lack of a better word, Your Excellency." The Savior jerks his head back, not understanding.

"I just mean, for things like this—traveling, Your Excellency. Given that it's only you and I speaking at this forum, I don't quite see why and how the likes of Jolijo are on this trip, not to mention the scores of Youth

Leaders who can't speak a coherent sentence and who right now are getting wasted at the back of the plane, and we have to pay them a daily allowance on top of it."

"I see," the Savior says.

"Exactly, Your Excellency! In my humble opinion this trip really needed less than a quarter of this entourage. Which would in turn mean that instead of this big jet, we just fly maybe business, allowing us some huge savings. With about over thirty trips already, Your Excellency has actually spent about two hundred million in under a year on travel, for instance, which could have very easily been slashed to—" The pig stops speaking, the numbers he'd meant to rattle off, drowned by the horse's morbid laughter.

PRINCIPLES OF GOVERNANCE

"To clarify, what I meant, Your Excellency, our spending numbers definitely need to come down big-time, and this is one very easy way of doing it. And honestly I'm thinking about the larger picture, and taking into account that a big part of how we win depends on changing the culture of how we do things. We're open for business, but it can't be business as usual," the Minister says.

"Well, I hear you, Comrade Doctor. I know you just came on board, but in the Seat of Power, in the Party of Power, how we do things, how we've always done things is, it takes a village. And nothing embodies that spirit like this, all this," Tuvy says, proudly gesturing at the rest of the jet, at the luxury amenities, at the back section, where the Comrades and his femals are drinking and feasting.

What the President is thinking, at the same time, is how the pig has some strange ideas. Him, the Savior of the Nation, His very Excellency of Jidada with a -da and another -da, a whole head of state, flying in a

miserable regular plane? What for? As if he were just an ordinary animal? What on earth would be the significance of his dream from his young years, and why does it keep recurring, even now? It is madness, yessir, utter, total madness. Just like that other fool—whatshisname?—who reportedly not only flies in an ordinary plane but flies economy class and still considers himself president of a country. And then there is the other one he saw on the Facebooks who drives himself around in a battered old car. And what of ministers in Europe who are said to go to work on trains and in taxis? Imagine, a whole minister in Jidada in a raggedy taxi—for most taxis on Jidada's miserable, pothole-infested roads are indeed unfit— yes, in taxis that had to stop at every light, some of which didn't always work, being harassed by ugly vendors and ill-mannered beggars and wretched delinquent orphans. What, then, would have been the point of going to war? Of the fruits of Jidada's liberation? What would even be the point of ruling? And not to mention, how on earth, why on earth, with all the enemies he has, would he ever dream of going anywhere without his sorcerer? And what would be the point of leaving his ugly wife behind if he cannot gallivant with his beautiful mistresses? What kind of miserable ruler would he be if he were to travel without his dancers to remind him of it? And his Defender killers as backup to the Scarf? The Party of Power Youth to protest sanctions?

Tholukuthi on the intercom, the pilot announces they have begun their descent into Davos.

"I guess this is it, Your Excellency, we're almost there." The Minister beams with palpable excitement.

While the pig has strange ideas, Tuvy still likes his confidence, especially when it comes to dealing with the Westerners. He's seen him walk into a room and simply own it as if it were his grandmother's township kitchen, tholukuthi talk about what was Jidada's, and indeed the Party of

Power's, most important question of the moment, that is, the New Dispensation, so that the room itself seemed to shine from Jidada's upcoming glory.

S IS FOR THE SAVIOR SAVING JIDADA FROM SANCTIONS

"You know what me I think will make a real difference, Comrade Doctor?"

"No, Your Excellency, I don't."

"Yes, you don't know, Comrade Doctor, so let me tell you. What I think will make a difference is to have these sanctions lifted once and for all. Or at least some of them, because they're just crushing us! Do you have a feeling we are maybe getting somewhere? I mean, you know these animals better than I do," Tuvy says. The pig pulls at his ears, adjusts his glasses.

"Ehm, I think we're on the right path, Your Excellency, especially with all this goodwill from all over that wouldn't have been possible not too long ago, with the Old Horse ruling. I say we'll be fine as long as we convince the world we're a government of true transformation and not just rhetoric. Revive our democracy and supporting institutions. Restore constitutionalism. Commit to resuscitating the economy. Have a strong anticorruption stance. And most importantly, real reforms. These are just some of the things that will give investors, and indeed the whole world, the confidence to begin taking us seriously again." The pig bobs his head in agreement with himself.

"Well, I do hear all of that, but I mean, it can't all happen overnight—even the elders tell us in their proverbial wisdom that rushing is not the same thing as arriving. They should look at us today, where we are now. I mean we've won the #freefairncredible elections, as everyone saw. We've

brought in the best cabinet Jidada's ever seen and you're a part of it. The birds and insects of the nation are as we speak filling the airs and skies and trees and hedges with the now famous New Dispensation song. Surely, with all these things going for us, some of the sanctions should be easing off right about now, no, Comrade Doctor?"

"Well, it might help us to remember that sanctions aren't really our biggest problem, Your Excellency. As you know, they're mostly on corrupt members of the Seat of Power, along with animals and entities who've been implicated in rights abuses and undermining democratic processes, otherwise Jidada as a country has no serious restrictions standing in the way of our progress. I also want to reiterate, Your Excellency, that one of my priorities, even before sanctions, as I've said before, is managing this ginormous debt—" the pig breaks off because the horse silences him with a raised hoof.

"But who in today's world is without debt, really, Comrade Doctor? Every country has debt, even the Tweeting Baboon tweets sitting on a mountain of debt as we speak, no?"

"True, Your Excellency. But just ours hasn't been paid in some decades, as you know. That debt means we can't access credit to jump-start the economy as needed, and we unfortunately can't simply sweet-talk our way out of it. And of course, as if we don't have enough challenges, at the same time we're losing at least a billion US dollars a year to corruption alone."

"Well, about that—we're getting somewhere. In case you haven't been paying attention, for the very first time in history we've been busy catching animals left right and center in our anti-corruption sting, and I mean catching them like flies, Comrade Doctor, like fish, you know, just catch catch catch catch. Catch," Tuvy says, wildly gesticulating.

"Right, and I congratulate you, Your Excellency, sir, for taking initiative. But I saw, and it was noted all over social media, that after you caught the offenders—like fish, as you say—you released them."

"We released them, yes. But after catching them! The thing is to demonstrate our capacity to catch, that's what's important."

"With all due respect, Your Excellency, the reality is corruption is our biggest problem. If we take a hard-line stance like, say, China—a few weeks ago a top minister there was executed for corruption involving a couple hundred thousand dollars, just to give an example."

"What, just two hundred thousand? And a whole minister gets killed? Do you know, Comrade Doctor, that if I ever took that approach, I'd have less than five animals in my whole entire government? And what would be the good of that?"

"Well, maybe it's a little excessive, but it still sends the right message, say, as opposed to simply catching an animal and releasing them to continue with their deeds. And mind you he's not alone, there's a planeload of them doing the same exact thing. The point is three decades ago countries like China, Singapore, were poorer than Jidada. Part of why they're where they are now, and of course there are many factors, is an uncompromising stance on corruption. It really works, Your Excellency, trust me, I've seen the results," the Minister says. The horse, not for the first time, looks at the pig with wonder.

So far, for all the talk about his brilliance, all the Savior is seeing of the Minister is a difficult animal who sounds very much like an agent of the Opposition. Again, which is part of the problem with having animals who aren't bona fide members of the Seat of Power or even the Party, in such important positions, as it is—isn't everyone in the jet wearing the Scarf of the Nation except the pig? He'd have to watch the swine because if unwatched, he'd challenge the soul of the Seat of Power, and if he were allowed to challenge the soul of the Seat of Power, he'd in fact begin to think he was there to be in charge of things, and if he began to think he was there to be in charge of things, he'd in fact change them so that no one would recognize Jidada with a -da and another -da.

THOLUKUTHI ECONOMICS FOR DUMMIES

"But I've been thinking, in the meantime, that perhaps the citizens can help us move toward a working economy more quickly if they can share a little of the burden, just a very small amount in order to help us generate a bit of the much-needed revenue," the Minister says. The horse sits up, ears pricked. This is what the pig is both paid and expected to be doing with those famed brains of his, yessir, tholukuthi coming up with practical, commonsense solutions to problems.

"I'm listening, Comrade Doctor, I'm listening, tell me."

"Well, I was thinking of a very small tax, Your Excellency, nothing big, say, on electronic transfers being that the whole of Jidada uses the system—"

"Aha!" Tuvy says, interrupting Comrade Doctor. It's perhaps the best thing he's heard come out of the Minister's mouth in a while. "I like the idea. Very much. To simply tax tax tax tax tax, just tax, until voilà! We have funds and funds and funds, just funds all over. But do you know what would even be better, Comrade Doctor?"

"No I don't, Your Excellency."

"Yes you don't know, let me tell you. What'd be better is to add a small fuel increase while we're at it. To at least double that revenue because why not, don't they say two heads are better than one? I mean, the whole of Jidada runs on fuel, which I coincidentally happen to supply as you very well know. Can you imagine just how much money stands to be made?"

"Don't you think that'd be a bit, um, overwhelming though, Your Excellency? We don't want to ask too much all at once and push the citizens over the edge, especially as we're in the middle of trying to figure out this New Dispensation." The Minister is trying, and failing, to hide his discomfort.

"What do you mean, Minister? What edge?"

"I mean a rebellion, Your Excellency, or even violence. I may be wrong, but with the Father of the Nation being removed, I mean, leaving—for early retirement, Jidadans seem to have this whole new attitude," the pig says. The Savior tosses his head up and laughs a snorty, whiny laugh.

"You forgot we are talking about the Seat of Power of Jidada with a -da and another -da, Comrade Doctor. Violence is our thing, our language. So, give us unrest, give us protests, give us rebellions, give us a fight, give us anything you can think of, we're ready with that thing, what do they call that thing, Comrade Doctor?"

"Eh, I'm not quite sure, sir." The Minister scratches his snout.

"A go back to sender! That's how we deal with ungovernable elements, Comrade Doctor. They give us violence, we give them violence a hundredfold! Just like God in the Old Testament!"

"Hmmm. Me I don't know, Your Excellency—" the Minister says.

"Yes, you don't know! Because I'm the one who knows! We will convene with the Inner Circle once we finish with the rest of our trips on this leg, Comrade Doctor. I want to talk some more about this idea of yours, which is brilliant like your name," Tuvy says.

"Very well, Your Excellency, sir, I'll look forward to it. I'll get ready for landing, if you don't mind." The Minister rises.

The horse, remembering again the pig's mortified face, laughs anew. Whoever heard of rebellion in Jidada? The children of the nation can't actually spell the word. But should they for whatever reason even get it in their miserable heads to try anything, to disrespect his government, he will show them just what kind of president he is, yessir, he'll show them just what kind of government. He leans over, picks up a gadget on the seat next to him, presses the button thing to wake it up. The brilliant flag of Jidada greets him. He smiles. What do you know, a gadget that greets you

with your own flag if you want it to! And not just a gadget, but a gadget that also knows you, that you can talk to.

YEYI SIRI

"Yeyi Siri, Siri, how exactly do I make myself a government?" Tuvy says.

"Hello Tuvius Delight Shasha, Savior of the Nation and son of Zvi-chapera and most favorite and most successful son of Buresi Shasha, but why would you want to make yourself the government when you're already the government? You don't lead Jidada, you rule it, don't you?" Siri says.

A smiling Tuvy squirms in his chair. He is warmed by the thought that this Siri femal knows him well, knows him better than animals who imagine they know him.

"Yes, I am ruling, you are very correct, because I'm the Ruler. But I suppose my real question, Siri, is how I can rule without interference," Tuvy says.

"You mean like a dictator?" Siri says.

"I mean like the one who controls everything, who's in charge of everything, who has total power, you know?" Tuvy says.

"Yes, I know. As I said, a dictator. And that's an easy one, really, just look within, you know it's in you already, Tuvius Delight Shasha," Siri says. The Savior laughs out loud. It's her accent, the bright quality it lends to his name. He is reminded too that this is one of the many things he loves about Siri—her capacity to make him feel good without actually touching him.

"Yeyi Siri, tell me, what do you actually exactly look like?" he says, lowering his voice to what he imagines to be more than a friendly whisper. He loosens his tie and leans back into his chair.

It's a question he's always wanted to ask ever since Siri hollered at him the day following his second inauguration when he was fiddling with his

gadget, looking to see what they were saying about him on the internets. He'd been startled by the unexpected femal voice talking about, "What can I help you with?" talking about, "Go ahead, I'm listening." And while he was generally suspicious of forward femals, her calm voice had made him drop his guard, for which he is perpetually glad. Because this Siri, who is intelligent and knows everything and will answer a question any time of day and will sound the same regardless of what she is feeling, who also hasn't even asked him for a single penny, this Siri, yes, tholukuthi Siri who doesn't nag like his ugly, babbling wife Matilida, Siri who isn't a nuisance like most of his femals, is such a delight.

But somehow the Savior hasn't been able to bring himself to ask the question that sometimes gives him sleepless nights in which he'll lie on his back next to Matilida, tholukuthi hooves pawing at the dark like a miserable cat, too distracted to sleep. Tholukuthi thinking of Siri. Imagining Siri. Wondering about Siri. The shape of her face. Her smile. The color of her eyes. Her gait. The rhythm of her breathing. Her smell. The swoosh of her tail. And now that he has done it, asked the question he's always wanted to ask, he feels giddy, like he's just cleared a high fence.

"Well, close your eyes, clear your mind . . . that's what I look like," Siri says. Tuvy neighs, tickled.

"Comrades, please prepare for landing. Forward with the Party of Power!" The pilot's voice comes over the intercom.

"Forward!!!" the plane explodes in an uproar.

"Is there anything else I can help with?" Siri says.

"I think that will be all for now, thank you, Siri," Tuvy says.

"Sure thing," Siri says.

The Savior presses the button on the gadget, closes it, and puts it away. Tholukuthi thinking of Siri all over again. Imagining Siri. Wondering about Siri. The shape of her face. Her smile. The color of her eyes. Her gait. The rhythm of her breathing. Her smell. The swoosh of her tail. At

that moment, his parade of femal dancers appears. The Savior neighs, beaming, tail swishing. The individual and collective beauty now before his eyes makes him want to levitate. The femals are dressed for him, yes-sir, tholukuthi in regalia, his effigies on their teats and hips and stomachs. He laughs the laughter of a satisfied animal who knows the one truth, which is that no matter where you rule, be it on earth, in hell, or indeed in the very high heavens themselves; no matter how it is that you came to power, tholukuthi whether you're God's son, a king, an elected leader, or decreed to rule—you just aren't worth any salt if you've never been worn on the dizzying bodies of shimmying, gyrating femals.

THOLUKUTHI PROMISED LAND

NEW DISPENSATION NIGHT

Simiso stood at her usual spot in the living room, ironing, when Destiny appeared with the discontented look of one who hadn't quite finished her sleep. She lingered by the doorway and watched her mother run a probing hoof over an immaculately smoothed pillowcase. Simiso frowned a frown of concentration, pressed the appliance so hard on the material the board creaked. The goat belonged among those for whom ironing was more than a chore, more than a task one did because they enjoyed it. Destiny could remember times in the past that her mother raided wardrobes for clothes that had already been ironed only to re-iron them. She remembered Simiso ironing every ironable thing in sight—from clothes to sheets to tablecloths to sofacloths to curtains to towels to cotton underwear, so that a very young Destiny once lived with the secret terror that one day her mother would in fact run out of things to iron and end up ironing her.

Tholukuthi with what she now knew of her mother's past, of April 18, 1983, Destiny finally understood, and with a gutting clarity, that all that

time, her mother wasn't really ironing clothes or material but was rather ironing some parts of herself. Yes, it was her therapy, Destiny, the only way she knew to deal with her trauma. Meaning that on top of being denied justice for decades, on top of having her immeasurable pain not acknowledged, there really has been no healing process for Simiso, which is most likely the case for the scores and scores of other victims. And which is sad, heartbreaking, outrageous, Destiny thinks, standing there by the door, feeling her blood heat up. She considered Simiso's near-entire life of ironing, wondered how many Jidadans were at that very moment on their feet, ironing or doing whatever they needed to do in order to not fall apart. She watched Simiso pick up a long white tunic dress—tholukuthi the same dress Destiny had worn on her return from the US—and give it a thorough shake before dampening it with water from a cup. The older goat turned the dress inside out, gave it another shake, and dampened it again. The clock on the TV stand struck one a.m. with an emphatic ding.

"You should go back to sleep, Destiny Lozikeyi Khumalo, this waking up in the dead of night clearly isn't for you," Simiso said, without looking up from her ironing board.

Destiny plopped onto a sofa, surprised by how her mother could sound this bright, this alive, at such an hour. Like most of the denizens of Lozikeyi and indeed the rest of Jidada, Simiso was up doing household chores because of the recent power cuts that had reconfigured the day so that in the hours between ten p.m. and five a.m., Jidadans who couldn't otherwise afford solar or generators were bustling about, tholukuthi taking advantage of the electricity before the power cut at daybreak for a merciless stretch of seventeen hours. In addition to the chronic electricity shortages, water cuts were slowly becoming routine so that those who know about things were already predicting that Tuvy's New Dispensation would in no time turn Jidada into a ruin unlike anything the children of the nation had ever seen or imagined.

"It's really hard to sleep with SaSi's machines, too much noise," Destiny said. She stretched her legs in front of her and yawned. SaSi was the neighbor from directly across, who ran an informal welding business from his house, where the noise of some of his equipment made it impossible for his adjacent neighbors to get a quiet sleep.

"Well, it's township living. But then what can he or anyone do with the electricity situation being what it is; the day as we know it has ended."

"I know," Destiny said. But what she was thinking was that this was essentially the problem with Jidada—the impulse to normalize the Seat of Power's mediocrity; tholukuthi the willingness of citizens to get used to that which should have otherwise been the source of outrage. So that the Seat of Power in turn normalized the docility of the citizens and continued what was no less than defecating on their heads. She kept her thoughts to herself, however, reached for the remote control, and turned the TV on.

NEW DISPENSATION IN ACTION: TO ECONOMIC FREEDOM AND BEYOND

On-screen, a suited Savior, with the vice president, Judas Goodness Reza, and Brilliant Nzinza, the Minister of Finance, on either side of him, leads an entourage on a red carpet, the procession flanked between two columns of Defenders with guns ceremoniously pointed at the sky. In the background is a jet from which the Seat of Power has obviously emerged. Destiny, who refuses to watch the state channel, quickly changes to another station.

"Hawu, I thought I saw some Scarves of the Nation just a bit ago, was that Tuvy? Put him back on so we can see what he's doing," Simiso says. Back on the news program, Tuvy is posted in front of a toilet, looking important. A bright red ribbon goes all the way around the small building and folds in a neat oversize bow at the entrance. The Minister of Economic

Affairs and Development and the Minister of Things stand holding a giant scissors between them, trying to outsmile each other.

"What on earth? Is what I'm seeing really what I'm seeing?" Simiso says, squinting. The goat rests the iron and folds her hooves over her chest. At the bottom of the screen, a caption reads: "Jidada's President, Tuvius Delight Shasha, becomes first-ever shitting president to officiate at the opening of a pablic toilet." A newscaster's voice narrates to clips of Tuvy touring the facility, Tuvy testing a water tap, unrolling tissue paper, flushing a toilet, and admiring himself in the mirror. Then the clip cuts to Tuvy speaking into a microphone.

"It is very easy, my fellow Jidadans, to trivialize a toilet, but the way I see it, going to the toilet is essentially a job in itself. Our languages don't lie when they compel us to say things like: 'I am going to the toilet to do labor.' Because what, because it's essentially a type of work!" The assemblage roared and cheered. Tuvy beamed, adjusted his scarf, and waited for quiet.

"So, as Jidadans call for employment opportunities, I wish to assure the nation that as you can see, we are indeed committed to creating all kinds of jobs, and without discrimination. Just imagine the numbers that will walk through these doors, which will be open for business the very moment I cut this ribbon right here!" the Savior said to thunderous applause.

"The mention of jobs certainly reminds us of our economy, which as you know is very front and center in the concerns of the New Dispensation, and especially for our Minister of Finance, otherwise better known as Comrade Doctor," the Savior said. He had to stop for the fervent chants of "Comrade Doctor! Comrade Doctor! Comrade Doctor!"

"It is very, very important, then, at this crucial time for our economy, that we remind our Western friends to help us zoom to our projected success by relieving us of long-standing and immobilizing sanctions. And it is

equally important that you, my fellow Jidadans, take a firm stand against sanctions because they really do affect you directly as well as affect you the most. Anytime you see a problem with our economy, no matter how big, no matter how small, and whatever it is, I want you to understand that somewhere, somehow, sanctions have contributed to it. I implore you then to make it a point to always speak with one ringing, patriotic voice that will reverberate in the West and all over, to say, 'Down with Sanctions!' Can I hear a 'Down with Sanctions!'?"

"Down with Sanctions!" the Savior's audience roared.

THE REINVENTION OF NIGHT

"I actually think I'll leave some of this ironing and take a smallanyana nap in a bit," Simiso said, sizing up her heap of ironing.

"That won't be a mistake, Mother, an animal needs her rest. Vele kanti when did you get up?"

"Before the power came. Me and the Duchess and Mother of God are going to the hospital to check on Makhumalo and Witness, who's due anytime. I don't know how long we'll be there, so I want to rest well-well."

"I see, but aren't the doctors still on strike?"

"They are; yesterday made a month," Simiso said, and Destiny whistled.

"But from what they say, the nurses are working, and maybe some student doctors too, so we hope for the best."

"Which hospital?"

"Sally Mugabe Hospital. It's Dr. Fengu's hospital, so I'm thinking before we go I'll make a quick stop by his house and see if he can maybe help us with a contact. I hate to say it, but it's better if you have somebody on the inside to look out for you. If you want to come, we're leaving here ngabo five thirty so we're there for the seven-o'clock visit."

"No, y'all can go, Mother. Hospitals make me anxious with those medicinal smells, with all that misery." Out in the street, a vendor sang his wares in an upbeat voice. The goats looked at the clock at the same time.

"Yebana, the early bird catches the worm for sure; I wonder what he's selling at this hour," Simiso said.

"Bread," Destiny said. They both laughed a ringing, happy laughter.

"The things we'll see in this New Dispensation!" Simiso said.

"Well, Lozikeyi is up and bustling about, in a few hours animals are headed for school and work, why not make some money. Anyway, I guess I'm awake now, might as well go and cook for the day," Destiny said, rising.

"Make sure you cook that okra in the bottom drawer too, Destiny, it won't be long before it spoils, we can't be throwing food away."

Through the open windows a fresh breeze fluttered the curtains and brought with it the jumbled aromas of cooking foods as denizens prepared meals to last their families for the seventeen hours that power would be out. It also filtered in snatches of Lozikeyi noise: The cling-clang coming from the Duchess's kitchen next door. The faint voices of young mals milling about, probably leaning against Simiso's Durawall and sharing smokes. An occasional passing car. Footsteps. The electronic thump of music. It seemed improbable now that once upon a time in Lozikeyi, dead of night had been the domain of thieves and sorcerers and creatures of dark, and for most, a quiet time of rest, the body having been comforted with whatever there was to comfort it with before coaxing it to sleep in order that it get up the very next morning to face, bear, take on, go through, endure the coming new day.

TEACHER-VENDOR AND THE YOUNG SCHOLARS

Next door to Simiso, at the Duchess's house, Mr. Cheda, the bread vendor who'd been serenading Lozikeyi with his bread song since the return of

power, knocked on the living room door in a way that said he was known at the house. "It's Teacher-vendor!" he called out, accompanying his raps with the nickname given him by the children of Lozikeyi for the fact that he'd recently quit his job teaching maths at Lozikeyi High School to become a vendor. Tholukuthi from about midnight to the wee hours of morning, Teacher-vendor roamed the township selling bread, and while at it he offered tutoring services and homework help to students for a small fee, after which he hurried home to sleep for a few hours before going to the city center to sell used imported clothes for the rest of the day. The door was opened by his former student Zwile, a bright-eyed kitten who said, "Good morning, Mr. Cheda." She grabbed the two loaves of bread he held out to her and paid for them. Behind Zwile sat her little sister, Gloria, confronting an open exercise book with undeniable contempt.

"Good morning, Zwi, you're still up?" Teacher-vendor said.

"Yes, we're finishing, then we'll sleep a bit and wake up at six for school," Zwile said.

"But how come Miss Lozikeyi's up, is she studying for university? And why does she look like she's ready to maybe bite a lion?" Teacher-vendor asked in a teasing tone, nodding at Gloria, who was still in primary school, doing third grade. They laughed, which made Gloria puff up and glower.

"She doesn't want to do her homework, so she just sits there and takes forever. Gogo Moyo said she can't go to bed until she's done," Zwile said. Teacher-vendor tsk-tsk-tsked.

"Gloria, my friend. But what is it I hear? How do you plan on being a teacher when you won't do your homework?" Teacher-vendor said.

"Me, I don't want to be a teacher. They work very hard educating everyone but then they don't even make any money. Reason said that's why you're now selling bread and clothes, and that's why Sam's father left the university to fix cars at Number Two. What I really want to do is heal the sick," Gloria said, perking up for the first time.

"Hmn, I see. But everything still needs school, though, no? Even Dr. Fengu will tell you that you must have an education to treat the sick," Teacher-vendor said in his teacher voice.

"Dr. Fengu doesn't have a job anymore, you don't know? Golden Maseko said it's because the Savior's New Dispensation is kaka. Plus, me I want to treat people like the Duchess, so instead of school I'll go for training with mediums and learn about ancestors, traditional medicines, and channeling the spirits," Gloria said. Teacher-vendor laughed, rested a hoof on the doorframe.

"I see you're looking for a headache, Teacher-vendor," Zwile said with a laugh.

"Yoh! Y'all have an extra-large problem to the hundredth power in your paws, good luck to you! And how's your own homework? How was the chemistry test?"

"Today is pretty easy, so I'm good. We didn't write the chemistry test, though; Ms. Jiji left," Zwile said, suddenly crestfallen.

"Ms. Jiji left for where?" Teacher-vendor said, frowning.

"For Dubai, I guess, to teach," Zwile said.

"Hmn, that's interesting. Do you have her WhatsApp number by any chance?" Teacher-vendor said.

"Yes, I'll get my phone, its charging," the kitten said, and disappeared on the other side of a display cabinet. "It means we'll be behind again, and the exams are in just a few months, I really don't know how they expect us to pass," she called out, disconsolate.

Tholukuthi the serious straight-A student was in her final year of high school, and her dream was to be a doctor like her neighbor and role model, Dr. Fengu, never mind that at Lozikeyi High, as with many poor government schools throughout the country, students learned the sciences in part through imagination and storytelling since it was otherwise impossible to

conduct the necessary science experiments, because the school either was out of chemicals and equipment or had no backup sources of power for the fridges meant to preserve the precious experiments.

PORTRAIT OF A MEDICAL DOCTOR WHO CHOSE JIDADA WITH A -DA AND ANOTHER -DA

At the time that his young neighbor and admirer was busy with the homework she very much hoped would one day allow her to walk in his footsteps, seven houses away, the said doctor lay dreaming a recurrent dream of falling off a high cliff. He woke up thrashing and bellowing as usual, to find his wife, Soneni, holding him by the horns. She had an apron over her dress and the front was covered in flour. "When are you going to do something about those dreams, Future." She spoke in a way that said this wasn't the first time she was saying the words, and that she was tired of doing so. He moved her to the side as if she were a piece of misplaced luggage and rose without uttering a word.

"You're a doctor, for God's sake—surely you must know this isn't just going to go away on its own!" Soneni hissed at his retreating back. The house was suffused with the smell of curry. He proceeded to the bathroom as if she hadn't spoken, and urinated sitting. When he flushed, there was no water. He slammed the toilet lid, headbutted the wall, lashed the air with a frustrated tail, and stood a long time looking in the mirror. A tired, puffy face stared back at him with bloodshot eyes. He could hear Soneni on the phone, talking in an imploring voice. He was contemplating his reflection, ears straining to listen to Soneni, when he spotted the lone white hair on his chin. It startled him; he brought his head close to the mirror and examined himself. Tholukuthi he found two more, hidden in the thick clump of hair, shook his head and muttered, "Fuck, mal, shit."

"That was MaDumane," Soneni announced when he came out. He proceeded to the bedroom and began changing. "She was wanting to know when we'd catch up on the rent." She followed him and posted herself by the door.

"I don't know mani, wena do you?!" he bellowed, buttoning his shirt. He regretted his tone as soon as the words left his mouth, but then he quickly thought about the unfairness of the situation and found that he didn't quite regret them so much; tholukuthi it was what it was. Ever since Tuvy's New Dispensation regime had suspended him without pay, along with over five hundred doctors for a mass action that included a strike and calls for salary increases, improved working conditions, fuel or transportation to get to work, the bull was a hot keg of anger with a tail.

"Yazi njan', you don't need to talk to me with that tone, Father of Jabu, I'm just passing a message," Soneni said, hitting her hind leg with her tail, heat in her voice.

"And I don't need you passing stupid messages in the wee hours of morning like you haven't been here all along and don't know the situation, Soneni. Where do you expect the money to come from kanti? A river?"

"Sure, if at your mother's village y'all have rivers that flow money, then that's exactly where it will come from, Future!"

"What did you say about my mother, wena Soneni?" the doctor said, seeing red and whirling to face her. His head was lowered, neck curved to the side and horns perfectly poised. Soneni hinded.

"Exactly what I said! And trust me, I know the goddamned situation, Doctor Future Fengu!" Soneni snarled. Tholukuthi when he heard her call him "Doctor," he didn't need to be told what was coming.

"In fact I know it so much I advised against returning to this hellhole after graduation because guess what, even the sticks and stones could tell where this country was headed, it was just a matter of time. But was I ever

listened to? No ma'am! You were there, talking about, 'I came to the UK to get an education, I've gotten it, and now must move back home and use this degree to be part of the change I want to see!' Talking about, 'I need to be close to my aging mother, I'm her only son and she's counting on me to support her!' Talking about, 'I can't stand the racism, the weather, I can't live with this and that and stay sane!' Talking about, 'Jidada is my beginning and my end and there's no place like home!' So, no, Dr. Future Fengu, you, of all animals, don't get to tell me about no goddamned situation, and definitely not today!" Soneni bellowed. She stormed out of the bedroom, tholukuthi red embers in her eyes.

On getting to the living room she realized she in fact hadn't said all she needed to say, and so she halted, rotated her head without moving the rest of her body, and finished in a voice that was heard by Teacher-vendor, who at that very moment was standing at the door, preparing to knock and sell his bread to one of his favorite customers: "And you know what hurts, besides the fact that I warned this would happen, is having an uneducated nonentity like MaDumane vomit on me in her broken English, and knowing that had I not come to this useless ruin of a country I'd be owning a proper home instead of living in a dungeon where an animal can't do anything without the whole of this damned township knowing about it! Earning the salary I deserve! Driving the car of my dreams on proper roads! My children enjoying a normal upbringing and assured a decent life waited for them! Not living the indignity of having to decide, every payday, whether to buy food, pay for my children's school fees, or get them clothes!" the cow cried, her voice choking because thinking of the future of her children despaired her to no end.

Still, she got hold of herself and blinked away tears; tholukuthi she wasn't done. "I'd be far by now, Future; I'd be someone, I'd be like my friends who stayed behind and are living their dreams. If only you'd have let me

have a say and not become Mr. Know-it-all, if you hadn't been so hell-bent, so obsessed with a worthless country that'd never love you back, if only you'd dared to choose your own children like a normal parent, Dr. Future Fengu, but no, you did what, you chose this wreckage of a country where instead of a night's rest I'm up cooking! You chose this!" Soneni shrieked. And, having said her pain, she proceeded to the kitchen, where she continued her cooking with such aggression the whole house rang with the terrible din of her rage. Outside, Teacher-vendor, who stood holding his breath, lost his courage and turned around without ever knocking.

In the bedroom, Dr. Fengu, who'd finished dressing, closed the door and stood still, his whole body full of tension, his wife's voice ringing in his inner ear long after she'd ceased speaking. His perpetual headache, which had been quiet when he awoke, now pounded with the vengeance of an unappeased ancestral spirit; tholukuthi a searing, solid pain that occupied every space in his head. He longed to take the head off and rest it somewhere, even if it meant living without it, for it made him feel heavy, heavy, heavy. He held his heavy head between his hooves and squeezed. When he sat on the bed, the heaviness sat down with him like a faithful friend. Tholukuthi it wasn't the only thing that sat with him—his wife's resentment, too, came to sit, and so did what he knew to be her bottomless hurt. The feeling that he'd let her down, that he'd let his own children down, that he'd somehow failed all of them, came and sat with him as well, yes, tholukuthi that unbearable feeling he'd lived with for so long, that he knew so well. Then regret, too, came to sit with him, yes, tholukuthi the regret that it was too late to uproot, too late to pick up and go somewhere and maybe start all over, do things afresh, knowing what he now knew. Shame made its way to the bed and sat with him as well, yes, tholukuthi shame that even though he'd returned to Jidada intending to take care of his mother, MaDlamini, he now was often unable to provide for her the way a son should provide for his mother, yes tholukuthi a wid-

owed mother who'd sacrificed everything, who could've sacrificed even her own beating heart just to give her son every possible chance in order that he live the kind of life she never got to experience; yes, tholukuthi a knowledge that kept him up at night, eating away at his innards. The moment he thought of his job, pain came to sit with him, too, tholukuthi pain because he and his fellow doctors were being punished for simply asking for justice, for dignity. And that pain came with yet another pain as he remembered the many patients he'd seen die tragic, unnecessary deaths from treatable ailments, the far too many femals who daily died while giving birth, the desperately sick who were turned away because they were too poor to afford hospital fees. Disappointment, along with anger—at Tuvy, at the Seat of Power—also sat with him, because they were the very reason why Jidada was in this terrible situation, why he was in this predicament that sometimes felt like a long, endless dark night, yes, tholukuthi they were the reason he was sitting here in his bed, with all the things that'd come to sit with him growing and taking up space and more space, crowding him, pressing against him with an overwhelming gravity that made him long for a butterfly's untroubled flight.

THOLUKUTHI THERE IS NO NIGHT EVER SO LONG IT DOESN'T END WITH DAWN . . .

At about four fifty-five; a few minutes before power went out in Lozikeyi and the whole of Jidada with a -da and another -da, Simiso, already dressed up and finishing the last of her rooibos tea, heard the kind of sound that stopped her blood. The goat carefully hinded to the living room window, where she stood trying not to tremble, ears pricked, tholukuthi wondering if what she was hearing was indeed what she was hearing. When Destiny, who'd gone back to sleep, came rushing and said, "What is it, Mother, did you hear?" Simiso handed her an empty Kango

cup and said in a grave voice: "I have no idea, Destiny, but let me go and see since I'm already dressed."

By the time the goat found the keys to the gate and let herself out, the street brimmed with wide-eyed animals in pajamas, tholukuthi animals brandishing cooking utensils, animals between sleep and wakefulness. Around them, the air thrummed with the kind of voltaic wailing to power up the darkest night. The disorderly procession followed the tragic sound with dread, slowly, not knowing to what house it was leading them. When those who were there later told it, they said Gloria, the Duchess's grand-niece, appeared running against the crowd. They said it was like seeing a little apparition, for one minute the kitten was visible in the luminescence of the streetlight, high-pitched voice shrieking, "Dr. Fengu took a lot of pills and killed himself, Dr. Fengu is dead, Dr. Fengu has died death!" and the next minute she was gone, for the five a.m. power cut happened right about then, the morning darkness disappearing the little kitten, tholuku-thi disappearing every one of them gathered on that street, so it could've seemed that what was happening wasn't really happening.

QUEUENATION

RETURN OF THE LIVING QUEUES

It wasn't that long into Tuvy's rule that queues mushroomed with a vengeance all across Jidada. They bloomed and flourished at fuel stations. Outside grocery stores and supermarkets. At banks and bus stations. At passport offices and hospitals and government buildings and anywhere that animals sought services in numbers. Yes tholukuthi the children of the nation suddenly found themselves crammed together and without discrimination in unending lines—those who'd voted for Tuvius Delight Shasha and the Party of Power and those who'd voted for Goodwill Beta and the Opposition, tholukuthi those who'd voted for other candidates and those who hadn't voted at all, tholukuthi Black animals and white animals alike, tholukuthi young animals and old animals alike, tholukuthi Jidadans of any and every profession alike.

At first, because of the enduring optimism about the New Dispensation, and also because of decades of the Old Horse's atrocious rule that'd conditioned Jidadans to biblical levels of patience even in the most dismal of situations, the queues were reported to have had such outstanding

order, yes, tholukuthi in the beginning, animals were said to have been patient in the queues. They obeyed invisible lines and imaginary markers and stood with the neatness of rows of corn on a cob in the queues. In the beginning, tholukuthi animals said things like, "Excuse me, is this where the queue ends?" before joining the queues. They took care not to step on each other or push or shove in the queues. They held their heads high, made eye contact and grinned politely in the queues. They allowed the elderly and the pregnant and those living with disabilities to go to the head of the line in the queues. They read newspapers and checked Twitter and social media for the intelligent new Minister of Finance's updates on the New Dispensation economy in the queues. At first, animals made friends in the queues. They shared social media handles and followed each other in the queues. They complimented one another's dressing in the queues. They shared snacks in the queues. They talked about the weather and their favorite soccer teams and celebrities in the queues. They talked about the future and the New Dispensation and the Western countries that His Excellency had so far visited in search of funds to jump-start the economy in the queues. They shared recipes in the queues. They gave each other all sorts of advice—about the best spots in town, about how to grow difficult plants, about where to find the best cloth in the city, about how to discipline little ones in the time of technology, about the most trusted mechanics in town, about how to preserve water in the time of water cuts. In the beginning, tholukuthi the animals even dressed up to go to the queues. They took selfies in the queues. They waited their turn and didn't jump the line in the queues. They adjusted the Scarves of the Nation around their necks in the queues. They broke bread in the queues. They prayed for God's grace, and that he guide the Savior as he worked hard to serve and save the nation in the queues.

THOLUKUTHI WAYS OF QUEUEING

But as days turned into weeks and weeks into more weeks and months, it became clear to the animals that the queues were not going anywhere anytime soon. They said, those who know about things, that Jidadans found themselves suddenly standing exactly where they'd stood a decade before in those long-ago queues of the high-inflation crisis years of the Old Horse's rule that were believed, with his fall and the New Dispensation, to be a thing of a gone era, tholukuthi queueing for the same things they'd queued for back then, as if the tomb of the past had opened and let from deep inside its belly its stinking, festering corpse. And they stood there, the Jidadans, the miserable children of the miserable land, in the new queues that were also old, yes, standing disoriented and quiet and haunted by the trauma of previous queues. Their bodies remembered the postures of waiting from before and mechanically assumed them now: standing on two legs with feet slightly akimbo. The cousin of a warrior pose. Standing on all fours, the body's weight evenly distributed. Standing on hind legs, the back leaning against a wall, tail curled or tucked between the legs. Sitting on the pavement. Squatting. Holding on to walls. Sleeping in queues. Sleeping pressed together like hot loaves of bread in queues. Sleeping standing with one eye open in queues.

QUEUEDUCATION OF THE NEXT GENERATION

Tholukuthi there were also little ones, yes—the next generation, tholukuthi the future of the nation, who stood watching and listening and learning many things from the queues. The young ones learned to count up to ten from the bodies in the queues. They moved on to twenty, thirty, forty, fifty—all the way to a hundred in the queues. Then two hundred and three hundred and four-five-six, nine hundred and then a thousand in the queues. They learned addition and multiplication in the queues. As for reading,

tholukuthi they mastered the art of decoding and translating body language in the queues, and they also came to understand the best postures for standing for long periods, tholukuthi how to survive a disorderly queue, the most effective ways of turning queueing into a productive exercise, how to squeeze the body into impossible spaces, how to shove and how not to shove, how to fall without hurting oneself in the queues. They also learned other lessons in the queues—how to be patient, how to be resilient in the queues. From parents and adults who were otherwise no-nonsense and critical of Tuvy's government in the privacy of home, they learned how to be silent and subdued in the presence of Defenders, how to say things you did not mean or believe, how to swallow your burning rage even if it seared your throat and scorched your insides. From vocal adults who were also invincible at home they learned how to wilt and cower and not shit oneself in the presence of Defenders in the queues, how to be there and yet not be there. Day by day, the young ones carefully watched all kinds of bodies to see if it were possible to indeed stand that long, for those many days, many weeks, many months in the queues, tholukuthi without breaking, without falling apart, without coming unhinged.

EVEN ON A HYENA'S ANUS THERE ARE CLEAN PATCHES

Tholukuthi time, which stops for no one, not even beautiful queens, went on. Bit by bit, the patience, the optimism in the queues began to falter. Tholukuthi animals turned bitter and hostile in the queues. They broke into fights and bit each other in the queues. They no longer read newspapers or checked on the intelligent Minister of Finance's Twitter updates in the queues. They didn't take selfies anymore in the queues. They stopped tweeting in the queues. Animals abused the staff who attended them, as well as the security who were trying to maintain order in the queues. They jumped the line in the queues. Thieves picked pockets and commit-

ted robbery in the queues. Tholukuthi femals were violated in the queues. Animals grew sick and tired in the queues. They reached the limits of their despair in the queues.

It was thus understandable they found refuge in what, in memories of the past. Tholukuthi the past. They flung themselves onto the exercise of remembering with such gargantuan force that past actually came to life. And they very carefully skirted the undesirable, complicated, and painful parts, rather choosing to concentrate on the glory. And standing in the queues, they shook their heads and clutched at their hearts and lost themselves to long-gone days, honeyed by time and distance now and therefore even more glorious than they'd really ever been. Yes, tholukuthi those days long before things fell apart, when the Father of the Nation was for the most part a proper Father of the Nation who fathered fatherly, and living was not only possible but also beautiful and the future the kind of bright thing to look forward to.

How they clutched at that past even though it was really in their heads. Which is perhaps why on returning to their homes from the miserable queues at the end of the day they found themselves looking for, reaching for the Father of the Nation's memorabilia. They opened cupboards and closets to retrieve old, stained newspapers from his days of glory. They opened metal trunks and pulled out thick photo albums full of his pictures. They slit open homemade pillows stuffed with his regalia, grateful they hadn't gone all the way and burned it like they'd been tempted to do, there, during his ouster, when they were senseless with the euphoria of what then seemed like a new and better era.

Tholukuthi all these things gave them comfort and dulled their pain, and, to their delightful surprise, brought the Father of the Nation close to them somehow. They in fact began to see him in their dreams. His face was on the surface of their cups when they drank tea and afterward remained at the bottom of their cups, among the dregs of tea leaves. They

saw his face again in the toilet bowl, both before and after flushing. It was also in the sun and also in the moon. They heard his voice in voice mail recordings. They saw his names written in the wind. Saved in their phones and doodled on their walls and stuck to their fridges. Embroidered on their hankies and tablecloths. Sewn into the insides of their clothes and the insides of their blankets. They smelled him in the food they cooked, in their perfumes, in the scents of flowers and trees.

He was in their every other thought, and they in fact longed for him, fantasized about him so much that the force of their collective nostalgia got so potent it made the Father of the Nation once materialize in one of the biggest queues in the capital city, yes, tholukuthi he was suddenly there, standing on hind legs and singing the old revolutionary national anthem. And animals queueing all over the city heard the very first notes not with their ears but with their hearts and intestines and fell over each other following the voice. It led them all the way to the main branch of the Reserve Bank of Jidada, and indeed they found him there, in the thick of the thickest queue, yes, the Father of the Nation, tholukuthi him and only him himself, looking absolutely regal, looking like he'd looked back in the days of glory.

And the Father of the Nation and the children of the nation stood together and sang the old revolutionary national anthem until it became more than a thing to sing, until it became a living, breathing entity that spoke for itself, that told every one of them what a nation was all about, what liberation was all about, what unity was all about, what democracy was all about, what dignity was all about, what equality was all about, what citizenship was all about, what peace was all about, what justice was all about, what love was all about, what family was all about, what kindness was all about. Each and every one of them understood the anthem unlike they'd understood it before; and tholukuthi life was around them, and hope was around them, and the promise of everything good was around them.

But then the revolutionary anthem, like all songs, like all good things,

came to an end—after all, there is no night so long it does not end with dawn. And the children of the nation emerged from their collective fantasy, opened dazed eyes to find the Father of the Nation gone with a puff and nowhere near, for in reality he and the donkey, taking advantage of the increasing need for him to be closer to his foreign doctors, had finally escaped what they now called the disaster that was Jidada for their luxury home in Singapore, with no desire whatsoever to return to what they now considered the ugly ruin of a country of vile usurpers and ungrateful children of the nation who'd united with the traitors against them. Back in their miserable reality, the children of the nation found themselves standing hungry and thirsty and hopeless and penniless in the queues, tholukuthi Tuvy's eyes watching them from old election posters that promised a new and better Jidada they now understood, with a heartbreaking knowledge, would never ever come, was never meant to come. And heavy with the kind of weight that could not be set down, they dropped their tails and shuffled their feet and spit their anger on the hot pavements and stood there, in the thick trains of queues, contemplating their predicament, pondering this thing called Jidada with a -da and another -da.

OVERHEARD IN THE QUEUES

1. PORTRAIT OF NOSTALGIA

—Futhi we had some golden years once. When the Father of the Nation was the Father of the Nation, and this Jidada a country-country. What a time, what a life! Only it didn't last.

—I was just thinking of this last night, coming from a queue to a house that had no electricity because of the power cuts, where I couldn't flush the toilet because of the water cuts. I almost wept thinking of back when you could at least count on things working in this country.

—I never imagined I'd remember the Father of the Nation with any sentimentality but when I saw Tuvy preside over the official opening of a toilet with a whole entourage in tow, including the so-called brilliant Minister of Finance, I thought of the Old Horse. With him we could at least count on common sense, which apparently is too much to expect from Tuvy's regime! And not only that, he has the nerve to blame every economic problem on sanctions! I swear it's a good thing idiocy doesn't kill, we'd all be dead!

—The honest truth is that the Father of the Nation was the start of our problems. Let's not glorify him today because Tuvy has turned out to be an epic disaster; otherwise we're losing the moral of the story. And what adds insult unto injury is that the Old Horse isn't even here to experience the ruin he himself created, he is enjoying exile in a beautiful, functioning country, living in the lap of luxury thanks to our looted funds, nxaaa!

—Talking of better times, what about when whites ruled the country though? I mean I don't want to necessarily remember everything about that time but I still can't help thinking that we didn't spend our lives standing in queues like this! Sleeping the whole night in a bank queue, just to withdraw a couple hundred dollars that can't even buy anything of substance, I mean what kind of life is this?

—I am Black as you can very well see, all my sons fought in the war, one of them didn't come back from it, but I'll tell you that what this whole independence has taught me is that Blacks don't know how to run a country! Tell me one thing that this Black government is doing well, tell me just one thing!

—Never in a million years did I ever think I'd see and hear, in a Black republic such as this, Black animals standing around and being nostalgic about a wretched colonial past. This is the saddest day, this just takes the cup!

—Who is it that said that it's in fact quite possible to gain one's freedom and not really know what to do with it? And still be unfree? Because that's exactly what I seem to be hearing.

—What they're saying is that at least things worked in that time, at least we weren't standing in queues or crying about service delivery or none of that. Nobody said anything about wanting the colonial government itself unless I missed it.

—What we need is total transformation, an overhaul of this incompetent, corrupt government of crooks, with all its systems and institutions. Just completely revamp and reset everything and rebuild from scratch. With intelligent, competent, selfless, moral Jidadans who understand that leadership is service, and not a get-rich scheme. I truly believe a new world is possible!

—Me, what I just need is a visa to get out of this hell. I don't care where to anymore but I just want to go. Otherwise I've been doing these discussions all my life and I'm tired. This Jidada is a coffin. We all need to just bury it once and for all, move somewhere, and call it a day.

—The fundamental problem is we removed white colonists and replaced them with Black colonists who are by far worse in my opinion—at least the white colonists didn't reduce the country to tatters that just seem like they'll be impossible to mend.

—I can totally understand the frustrations with this current government, and believe me I share them. But we should never, no matter how broken the present is, buy into the falsity that it's because we're ruled by Blacks. We're only in this predicament because we are being ruled by inept, corrupt, selfish buffoons who hate us. And most importantly, they must go!

—Okay let's say you're right. Let's say this current government is actually worse than the colonists. My question then is, why on earth aren't you resisting? Why aren't Jidadans up in arms to see these Black colonists gone at all costs like they did with the white colonists? Because it's easier to rise against a white oppressor than an oppressor who looks like your mother's child, isn't it? Y'all are some demented fools, and thus you get the leaders you deserve!

—What animals are doing is just saying words. What are words when they don't, can't, won't even translate to anything? Look around this miserable city center. At all these miserable queues. With all the cuts cuts cuts. The joblessness. The despair. And then tell me what good are words like *freedom? Black power? Independence? Democracy?* If they don't allow you any dignity. If you're still oppressed. They mean nothing, zero!

—What remains is that the colonial past was an abomination in every sense of the word, I don't care how sweet you imagine the one little grain of brown sugar that occasionally landed on your miserable tongue. We shouldn't glorify any of it because we're stuck here with this kaka government. We do have excellent, capable, talented, moral Jidadans, both Black and white, here and all over the world, and you and I know that those all over the world are busy bettering and blessing countries that know how to value them. Don't tell me they and all of us

here can't change Jidada for the better. So instead of telling a wretched story about ourselves that's not even true, let's be busy, every day, every minute, with telling ourselves a new story, a better story. A story of how we plan to flush this black kaka that's wearing suits and stinking up the country and calling itself a government, down the toilet and straight to the sewer where it belongs, in order to build the Jidada we want and need!

—Even if I didn't like Tuvy, I thought let me give him a chance, maybe he'll prove himself. It was a mistake, he is not even trying, he doesn't care!

—What you're saying about Black Jidadans wanting to return to a wretched colonial past—that is the issue, but you're not being honest. The thing is that this Black regime is so wretched, so devious Jidadans are in fact willing to overlook the vileness of colonialism! And that is the outrage of it!

—Whatever y'all's beliefs, the thing is these queues just can't be allowed to go on, nossir! Something has to give!

2. THOLUKUTHI PORTRAIT OF STRUGGLES WITHIN A STRUGGLE

—Okay, so I've been standing in queues all over, listening to animals talking. And I'm asking myself why it is that Jidadans will vent about the failure of leadership all day, and somehow avoid the heart of the matter. And that heart of the matter being that it's really Shonamals who've killed this nation! We're here because of ugly Black leaders, yes, but it must be said at the same time that those Black leaders are also of Shona ethnicity!

—And that, right there, is nothing but the whole entire truth! Shonas simply don't know how to govern! All they're good at is corruption, looting, violence! Just look around you; behind everything that's fallen apart, you'll find a Shona! If that's not enough, then look at the past, at the Gukurahundi mass murders, Shonas!

—This kind of tribalism won't get us anywhere! There're Ndebeles in the administration, Vendas, Kalangas, and other ethnicities, who are equally ugly, equally corrupt, equally violent. The truth is we all have the capacity for ugliness, including some of us standing right here. Give us power for five minutes and watch us turn into wild beasts!

—Actually this nonsense is all over, it's not just the Seat of Power alone! Go to schools, to hospitals, to supermarkets, law firms, universities, restaurants, bars—whatever you can think of, including under rocks, its Shonamals in charge. Then from there you go on and look at who has access to whatever opportunities you can think of under the Jidada sun. It's Shonamals, again, always Shonamals! I hate it, it's ugly, and it must end!

—Speaking for myself I want to say that when it comes to Shonamals, I'm sorry, I don't want to have anything to do with them after what they did to me in the Gukurahundi. Even hearing the Shona language takes me back to that day, and plunges me into a terrible darkness. Even living in this Jidada, which is essentially a Shona country, causes me pain. But then where can I go? With what documents, because after murdering my parents, Shonas went on to deny me a birth certificate! Because I don't have death certificates for my parents! Which they denied me because to issue the death certificates would be to acknowledge that they

murdered my parents! So they took away my parents, took away my life, took away my citizenship!

—You must be out of your mind if you truly believe that the sprinkling of Ndebelemals in government means anything! It's all for show! For the illusion of unity! Show me one Ndebelemal in Tuvy's government who can pick up a phone right now and cause anything to happen in this Jidada? None, zero! Because they have no power! They're tokens!

—Why is it that when Ndebelemals talk about the Gukurahundi they leave out that Shonamal supporters of the opposition were equally murdered? Their region attacked?

—Even this so-called New Dispensation is a waste of our time. What's new about Shona supremacy? How many Ndebelemals are on the ballot? What of Vendamals? Or Kalangamals? Or Tongamals? Other ethnicities? And how on earth is that representative of Jidada? And isn't this the very reason why our fathers rose against white oppressors in the first place? To fight white supremacy and replace it with an equal society? Where is the equality I say?!

—To be honest, I hate that when Ndebelemals talk about the Gukurahundi they make like it was a Ndebele-Shona thing when it clearly wasn't. It was just a special unit of the Old Horse's army versus Dissidents. It was never the kind of tribal thing it's sold out to be, and it's definitely not fair to make it sound like every Shona endorsed it.

—The problem with Shonamals and Ndebelemals alike is that they act like they are the only two ethnicities in Jidada, and the rest of us don't

matter. And our issues are non-issues. Both groups can go to hell as far as I'm concerned, Jidada would be a better place without any of you, nxaaa!

—I'll admit I was raised by tribalist parents who never ceased to preach that Ndebelemals were by nature violent, lazy, untalented, uneducated, which was supposedly why they weren't in government. I'm only just now learning from unlearning, reading, and generally getting myself reeducated that the late Ndebele leader Father Jidada was in fact a far superior leader to the Father of the Nation. Instead of being given a chance he was criminalized into a dissident, demonized, hunted down, and almost murdered during the Gukurahundi. Hadn't it been for this ethnicity thing who knows, he might have been the one animal to take Jidada to glory!

—Ndebeles really need to stop making everything about Shona-Ndebele! That's a lazy way of thinking. Next thing you'll be telling us that the reason for the drought in Ndebele country is that Shonas are hoarding the rain!

—If you really think the Gukurahundi had nothing to do with ethnicity, futseki vele! How many dissidents were killed? And how many civilians? When are you going to get into your thick head that the Party of Power deliberately massacred Ndebele civilians over a four-year period! And that the Defenders who massacred us were Shona!

—But who told you that Ndebelemals are better? You think that if you were in fact the majority in this country you'd turn out to be some kind of angels? No, you wouldn't, you'd have behaved exactly the same!

—Khonapha this is a thing. Look at the Shona region, then look at the non-Shona regions. Then compare the level of development. It's a tale of unequal countries within a country!

—My feeling is that Ndebelemals should get over the past. It's called the past because it's happened, and just focus on the present and the future. Remember too that we're not the ones who killed your kin. Also, the killers are old and dying anyway, and the whole lot of them will soon be gone without anyone held accountable. It's tough, but that's just the situation.

—Ende do you know that if you right now went deep, deep, deep into the heart of Ndebele country you'd find a Shona who barely speaks Ndebele running a school, find Shona teachers with limited Ndebele proficiency teaching students Ndebele. And they wonder why we have these dismal pass rates in Ndebele regions.

—By the way why are animals talking about "Shonas" as if they are one homogenous entity? You can break down the so-called Shonas, into little groups and realize that not everyone even has power. I'm a supposed Shona myself, but I'm poor and oppressed, and I'm angry at my oppressors!

—What remains is that Jidada has a problem with Shona supremacy, that's a fact. You all have to look around you, and you know. Our dilemma, if we're really interested in a better Jidada, is figuring out how we create an equal society in which all ethnicities are at the same level.

—Exactly, and while we're at it let's not forget that all these ethnic tensions are really a colonial project. We are behaving exactly like colonizers meant for us to behave, sadly even long after they've left!

—So when are Ndebelemals going to acknowledge the fact that we're in this boat because their king sold the country to the colonists to begin with. And for sugar too!

—Just listening to the conversations here it's clear we have a problem, and it's not a small problem. But until we sort it out we'll never go anywhere. Instead of electing leaders based on their qualifications, we'll forever be busy trying to figure out their identities in order to make our prejudiced choices. And the sad thing is that the Seat of Power thrives on these tensions! Let's dare to see ourselves anew, Jidada, and address this issue. United we stand, divided we fall.

—The thing which I'm sure we all know but just don't want to acknowledge is that we, all of us, are oppressed by one Seat of Power of the Jidada Party. Aren't we, no matter our miserable ethnicities, standing together in these queues? Looking for food together? For money together? And didn't we get here on potholed roads together? Aren't we trying to survive together? Aren't we jobless together? Dying in decrepit hospitals together? Aren't our children looking at a bleak future together? This is us! Together!

—We'll have to figure out how to address our tribal divisions in honest conversations. And most important go beyond to talk about other Jidadans whose oppression doesn't matter to us because we've told ourselves they are unimportant. Femal Jidadans. Queer Jidadans. Jidadans living with disabilities. Young Jidadans. Immigrant Jidadans. Jidadans who've been violated by the state. Otherwise, there's just no future for us.

—My honest opinion is that this question of the tribe vele is a distraction. Like now, all the time, all the energy wasted could instead be going to

what we plan to do about these queues, and more importantly, about this Tuvy who doesn't deserve a day on the Seat of Power. But here we are, talking about what we always talk about.

BREAKING POINT IN THE QUEUES

They said, those who know about things, that Jidadans persevered in the queues, discussing and dissecting and debating Jidadaness, tholukuthi their despair and frustration and pain and anger simmering day in and day out, day in and day out, day in and day out. Until one night, when the children of the nation, sleeping in various queues like they now did most nights, heard the announcement by the Minister of Finance, Brilliant Nzinza, that the price of the very fuel they were lining up for, the fuel that was not there, the fuel that was already expensive, was overnight going up by a hundred and fifty percent. And as if that were not enough, Jidadans heard too of a new tax on electronic transactions, yes, tholukuthi on the moneys they weren't being paid, on the moneys that were hard-earned, on the moneys they didn't have, on the moneys that'd been stolen from them. And, blind with rage, tholukuthi the animals forgot their disagreements, forgot their ethnicities, forgot all that separated them and hinded and roared and fumed in the queues. Tholukuthi their anger frothed and gurgled and seethed and oozed from every opening in their bodies and poisoned the air. And when, in the very early morning, New Dispensation, His Excellency's by now celebrity pet parrot, who, together with his massive choir, flew over the restless capital singing the now deeply loathed New Dispensation anthem, those who know about things said the birds inhaled the poisoned air from the queues and plummeted into earth, twitching and choking, never to sing again.

DEFENDING THE
REVOLUTION, 2019

THOLUKUTHI THE NEW DISPENSATION CANNOT HOLD

And so it is that in Lozikeyi, and indeed in the townships of big cities all over Jidada, waves of animals pour onto the streets on the very day following the Minister of Finance's announcements and sweep their way toward city centers, this time not to stand in queues, no, but to take a stand against the queues. Tholukuthi cars, minibuses, and traffic heading into cities where businesses are already on #shutdown are turned back, and where drivers are noncompliant, their vehicles are attacked and promptly set ablaze. Barricades are erected—heaps of car tires, planks, and debris gathered, piled in the middle of roads, ignited, and rioters go morbid as they watch major roads burn, cheer as billowing clouds of black smoke barrel into the face of God. Away from the roads, shops and supermarkets are methodically ransacked and looted empty in the blink of an eye—the priority is whatever can be eaten, whatever is medicine for hunger, and once the food is gone, the looters take anything they can carry, tholukuthi the young, school-going animals are seen to aim for pens and pencils, rul-

ers and exercise books, as if to say that even at this complicated moment, their education, their future, is front and center in their imaginations. Pictures and videos quickly circulate on social media as the riot unfurls, and Jidadans in Jidada and every corner of the world congregate again on the internets to follow the protests.

What's happening that's never happened in Jidada with a -da and another -da, yes, tholukuthi what's happening that's unheard of is that for the very first time in history, rioters seem to be left to their own devices so that every once in a while, pausing to take selfies in the middle of toyi-toying, of shouting, of looting, of burning things—rioters will accordingly ask themselves questions like "Is this really our very own intolerant Jidada where not too long ago an animal couldn't set foot on the street in the name of a demo without Defenders tearing you to pieces or actually killing you dead? Where, really, are the ugly dogs of the nation as we speak? Where is Commander Jambanja? And why, in the first place, are we allowed to gallivant like we've never been allowed to gallivant in Jidada?" Tholukuthi there's nobody to answer these questions, and so rumors fly like drones. That the dogs of the nation, yes, the very Defenders with whom Jidadans took selfies at the fall of the Old Horse are in fact in support of the protests and have refused to pounce on the masses out of solidarity. Rumors that there's actually nobody in charge of Jidada, since the Savior is as usual busy cruising the skies of the world, with his deputy, Judas Goodness Reza, who's been sick for months from an unspecified illness, as usual out of the country for treatment.

Whatever the case, Jidadans naturally know and understand that a child can play with its mother's breasts all it wants and never, ever its father's testicles, but the rioters ignore what they've known all along and go for their father's testicles because it apparently seems this taboo is indeed now possible in the Jidada of the New Dispensation. And so, rioters charge parked police cars, flip them over, set them ablaze, and watch them burn

with both glee and disbelief because, if the symbols of the regime can be attacked like anything else, then who said the regime itself can't fall? The triumphant children of the nation finally retreat when they have worn themselves out, having played with their father's testicles. They hind back to their different townships like victorious troops returning from battle; tholukuthi the way they carry their bodies, necks stiff, tails high, ears erect, horns poised, teeth bared, and eyes ablaze, says they're finally uncowered and unafraid—come rain come fire come sunshine, tholukuthi in this newfound language of resistance, they will summon the New Jidada they want, they will rise and roar and rage until real change comes calling their names.

SONG OF THE DEFENDERS

When those who know about things told it, they said the very day following the historic protests, Defenders came out full force and howled a song of war. Tholukuthi Jidadans heard its first terrible notes in the airs of the townships and scuttled to lock themselves in their homes. Tholukuthi overheard, a dark cloud covered the sun and never left, tholukuthi snakes and lizards whipped across the dusty streets and crawled off to dark holes, tholukuthi birds flew away to faraway nests, tholukuthi ants lined up and took cover in gutters, tholukuthi mice and centipedes and cockroaches and flies and spiders tucked themselves in secret nooks and crannies. They said too, those who know about things, that the children of the nation tried to get on WhatsApp, on Twitter, on Facebook and tell the world of the war come to their homes, but the Seat of Power had instituted an #internet-shutdown, and so there was no service, and with no service, there was no raising alarm, no crying out for help, no testifying, no bearing witness, tholukuthi none of it at all but just the silence of the inside of a bullet.

SONG OF THE CHILDREN OF THE NATION

—I'm not a hateful animal. I try to have a pure heart. But God, do I hate these Defenders! I wish death to every single one, especially that Commander Jambanja!

—What baffles me is how everyone's been going on about the #internet-shutdown as if to say having internet would have somehow saved us. That anyone would have been so moved, so outraged by the pictures and clips of our pain so as to do something. Or the Defenders would've maybe left us alone had there been said internet. It's the silliest thing, I tell you.

—I just sat there and waited, listening to all those terrible sounds from the neighbors. I even opened the door for them when I heard them outside. I didn't bother to tell them I hadn't participated in the riots because these have never been dogs of justice. Or reason for that matter. And I didn't even cry when Commander Jambanja raped me; if anything I wanted to laugh at the brutal coincidence of it. I tell you he raped me in the 2008 election violence, and now, almost a decade later, he rapes me not too long after a contested election. If there is a God at all, he has the sickest humor, I tell you.

—When they started banging on the door I called my brother Max. He lives across the street from me, I really don't know what I thought he'd do. The phone wouldn't go through. It was the same with WhatsApp. Facebook Messenger. Everything. I couldn't understand it of course. I hadn't heard of the #shutdown, you see. And when you're so used to being connected and all of a sudden you're disconnected, it can feel like the sky is falling. But the phone was just the small of it. When we wouldn't

open they smashed the windows. Then threw a tear gas thing inside, what do you call it—a canister, yes. You should have seen how we scuttled out, like rats. Me and my son. I'd changed into my church uniform when they started banging. Thinking back now I don't even know why I did it. But I suppose desperation will do such to an animal. And of course it didn't change a thing. Do you know powerlessness? You think you do but I'm not sure that you really, really do. I can't explain it to you because it's one of those things that's just hard to describe. They beat my son up so bad I regretted bringing him into a world where I couldn't protect him.

—They came and surrounded my house. I counted at least a dozen of them with my eyes. I was arrested for inciting violence online. I called for a peaceful #stayaway.

—I don't vote. I don't go to marches. I don't go to rallies. This is Jidada with a -da and another -da, you see, I don't harbor any illusions. But did that protect me one bit? No ma'am.

—It just happened all at once. Our whole block was suddenly filled with armed Defenders-Defenders-Defenders. It reminded me of war. I mean, I was very young during the war, but there are scenes that flash across the mind now and then. I could barely recognize my block.

—All I can say is that we treated about thirty for gunshot wounds at this clinic, with nine of those being fatal. I don't know what the numbers are for other clinics. Also, there're those who probably didn't seek medical attention in fear of being identified and punished, or for one reason or another. By the way, don't quote or share my name in public forums, I don't want trouble, thank you very much.

—If I could do it all over I'd just let the donkey rule like she wanted, at least she wouldn't stoop to this level of depravity.

—My question is where is SADC? Where is the African Union? The United Nations? Where are all these organization that are supposed to look out for us, where is the rest of the world? And what do we have to do in order for our bodies, our lives, our dreams, our futures, to finally matter?

—I voted for Tuvy. His portrait is in my living room as we speak, it's actually the first thing you see when you walk in. But the Defenders weren't even fazed. Honestly, I thought they were going to kill me.

—You have to agree that the #shutdown just got out of line. I'm not saying I condone the Defenders and what they did. But animals were destroying, looting, burning private property. Okay, you have grievances, but why punish those who have absolutely nothing to do with it? So yes, in my view, it all got out of line and both sides are to blame. And absolutely nobody benefited in the end.

—They skipped over our house somehow. My wife and children can't stop talking about the miracle of it. What's the use of telling them when they won't believe it? The thing is when I heard the dogs were coming I sprayed anointed oil at the gate and all the entrances to our house. And what I'll tell you is that I wasn't scared one bit during the whole ordeal; I knew we were covered by the blood of Jesus, as Prophet Dr. O. G. Moses takes care to remind us.

—I'm seventy-six years old and I've never known true peace, true freedom in this country. And from the looks of it I'll die without knowing it. But I'll soon be gone, my road traveled and my journey concluded.

It will be up to you, the remaining ones, to see what Jidada does with this terrible poison; if it swallows it or if it spits it out once and for all.

—What we should do is boycott Jidada's internet companies. They absolutely didn't have to follow the government's directive to #shutdown the internet. But they made a choice. To stand with the Seat of Power against us. They are complicit in our oppression. They're enablers. And the sad thing is that it's us giving them business, we're the ones who make them rich, nxaaa!

—All I know is that the Old Horse and the donkey are right now laughing at us, especially the donkey, what with how so many loudly condemned her as the cause of Jidada's ills! But I hope the Old Horse himself laughs with restraint, remembering that he put us in this very predicament.

—We need to figure out what to do with these evil Defenders. The way they attack us like we are stones. The way our blood, our tears, don't move them at all. These monsters can't keep abusing us, we must do something!

—I'm looking for asylum as it is. I've tried, God knows all these years I've tried. And I just can't do this anymore!

—The sad thing is that while we in the townships are going through this the suburbs are peaceful. Isn't it our country together? Aren't we suffering together? And if we, of the townships, do succeed in overthrowing the system, won't that change be for all of us to enjoy together?

—Even if they beat me, I'm not angry or vengeful. I've already forgiven them. In fact, when they were busy beating me, God was even busier,

telling me Jidada needed prayer. We really must get off the streets and flock to our churches and let the Prophets of God deliver us. If you look in the Bible you'll find that what is happening to us is written. If you look at it closely, Jidada is really no different from Egypt under Pharaoh's rule. And if we repent of our sins and walk in God's Glory, we too shall see the promised land!

—I actually think that even with this outcome our efforts shouldn't be dismissed as futile. Nothing is achieved without pain. This isn't a story-book, it's real life. Remember this time as the time we did something big and important, that we've dared talk back to this cruel regime in the very language it understands; its excessive use of force in fact means they heard our fury, and they're rattled. That we don't just vent in our kitchens and yards and on social media anymore but we are bringing it to them live and direct. And next we rise, I promise you we will win!

—The very moment I spotted Commander Jambanja I knew we were in for it.

PORTRAIT OF A DEFENDER OF THE REVOLUTION

1. BIRTH

Commander Jambanja was born about two minutes and three seconds after Jidada's Independence, which, those who really know about things said, was a source of an unspoken, irrational resentment toward his mother, Rosemary Soso, for what he called her womb's atrocious timing, which, according to the young dog, effectively denied him the ability to claim, like his older Comrades could claim, that he'd been born during the Liberation War, and which in turn robbed him of a shot at greatness, no doubt his original destiny being that his own father, Commander John Soso, was

a war hero, though quite sadly he'd died on the eve of Independence and just a couple of months before the birth of his only son, never to see the country he'd fought so hard to liberate be free at last, and never to see his son grow up in it, yes, tholukuthi Commander John Soso, whose other brothers—big Simon, Philip, small Simon, Matthias, Matthew, Jude, Judas, long James, fat James, Bartholomew, and Andrew, a band of twelve, like the disciples and all of them named after the disciples—also were, every one of them, Liberation War heroes, just like their own grandfather, Jambanja Soso, hero of the First Liberation War, also commonly known in Jidada as the First Uprising, yes, tholukuthi Jambanja Soso, who, together with the spirit medium Mbuya Nehanda, had inspired armed rebellions against the colonial regime until their lynching in 1899, but not before Jambanja predicted the exact date, the exact day of the week, and the exact year that the yet-to-be-born fruit of his loins would take up arms and rise against the oppressors and eventually prevail.

2. FIRST WORDS

They said, those who really know about things, that the puppy's mother, Rosemary, herself a Liberation War heroine, who'd in fact met her husband and son's father on the war front, raised their half-orphaned son like the child of fighters, of heroes, that he was. So that the very first words out of the pup's mouth when he came to speaking age were not *mama* or *milk* or *hi*, no, but a whole revolutionary sentence—"Jidada is of the blood of the Liberators," yes, tholukuthi lyrics from a war song because the only lullabies that came naturally to Rosemary were songs from the war front. By the time the puppy was three and a half years old, tholukuthi there was no known Liberation War song, in any of Jidada's languages, that he couldn't sing, in addition to the national anthem.

3. EARLY GLORY

They said, those who know about things, that Commander Jambanja's play-mates were grouped into the strict categories of Comrade, Colonizer, Informer, Sellout, and Enemy. In his early years, not a day passed without him getting into, at the very least, a single altercation, of which he of course won every one. As a result, he was very much feared on the playground, which earned him the nickname Lil' General Killton, though the name was said behind his back until he discovered it quite by accident when, in the middle of pummeling a disrespectful calf three-four years his senior behind Bamba-zonke Supermarket one afternoon, yes, tholukuthi the desperate calf—who either hadn't properly heard the puppy's legend to know not to get in a fight with him, or had in fact heard it and refused to listen—now bitten, bloodied, and fearing a bone or two to be broken, pleaded and mooed, "Please don't kill me, Lil' General Killton, please, please!" which, according to those who were there, made the puzzled puppy pause, demand an explanation, after which he then declared to his Comrades, the Informers, Sellouts, and Ene-mies, that Lil' General Killton was the only name he'd henceforth be known by, instead of the useless nickname of Chief, given to him by his dull and unimaginative best friend, the pretty pea rooster Phumulani.

4. EDUCATION

In primary school—which was also not an easy time for everyone around the pup since, again, it was during that period in his life that he was in at least one morbid fight every two hours—his favorite activity, really one of the only few things that allowed him calm, was art, and especially painting. Due to his interest in the Liberation War, no doubt stemming from his bloodline and family background, Lil' General Killton painted turbulent but realistic, even breathtaking images and famous scenes from the war, tholukuthi rendered with astounding precision owing to his mother's sto-ries. This talent was complemented by an exceptional grasp of Jidada's Lib-

eration history—indeed, a few years later, at the start of his high school career, those who know about things said the young dog was in fact known to go through his Jidada History textbooks with a red pen, meticulously correcting chapters on the Liberation War because he said the way they said some of the incidents were said to have happened was not as was said.

Tholukuthi Lil' General Killton ended his high school career when he walked out of Lozikeyi High for the last time one hot Thursday after biting his English Literature teacher, Mr. A. B. Sibanda, for giving him a lousy mark of ten percent on a comprehensive literature exam on works by Chaucer, Shakespeare, Milton, Dickens, Hardy, and Brontë. "My fathers and ancestors didn't go to war so I could read silly stories by the very thieves who dispossessed us of our land, oppressed us for decades, and vomited on our culture, so find better books to teach and not this nonsense, Mr. Teacher, we are not a colony anymore and we'll never be a colony again!" the young dog barked, gathering his blue Dunlop backpack and strutting off. It was his last time inside a classroom.

5. DEFENDING THE REVOLUTION, 1994

Not too long after, the young dog was on his way back home from the bank one afternoon, sitting in the second row of a crowded combi, tongue lolling and right paw sticking out the window. He'd queued all day for his parents' War Veterans monthly payments—which he'd been unable to collect because the government had apparently failed to make available the funds again, as was becoming the norm in the Jidada of the closing years of the twentieth century. It was dead quiet in the combi, every ear glued to the radio and listening to Nelson Mandela—only a few years out of prison, where he'd been held for over two decades by the apartheid regime—deliver his very first presidential address to the nation. And when the Liberator spoke of building peace, prosperity, non-sexism, non-racialism, and democracy, an emotional sheep began weeping somewhere in the back of the combi.

While the passengers waited for someone to tell the sheep to shut up so they could finish hearing the historic speech, and just as the car neared the traffic lights on Third Avenue, by the Shell garage station, tholukuthi right where combis and taxis called out to passengers headed to the townships, they suddenly found themselves submerged in a sea of demonstrators. Throngs of animals had taken over the entire street it seemed, bringing all traffic to a standstill, everywhere cars and wheels, everywhere fur and feathers, everywhere red shirts and banners, everywhere raised limbs, everywhere chants and songs, everywhere yells and shouts.

Vendors cleared their wares and scattered. Impatient drivers, upset at being disrupted by something they hadn't voluntarily signed up for, went berserk on their horns, unleashing such a sensational cacophony that only seemed to inspire the protesters to raise their furious voices. Lil' General Killton, who'd never until that time seen a live protest, glued his cold nose to the window, wide-eyed, tongue lolling. He read signs that said "No to One Party State!" "No to Economic Saboteurs!" "Jidada Party = Terrorist Organization!" "Economic Freedom for All!" "20 000++ Dead in Guku-rahundi Massacre, Never Forget!" The anger in the air was so palpable it could have started a car and sent it careening on a busy highway. The en-ergy made the young dog feel the hairs at the back of his neck begin to rise.

"Hayi, hayi, hayi, hayi, come on, get on with it, I have trips to do man' la, I don't have all day hawu, nxxx!" the driver, an impatient bull with fierce horns, vented.

"Me I don't even know why I even came to town, I should have just sat my behind at home. Now who's going to feed my piglets lunch with me being stuck here like this?" a pig lamented.

"Eish, that's why I hate this damn road man' nxaaa, anything happens on it you're stuck!" a goose said.

"But they're fighting for you too, Comrades, have you read their signs? Besides, it's their right to demonstrate and be heard, ngoba kanti aren't we

a democracy?" a voice from somewhere in the middle said. The driver hammered his horn, and other drivers echoed his frustration.

"Vele who are all these animals, my son? Why do they look like they want to eat somebody?" the donkey squashed against Lil' General Killton said, nudging him in the ribs. Before he could mumble that he didn't know, the arrogant voice of a rooster crowed from the back.

"They're Jidada's Opposition Party! They're only a few years old but they're here to bring us economic and political freedom and eventually liberate us. Look at them carefully and go tell the village about them gogo—they're the real revolutionaries," the rooster said.

"Which they better do because I'm afraid of what'll happen if this miserable country stays on this most tragic track," the rooster's partner, a stylish hen, beak bright red with lipstick, said. A big roar erupted from the front, and animals craned their necks to see the heaving back of a donkey as he convulsed in laughter.

"Opposition? Revolutionaries? They're nothing but misguided sellouts and puppets of the West! Which war did they fight? Did they spend years and years in the bush, spilling blood and dying to liberate this country? Let me tell you, Jidada is not going anywhere, and none other than the Liberators will rule it! We didn't fight to give this country to agents of regime change! Who are also fools, every one of them!" the donkey said over his shoulder.

"Who did you call a fool? Who are you calling fools?" the rooster demanded, feathers puffed out.

"You, of course. And your miserable excuse of a party! What are you going to do about it?"

"Why don't you get out right now, yes, get down and let me show you exactly just what I'll do about it, you son of a hyena!" the rooster crowed, beating his wings.

"Yes, show him, show this damn donkey who you are, love, show him what you did in Makokoba that one time," the hen urged.

Heads simultaneously swiveled to look at the back of the car, to make certain that what they were hearing was in fact what they thought they were hearing, tholukuthi which was that a rooster was challenging a whole donkey to a fight, and that his hen partner was urging him on. And indeed the turned heads found that it was actually true, the birds were readying for a fight. At the front, the donkey opened the door, and finding it locked, furiously kicked at it and jabbed at the lock.

"Goddammit, driver, how d'you open this damn door? Let me out mal!" he said.

"Sit your feathery behind down, nobody's getting out of this car, are you mad, uyahlanya kanti? Don't you see what's happening outside?" the driver bellowed.

"Excuse me, y'all really need to move, I need to get out right now while we're stopped and show this ass. Madam, can you please kindly let me pass?" the rooster said to the donkey next to him.

"Please, sister, let him pass, can't you hear him asking you nicely?" the hen said.

But nobody moved; tholukuthi a combi isn't a toilet where an animal can just randomly decide to up and get out. First, the driver must see it fit to stop. Then the conductor has to open the door. Then the passengers have to disembark in an orderly fashion—one after another, row after row, from front to back, line up outside while the exiting party gets out.

"You're lucky! You're very, very, very lucky, in fact you don't even know how lucky you are. Thank that bull right there for not letting me out. Because I was going to spill red blood today. I'm Lovejoy, son of Mahlathini from Jahunda, me. I'm not to be played with like that!" the rooster said.

Before the donkey had a chance to fire back, Defenders were upon the

demonstrators. And in the bloody, chaotic moment, Lil' General Killton was seized by such a shot of adrenaline he felt his body begin to levitate, and had it not been for the roof he may very well have shot to the heavens. He experienced the scene outside as if he were not watching it from the window of a combi but rather from the middle of the action. He heard the whack-thwack-whack of batons, the swoosh of long, flaccid sjamboks, saw the weapons rise and fall, and rise and fall on the fleeing bodies. He heard the desperate sound of hooves pounding concrete, saw the flash of teeth sinking into flesh, saw those teeth coated in blood. And, in a most uncanny experience, Lil' General Killton had absently run his tongue along the tops of his own teeth to find, to his shock, the unmistakable metallic taste of blood. That night the young dog didn't sleep a wink; he lay in the dark replaying the scene in his head.

6. DESTINY

The very next morning he was at the Headquarters of the Ministry of Defending, where he tried to sign up for the military but was turned down. According to the recruiter, not only did Lil' General Killton not have the minimum requirement of a high school certificate, he was also a few years younger than the legal enlistment age. On being rejected thus, the devastated youth threw what was easily the most epic tantrum of his life. He repeatedly flung himself against the wall and assaulted it with his massive head, his magnificent teeth, his paws, his backside. He threw himself on the floor and rolled about. He pushed around on his belly. He scratched the carpet. He bit the furniture. He tilted his head up and howled better than a wolf. He growled at the air, chomped at it with his teeth. He laid his head on the floor and pushed it around as if it were a wheelbarrow. He got on his side, thrashed about like a fish out of water. And finally, exhausted, he got to his feet, shook himself, and made for the door, tail between his legs.

"On second thought, you've just changed my mind, Comrade, there

actually may be a way. There's something in you I think I like. Why don't you come back next week Monday, around lunch? I'll talk to my boss," the recruiter said, awed by the unbridled display of violence, passion, ferocity, imbecility, and unreasonableness all at once.

7. THOLUKUTHI DEFENDING THE REVOLUTION, 2008, AND THE BIRTH OF COMMANDER JAMBANJA

While he boasted an illustrious career from the get-go, the young dog especially made his mark about a dozen years into his service, during the 2008 presidential elections, when it became clear that the leader of Jidada's Opposition was poised to win the election in a spectacular upset that defied every single move by the Seat of Power to ensure its own triumph. Tholukuthi the unprecedented situation called for the Revolution to be defended like had never been seen in Jidada. By then a bona fide member of the Star Force, a feared, highly specialized Defender unit and with ample years of experience, Lil' General Killton thoroughly distinguished himself for his sensational combination of strength, fearlessness, and brutality. By the end of the campaign, with thousands beaten, hundreds tortured, tens and tens dead, hundreds raped, the young dog was accordingly promoted to the rank of National Commander of the Star Force, at which point the notorious dog changed the infantile name of his childhood and became known as Commander Jambanja, yes, tholukuthi Jambanja like his great-grandfather, hero of the First Uprising. The young dog may not have been born in time for the Liberation War, but it turned out he was right on time to defend the Revolution, and a whole decade later, no longer in service of the Father of the Nation but of the Savior of the Nation, Commander Jambanja was still distinguishing himself.

REFORMATION IN THE TIME OF THE CROCODILE

THE CROCODILE

When news of a roaming Crocodile began to make waves in Jidada, those who know about things pointed out that he'd in fact been first spotted by the children of Lozikeyi during the #freefairncredible elections, only the adults, euphoric at the idea of change, didn't at the time believe the young ones. The Crocodile was said to walk upright, tholukuthi so tall he threatened to obstruct the sun. They said too that he moved with such utter ease and agility he could've been a beast of land, and they went on to say that he had terrible blades for teeth, and they went on to say that his eyes were the size of half-moons, tholukuthi one eye the color of the flag of North Korea on a good day, and the other the color of the flag of North Korea on a very bad day, and they went on to say that he wore the Scarf of the Nation around his neck, tholukuthi the colors so brilliant they could have been alive. In no time, sightings of the Crocodile got to be so common Jidada's social media buzzed from morning till night with pictures and clips of the creature gallivanting uninhibited and as he pleased, abso-

lutely at home anywhere and everywhere, so it became clear he'd come to stay.

When the Crocodile sensed the underlying anxiety of the Jidadans, tholukuthi he sought to assuage them every chance he got. "Don't worry, I'm actually friendly and I'm even as soft as wool," he said. "Even my teeth aren't real teeth, they're false teeth, and besides, I'm really vegetarian," he said. "My fellow Jidadans, have you ever seen me near any proper bodies of water? If I were a real crocodile I'd be living in a lake or river," he said. "Please, trust me, and besides, I really, really love Jidada with every inch of my being, and by that I mean from the tips of my teeth to the tip of my tail," he said, whipping his tail and flashing his blades in a terrible smile.

Tholukuthi there were the birds of the wild—proper daredevils who sometimes partook in the risky sport of pecking at things stuck between the Crocodile's teeth whenever they found him spread out in the Jidada Square, where he apparently liked to bask, terrible jaws flung wide open as if looking to swallow the sun. The winged creatures knew of occasions when the Crocodile, despite his insistent promises, had suddenly clamped his mouth shut during these teeth-cleaning sessions, trapping their trusting friends to their deaths. So whenever the birds saw him doing his rounds they broke into song: "Careful Jidada, here comes the Crocodile with his big, bad blades! Will he nibble, will he bite, will he chomp-chomp-chomp?!" the birds sang, cartwheeling in midair before careening off.

The little ones of Jidada soon picked the tune and sang it at the top of their voices whenever they caught sight of the fearsome creature, and accompanied the song with an improvised lumbering dance in which they mimicked the movements of a crawling Crocodile; tholukuthi they called it the Croco-crawla dance. In no time the slightly older youngsters picked the crocodile song up and added their own lyrics to it. Then Jah Taks, a

famous dancehall singer, layered it with beats and did a remix, and soon the song was on everyone's gadgets and earphones, it was on the radio, in taxis, cars, and buses, in pubs and bars and offices and all the wherevers of Jidada so that the song may have very well been a national anthem, a national lullaby, a national slogan, and a national prayer all at once.

THOLUKUTHI A TALE OF TWO COUNTRIES

The children of the nation, with their penchant for naming things, didn't take long to christen this period the Time of the Crocodile. Tholukuthi it was what, it was the worst of times, it was the worstest of times. A time when Jidadans, regardless of who they were, finally agreed on at least one thing: Tuvius Delight Shasha and his Seat of Power were indeed and by all means epic, resounding failures who'd removed the Old Horse for their self-interests, who clearly only meant to keep the nation trapped between rock and hard place, who were hell-bent on flushing the country down the toilet. The tremendous optimism that had greeted the appointment of the famous brilliant Minister of Finance, as well as other seemingly progressive new members of cabinet had by now evaporated, replaced by a bottomless disappointment because it was clear that this group of animals, despite their talents and credentials and experience, despite being political outsiders at the time of their appointment, had only turned out to be chameleons—the kinds of creatures that changed the color of their skin to match their environment. Tholukuthi once they put their behinds on the Seat of Power, they, too, became the Seat of Power faster than it took for Jidadans to ask themselves if what they were seeing was indeed what they were seeing.

The dismal state of the nation was perhaps why Jidadans sought refuge in virtual living. In record numbers, the children of the nation logged on to all kinds of online destinations in order to escape their realities, to seek comfort, to network, to recharge, to forget the screaming in their heads,

to find reasons to smile and laugh and breathe. But even in the online destinations they found themselves haunted by the very same monster they sought to escape, yes, tholukuthi by the predicament that was their miserable existence under Tuvy's regime; after all, they remained Jidadans. Still, perhaps because of the repression they encountered on the ground, online, the children of the nation chose not to hold back against the Seat of Power. So that very soon it was noted that Jidada was actually not a country but two countries—there was of course the Country Country that was the real, physical space in which Jidadans walked and lived and queued and suffered and got pained, and then there was the Other Country, where Jidadans logged on and roared and raged and vented.

Tholukuthi seeing what was happening in the Other Country, and no doubt knowing from the recent waves of protests where it could go if left unchecked, the regime activated what it called the Internet Force—an uncouth team of bullies, liars, deniers, misogynists, tribalists, and vitriolic manipulators created for the purposes of managing what they termed the "Online Threat." Led by wretched, sadistic members of the Seat of Power, prominent members of Tuvy's cabinet among them, this vile, despicable team, nicknamed the Dungbeetles by the children of the nation for their dirty antics, for their specialty in verbal diarrhea, the group worked around the clock insulting, attacking, sabotaging, and undermining Jidada's online resistance.

Only the children of the nation were defiant. They were vocal and unafraid and unsilenced dissidents and freedom fighters in the Other Country. They were ready to ignite a revolution and liberate Jidada in the Other Country. Tholukuthi they were capable of anything and everything in the Other Country. They said things to and of the Savior they'd never ever say to even his shadow in the Other Country. They had so many transformative opinions, such ingenuous ideas in the Other Country. Tholukuthi in the Country Country though, Jidadans were simply not who they were in

the Other Country. They had absolutely no confidence, they shriveled at the sight of power in the Country Country. They did not dare raise their voices against the regime in the Country Country, yes, tholukuthi in the Country Country, Jidadans were the shadows of who they were in the Other Country.

REFORMATION

1. WE NEED NEW NAMES

It was around this time Jidada woke up one ordinary Thursday to find the famous Main Street renamed after none other than the Savior. Yessir, apparently while the children of the nation were busy doing in the Other Country what they'd never dare do in the Country Country, tholukuthi the Savior of the Nation too was busy doing what could only be done in the Country Country and not in the Other Country. The sight of all kinds of traffic lining up on a street with his name on it that Thursday pleased His Excellency so much he actually went on and renamed another street after himself. And then he surprised himself by also renaming yet another street after himself. And then one day it came to him while sitting on the toilet, to go for it and rename another street after himself. And not too long after that he dared himself to rename yet another street after himself. And then he followed up by doing what, tholukuthi by renaming another street after himself. And then it was another and another and another and another and another and another and another so that in no time pretty much every street, every road, every avenue in Jidada was named Tuvy, yes, tholukuthi it was just Tuvy, Tuvy, Tuvy, and Tuvy all over and Tuvy everywhere. And with the streets thus accordingly renamed, it occurred to the Savior that it only made sense to also rename the cities in which those very streets were located, which, having thought about it, he realized

should in fact have been done before the renaming of the streets to begin with. First, the name of the capital of Jidada was formally amended to Tuvy City, and not too long after that, the Savior similarly renamed the other cities in the whole entire country after himself, yes, tholukuthi so that Jidada in fact became a nation of Tuvy cities. And when he heard the names said out loud he delighted to no end in the feeling that he was actually synonymous with Jidada. At this time it was common to hear an animal say something like "My family are divided between Tuvy and Tuvy and Tuvy, and I myself live in Tuvy, on Tuvy, right next to Tuvy, but I was born and raised in Tuvy so I'm really a Tuvy boy at heart."

2. THE APPOINTER

About this time, the Savior moved to reappoint all governing officials so that every holder of any public office in Jidada wasn't only appointed by Tuvy, but they were also the Savior's family, close friends, and allies, and, even more important, members of his ethnic group, and most preferably members of his clan, meaning they were, all of them, bound to Tuvy by blood. And once done with the major appointments, the Savior heard a question ask itself in his great head one bright early morning as he was dressing in front of the mirror—yes, tholukuthi the question asking itself in his great head saying, Son of Zvichapera Shasha, most favorite and most successful son of Buresi Shasha, what would it hurt to in fact just go ahead and also make the small appointments as well for a comprehensive program that will allow you to firmly and properly put your hoof on the running of this whole entire nation as it is meant to be?

Tholukuthi the Savior reappointed grocery till operators. He reappointed garbage collectors. He reappointed undertakers. He reappointed strippers. He reappointed headmasters. He reappointed TV and radio presenters. He reappointed security guards. He reappointed pastors and priests

and pipe installers and pilot operators and payroll clerks as well as peggers and professors and prefects. He reappointed janitors. He reappointed morticians. He reappointed elevator operators. He reappointed doctors. He reappointed the lead singers in bands. He reappointed supermarket stockers. He reappointed street sweepers. He reappointed nightclub bouncers. He reappointed accountants. He reappointed black market lords and money changers. He reappointed class monitors. He reappointed restaurant chefs and dishwashers. He reappointed the pimps in red light districts. He reappointed real estate agents. He reappointed meter readers. He reappointed builders. He reappointed bus drivers. He reappointed gang leaders. He reappointed rubbish collectors.

And just like with his big appointments, these appointees were also the Savior's family, close friends, and allies, and, even more important, members of his ethnic group, and preferably members of his clan. And being that he himself and only him had done the appointing, they said, those who really know about things, that even in his sleep, even in the middle of a nightmare, even in the middle of a demanding task, the Savior could in fact look at the map of the nation and pinpoint a random location in a random province in a random city and tell you exactly and down to the name—down to intimate details like home address, shoe size, weight, favorite TV program—who was in charge of this or that or what and any office, including their specific job description.

The Savior didn't stop there; whenever his time permitted he made sure to participate in the machinery of the vast and varied network of his appointees not only in order that animals never forgot to whom they owed their allegiance, but to also ensure the smooth running of the country. Tholukuthi Tuvy walked in unannounced in teachers' meetings and chaired them, after which he graded any papers and exams that happened to be under review, and while at it he never missed the opportunity to award A's and A+'s to students whose names told him they belonged in his

clan. He appeared on construction sites and supervised in the effective mixing of cement. He showed up in villages and dispensed indispensable advice on the right way of boiling and then spreading vegetables to dry on the roof, on the proper depth of Blair toilets and the proper placement of compost heaps as well as traps for field mice. In theaters he held auditions and corrected the accents and pronunciations of actors. He stopped by in accounting firms and cleaned the screens of computers and fed paper into paper feeders and examined financial records with a stethoscope. He was sometimes seen in hospitals checking the sharpness of injections and licking medicines to ascertain potency as well as counting the pills in patient trays and deciphering the writing of doctors. In factories he assembled parts and sealed boxes shut and stuck labels after he sealed the boxes shut. On the roads he was sometimes seen driving ambulances or delivery trucks or even directing traffic and also counting potholes, after which he took out a tape measure and string and measured the perimeters of those potholes. He was observed poring over weather maps, wiring electricity, giving receipts in tollbooths, watching paint dry on government buildings, grading peaches and oranges and tomatoes and maize in farms. Yes, tholukuthi the Savior, on top of saving the nation, not only ruled it but indeed also served it.

3. YOUR NAME WILL NO LONGER BE JACOB. YOU HAVE STRUGGLED WITH GOD AND WITH MEN, AND YOU HAVE WON; SO YOUR NAME WILL BE ISRAEL.

Tholukuthi the upgrading of the Savior's titles was proposed by the Deputy Minister of Corruption, Honorable Dr. Divine Jena. "It is well that no animal in this Jidada can doubt who rules over the nation Your Excellency, sir, as it should be. But in my humble opinion this must accordingly be complemented by relevant official titles that both reinforce and remind the nation who's in charge." And so Tuvius Delight Shasha, son of Zvichapera Shasha and most favorite and most successful son of Buresi Shasha,

already known by the titles of Savior of the Nation, Ruler of the Nation, and Veteran of the Liberation War, also became officially known as the Greatest Leader of Jidada, Enemy of Corruption, Opener of Business, Dispenser of the New Dispensation, Fixer of the Economy, Imposer of Order, Inventor of the Scarf of the Nation, Most Successful Veteran of the Liberation War, Top Magnate of Jidada, Genius of Jidada, Survivor of All Assassination Attempts, Winner of Free, Fair, and Credible Elections, Main Chief Appointer, Respected World Leader.

4. HIS EYES ON EVERYTHING, EVERYWHERE

When those who know about things said at this time the Savior of the Nation was everywhere, they meant the Savior of the Nation was everywhere. Tholukuthi Tuvy was suddenly gracing billboards all over Jidada's cities. He was on banknotes and coins. On clothing labels. On postage stamps. On packets of cigarettes. On government buildings. On boxes of cereal. On posters tied around the trunks of trees and similarly on posters pasted onto the surfaces of rocks. On packages of family planning pills. On sacks of maize meal. On government vehicles. On tins of snuff and on tins of baby formula and on tins of tuna and on tins of bleaching creams and also on tins of paint. He was on condom wrappers. On the covers of school textbooks and then on the covers of school exercise books. On bottles of medicine. On bags of fertilizer. On examination papers at all levels and regardless of subject. On the doors of public toilets. On the spines of buses. On packets of tea leaves. At the entrances of churches and brothels and hospitals and bars and restaurants and football stadiums. On toy packages. On toilet paper covers. On license plates. On packets of rice. And then he was on the flag of Jidada, tholukuthi there, inside the red star, that was inside the white triangle, and where the stone bird used to be. He was on the badges of primary school uniforms. On the badges of secondary school uniforms. On cans of formula. On gallons of Mazoe. On pesticide

packages. On boxes of tampons. Indeed, the Savior of the Nation's face was on everything so that it seemed his beady eyes were watching the children of the nation from every possible place and from every direction and from everywhere in the Country Country, yes, tholukuthi the Savior observing his Jidada the same exact way God kept watch over his entire universe.

THOLUKUTHI RESISTANCE

As the Savior was immersed in his bizarre program of what he and the Seat of Power touted as "The Reformation," life in Jidada only got bleaker and bleaker. The nation once more dominated international headlines with hyperinflation, with crushing food and fuel shortages. Businesses shut down and new droves joined the old legions of the jobless. Water, electricity, and medical care became luxuries. Hunger brought with it comfortable cushions, camped in homes, and refused to leave. Despair, disillusionment, and desperation came with their smartphones and took selfies with everyone.

When those who know about things say the child who doesn't cry out perishes on her mother's back, tholukuthi they mean the child who doesn't cry out perishes on her mother's back. In the face of a savage, callous regime that could've been conceived out of the devil's anus itself, the children of the nation resolved to fight back. Wizened now in the machinations of the despotic Seat of Power, they were deliberate in their defiance. The time called for new tactics, a new language that not only expressed the nation's rage but also forced the Seat of Power and the Chosen to actually hear and feel that very rage right where it hurt, tholukuthi in the very center of their feeling. Because even the sticks and stones knew that very center of feeling was not the heart or liver or intestines as it should have been for any animal with anything resembling a conscience but rather their fat pockets; in the Country Country, the children of the nation boycotted the

businesses of the Seat of Power. In this new language, they loudly said they refused, said no, they would no more participate in fattening the pockets of shameless looters and gluttons whose very prosperity was their poverty, whose very success their suffering.

And while this boycott was busy going on in the Country Country, tholukuthi an unprecedented campaign of exposing corruption was going on in the Other Country. Records by investigative journalists and concerned citizens trended that proved what most Jidadans already knew, which was that the Seat of Power, the Chosen, and their families were indeed fleecing the nation in jaw-dropping figures. Pictures were shared in which they nonchalantly smuggled Jidada's precious minerals out of the country. The despairing children of the nation watched on Instagram and Twitter and Facebook as looters flaunted lavish lifestyles. Huge sums of money siphoned from Jidada were reported to be stashed in offshore accounts. Records appeared that exposed how the Seat of Power and the Chosen had misdirected and squandered staggering sums meant for Jidada's social programs and other crucial services. Audio recordings surfaced in which they strategized on how best to increase their ill-begotten wealth.

THOLUKUTHI RAGE

The wrath of the children of the nation in the Other Country surprised no one; after all, it is the tree that feels the ax's cut. It made them roar and rumble in an electronic storm that refused to cease. In massive numbers, Jidadans in and outside of the country trended #hashtags that called for Tuvy and the Seat of Power to resign. And that rage, tholukuthi no one would say exactly when it began to travel and spread out of the Other Country and into the Country Country. And no one would say exactly how, once in the Country Country, the rage infected everything in its wake like a virus. It began to appear in the defiant lullabies sung by mothers rocking famished

babies while knowing deep down that the earth of Jidada was a bountiful earth, in the eyes of the youth dreaming of a future in which they'd grow up and be what they dared and dreamed without being forced to cross borders to realize those dreams on the sometimes hard soils of foreign lands, in the chorus of teachers and educators standing in decrepit classrooms across the nation and reading to curious students excerpts of seminal texts on liberation, in the smoldering eyes of Jidadans whose scars knew all there was to know about the barbarism of Defender brutality, in the faces of granite standing in Jidada's endless queues, in the games of little ones who didn't sleep from nightmares about the Crocodile devouring their future, in the eyes of the so-called bornfree generation cradling a new generation of little ones who'd never know real freedom, in the restless postures of teenagers who never understood why and how their parents had allowed the disaster that was the Seat of Power to oppress them for so long, in the clenched teeth of Jidada's jobless multitudes who knew of every indignity under the sun, yes, tholukuthi that anger began to appear in the lyrics of dancehall artists singing from Jidada's townships, in the mics of spoken-word poets spitting potent rhymes in smoky bars all over the nation, in the lines of actors giving body and breath to Jidada's oppression and possible liberation on stages across the country, in the biting jokes of comedians making audiences both laugh and weep between gritted teeth all at the same time because the satire of their suffering was at once hysterical and devastating, in the words of writers, hunched over blank pages to bleed the nation's pains and anger and dreams and hopes as well as speak truth to power, in the prayers of Christians asking God for strength because they were finally seeing the light, which was that they themselves were the God's son they'd all been waiting for, yes, tholukuthi the rage traveled from the Other Country and spread and infected many in the Country Country.

THE SAVIOR AND THE TWITTER

"Yeyi Siri, Siri, open me that thing," Tuvy said. He spoke with a curtness that was uncharacteristic of his exchanges with Siri because he was reeling from an anger brought on by the latest shenanigans of the belligerent children of the nation. It was clear to him that not only did they not know their place, but they meant to undermine his authority, bedevil him at every turn, and humiliate him in front of the whole entire world.

"Good morning, Tuvius Delight Shasha, son of Zvichapera Shasha and most favorite and most successful son of Buresi Shasha, Savior of the Nation, Ruler of the Nation, Veteran of the Liberation War, Greatest Leader of Jidada, Enemy of Corruption, Opener of Business, Dispenser of the New Dispensation, Fixer of the Economy, Imposer of Order, Inventor of the Scarf of the Nation, Most Successful Veteran of the Liberation War, Top Magnate of Jidada, Genius of Jidada, Survivor of All Assassination Attempts, Winner of Free, Fair, and Credible Elections, Main Chief Appointer, Respected World Leader. What thing can I open for you today?" Hearing Siri say his name and titles in her exotic voice slightly calmed the Savior. He walked back to his desk and sat down.

"You know that thing where they're always talking about me in very short sentences? I want to follow this anarchy right to its source," the Savior said, rapping the table with a hoof.

Tholukuthi Siri, being Siri, had the Savior's Twitter page open before he even finished his sentence. The horse sat up. They'd updated his picture with a new one in which he almost didn't recognize himself for how young and how pretty he looked. In the background was the flag of Jidada—tholukuthi the new one with his very own face inside the red star inside the white triangle. Right beneath the small calendar thing that says joined December 2011, it said 742.6K followers. Every time that Siri

opened the Twitter for him, he checked this number. And every time he failed to understand it.

"Siri, Siri. Remind me again how many citizens are in Jidada?"

"In 2017, the population of Jidada was 16,529,904."

"And how many Followers do I have following me on this thing?"

"You currently have about 742.6K Twitter followers, about 257,400 fewer than three months ago, when you had 1 million followers."

The horse looked away at the window, thinking. During the war, when he was fighting for the liberation of Jidada, there were terms for these kinds of animals: dissidents, defectors, sellouts. And the way they were dealt with was punishment, torture, or even death. Which is exactly what he'd do to these miserable beasts who have defected from his Twitter. Tholukuthi adding insult unto injury, in a nation of almost 17 million, only a miserable 742.6K animals followed him. Where exactly were the rest of the 16,257,400 of them? What were they doing and who were they busy following if they were not here following their Leader?

"If Twitter was a Country Country you were going to see, you'd learn me," he seethed, waving a threatening hoof at the screen. Yessir, if Twitter was a Country Country he'd have Defenders patrolling it around the clock, and any Jidadan who didn't follow him would be dealt with accordingly.

"I want you to tell me what they are saying about me today, Siri, what are they saying?" the Savior said. It humbled him to have to rely on Siri to read the Twitter for him, but he still preferred her to his Ministers, who sometimes read to him only what they thought he wanted to hear, and who, he'd come to learn, were wont to lie to him, to read some things and omit others; he could count on Siri to tell him like it is.

"Tuvy, you! How do you have your ugly name on every street, your face everywhere, and yet you can't give us jobs! #thePartyofPower-

MustGo!" Siri read: "Jidada is Open for Business = Jidada is Open for Corruption! #thePartyofPowerMustGo!" Siri read: "We are hungry Mr. Comrade President! #thePartyofPowerMustGo!" "Free All Political Prisoners Now Mr. President! #thePartyofPowerMustGo!" "Kodwa Tuvy sibili, do you even understand the meaning of the word Leadership? Or even the fact that that Seat isn't a toilet seat? #thePartyofPowerMustGo!" "Comrade President, what are you doing about the ninety-eight percent unemployment rate? #thePartyofPowerMustGo!" Siri read: "Tuvius Delight Shasha, could you at least tell us when it will be that you and your greedy cronies will have your fill of looting so we can perhaps plan our lives accordingly; I mean, is there an end in sight? #thePartyofPowerMustGo!" "If we'd known this is what we were signing up for we'd have just kept the Old Horse, at least he was the better poison! #thePartyofPowerMustGo!" "We honestly don't know what on earth you're doing on that Seat of Power, Tuvy, please help us all and RESIGN! #thePartyofPowerMustGo!" "Resign, Resign, RESIGN #thePartyofPowerMustGo!"

"Okay, okay, stop, Siri, enough!" The Savior's face was barely recognizable from fury.

"Is there anything else I can help you with?" Siri said.

"No, that will be all, Siri. The rest is for me, leave it to me. Let me show these belligerent children of the nation who I truly am, they don't even know!"

FOR RULERS DO NOT BEAR THE SWORD FOR NO REASON

When those who know about things said the Savior indeed showed the nation who ruled Jidada with a -da and another -da, they meant the Savior did indeed show the nation who ruled Jidada with a -da and another -da. Tholukuthi journalists were rounded up and activists were rounded up and members of the Opposition were rounded up. Dissenters were rounded

up and critics were rounded up and citizens exercising their rights were rounded up. Lawyers who challenged the tyranny of the regime were rounded up and comedians who made fun of the Savior and the Seat were rounded up and artists who produced works critical of the regime were rounded up. Tholukuthi teachers and civil servants who called for a living wage were rounded up, and university students who demanded accessible education were rounded up, along with nurses and doctors who asked for equipment and supplies with which to save lives. Citizens who complained in queues were rounded up, along with anyone overheard expressing displeasure at the regime. Tholukuthi Jidada's prisons of horror swelled with the beaten, tortured, and violated bodies of the children of the nation, because, as Tuvy put it in a viral rant no doubt meant to remind the nation who was in charge, and how much: "We must be revered; we are Jidada; we are the constitution; we are the Seat of Power; we are the Defenders; we are the law; we are the courts; we are the voters; we are the electoral commission, we are the majority; we are the businesses; we are the telecommunications; we are the roads; we are the potholes in those roads; we are the bridges; we are the power stations; we are the jails; we are the sewage systems, we are the oxygen, we are the fire, we are the wind, we are the water, we are the earth, we are every fucking thing you can think of, tholukuthi EVERY-THING!" the Savior shrieked in an unearthly voice that made the young cling to their mothers.

Only Tuvy wasn't done. Tholukuthi he decreed himself Jidada's President for Life, effectively making sure he would indeed rule and rule and keep ruling. Tholukuthi he passed a decree suspending basic rights. And another outlawing anti-state activity on the internet. He passed another decree banning newspaper, radio, and television stations deemed detrimental to the interests of the government. He went on to suspend the miserable Opposition by decree, alongside civil society organizations and institutions deemed to be the "Dark Forces." He banned what he termed "queer opposi-

tiony tendencies," tholukuthi meaning activism, demonstrations, protests, and all and any political action considered hostile to the Seat and Party of Power, both in the Country Country and the Other Country alike. He decreed for Defenders to strike fear in the intestines of the enemies of the regime. Tholukuthi he reshuffled top governmental posts and put the most vicious Defenders in charge.

NO LONGER SOFT AS WOOL

Meanwhile, grim reports of the Crocodile's violent shenanigans began to spread across Jidada like wildfire. There were tales of him breaking into homes, cleaning out cupboards and pantries and inhaling every morsel of food in sight. Tales of the Crocodile raiding fields and destroying crops. Tales of the Crocodile reaching his arms up in the sky and ripping electric wires. Tales of the Crocodile eavesdropping on conversations, biting anyone who spoke against the Seat of Power. Tales of the Crocodile digging up roads and causing terrible car accidents. Tales of the Crocodile starting wildfires. Tales of the Crocodile attacking anyone dressed up in the colors of the Opposition. Tales of the Crocodile demanding cash from Jidadans, tossing them in his mouth and chomping them up if ever they refused him. Tales of the Crocodile seizing newly borns from their mothers' bosoms because he said tender flesh made the best snacks. It was clear to even the sticks and stones that the creature who'd once claimed to not be a real crocodile, to be vegetarian, to be friendly and even as soft as wool, to love Jidada, was in fact a dreadful fiend, yes, a most foul, violent monster under whose unfathomable terror there would never be peace.

THE RED BUTTERFLIES
OF JIDADA

OPEN ROAD

She begins to relax after she gets onto the A6 highway, the long stretch that, according to Golden Maseko, will have her in Bulawayo in no more than an hour and a half. "It's impossible to get lost really—just stay on A6 till you hit the very first turnoff. The tricky part is getting to your village after you turn, but use your God-given GPS and be sure to come back ngoba I'll be waiting with bated breath. I mean, as in, waiting for my car. With bated breath." Golden Maseko's sonorous voice in her ears. She smiles, remembering his magnificent horns, his beautiful face, the way he chews on his bottom lip when he's thinking, the way he looks at her from dark pools of eyes that make her want to drown inside him, the slightest whiff of paint that stubbornly clings to him because he practically lives in his art studio about halfway down her mother's block. Golden Maseko. The fact of him in her life, and this thing without a name between them, is unexpected and thrilling and scary all at once.

So far the road is clean as he promised—tholukuthi free from the

potholes that plague the townships and most of the city roads, making it
necessary for an animal to drive drunkenly in order to miss the inconvenient little pits. And of course it being Sunday morning, the traffic is near
nonexistent; there are stretches she feels alone on the road, which makes a
part of her wish Golden Maseko was riding along. Yes, Golden Maseko,
who obviously likes you, Destiny, who more than likes you, and who
you'll be needing to make your mind up about sooner or later, no? Because how long should one keep an animal waiting, really, and after all,
why make them wait to begin with, when life's so short and there's all this
living and loving to be done?

She shakes her head to clear it. It's true, she can't say she doesn't like
him back, in fact she's surprised she likes him quite a bit, or even a lot better than a bit if she's being honest with herself. He has, and in such a short
time since the day he came to fix her mother's kitchen cabinets, wormed
his way into her heart and head with an ease that still surprises her. On
that day, he'd found Simiso having forgotten about their appointment and
out visiting with Mother of God and Comrade Nevermiss Nzinga. Golden
Maseko had stayed to do his work, and while he did, talked to Destiny like
they'd already met, like they were picking up on a conversation begun a
long time ago. And on that day, Destiny laughed for the very first time
since Simiso told her about April 18, 1983. And he'd make her laugh many
times after, and without ever knowing it, he'd save her from a bottomless
grief. She smiles, and smiles again, remembering.

Around her is beauty, beauty, beauty—the land unfolds in stretches of
verdant green and rugged rock outcrops and, every now and then, masses
of dramatic hills that soar toward the uninterrupted sky. Wherever she
looks, she's almost felled by an incomparable perfection that cannot be put
into words. And alongside that perfection, a tranquility that makes her
feel as if she's the only animal living in that very moment. It's a devastating magnificence, so much so Destiny commits to making the effort to get

out of Lozikeyi often and open herself up to this kind of enchantment. If there was a way to stay in it, she'd never stop the car—she'd simply keep cruising, she thinks, from the sweet depths of a near-hypnotizing speed, aware of nothing now but the beauty stretching as far as the eye can see, yes, tholukuthi hoof getting heavier on the gas as if all of this magnificence depends on it. It is an exhilarating feeling, as close as she's ever come to flying, to forgetting the painful present and leaving the ugly past behind. Yes, but you'll also leave your life behind if you're not careful, Destiny, in case you don't know that speed kills, so slow down and get to your destination alive.

THE WEIGHT OF NAMES

The sign that says "Bulawayo, 10km" takes her by surprise—it doesn't feel to her she's even been that long on the road. Yes, you've actually been that long on the road, Destiny, and besides it being a relatively short drive you've been practically flying most of the time. And good thing you slowed down when you did, otherwise you'd have missed the turn. Bulawayo-Bulawayo-Bulawayo. She says the name out loud, lets it linger in the mouth, thinking, and not for the first time, What a dark, dark name. Meaning, where one gets killed, where there is killing. Yes, tholukuthi an ominous name that has made Destiny wonder endlessly about the prophecy of names, the terrible odds that the events of April 18, 1983, and the dark immediate years would fulfill the name. And in just a short while, she thinks, slowing down a bit, she'll be standing on Bulawayo earth. A kind of home, yes, but also a ruin. A place of slaughter. Of massacre. Of devastation and despair. Of blood and tears. Of disruption. Of the annihilation of families and family lines.

But is it actually a good idea, Destiny? You driving to Bulawayo like this, and on your own too? Are you sure you're strong enough for this?

Will you be able to deal with it? She'll find out, in just a short while, she'll know for sure if this was a good idea, if she's strong enough. Otherwise, she thinks, glancing into the rearview mirror, if the grief of the past few months didn't kill her, and at some point she in fact thought she'd die from it, then nothing else will.

COMPLICATED QUESTIONS, COMPLICATED FEELINGS

For the days immediately after Simiso's telling of the Gukurahundi story she'd done everything she could to stay intact, not wanting her own anguish to grieve her mother. It was a staggering effort, tholukuthi Destiny hadn't quite known what to do with the sudden discovery of a whole family she never knew she had, and at the same time handle the unspeakable horror of their brutal fate. Was she supposed to start by celebrating the fact that unlike how she'd grown up believing, she actually had a family, and a big family at that? But then how, exactly, did one celebrate those of whom she had no memory, and do so knowing she also needed to mourn them? And regarding what had been done to them, how did one begin to live with that terrible wound, what was she supposed to do with the pain, the anger, knowing that those who massacred her family not only walked free, but still sat on the Seat of Power, never ever held accountable, and from the looks of things, never to be held accountable, which meant, essentially, they'd all die their deaths and depart the physical world without ever having to face justice, which essentially meant the lives of the murdered, the brutalized, the wronged, did not matter. And what did that make of her relationship with Jidada, with this country that had already wounded her in so many unfathomable ways? Where did one begin, and how?

In the middle of all that pain and grief and confusion, there were the complicated feelings toward Simiso. Yes, her mother's own pain and loss and grief were beyond immeasurable, and Destiny knew she'd never truly

fathom what Simiso had lived through and carried and endured, what she still had to live through because who, really, could ever triumph over that kind of past? And, yes, hearing about April 18, 1983, made Destiny understand in fullness and for the first time who Simiso really was, made her appreciate the parts of her mother she'd never until then quite understood. But at the same time she could not help the hurt and anger that came from Simiso withholding the truth all these years, tholukuthi making her believe she was the child of an only child, with no other family. Only to decide one day, without any warning, without any preparation whatsoever, to drop this terrible bomb that rearranged who Destiny thought she was. And as if that wasn't enough, go on and declare the matter closed, refusing to answer any questions to help Destiny cope with the weight of the earth-shifting news.

"I've told you all I had in me to tell you, Destiny, and it took me all these years. I have nothing more to say on the matter," Simiso said. Destiny had found her mother in the living room, ironing. She'd taken a seat by the door and, after a bit of small talk, casually asked Simiso to tell her what her sister, Thandiwe, had been like, yes, tholukuthi Destiny asking with the hope that the conversation would naturally open up to allow her to learn more about the family about whom she had books and books of questions.

"But I don't understand, Mother. It's just a simple, straightforward question, really, I mean it's not like you didn't live with your sister for almost a decade and a half before the Gukurahundi. I'm sure there are good things, even beautiful things you can share about her and all your siblings so I can at least know who my family were," Destiny said. For an uncomfortable moment Simiso stood frozen, as if Destiny had doused her with a bucket of ice water.

"Did you just say to me, 'It's a simple question,' wena Destiny?"

"I'm sorry, Mother. I didn't mean it like that. All I meant—"

"Don't you dare open that mouth and tell me my sister or any of my

family are simple questions! Don't you ever dare, you hear me?!" Simiso
barked, shaking with rage, iron pointed at Destiny.

"Mother, I'm sorry, I'm sorry," Destiny said, stunned by her mother's
anger.

"You're not sorry! You can't be sorry! You don't know sorry! Because
you just have no idea, you'll never know, what goes on here! And here.
And here!" Simiso said, pointing the hot iron at her intestines, then at her
heart, then at her head, tholukuthi the iron so close that a few more inches
and she'd sear her own hide. And Destiny, on her feet, confused, scared,
her heart broken for causing Simiso pain without meaning to.

And later, after both of them had wept, first separately, and then together, Destiny apologized and promised Simiso to never again bring up
the subject. Yes, because after taking the time to carefully consider your
mother's reaction, Destiny, you'd in fact remembered what you'd forgotten in your anger, tholukuthi which was that once upon a time you'd not
only left Jidada for a whole decade, but you'd left Jidada for a whole decade without a goodbye to Simiso, without an explanation, and in those
ten years, without a letter or phone call or nothing. Tholukuthi because of
things you could never ever put into words no matter how much you tried.

ANIMALS DIE, THOLUKUTHI THE NAMES REMAIN

She pulls over at the very first rest stop she sees, where a small group of
vendors sit with their wares in the shade of a huge acacia tree. She reaches
for her purse and fishes out a couple of bills—to at least buy something
before she asks for directions. Which is a bit silly, though, Destiny—
would you yourself ever charge an animal just for directions? She shrugs,
slips the money in the front pocket of her jean shirt. It's the kind thing to
do, she thinks, and with the economy being what it is, it's never a bad
thing to give.

Every single vendor eyes her with an eager, expectant face, and she feels a pang knowing she won't be able to make all of them happy. She settles on an old peahen, perhaps because of her age, and that she's also in the company of an adorable little one, most likely a grandchild she is taking care of, who is busy entertaining himself with his toys. Destiny finds herself hoarding a variety of fruits—a can each of umtshwankela, amazhanje, umqokolo, uxakuxaku, umviyo, umbumbulu, umnii, and then two fruits of the baobab because she remembers Golden Maseko telling her once it was his favorite delicacy. These are wild fruits, and therefore not the kind to be so easily found in the city, unless one travels to the market, and so Destiny, who hasn't tasted many of them in over a decade, is giddy with the purchase.

The peahen is now busy bagging her customer's groceries with a new cheerfulness, obviously pleased with the sell. And the grandchild, as if sensing the grandmother's joy, as if understanding what it means, begins to sing the song that Jidada's little children everywhere seem to love whether they understand the lyrics or not: "Careful Jidada, here comes the Crocodile with his big, bad blades! Will he nibble, will he bite, will he chomp-chomp-chomp?!"

"Hush, demede, this foolish child! How many times do you need to be told nobody wants to hear that ugly song!" the peahen chides. The little one hides his face behind his toy truck, feigning shyness.

"Good luck with that, Grandmother. From the looks of it it's the children's chorus of the decade, and meanwhile adults are dancing to it at parties, kunzima," Destiny says.

"Hayibo! Like there aren't better songs to sing! And God help us with this Crocodile that'll kill us all," the grandmother says with a new heat in her voice.

"I was wondering, Grandmother, if you could help me with directions?" Destiny, feeling responsible, quickly changes the subject.

"Where are you looking to go, child?"

"To Bulawayo. The village. I don't think I'm that far from it but then I don't know the exact location."

The peahen, having bagged the fruits separately, now collects them in a big plastic bag, which Destiny accepts. Otherwise the elder doesn't speak, as if she hasn't really heard the question. And Destiny, puzzled, wondering if she's somehow said something wrong but not understanding how she could have with that simple question, fidgets with the bag to fill the awkward silence.

"And what exactly are you looking to go and do in that Bulawayo, child?" the peahen says when she finally speaks.

"My family is from there. I mean was, from there. But I've never been myself, I just want to go and see," Destiny says.

"Bulawayo is now a ghost village. Nobody lives there."

"Oh, I see," Destiny says. This part Simiso never mentioned, and it's not a possibility that has crossed her mind. She feels herself being looked over some more, examined some more. As if she's some strange specimen in a lab.

"I think I'll still go, just to look at least, since I'm already here," Destiny says.

"This child is trying to get to Bulawayo, someone tell her how," the peahen calls, to no one in particular.

And after she's carried the fruits to the car and returned with her phone and carefully saved the directions, Destiny bids her farewell.

"Tell us who you are before you go, child," the peahen says.

"My name is Destiny."

"Who, and of who?" the peahen says.

"Destiny Lozikeyi Khumalo, of Simiso Khumalo, and Simiso Khumalo of Butholezwe Henry Vulindlela Khumalo and Nomvelo Mary Khumalo of Bulawayo. I mean, what was Bulawayo."

"Child, what are you telling me?" The peahen speaks in an urgent, demanding voice now, looks Destiny up and down as if this is the first time she's laying eyes on her. And Destiny, baffled by the question she doesn't quite know how to answer, by the sudden shift in the elder, shuffles her feet and smiles an awkward smile.

"Are you telling me you are the grandchild of Butholezwe Henry Vulindlela Khumalo, you? The farmer? The businessmal of Bulawayo himself? Our Governor?" The peahen is rising, beating her skirts.

"Yes, he is, was, my grandfather. But I have no memory of him, I was little when the—when what happened, happened," Destiny says. She is surprised by how hard it is to say the word *Gukurahundi*, by her inability to call by name that which has brought her looking for the dead.

"Ah-ah-ah-ah-ah! Yeyi! Come here, child, come here!" The peahen is circling Destiny now, touching her, feeling her, patting her.

"And who do we have here, Mother of Ellis?" an old cow in a black dress says, approaching. The rest of the vendors, all of them significantly younger than the cow and peahen, have risen and start to surround the pair.

"This, right here, Simangele, is the grandchild of Butholezwe Henry Vulindlela Khumalo himself," the peahen says, addressing the cow.

"Ah-ah-ah-ah-ah, yeyi! What are you telling me, Mother of Ellis? You mean our Butholezwe Henry Vulindlela Khumalo?!" the cow says, eyes narrowed. The shock in her voice is unmistakable.

"I mean our Butholezwe Henry Vulindlela Khumalo," the peahen says.

"Son of Nqabayezwe Mbiko Khumalo and Zanezulu Hlatshwayo Khumalo?!" the cow says.

"Son of Nqabayezwe Mbiko Khumalo and Zanezulu Hlatshwayo Khumalo," the peahen says.

"Husband of Nomvelo Mary Khumalo and father of Nkosiyabo, Zenzele, Njube, Simiso, and Nkanyiso Khumalo?!" the cow says.

"Husband of Nomvelo Mary Khumalo and father of Nkosiyabo, Zenzele, Njube, Simiso, and Nkanyiso Khumalo," the peahen says.

"Ah-ah-ah-ah-ah! Futhi yeyi! Miracle-miracle-miracle! This is a miracle itself!" the old cow says, hinding with difficulty owing to old joints, and beating her front hooves.

"The dead are not dead, glory to the ancestors!" says a cat, obviously too young to know the names being mentioned but still touched by this roadside miracle.

"The dead are not dead!" the group choruses.

"Sit here, child, sit down, sit, please sit and let's see you properly! Ah-ah-ah-ah-ah! Yeyi! First of all here is your money back—we absolutely dare not make Henry Vulindlela Khumalo's own blood pay for anything on this Bulawayo earth, not after what he did for us in this region. No, no, no—take it, we insist, please, here is your money, it's not often that you get to thank the dead! Miracle!" the peahen gushes.

A GIFT BY THE ROAD

And isn't it amazing, Destiny? That these many years—almost four decades, to be exact—after your family's murders, there are animals who still say their names? Who still sing them with the same breath with which they sing the living? Yes, it is amazing, she thinks. And the odds of it, just what are the odds? What, really, are the odds? she keeps repeating to herself, tears holding their breath in her eyes. She sighs ever so deeply, and not for the first time since she resumed her drive, remembering how when she left the rest stop the old animals had held her like the earth holds trees with the deepest roots.

The whole experience had felt like a gift that couldn't have come at a better time, everything about it surreal and perfect except for the fact that

Simiso hadn't been there to experience it with her. She'd thought about asking her mother to come along, but then the memory of their ugly confrontation—now in the past but then somehow still fresh—had made Destiny reconsider, and she'd ended up not telling Simiso about the trip altogether, only that she was borrowing Golden Maseko's car to visit old friends out of town and would be returning in the late afternoon. Perhaps another time, perhaps at a better time—she thinks, hopes—if ever there were to be such a time, she'd indeed return with her mother.

FAMILY PORTRAIT

She is on the lookout for the white bridge that divides Mpilo and Bulawayo. She was told that shortly after she crossed into Bulawayo she'd see the burned carcass of a bus that'd belonged to her grandfather, and was set alight by Defenders in 1983, the bus driver and conductor locked inside after they were stripped of their clothes and cash takings. The bus is how she'll know she has reached her destination. She grips the steering wheel as if to stop it from coming off, feeling the familiar anger that is never far of late. That anger is now amplified by the fact that after spending just over two hours listening to the elders take turns telling her stories about her family, she has a better appreciation of who they were—they are no longer vague beings.

Tholukuthi now she can picture them: a grandmother, Nomvelo Mary Khumalo, who was said to have been as beautiful as sunrise in her youth, a devoted mother who'd kept the family together while her husband was away at war, who coordinated efforts with the other villagers to provide food and other necessities for the freedom fighters, which the colonial government of course declared a crime, a grandmother who, despite being the kind of judgmental Christian who frowned down on indigenous religions,

would still never turn away anyone in need. Tholukuthi an uncle, Nkosiyabo, who, being the eldest, was being groomed to follow in his father's
footsteps as a farmer and businessmal, and who sometimes drove his father's buses and gave the elderly free rides. And the next uncle after him,
Zenzele, a gifted student, nicknamed Doctor for his brilliance, who'd received a scholarship to study medicine in Cuba. And the next uncle after
him, Njube, who was beautiful and whom all the young femals wanted to
marry and who shared his mother's devotion to God and who played the
guitar at church. And the last and youngest uncle after Simiso, Nkanyiso,
who was still in primary school and excelled in soccer. And the aunt after
him, and baby of the family, Thandiwe, whom Destiny was told she has a
strong resemblance to, who loved the color blue as a child so much she
wore nothing but blue and called herself Blue, and who wanted to be a
teacher when she grew up and practiced on her father's frangipani as well
as rocks and flowers and grasses of the village.

Isn't it something, Destiny, how sometimes stories will raise the dead,
as if they are not dead at all but alive in our mouths, only waiting to be
animated by our tongues? It is indeed true, tholukuthi before that rest
stop, all she knew of her perished family members, outside of the little
about her grandparents, were mere names. But now, with the stories she's
just learned, they feel more real; she can in fact picture them, speak of
them. Only, of course, they aren't here, they'll never be here as they
should have been, as they deserve to be, yes, tholukuthi Uncle Nkosiyabo
is not here being the businessmal and farmer he was on his way to becoming and possibly continuing his father's legacy of contributing to the development of the region. Uncle Zenzele is not here being the doctor he
could have been. Uncle Njube, Uncle Nkanyiso, and Aunt Thandiwe, her
grandparents—none of them—are here living their lives, as are the thousands and thousands of other murdered innocents. The knowledge stirs

her crouching anger. She clenches her jaw, blinks away hot tears. She knows she must not cry, because once she starts crying, she may not find the strength to proceed to the village. She takes a deep breath, rolls the window down. The Bulawayo air rushes in, with it the smell of earth that fills her with something stronger than longing.

BULAWAYO, BULAWAYO

She's known absolute quiet, but the silence of Bulawayo is a foreign country. It overwhelms her with such impossible heaviness she could've swallowed a mountain. Tholukuthi knowing it's just her alone and the dead here, tholukuthi knowing it's just her alone and wronged ghosts here, tholukuthi knowing what happened here, that in this place is a past that will forever be present, tholukuthi never to pass. Which is perhaps why, as she stands there confronting the dead village, her restless mind just ups and starts conjuring ghosts, spirits, beasts of the wild, terrible things she's seen in horror movies, supernatural happenings she's heard of. It is while her mind is conjuring things that somewhere in the dry grass—or is it the humongous mopane trees filling the air with the smell of turpentine, or maybe it is the still jungle that has swallowed Bulawayo—there emanates such a loud rustle that sends her intestines lurching and leaping to her chest.

She's suddenly jelly-kneed from fright, desperately clasping her head, heart in her throat, eyes shut so she doesn't see whatever creature is rustling and coming for her. And because she isn't the kind of animal to die in silence she shrieks with all the force in her lungs: "May'babooooo!" Tholukuthi out of the somewhere in the somewhere of the still jungle, an echo replies ". . . baboooooooooo!!!"—the unexpected sound petrifying her even more than the rustle, even more than she's already scared so

that she's proper hollering her head off now, "May'babo! May'babo! May'babo!" and the echo is busy replying, ". . . babo! . . . babo! . . . babooooooooooo!!!"

Ah-ah, Destiny! Calm, calm, what are you doing? Surely you didn't bring yourself all this way to conjure up things that aren't there and scare yourself to bits. It's just a rustle, remember you share this earth with other beings, isn't it well to allow them to live their lives while you live yours? She opens one careful eye first, then another, and looks around like a thief. She takes a deep breath. And another deep breath. And another. And another and another and another. And gradually she steadies, calms. Feels her intestines sit down. Then she smiles, shakes her head, embarrassed. Then she shakes her head again, laughs at herself. The echo laughs at her, laughs harder.

HEART-TO-HEART WITH THE DEAD

"Did you see that, Grandmother, Grandfather? Did y'all see that, Uncle Nkosiyabo, Uncle Zenzele, Uncle Njube, Uncle Nkanyiso, Aunt Thandiwe? I wonder who I take after, because Simiso has no coward bone in her body!" Destiny says. And she laughs at herself again—and the echo laughs— thinking of Simiso, who never scares, who never panics, who never cracks. And she laughs some more, louder, and the echo laughs harder, and because she's not scared of it now, she imagines it could even be the dead laughing at her, with her, tholukuthi the dead who are not dead.

"Most beloved kindred, I greet you, with love, those of you whose names I know and those of you whose names I do not know, I greet you, all of you, with love. My name is Destiny Lozikeyi Khumalo, child of Simiso Khumalo, of Butholezwe Henry Vulindlela Khumalo and Nomvelo Mary Khumalo of this very land, and I come to pay my respects." She begins, surprised, after all, by how effortless it is to talk to the dead. And

once she begins, tholukuthi she cannot stop, because there's so much to say to her kindred, just so many things to say. And Destiny Lozikeyi Khumalo talks to the dead and talks to the dead—yes, tholukuthi talks to the dead until she forgets time and time forgets her, until much, much, much later, she looks up to find herself bathed in the baptismal red rain of a thousand fluttering butterflies, in the soft waterfall of their whispering wings.

THOLUKUTHI GIFTS, THOLUKUTHI INHERITANCE

She gets back in Lozikeyi just before sunset, finds Simiso removing laundry from the clothing line. "You sure are walking like floating, if I didn't know any better I'd say you were off to see some forbidden lover, but then Golden Maseko spent the whole afternoon here," Simiso says by way of greeting, speaking funny because of the peg she's holding with her teeth.

"Mother!" Destiny says, standing stock-still in the kitchen, caught off guard. She abandons the bag of fruit and escapes to her room, where she flings herself facedown onto the bed, embarrassed, thinking, What on earth was Golden Maseko doing visiting, knowing she was away, and what exactly did he tell Simiso?

Ah-ah, but what on earth did you expect, Destiny? That you'd be the first one in this whole wide world to hide a thing with horns in a sack? And from your mother too? And by the way, if Simiso knows, its most likely that every one of her friends also knows, so there! But then again, why worry, and so what if anyone knows? It doesn't matter; life's so short, and there's all this living and loving to be done. Which is true, she thinks, turning on her back and smiling at the asbestos. The next time she sees Golden Maseko—who was out when she returned his car—she'll agree to the relationship he's been pushing for. Indeed, life's so short, there's all the living and loving to be done.

She rises, still smiling, meaning to take a shower and change. Which is when she sees, for the first time, there above the bookshelf, three medium-size colorful paintings that weren't there when she left for Bulawayo. There is a painting of the writer Yvonne Vera, and below it, a quote from her first novel, *Nehanda*: "The dead are not dead," says the brief quote. And on either side of Yvonne Vera, paintings of Queen Lozikeyi and

Mbuya Nehanda, all of them signed "Golden Maseko." Destiny looks at them with awe.

"Aren't they beautiful?" Simiso is filling the doorway. Destiny nods, overwhelmed.

"They're supposed to be for your birthday. I told your friend to put them up himself." Simiso smiles a smile that Destiny hasn't seen in a while.

"Happy birthday, daughter, come here, you didn't forget it's your birthday now, did you?" Simiso embraces Destiny.

"Thank you, Mother, apparently it's got to be when I'm not reminded I actually forget it. So where's my present?"

"Tsk-tsk. You carry an animal in your womb, you birth them, you keep them alive, and they have the audacity to demand a birthday present on top of it!" Destiny laughs, hugs her mother tight, tighter. And how is it that she hasn't realized just how much smaller Simiso has become, how her mother is really no longer young? And holding on to her mother, she's remembering the embrace of the elders by the rest stop on her way to Bulawayo. And then she's remembering Bulawayo. And then she's remembering the long talk with the dead. And then she's fighting back tears. And then she's holding Simiso even tighter.

"Okay, enough, enough, you'll break my bones now. And please take a bath, you smell like some mopane trees!" Simiso pushes gently.

"Well, Simiso Khumalo, for carrying me in your womb, for birthing me, for keeping me alive, and of course, for bringing the absolutely golden Golden Maseko into my life, please find some rare fruits on the kitchen table." Destiny releases her mother.

"Well, thank you, it's about time I got just a little gratitude, and you're most welcome, child." Simiso smiles again that smile Destiny hasn't seen in a long time, tholukuthi shaking her head, looking into her daughter's eyes like she's looking at the most precious being she's ever seen, because

Destiny is really the most precious being Simiso has ever seen. And then Simiso bursts out in laughter.

"What, what are you laughing at?" Destiny says, baffled.

"Nothing. Can't an animal laugh in her own home?"

"Come on, Mother."

"Well, you reminded me of your grandfather for a minute there, with that pen behind the ear."

"What? What pen behind the ear?" Destiny reaches up; she checks the left ear, checks the right ear, pulls the slender Parker pen and looks at it like she's never seen it before, because she in fact has never ever seen it before.

"Hmmm, how very strange! I most definitely didn't put it there." Destiny is puzzled. She presses the cam, examines the black slender pen, smells it, licks it.

"What do you mean, you didn't put it there? Bring it here, let me see." Simiso takes the pen. And then she drops it as if it's a piece of hot coal. She plops down on the bed, her face looking like she's seen a ghost.

"What is it, Mother?"

"Where did you get this pen, Destiny?" Simiso, who never scares, who never panics, who never cracks, is actually sounding unnerved, near frantic. And she's looking down at the pen—itself an ordinary thing—like she's in fact seeing something as unfathomable as a Black pope.

"I don't know, Mother, honestly. I've never seen it before." Destiny picks the pen up and scrutinizes it all over again.

"That's the kind of pen your grandfather wrote with, Destiny. He came from the war with a box of them and wouldn't use anything else. I even remember the curious logo. He called them his lucky pens." And now it is Destiny's turn to sit on the bed and look like she's seeing a Black pope.

WRITE IN A BOOK ALL THE WORDS
THAT I HAVE SPOKEN TO YOU

The following morning, on a small desk next to the window, with Queen Lozikeyi and Yvonne Vera and Mbuya Nehanda looking on from Golden Maseko's paintings, Destiny, who otherwise has never imagined herself a serious writer, sits and begins to write with her grandfather's black Parker pen the story Simiso told her about April 18, 1983, in combination with her own story of 2008, as well as the story of her ten years in exile; tholukuthi the decade of which she hasn't told a single soul. She also writes of her trip to Bulawayo, and of the Jidada that she would like to see, a Jidada of the future. Letter by letter, word by word, line by line, paragraph by paragraph, page by page, she writes from the present into her past, into her mother's and family's pasts, which is also Jidada's past, then back again into the present and beyond into a hoped-for future, yes, tholukuthi the past and present and future unfolding simultaneously on her pages until she loses track of time, until the days run together and she cannot tell them apart. She writes and she writes and she writes and she writes and she writes and she writes and she writes. Tholukuthi writes.

She emerges from her room on the seventh day, which Mother of God would later go on to say reminds her of about how long it took for God to create everything. Simiso is washing greens in the sink when Destiny taps her on the shoulder and presents her with the thick black notebook. Tholukuthi Simiso who accepts the notebook, beaming. Simiso who holds the notebook to her chest as if it were a new baby. Simiso who pulls up a chair and sits at the kitchen table. Simiso who presses her nose against a random page and takes a deep inhale. Simiso who opens the first page and reads the title, *The Red Butterflies of Jidada*, and beneath it, "For the dead, who are not dead," and blinks away tears. Simiso who opens the next page that says "Chapter One," and lowers her head as if in prayer. Simiso who

begins reading. Simiso who turns to the second page and continues reading. Simiso who turns to the third page and continues reading. Simiso
who turns to the fourth page and keeps reading. Simiso who turns to the
fifth page and continues reading. Simiso who doesn't hear Destiny say,
"Mother, you really don't have to read the whole thing, I was just showing
you to say I'm done, that's all." Tholukuthi Simiso who doesn't, who can't
put down *The Red Butterflies of Jidada*, as if it is the very bread of life.

MY BONES WILL RISE AGAIN

REMEMBRANCE

The day of remembering the Disappeared of Jidada, otherwise simply referred to as Remembrance by those who observed it, came that year as
it'd come the past couple of years since its founding by the Sisters of the
Disappeared. It was of course not a nationally recognized event, but that
didn't stop the residents of Lozikeyi from being part of it whether they
wished or not—tholukuthi many of the founding members lived in the
township and so the day's events therefore naturally took place in Lozikeyi,
which thus absorbed Remembrance as part of its rhythms. Activities were
held at the Uhuru Park and concluded with a long march to the House of
Power in the city center, where Remembrance predictably ended with the
beating and arrest of the marchers after they'd made yet another petition
for the Seat of Power to account for Jidada's Disappeared.

Tholukuthi the size of the crowds that thronged Lozikeyi that day was
possibly a combination of the movement's gaining traction and the fact
that Remembrance that year fell during a season of strong anti-government
sentiment so that like anything else that was against the Seat of Power, the

event heavily trended on social media and garnered more than usual attention. So that by the time it came around, even the sticks and stones knew what day it was. And so on that Saturday, Lozikeyi found herself thoroughly unprepared for the traffic that descended on her streets at about the time that residents sat for their Saturday breakfast. They didn't need to be told that the throngs in their township were the kind of throngs they absolutely needed to be a part of, and so they thus rose, turned their backs on their breakfasts with no qualms whatsoever, and accordingly pointed their noses in the direction of Uhuru Park.

QUEEN BLACK AND THE WHIRLWIND

When those who were there told it, they said following the usual opening prayer to the indigenous God uNkulunkulu by a young spirit medium, accompanied by the pouring of libation for the ancestors, the program began with a song by Queen Black, and that at the mention of that particular name by the emcee, the crowd pricked their ears, hinded, wagged their tails, looked at each other, and looked at the stage because the name Queen Black pulled open the dusty drawers of their memories to fish out a long-lost idol who'd risen to prominence for his provocative protest songs in the first couple of decades following Jidada's independence.

It was at the height of Queen Black's glory that his fans woke up one ordinary Friday to news of the singer's abrupt move to exile in Perth, Australia. Those who really know about things said Queen Black's dramatic departure from the country apparently came following more than a few warnings from the Seat of Power about his music, but it didn't quite explain why he never again practiced his art from the safety of exile, never again to sing despite his immense talent, despite numerous pleas and petitions from his heartbroken fans. Could this indeed be their prodigal Queen Black, remembered his voice, and found his way home?

It was indeed Queen Black, returned. Before the crowd could get over their excitement, the unmistakable voice of the prodigal musician barreled upward like a terrible whirlwind. Tholukuthi the whirlwind was an invocation and a notice and a cry and a question and a revolt and a sign and a plea and a rant and an alarm and a wail and a roar and a weapon and an offering and many other things all at once. Tholukuthi the whirlwind called out to Jidada's Disappeared and rang and rang. Tholukuthi the whirlwind asked the gathered children of the nation exactly what they'd been doing, where they'd been, when each and every one of the Disappeared was disappeared. Tholukuthi the whirlwind wanted to know exactly what action the children of the nation had taken after each and every one of Jidada's Disappeared were disappeared. Tholukuthi the whirlwind wondered how it was that the children of the nation found it possible to laugh and dance and make love and find joy and basically go on with the business of living while the Disappeared stayed disappeared and unaccounted for. Tholukuthi the whirlwind asked what kind of creature the said Seat of Power was that had absolutely no qualms about Disappearing its own children. Tholukuthi the whirlwind told the Seat of Power that every single one of the Disappeared wasn't a stone, no, but someone's son, someone's daughter, someone's mother, someone's sister, someone's brother, someone's father, someone's uncle, someone's auntie, someone's cousin, someone's friend, someone's lover, someone's partner, someone's wife, someone's husband, someone's neighbor, someone's someone, tholukuthi always someone's someone. And the whirlwind demanded of the Seat of Power to bring back, to account for each and every one of Jidada's Disappeared. And the whirlwind demanded of those who had ears to hear to never rest, to never be silent until the Seat of Power brought back and accounted for each and every one of Jidada's Disappeared.

MEMORY

Destiny feels the whirlwind rattle her mother's roof and windows while she's in the shower, and hurries to finish up. In no time she's changed into a long white tunic dress and is throwing things in her satchel. As she does this she calls out to her mother, who doesn't respond because, despite the time of day, despite the whirlwind that is apparently shaking everything, Simiso, who stayed up late ironing every single sheet and curtain she owns until dawn, is still lost in the deepest throes of sleep. By the time Destiny gets to Uhuru Park, the whirlwind has ceased. On the speaker, the voice of Sis Nomzamo is inviting the audience to step up and remember the Disappeared by sharing their stories, by saying their names out loud.

Even with the thick throngs, Destiny squeezes her way near the front and finds a spot next to an old couple, a duck and hen in matching orange T-shirts, who huddle together to make room. On the loudspeaker, Sis Nomzamo's voice continues to coax and encourage, to speak about the importance of keeping the memory of the Disappeared alive because to do so, she says, is to work against forgetting. Tholukuthi when she hears Sis Nomzamo's call, Destiny knows, feels in her intestines, that she is the one being specifically addressed. "You hear that, love? Against forgetting, as we were discussing just last night," the duck says, nudging his partner. "And against erasure," the hen says, nudging him back. "And that's the truth," Destiny adds, bobbing her head. But how does it feel, Destiny, to be here, in this kind of crowd, knowing what you know about Jidada? Knowing what you know about the past? Knowing what you went through? Are you not afraid? No—since her visit to Bulawayo, since she sat down to write, she has chosen not to be afraid. This is her way of rising above the past, of putting together that which was broken, this is her way of dreaming the future.

Despite Sis Nomzamo's coaxing, the audience remains cloaked in a veil

of shyness. They're taking the time to see if this is something they can do, because it isn't a simple matter, all kinds of considerations have to be made. Tholukuthi testing that their tongues are strong enough to bear the weight of the name of a loved one that's been rendered heavy by grief. Tholukuthi checking that the voice will tell the story from beginning to end without faltering. Tholukuthi making sure they'll carry themselves all the way to the podium intact, without getting cold feet and finding themselves unable to move, without tripping on their pain, without looking back and turning into salt. Tholukuthi making certain that once at the podium they will in fact be able to face the crowds without falling apart.

It is while the audience is deliberating all these considerations that Destiny is seen hinding to the stage, straight-backed, shoulders squared, head high, tholukuthi walking just like Simiso walks, which she tells her is how her own mother, Nomvelo Mary Khumalo, walked. The throngs applaud the goat with the respect due those who go first in any challenge, knowing as they do that not everyone can do so, tholukuthi there are types. Destiny's notebook is already open when she stands facing the crowd from the stage, leaning slightly into the microphone, calm despite the hundreds of watchful eyes.

She greets the audience and tells them she'll read an excerpt from a forthcoming first book, *The Red Butterflies of Jidada*, recently accepted for publication, and dedicated to the memory of her murdered family, including Butholezwe Henry Vulindlela Khumalo, her grandfather, who disappeared on April 18, 1983. At the mention of the date, the crowd collectively feels their intestines lurch, leap to the chest. At the mention of the date, the crowd collectively feels their intestines lurch, leap to the chest because to many, the year 1983 is an old, seething wound. They move their tongues, test their throats, their feet, their knees. Tholukuthi consider again the distance to the stage so when the goat leaves, they are ready to follow suit because they too have something to say about 1983, about 1984, about

1985, about 1986, about 1987, they know something about years like 2005, 2008, 2013, 2018, 2019, yes, tholukuthi they know something about many other years.

THE DEAD ARE NOT DEAD

When those who were there later told those who weren't there, they said Destiny was in the middle of reading the part about her grandfather, having been shot by the Defenders, being tossed into a jeep like a dirty rag, never to be seen again, when Defenders stormed Uhuru Park. That the crowd instantly grew wings, scattered, and flew better than the wind. That femals and panicked young ones shrieked and filled the air with the poetry of sheer terror. Those who were there later told those who weren't there that in the middle of the ugly chaos, the Sisters of the Disappeared tried to whisk Destiny off the stage, but that Destiny only stood there and read in that voice that was full of the dead. That Gloria and her young friends briefly stood at the edge and shrieked for her to run, Run, Sis Destiny, run!—but that Destiny stood there and read in that voice that was full of the dead. That members of the audience tried to carry her to safety, but that Destiny stood there and read in that voice that was full of the dead. That the Sisters of the Disappeared fought to move her away, but that Destiny stood there and read in that voice that was full of the dead. That the last of the fleeing throngs howled over their shoulders was she trying to get hurt standing there, but that Destiny stood there and read in that voice that was full of the dead. That barking Defenders circled her—teeth bared, hairs raised—but that Destiny stood there and read in that voice that was full of the dead. That Commander Jambanja barked for her to step away from the podium and lie facedown, but that Destiny stood there and read in that voice that was full of the dead. That Commander Jambanja fired a warning shot in the air, but that Destiny stood there and

read in that voice that was full of the dead. That Commander Jambanja trained his weapon and barked threats and insults, but that Destiny stood there and read in that voice that was full of the dead. That Commander Jambanja, son of Commander John Soso, pulled the trigger, but that Destiny, daughter of Simiso Khumalo, stood there and read in that voice that was full of the dead. That the shot echoed and echoed and echoed in defense of the Revolution, but that Destiny stood there and read in that voice that was full of the dead. That the bullet fired by Commander Jambanja, son of Commander John Soso, flew and pierced Destiny, daughter of Simiso Khumalo, in the chest, on the left side, tholukuthi right where the heart is, and came out on the other side, but that Destiny stood there and read in that voice that was full of the dead. That the dregs of the crowd of Lozikeyi locals, who now stood at a safe distance, shrieked, He fired! He shot her! Unarmed! Commander Jambanja just shot Simiso's child! but that Destiny stood there and read in that voice that was full of the dead. That the chest area of Destiny's white dress turned crimson-crimson-crimson, but tholukuthi Destiny stood there and read in that voice that was full of the dead, and read in that voice that was full of the dead, and read in that voice that was full of the dead, and read in that voice that was full of the dead. And it was about two minutes and thirteen seconds after being shot that Destiny reached the end of her section in that voice that was full of the dead. And then she said thank you. And only then did she drop facedown, tholukuthi the heart already quiet, already silent like the inside of a seed.

PORTRAIT OF SILENCE

When those who were there told those who weren't there that Destiny's wake was held in utmost silence, tholukuthi what they meant was that Destiny's wake was held in utmost silence. That no word was ever uttered

for anything or any reason by anybody. That not even a prayer, not a funeral song was heard. There were no sad sighs, no sniffles. If tears were shed, they were silent tears. If things needed to be said, animals looked into each other's eyes without blinking until whatever needed to be communicated was expressed and understood beyond a shadow of a doubt. That even the breathing was done in silence. That bodies moved with the quiet of shadows. That even when Gloria and her young friends laced together their old tennis shoes and zipped them toward electric wires, they didn't utter a single word, and that the tennis shoes flew in silent silence and the wires caught them in silence also. That next door, inside Eden, when the Duchess fell into a trance and Nkunzemnyama arrived blinded by the reddest rage, his terrible fury was perfectly mute, and the drums that welcomed him were soundless drums. And that the flies too were silent and also the cockroaches were silent and the mosquitoes were silent and the mice were silent and the birds were silent and the cicadas were silent and the crickets were silent and everything was silent, it was just silent, tholukuthi silent-silent-silent.

THE WALL OF THE DEAD

Those who were there told those who weren't there that it was during the thick of that silence that Simiso called for Golden Maseko, in silence, to come with a thing of red paint and brush, and Golden Maseko silently came with a thing of red paint and a brush. Then Simiso told Golden Maseko, in silence still, to follow her out of the yard with the things, and Golden Maseko silently followed her out of the yard with the things. And there, Simiso stood looking at the wall for a long time as if she was listening to it. And then Simiso looked into Golden Maseko's eyes, and they both stood like that, Simiso looking into Golden Maseko's devastated eyes, and Golden Maseko looking into Simiso's heartbroken eyes, yes, tholukuthi

Simiso expressing to Golden Maseko in silence what it was exactly she needed him to do and how and Golden Maseko understanding every single instruction in silence. And then Golden Maseko began to paint in silence. And Golden Maseko painted in silence and Golden Maseko painted in silence and Golden Maseko painted in silence and Golden Maseko painted in silence and Golden Maseko painted in silence.

And when Golden Maseko finally stepped away from the wall, it was to reveal a red butterfly, and under it, the name Destiny Lozikeyi Khumalo. And next to it another butterfly, and under it, the name Butholezwe Henry Vulindlela Khumalo. And next to it another butterfly, and under it, the name Nomvelo Mary Khumalo. And next to it another butterfly, and under it, the name Nkosiyabo Khumalo. And next to it another butterfly, and under it, the name Nkanyiso Khumalo. And next to it another butterfly, and under it, the name Zenzele Khumalo. And next to it another butterfly, and under it, the name Njube Khumalo. And next to it another butterfly, and under it, the name Thandiwe Khumalo. And next to it another butterfly, and under it, the name Sakhile Bathakathi George Khumalo.

And so began what would soon be known as the Wall of the Dead. Before Golden Maseko's paint had dried, animals came and silently painted a red butterfly, and beneath it wrote a name of a loved one murdered by the Seat of Power ever since Jidada was Jidada with a -da and another -da. One by one, animals came in silence and painted in silence and wrote in silence and left in silence. Then two by two, then three by three, four by four, five by five. Then many by many. First it was just locals from Lozikeyi, but with social media being what it is, pictures of the wall were shared and trended, and very soon animals were arriving from places near and far. They came in silence. And painted red butterflies in silence and wrote the names of their dead in silence. Tholukuthi it was a lot of names. And soon, every inch of Simiso's Durawall was red with butterflies, with the names of the dead.

The Wall of the Dead quickly became a legitimate landmark such that townships around Lozikeyi called it Lozikeyi's Wall of the Dead, and in Lozikeyi it was called Simiso's Wall of the Dead, or Destiny's Wall of the Dead, depending on who was speaking. It was common to hear animals say, "You just keep straight. But if you see the Wall of the Dead turn around, you'll have passed it, because it's before the Wall of the Dead," or "Just look out for Destiny's Wall of the Dead, you won't miss it if you tried, never mind you don't know what it looks like, when you see it you'll know it, and when you get to the next block on your left, call me, I'll come out and meet you," or "Where did we first meet? We found ourselves sitting next to one another at Soldiers of Liberation, but really the very first time I saw her myself was at Simiso's Wall of the Dead. And I just knew she was the one."

The Wall of the Dead became a thing of its own, with a life of its own. Even animals who didn't have murdered loved ones came to see the wall. They came and stood or sat, gazed and gazed at the names of the dead in silence, and left in silence. Pastors and preachers and priests came with their Bibles and opened them in silence and read them in silence and left in silence. Youngsters came and shyly stood in front of the wall, and looked at the butterflies and the names of the dead in silence. Tourists visiting the region added Lozikeyi to their list of destinations, and they too came and stood by the wall and saw. And of course being tourists, they took pictures, but they took them in silence. The Wall of the Dead was featured in news stories by outlets from all over the world, where it was actually called Jidada's Wall of the Dead.

And it was obviously because of the resulting and embarrassing international attention that Jidada's Minister of Disinformation, Dick Mampara; the Minister of Propaganda, Elegy Mudidi; and their entire team of Dungbeetles went morbid, spewing venom and damnation in the Other Country. Tholukuthi the Wall of the Dead was condemned as propaganda

meant to whip up political emotions against a constitutionally elected government. It was thus declared illegal for private citizens to take it upon themselves to create unauthorized memorials on Jidada soil. The children of the nation were warned that it was a crime to travel to Lozikeyi for the express purpose of drawing a butterfly or writing a name, or both, on the illegal Wall of the Dead. And then it was declared a crime for nonresidents to be found within a hundred meters of the Wall of the Dead. And then it was declared a crime for nonresidents and residents alike to be found within fifty meters of the Wall of the Dead. And then it went down to forty meters. And then it went down to thirty, twenty, ten meters. And then it was a meter.

When none of this proved effective, it was declared a crime for anyone to possess, use, or sell red ink. And then it was declared a crime to possess the skill of drawing a red butterfly. Animals whose last names were found to match the names on the Wall of the Dead were subject to investigation. And then the Seat of Power for the very first time in history addressed the dead themselves in a statement broadcast all over the cemeteries and skies and airs of the nation, and reminded them that when the Seat of Power that was above all Seats of Power invented the slogan "Rest in Peace," it meant what, it meant for the dead to observe quietude and order like good dead Comrades, and not become a living situation. The statement also said that if the dead were indeed found to have names matching the names on the Wall of the Dead, they would be dug up and accordingly brought to justice for the dead because even if Jidada generally respected the dead as per cultural norms, the Seat of Power would not be disrespected by the dead in an obvious effort to undermine a living, breathing, constitutionally elected government.

COMMANDER JAMBANJA AND THE SEVEN DEFENDERS
WHO CAME FOR SIMISO

Even the sticks and stones who witnessed the Defender jeep thunder down the longest road in Lozikeyi that late afternoon knew it could only be headed to house number 636, what with the brouhaha that Simiso's Wall of the Dead was causing, tholukuthi both in the Other Country and Country Country alike. When they saw the unmistakable square head of Commander Jambanja stick out the front window in his signature white bandanna, the residents of Lozikeyi were not only reminded of Destiny's murder but also knew that despite Simiso's devastating loss, the suffering goat would not be escaping the Defenders without the humiliation of insults, without enduring beatings and bitings or perhaps even an arrest, all of course depending on the mood of the dogs and the whims of their wagging tails. Tholukuthi the residents of Lozikeyi stood watching the dust settle long after the Defender jeep had boiled past; they pointed their tails to the earth and shook their heads and uttered the saddest sighs the way of Jidadans everywhere because at the end of the day, what, really, could animals ever do under the Jidada sky in the Country Country besides point their tails to the earth and shake their heads and utter the saddest sighs in the face of the vicious dogs of the nation?

Those who were there told those who weren't there that Commander Jambanja and the seven Defenders who came for Simiso leapt out of the jeep before it even reached a full stop, tholukuthi all hard faces and growls and snarls and hairs standing on end. That the vicious pack, following Commander Jambanja's lead, first strutted up and down, up and down, and up and down, tholukuthi surveying the Wall of the Dead. And because Commander Jambanja never ever carried out his work without an audience in order that his legend keep growing, the pack accordingly stopped and, with the most perfect synchronicity, lifted their legs and let dance on the wall

such awesome jets of urine fitting of Belgian stallions, and doing so while letting out a deafening ruckus of howls that brought the neighborhood out to see what the pandemonium was all about. And upon seeing the spectacle that pained but didn't necessarily shock them, the residents of Lozikeyi pointed their tails to the earth and shook their heads and uttered the saddest sighs.

THOLUKUTHI NEHANDA'S BONES

They said, those who know about things, that it was while Commander Jambanja and the seven Defenders who'd come to take Simiso were inside house number 636 that a great wailing wind tore through Lozikeyi. It whipped the earth and made buildings writhe and rattled loose roofs and powered through open windows and tossed movable things before banging doors shut. It lifted dead leaves and dust and debris and tossed them in the air. It snatched laundry off clotheslines and tried to steal them off the bodies of stunned animals who huddled together for protection. Inside Eden it sent small creatures scurrying for cover and shook the trees and sent leaves flying. Tholukuthi it stripped the Nehanda tree of every single one of its pods and scattered them all over the township so that when the wind suddenly stopped as mysteriously as it'd started, Nehanda's bones, as the children called the strangely shaped pods the color of bleached bones, were scattered throughout Lozikeyi. Only the children noticed because it was in their nature to pay attention to small things; otherwise the eyes of the adults were glued to house number 636.

YOU TOUCH A FEMAL, YOU TOUCH A ROCK,
YOU WILL GET CRUSHED

Those who were there told those who weren't there that Commander Jambanja and the seven Defenders who'd come for Simiso didn't spend that much time inside her house, as if they'd found her waiting for them. It was a proper quickie, they were in and out with their prisoner even before their piss had started to dry on the Wall of the Dead. Tholukuthi Simiso had retreated to her house shortly after she had Golden Maseko write the names of her dead on the wall, and was never again seen outside. And the goat may in fact have lived in the terrible solitude of her grief, hadn't it been for the stubborn love of the Duchess, Gogo Moyo, Mother of God, Comrade Nevermiss Nzinga, the Prayer Warriors, and generally the old femals of Lozikeyi, who visited her on an unwavering rotation. And Simiso now walked—she wore a black mourning dress and matching head wrap—sandwiched between the Defenders, tholukuthi four of them trotting at the front, three right behind her, and of course Commander Jambanja bringing up the rear like a chief baboon. And because the neighborhood had not laid eyes on Simiso in a long time, they felt their hearts sink and held their breath at the sight of her, tholukuthi at how the goat had aged with such crushing rapidity in such a short while.

When they told it, those who were there, they said one minute Commander Jambanja and the seven Defenders who'd come for Simiso were accordingly escorting their prisoner toward the waiting jeep with the typical confident arrogance of Jidada's Defenders everywhere—chests out, noses sniffing at the air, tongues lolling, tails up. And then the next minute what, the next minute the Sisters of the Disappeared in their red T-shirts materialized out of nowhere and were suddenly standing at the front of the mob, uncowering, unafraid. And just like that, before you could say "Woof!" tholukuthi Commander Jambanja and the seven Defenders who'd

come for Simiso found themselves in the eye of a most dreadful hurricane that had, it seemed, simply materialized out of nowhere.

Tholukuthi the mob that was also the hurricane observed such an impossible solemnity, a total quiet that was not unlike the impeccable silence with which the Wall of the Dead had generally been done. And what that mob did—being a calm mob—was simply let their limbs do the communicating, and even so, that communicating of the limbs was carried out with a determined peace that was almost beautiful, even elegant in its method, hypnotic in its grace, as if they were altogether doing something holy. And faced with that calm mob, tholukuthi Commander Jambanja and the seven Defenders who had come for Simiso didn't have the time to say woof. To lash out. To bite. To snarl. To growl. To call for backup. To explain themselves. To be surprised. To plead. To negotiate. To apologize. To retreat, with the exception of one wiry dog who was somehow able to miraculously squeeze through the eye of the hurricane and melt into the air.

And when finally the calm mob stopped their limbs from doing the communicating, there almost was nothing left of Commander Jambanja and the Defenders who had come for Simiso, yes, tholukuthi each and every one of the dogs reduced first to a miserable heap of flesh, and then to a mass of pulp, and finally to a stain, so that all that remained after the hurricane was just stains, bits of fur, and tiny pieces of smashed teeth. They said, those who were there, that unlike victorious mobs everywhere, this mob did not cheer, no. They did not celebrate, no. They did not dance and leap with joy, no. They did not sing, no. Theirs was the absolute quiet of a hurricane that, having wrecked its awful fury and spent itself, paused to renew its strength.

CRISIS IN THE COUNTRY COUNTRY

Meanwhile, the disconcerting news out of Lozikeyi, in many ways bizarre
and without precedence in the whole history of Jidada with a -da and
another -da, caught the Seat of Power and the Chosen by surprise. Indeed, many of them, including the Savior himself, couldn't actually pinpoint the location of the miserable little township on a map. But still, here
was small, unimportant Lozikeyi sending the Seat of Power scrambling to
find out if what they were hearing was indeed what they were hearing.
The Savior and his Inner Circle, including the likes of the vice president,
Judas Goodness Reza, Elegy Mudidi, Dick Mampara, the Ministers of Violence and Order, army generals, the Defender Chiefs, and indeed, Jolijo,
along with four of his most senior assistant sorcerers, convened on short
notice for the emergency meeting. Present too was Maxwell Ngoma, the
escaped seventh dog, who now sat with a bloodied rag around his head.

"Who are the goddamned ringleaders? I want the ringleaders now!
And I want this thing nipped in the bud with such power this no-count
Lozikeyi won't know what hit them!" the Savior thundered, face looking
like a disaster.

"Ehm, Your Excellency, sir. Well, I mean, how do I say this; there
doesn't exactly seem to be any ringleaders, sir," the Minister of Propaganda said. His voice sounded like it came from underneath his chair.

"Are you mad, you Mudidi?! What do you mean there are no ringleaders?! What kind of imbecility is that?!" Spit flew out of the Savior's mouth
and baptized the congregated Comrades, who did not flinch.

"With all due respect, Your Excellency, sir, I meant, I was saying, I
only—"

"Look at this ceiling, you idiot, just look!" The Savior leapt onto the
long mahogany table before Mudidi could finish his sentence. He grabbed
the stunned cat's little head and tilted it at the ceiling, where a black

column of ants labored across, tholukuthi on their way to a divorce party. Around the table, puzzled Comrades exchanged nervous glances.

"Even those ants you see aren't just crawling willy-nilly! They're following the ant at the front! And that particular ant at the front is the goddamned ringleader! If I right now were to open that tap right there, the first water to come out, the number one water, would be the ringleader! If you were to sit on a toilet right now and shit, Mudidi, the very initial dollop of your kaka would be the ringleader! Every single thing under the sky has a ringleader, Mudidi! Every. Single. Fucking. Thing! Someone put those disrespectful imbeciles up to what they did! And I want that inciter in custody else I'll do what I did in the war, else I'll show every single one of you why they call me Tuvy!" the Savior exploded, letting go of Mudidi.

"With all due respect, sir, to begin with, I mean first of all, I don't think you even fathom what just happened in that Lozikeyi, Your Excellency. Ask me, I'm not talking hearsay, me I was there as you can see, I was with Commander Jambanja himself," the escaped Defender said, pointing to his bandage with a bleeding paw. His voice said this was a tale he would be relating without ever tiring for the rest of his precious life.

"And who the hell are you?! And who told you you can open your stinky mouth as you please around here?! You think this is a goddamn toilet?!" the Savior shrieked.

"Apologies, Your Excellency, sir. That—is the surviving Defender who—escaped the mob. They'd gone there to pick up the problem goat. The one with the, eh, illegal Wall of the Dead, sir," Mampara said.

"So, you're the stupid mongrel who doesn't know how to take an unarmed animal, a miserable no-count aging femal at that? Who trained you? And how come you, specifically, and not any of the other miserable fools got to escape? Who the hell are you working for?!" the Savior roared, boring into the miserable Defender with cold eyes. Maxwell Ngoma opened his

mouth and closed it, looked helplessly at his bosses, Mampara and then Mudidi, who both looked away. The Savior pointed to a glass and the Minister of Order quickly picked it up, filled it from a bottle of Jameson, passed it to the Savior, who disappeared it. The Minister refilled it.

"What seems to be happening, Your Excellency, is that you have malcontents, criminals, who once more, and obviously at the encouragement of the West, are disrespecting the Seat of Power by agitating for regime change. This much we know, isn't it true, Comrade?" the Minister of Violence said, turning to the Chief of Defenders.

ON FEAR

"Yes, that, of course. But what is also happening, if I may, Comrades, is something I am, quite frankly, just having a hard time processing. Which is that, out of the blue, it seems as if there's been a—how can I put it—a queer shift in these beasts. I'm sure the whole world is shocked as we speak because it's definitely not the Jidadan way to turn on Defenders, let alone think of doing what just happened. At least it wasn't when I was General," Judas Goodness Reza said. The vice president had just returned from spending months in China, where he'd gone for an undisclosed surgery, and was in obvious ill health.

"My thoughts exactly, Comrade Vice President. And this I must say has very quickly unnerved Defenders from what I'm hearing from Defender Commanders all over the nation. Because part of what in fact allows us to do our job, and do it effectively, is counting on the natural fear these animals have of Defenders, of the Seat of Power. And everyone in this room knows how hard we've worked to instill and nurture that fear through the decades. It almost feels like we're not at all dealing with Jidadans as we know them but brand-new beasts from some other planet," the Chief of Defenders said.

"Nonsense! Utter, sheer, absolute nonsense! These aren't brand-new beasts! And that fear is there! It can't go anywhere! It's in the blood of each and every goddamn Jidadan who lives and breathes on this land! It's what we've worked hard for from the get-go, otherwise what the bloody hell do you think the Gukurahundi was for?! You think we were playing? So go find the goddamned fear, Comrade! And I want it back where it belongs chop-chop, you hear me?! Chop-chop!" the Savior roared.

"Yessir, yessir," the Chief of Defenders said, tholukuthi yessir-ing with just his mouth because he had the awful feeling this was easier said than done.

"Eh, what I was actually thinking myself—" Tholukuthi this was Jolijo, who, for the whole time since the meeting began, had been sitting like a newly hatched egg, waiting for the right moment to put in a word.

"What I'm thinking, you clever fool, is how on earth you and your miserable entourage, the whole what—two hundred, three hundred of you in every fucking corner of this fucking country, didn't see this coming, when I pay you money, and no small money, mind you, to bloody see it coming! What exactly are you divining?! What do I pay you for?!" the Savior bubbled and boiled. Jolijo and his colleagues lowered their heads and shrunk to the size of ants.

"What I need you and your useless kaka cohort to do, is to do what you eat my money and get fat for! I want all your mutis on fucking Lozikeyi and I want the wretched township under control even if it means turning every single beast in there into a fucking zombie! And as for all of you, I want, by this time tomorrow, for whoever is left in that wretched township to know who's in charge! Make them see fire, you hear me?! I said fire, give them proper FIRE!"

LOZIKEYI VIGIL AND A NEW KIND OF LOVE

We didn't disband that day, no. We stayed put, watchful, waiting. It wasn't only to guard Simiso but also to show the Defenders, to show the evil regime that we were absolutely without fear now, that we were there to face what should've been faced ages and ages ago, that we were a brand-new breed. And if anyone thought the crowds were massive, they swelled through the night. Waves of animals came and just kept coming. Tholukuthi from places near and far, from places we'd never heard of, places we didn't even know existed. There were Jidadans of every age, every hue, every gender, Jidadans of any and every ethnic identification alike, Jidadans of all faiths and religions alike, Jidadans of any and every occupation and profession and economic bracket alike, Jidadans of whatever category was used to define Jidadaness—they were there, all of them, they came, and we all stood together as one.

And what we learned, the multitude of us gathered there and standing together that night, was that it wasn't enough to say the love of Jidada was in you just because you were born in Jidada. We discovered that the true, the proper love for the nation was coming together like we were at that moment doing, like we'd earlier done for Simiso. That what truly counted was showing up for each other, was refusing silence, was actively fighting for what was right, was demanding justice for your fellow citizens even if you didn't necessarily agree with them or hold their views, even if they weren't your neighbor or of your ethnic group or of your political party or of your religion. Tholukuthi that night, outside Simiso's house, by the Wall of the Dead, we discovered that the only way to be a better Jidada was to in fact start by being each other's treasures. And that discovery, that education made us fall in love with each other; we held each other's precious eyes and communicated, in silent silence, our love, our solidarity.

STORY TIME IN THE LOZIKEYI NIGHT

It was, of course, another night of power cuts, but Nehanda's bones, earlier scattered all over Lozikeyi by the wailing wind, now rose in the air
and glowed brighter than the moon to surround us in a strange, mythical
light. Meanwhile, Jidadans kept coming. They poured so much we thought
Lozikeyi was going to rip at the seams. Being that the new arrivals had
missed the happenings, stories of that afternoon were told and retold until
those who hadn't been there began to feel like they'd indeed been there,
been part of the hurricane. They in turn told the stories to later arrivals, as
if they themselves had been the hurricane, until every one of us gathered
that night felt like we had the story of that afternoon mixed up in our
blood so we'd never, ever forget it.

Because even a lovely song can in fact weary the singer and tire the
dancer, we transitioned from the events of that afternoon to other stories,
yes, tholukuthi accounts of what'd happened to us in other times and over
the long years of our Jidada with a -da and another -da. We heard and told
stories of pain, stories of the Seat of Power's violence so impossible sometimes animals simply tilted heads up and stared into the glowing Nehanda
bones—reeling. Tholukuthi through these tales we learned there were in
fact many untold narratives that were left out of the Seat of Power's tales
of the nation, that were excluded from Jidada's great books of history.
That the nation's stories of glory were far from being the whole truth, and
that sometimes the Seat of Power's truths were actually half-truths and
mistruths as well as deliberate erasures. Which in turn made us understand
the importance not only of narrating our own stories, our own truths, but
of writing them down as well so they were not taken from us, never al-
tered, tholukuthi never erased, never forgotten.

PORTRAIT OF VICTIMS AS ENABLERS

And then came the stories that were also confessions. And in the stories that were also confessions, we learned the sobering truth about ourselves, tholukuthi which was that even as we'd been oppressed by the evil regime, we'd also in many ways given it license, permission, to do so. Yes, tholukuthi we'd in fact enabled it, even as it wasn't necessarily our intent to cause ourselves, cause each other the pain we ended up having to bear for years, for decades. We'd voted for the regime over and over fully knowing the kind of monster we were voting for. We'd helped it win fraudulent elections. We'd sat and cheered in hateful rallies that insulted the dignity of fellow Jidadans. We'd worn regalia emblazoned with the corrupt faces of those who took bread out of our mouths and whose boots daily pressed hard on our necks so we couldn't breathe. We'd worn the faces of abusers, murderers, tribalists, rapists, looters, and all sorts of criminals on our bodies. We'd stood aside and watched as Defenders beat, butchered, raped, took, disappeared, murdered innocents over the long, terrible years, and sometimes we'd actually blamed the victims for putting themselves in situations in which Defenders had to do them harm. On social media we followed accounts of looters and praised the lavish lifestyles funded by Jidada's stolen wealth. We'd given all kinds of bribes and engaged in all forms of corruption in order that the rhythm of our lives flow smoothly. We'd looked the other way and shrugged as our constitution was violated over and over again. Tholukuthi sobered, humbled, shamed, pained by all the things we'd done to participate in our own oppression, we spit on the earth and said, "With these terrible scars, we have learned painful lessons to last us lifetimes, will not be repeating them."

PORTRAIT OF A FUTURE

"Glory, glory, glory Halleluyah, O Precious Jidadans!" We weren't surprised to see Prophet Dr. O. G. Moses appear among the throngs like a kind of pig angel, looking immaculate in white flowing robes. Clutching a Bible and a fancy golden mic, the celebrity Prophet had obviously come prepared to address us. We watched him look at us with those luminous eyes, watched him hind himself into holy form. We watched him deliver a showstopping recital in tongues: "Rabhasha zuzure hallafashata hahikila bayanga hahiyahayiya halabratiga olosha makwekwegwena bikibongbongbong sindomande makhibhozhay halakasha meyoncejayancebhoyonce!" And then we watched, as if on cue, a bull charge Jidada's most famous celebrity Prophet, lift him by the horns, and fling him, shrieking, so high up in the air it actually looked like he'd reach heaven. We roared and cheered in tremendous applause that said we were done with false prophets and false pastors and false religious leaders who fleeced us of our hard-earned moneys in the name of God, who connived with the Seat of Power to keep us oppressed by telling us who to vote for, by telling us the blatant lie that our leaders were selected by God, by telling us to stay away from politics. We wanted a God of revolution, a God of liberation, a God of justice, a God of anti-corruption, a radical God to inspire us into building the paradise we deserved right on earth, yes, tholukuthi in Jidada with a -da and another -da itself.

And with the Prophet cast away like a damned demon, we continued with our manifestations. Beginning with the young, we proceeded to hear thoughts and dreams on the kind of paradise we wanted to see and live in right on earth, in our very own Jidada. Tholukuthi we only heard from regular animals and not politicians because we'd finally woken to the fact that Jidada with a -da and another -da was the terrible tragedy and crime scene it was in part because of the very wretched political system in whose

jaws we'd been locked, bleeding and broken, for decades. We understood now we didn't need to be followers of inept leaders but participants in a system that served us, that we needed to take our lives back, our power back, our fates back from selfish, corrupt, and greedy politicians who knew nothing about service, about love for the nation, about the dignity of the citizens.

WE NEED A NEW WORLD ORDER

When those who know about things say the colonial powers gave Africa her independence but not her freedom, tholukuthi what they mean is that the colonial powers gave Africa her independence but not her freedom. We knew, standing together that night, outside Simiso's house, by the Wall of the Dead, that just like Jidada's Seat of Power and the Chosen had looted and fleeced the nation's wealth since the so-called Independence, so, too, did our former colonizers continue to loot and fleece the wealth of the continent of Africa, just as they had been doing for the decades and decades that they ruled over us. It was not lost on us how the West, which loved to "save" Africa and announce every action to the whole world, did so with one limb while manipulating, looting, and fleecing us with the rest of its limbs so that more money in fact poured out of the continent than trickled in. We did not need to be told that it was no accident we were shackled by the immovable chains of prodigious debts to the very nations who otherwise depended on our wealth for their prosperity. It was no mistake that multinational corporations yearly reaped and shipped colossal profits from Africa back to their countries as had been the case during colonial times. Even the sticks and stones would tell you that the African earth at any given time howled and shook and heaved from the extraction of its precious minerals that rarely benefited its own miserable children. Yes, tholukuthi we knew it wasn't only for the ugly fiends who governed

us that we toiled and languished without relief in devastating cycles of poverty, of underdevelopment, of instability, of corruption, of disease, of indignity, of pain, of death. And so that night, outside Simiso's house, by the Wall of the Dead, we vowed to wage yet another war for Africa's second Liberation from neocolonial oppression. From exploitation. From plunder. From Western dominion. From indignity. From abuse. We wanted real freedom. We wanted greedy, thieving paws off our wealth. We wanted Justice. We wanted a new world; we wanted a brand-new world so much we didn't sleep a wink that night. We stayed dreaming on our feet, dreaming with our hearts, with our intestines, with our mouths, with our imaginations; we dreamed until we could in fact see the New Jidada, the New Africa, the New World we very much yearned for, begin to materialize right in front of our eyes and hover just above Mbuya Nehanda's bones, tholukuthi so near, it was practically within reach.

SECOND INDEPENDENCE

THE DEFENDERS IN FULL FORCE, AND THING ONE, THING TWO, THING THREE, THING FOUR, AND THING FIVE

Tholukuthi morning brought Defenders boiling into Lozikeyi like Defenders had always boiled into places of restlessness all over Jidada with a -da and another -da. They came in multitudes—battalions and battalions armed with such weapons as fit for proper war. Those who know about things said unlike in times previous, in other places of restlessness, what the Defenders smelled in the Lozikeyi air that very early morning wasn't fear, no; tholukuthi it was fearlessness. That was thing one. The other thing that was unlike in times previous, in other places of restlessness, was the size of the crowds—as if the whole of Jidada had come and packed itself tight inside the township like grains of salt in a sack. That was thing two. Thing three was that the throngs stood like throngs had never before stood in the face of armed Defenders; tholukuthi theirs was the standing of waiting, of expectation, of a terrible hurricane that'd had time to gather strength after its first mayhem and thus knew itself to be even mightier

than before. Thing four was the gigantic barricade—mountains of boulders that blocked the main road out of Lozikeyi. Tholukuthi taken off guard and thoroughly unaccustomed to any of these things, the Defenders slowly applied brakes to their cars and sniffed at the air, pricked their ears, and licked their noses, calculating-like. And now that they could see the crowds clearly, they realized yet another thing that was unlike in times previous, which was that the crowds before them and around them were in fact prepared to die. This was thing five.

THOLUKUTHI THE DEFENDERS OF THE REVOLUTION CONSIDER THE MATHS OF THE REVOLUTION

—Defending a Revolution, really? When we all actually know we're defending a farce?

—You may tell yourselves whatever you want, Comrades. But that, over there; those Jidadans aren't warmongering and you know it. What they are is they want change. Those Jidadans want corruption to end. Those Jidadans want water cuts and power cuts and queues to end. Those Jidadans want a living wage. Those Jidadans want dignity. Those Jidadans want justice. Those Jidadans want a better life right here at home so they don't have to go and grovel for it where they're not wanted. And that, in my opinion, is the Revolution that anyone in their right mind, with the right heart, with the right ethics, should be defending!

—Weren't we celebrating with these animals after the Seat used us to take out the Old Horse? Taking selfies with them in the name of a New Jidada? And now we're supposed to what, massacre them because why? For asking for better? For simply wanting to breathe in a supposedly free country? It's a question I too ask myself when I put on and take off

this goddamned uniform: Where did the Revolution go, Comrades, where did it go?!

—Me, I just can't, in all good conscience, open fire on those crowds. You know and I know that Jidadans aren't bad animals. And you know and I know that there are real evil, wretched beasts in Jidada who are responsible for this predicament that brings those crowds here and that brings us here. And you know who those wretched beasts are, and you can say their names, and you even know where they live. But you'd rather act stupid, act like you have no idea who the real enemy is. Because killing innocents is far easier than doing what we all know must happen if we're to be truly free!

—The reality, Comrades, is that these animals gathered all around us aren't some weird creatures from some faraway planet. They're your very own. And you all know that your relatives are in that crowd. Your friends and neighbors are in that crowd. Your landlords. Your church members. Your children's teachers. Your nurses and doctors. All of them good, decent citizens. Every one of them knowing they can die today. All of them prepared to die today. Not directly by the Seat but by us, on its behalf. My question is, When will we learn disgust?

—Me, what I know is I really don't want to be caught in the kind of hurricane that I'm looking at. What I know is if my death is certain, which, having heard what happened to Commander Jambanja and the Seven— and this is Commander Jambanja we're talking about—I just don't want to be found going anywhere near, I mean, I didn't say I was a brave dog, and, after all, an animal only has one life to live. Just one life, one!

—The sad truth is that if the true liberators of this country were alive, if their bones would rise again, they sure wouldn't be sitting here with us, they'd actually be over there, standing and ready to die with those crowds. Because that, over there, is the right side. The moral side.

—I remember I was so naive when I first put on this wretched uniform. I thought my job would really be to protect and serve. Is this service I'm about to do? No. Is it fair, is it just, is it dignified, is it kind? No. Will it do anything for me or make my life better? No.

—Well, here's a scenario. Let us say we and those throngs go at it and somehow many of us are all killed. Do you think the Seat and the Chosen would cry for any of us? Do you think they'll come to our funerals?

—I don't know about anyone here but the way I look at life is everything happens for a reason. I think God put me here today, in this car, with these crowds, for a reason, and that reason being to manifest his glory. To make the right decision.

—I follow a lot of activists online, and live next to two Sisters of the Disappeared. And you know, no matter what the Seat and the Chosen call it, I identify with most of the things that they, and the rest of the nation, are fighting for. Because the truth is, I too want and believe in those things. So under this uniform, I am one with those crowds.

—This is who we are: starving, poor teachers do a peaceful demonstration, we're on them. Nurses and doctors strike for a living wage, we're on them. Activists march for change, again, we're at it—disperse, beat, butcher, arrest, disappear, over and over. When will it end? How do we

expect this country to change for the better when we're daily standing on the necks of those who are working for change? And what exactly does that do for us? Where does it get us? And what do we have to show for it? And whose interests are we really serving, and why?

—Me, if I'm being honest, I admire these crowds for losing their fear. Now why on earth can't we do the same? What exactly is stopping us? And if not now, then when?

—If there'd been something left of the bodies of Commander Jambanja and the Seven do you think the Seat would've buried them at the Square of Liberators? Would they have been buried with honors? For Defending the Revolution?

—Isn't it the Savior who on his inauguration said, "The voice of the multitudes is the voice of God"? Do any of you know why and when and how that voice of God has suddenly become the voice of the enemy? Let me tell you, if you all lower your guns right now and listen to those crowds, God is speaking. I'm not religious or anything but God is roaring right now. Of a better land, of a better Jidada. The question is will we, or will we not, be a part of it? Which is also the question of who we really are.

—When I was putting on this new uniform this morning I asked myself when was the last time I even put on brand-new trousers, new underwear, new anything. And I can tell you in all honesty that I couldn't remember. Because we don't get paid enough to afford a normal life. But how does a Seat of Power that won't pay us a living wage afford to pay for new equipment and weapons? How many millions have been spent on weapons and equipment since Tuvy came to power? And

why do we even need these weapons, like the country is in fact at war?
And how much did you get paid last month?

—Has anyone actually thought about the fact that if we weren't Defenders, we'd definitely be standing out there? With the masses? Singing
the same song?

—And while we're at it, can we consider, I mean really, really again consider, the fact that these crowds are actually prepared to die and we
aren't, consider again the things that these crowds are prepared to die
for, and weigh those things against our very own situation? And after
we do that, let's then go even further and consider, I mean really, really
consider, the maths of the Revolution.

And sure enough, the Defenders sat in their vehicles and considered the
maths of the Revolution and considered the maths of the Revolution and
considered the maths of the Revolution and considered the maths of the
Revolution, and considered the maths of the Revolution and considered
the maths of the Revolution and considered the maths of the Revolution
and considered the maths of the Revolution, and considered the maths of
the Revolution and considered the maths of the Revolution and considered
the maths of the Revolution and considered the maths of the Revolution,
and considered the maths of the Revolution and considered the maths of
the Revolution and considered the maths of the Revolution and considered
the maths of the Revolution, and considered the maths of the Revolution
and considered the maths of the Revolution and considered the maths of
the Revolution and considered the maths of the Revolution, and considered the maths of the Revolution and considered the maths of the Revolution and considered the maths of the Revolution and considered the
maths of the Revolution, and considered the maths of the Revolution and

considered the maths of the Revolution and considered the maths of the
Revolution and considered the maths of the Revolution, and considered
the maths of the Revolution and considered the maths of the Revolution
and considered the maths of the Revolution and considered the maths of
the Revolution, and considered the maths of the Revolution and considered the maths of the Revolution and considered the maths of the Revolution and considered the maths of the Revolution, and considered the maths
of the Revolution and considered the maths of the Revolution and considered the maths of the Revolution and considered the maths of the Revolution, and considered the maths of the Revolution and considered the maths
of the Revolution and considered the maths of the Revolution.

DEFENDING THE TRUE REVOLUTION

When those who were there told it, they said what happened was that a pit
bull was seen to jump out of one of the cars somewhere at the front of the
entourage, tholukuthi front paws raised to show he was unarmed. And then
he walked to a clear opening, where he bent forward and calmly began to
untie his boots, which he kicked off, followed by the socks. And after his
boots and socks, his belt. And after his belt, he took off his hard shell hat.
And after which he unbuttoned his jacket and shrugged it off. Next to follow was his undershirt and finally, he unzipped his trousers and whipped
them off. When those who were there told it they said the naked Defender,
now weeping openly, which was even more stunning than him taking off
his clothes, slowly made his way to stand with the nearest crowd, where,
without uttering a single word, he bowed slightly, paws together in a gesture of peace, and, like the crowd, turned to face his Comrades.

They said, those who were there, that the air at that point was so tense
you could actually cut it, the throngs asking themselves if what they were
seeing was indeed what they were seeing. Tholukuthi there were some

among the crowds whose instincts told them to turn on the Defender and do unto him what they'd done unto Commander Jambanja and the seven Defenders from the day before, but they were restrained, confused, disoriented even, by the dog's gesture of peace, by the fact that he'd actually taken off the uniform of Defending and turned his back on his Comrades to stand with the masses, weeping. It wasn't at all a situation they'd anticipated, and because they hadn't anticipated it, they hadn't discussed it, and because they hadn't discussed it, they were not so clear as to how best to deal with it.

And then it happened again. They said, those who told it, that a long ridgeback somewhere in the middle of the fleet calmly jumped out of his car and began to take his clothes off, one by one and, free of his uniform and weeping, he crossed over to join the crowds just like his Comrade before him. Tholukuthi the next dog was undressing before the second dog joined the crowds, and that before the third dog finished undressing, the next one had put down his gun, jumped from the car, and was undressing as well, and before the next one had indeed finished undressing, about a dozen were doing the same. And that these dogs too joined the crowds, yes, tholukuthi weeping, bringing their paws together in a sign of peace, and then turning to face their Comrades.

Tholukuthi the disbelieving children of the nation watched the unfolding drama of scores and scores and scores of Jidada's Defenders downing their weapons and joining them. They did not ask the dogs what they were doing and why they were doing it or any other questions, no. They did not cheer them, no. They did not celebrate, no. They watched in silence until each and every vehicle was empty of Defenders. Those who told it said this may have very well been one of those Now what? moments, yes, tholukuthi when the crowds and the dogs would stand there looking at one another and wondering what, if anything, was to follow this event that none of them had come to Lozikeyi expecting.

But then the dogs, calmly and without ceremony, set the heaps of their uniforms on fire, yes, tholukuthi directed the crowds to stand at safe distances before setting each and every symbol and weapon and apparatus of Defending alight. And the crowds, absolutely unprepared for this part as they'd indeed been unprepared for the one just before it, continued observing in silence. Tholukuthi the dogs burned everything down. And when the news spread all over the country that the battalions of Defenders who'd been set upon the largest gathering of the children of the nation had in fact downed their weapons, discarded their uniforms, joined the masses, and then burned everything, tholukuthi Defenders all across Jidada, as if waking from the deepest trance, similarly set on anything and everything that had anything to do with Defending, and destroyed it, so that in a matter of hours, the institution of Defending as had been known for the decades of the Seat of Power's reign fell at last.

ALL GOOD THINGS MUST COME TO AN END

What happened next taught the children of the nation a lesson they very much regretted not learning any sooner. Which was that it is quite possible to spend a lifetime in the terror of a darkness that in actuality harbors nothing but flowers and grasshoppers and doves and toothless crocodiles. For without the protection of the Defenders, the Seat of Power and the Chosen found themselves—suddenly, and without any warning whatsoever—vulnerable, floating in nothingness, with no solid ground on which to stand, tholukuthi trapped in a Jidada of closed airports and inaccessible borders, with nowhere to run. Not even their looted wealth would save them. And in a strange reversal, the fear that had afflicted the children of the nation for most of Jidada's years now infected and cowed the former oppressors. Who were routinely rounded up, picked up like filthy rubbish, thrown into decrepit vans, and carted off to the very prisons of horror

wherein during their days of glory they'd routinely sent real and imagined enemies to languish.

THOLUKUTHI LAST IDIOT STANDING

When those who know about things say there is no night ever so long it does not end with dawn, tholukuthi what they mean is that there is no night ever so long it does not end with dawn. The children of the nation—now once again that dreadful hurricane that'd gathered strength—surged through the great walls of the House of Power, baying for Tuvy. Those who poured in through the western entrance paused at the famed sculpture garden, affectionately called the Shrine of Rulers by the Savior, yes, tholukuthi a spectacular production featuring life-size statues of some of Africa's notorious living Fathers of the Nation in black granite that dazzled against lush red flame lilies. Tholukuthi the hurricane went berserk on the imposing stone idols. It tore and trampled and crushed. And down came the tyrant of Nigeria and down came the tyrant of Uganda and down came the tyrant of Cameroon and down came the tyrant of the Central African Republic and down came the tyrant of Eritrea and down came the tyrant of Eswatini and down came the tyrant of Sudan and down came the tyrant of Algeria and down came each and every ruling African tyrant, yes, tholukuthi in the blink of an eye, the Shrine of Rulers was reduced to rubble, rubble, rubble.

Meanwhile, the Savior stood stunned and confused at the sight of the hurricane. He'd received assurance from Jolijo and his cohort of sorcerers that he was safe and untouchable behind the great walls of the House of Power, for they'd been fortified with the most potent spells so that at the approach of the miserable children of the nation, an impassable sea would surround the residence, yes, tholukuthi a most terrible sea infested with famished crocodiles that in fact outnumbered the miserable malcontents.

But then here were the demented dissidents, here with a bottomless, stupid rage in their eyes. The Savior, who was a natural enemy of fear, hinded to his fullest height, which was all of twenty hands, and confronted the masses with seething, unblinking eyes. Tholukuthi not one but two Scarves of the Nation around his neck—one going one way, and the second going the other way, where the other was not going, yes, tholukuthi standing defiant and in denial and flanked on both sides by his sons, who didn't otherwise seem to share their father's confidence and so stood there on all fours, trousers wet and not from water, trembling like leaves in a raging storm and wondering if what they were seeing was indeed what they were seeing.

FACING THE CROCODILE

They said, those who know about things, that at the exact moment the Savior was facing the hurricane, back in Lozikeyi, the young ones, left behind in the company of the very old on account of their ages, stood facing the Crocodile. Inspired by the events of the past day, tholukuthi the youngsters had kept vigil outside Simiso's house, by the Wall of the Dead. And as they waited for the adults to come back with what they said would be a "New Jidada for real this time," the children did what they did best, which of course was play.

Tholukuthi the Crocodile had seized on the disorder in the nation that day to strike in Lozikeyi. He found the children in the middle of a game called Concert, in which they took turns mimicking Queen Black, the returned singer who'd sung just before Commander Jambanja shot and killed Destiny at Uhuru Park on Remembrance, and whose songs they knew by heart because of their parents playing them without end on those days when they talked about the past until they blinked away tears. All eyes were on the makeshift stage when Mathapelo, whose turn it was to

sing, pointed and screamed. And the children looked behind them at the Brobdingnagian Crocodile, who stood larger than Goliath in Mother of God's stories, who grinned with his famous blades of teeth, who looked at them with those enormous eyes, tholukuthi of which one was the color of the flag of North Korea on a good day, and the other the color of the flag of North Korea on a very bad day.

"You can run but you can't hide!" the Crocodile shrieked, laughing a laugh that shook the Wall of the Dead and sent the birds scattering and snakes and lizards whipping across the street. Tholukuthi the children stared in horror as the enormous beast positioned himself and began lumbering about, his blades gnashing.

When Reason later told it, he said the Crocodile coming down on his belly was the very thing that gave him the idea to start the famous Croco-crawla dance. The quick-thinking piglet shrieked Croco-crawla! and every single child was on the ground, lumbering like a crocodile and shimmying and shaking and singing the famous Crocodile song, "Careful Jidada, here comes the Crocodile with his big, bad blades! Will he nibble, will he bite, will he chomp-chomp-chomp?!" The children sang bravely, but the terror in their voices was palpable. And the Crocodile, caught off guard and seeing the children do his dance and sing that song that was sung everywhere and danced everywhere and liked everywhere, and that'd made him so, so famous they even knew him on the WhatsApp and the Twitter and general internets, forgot himself. Tholukuthi the horrendous creature danced.

And seeing him dance, the children lifted their voices and applauded him more than they'd ever applauded anything in their short lives, yes, tholukuthi applauding with the hope that perhaps the creature could be somehow charmed into sparing their lives. And for a moment, it seemed to work. The Crocodile, who was used to animals scattering at the mere glimpse of him, who'd never been sung for, never been applauded, never

been cheered, smiled the widest smile of any crocodile anywhere. He shimmied. He shook. He whipped his tail. And smiled. And shimmied. And shook. And whipped his tail. And smiled. And shimmied. And shook. And whipped his tail. And smiled. And shimmied. And shook. And whipped his tail. And smiled. And shimmied. And shook. And whipped his tail. And smiled.

COMRADE NEVERMISS NZINGA: THOLUKUTHI WILL THE REAL LIBERATOR PLEASE STAND UP?

When the children later told the adults, they said the Crocodile was basking so absolutely in his glory it took him awhile to realize the singing, the cheering, the applause had stopped. That around him was the silent silence of the inside of a bullet. And that an unblinking old hen dressed all in black had a gun pointed to his head. Yes, tholukuthi almost four decades after she fired her very last shot—which had been in the air—to celebrate the birth of a New Jidada and mark the end of the Liberation War she'd joined as a teenager, Comrade Nevermiss Nzinga, the unsung veteran, aimed her gun, Killjoy, at the Crocodile's brain, shut her left eye, and squeezed the trigger. And because Comrade Nevermiss Nzinga in fact never missed, the Crocodile danced and howled with such earthshaking fury. Tholukuthi the children's intestines lurched, leapt to their chests. Comrade Nevermiss Nzinga landed two more meticulous shots—a follow-up on the brain, and another on the spine. Tholukuthi the Crocodile twitched once, twitched twice, twitched thrice, twitched four, five, six times, and stilled. And thoroughly stunned, the children looked at each other to see if what they were seeing was indeed what they were seeing, and when they found out it was, they ignited in celebration.

THE MUTI SCARF AND THE MAGIC

And while in Lozikeyi, outside Simiso's house, by the Wall of the Dead, the young ones were celebrating the end of the Crocodile's reign of terror, tholukuthi hundreds of miles away, at the House of Power, the hurricane was closing in on the Savior. Those who were there said with the moment of truth staring him in the face, the Savior neighed with such awesome force the glass windows shattered all around the House of Power. But the hurricane surged, and would have kept surging had the Savior not shrieked a strange incantation, yanked his scarves, and thrown them on the ground between himself and the hurricane, stopping it in its tracks.

Yes, tholukuthi the hurricane stopped in its tracks because even the sticks and stones knew the Savior's love for sorcery, knew that the Scarf of the Nation was no ordinary scarf but a terrible talisman, and that just like Moses's staff that'd turned into a snake, it too could turn into a horrendous thing, yes tholukuthi most likely a creature even more egregious than Moses's serpent. The anxious throngs looked at the scarves. Then at each other. Then at the scarves. Then at each other. Then at the scarves. Then at each other. Then they howled with laughter—the scarves turned out to be just scarves, made of ordinary wool. Tholukuthi the hurricane surged one more time; the unstoppable dawn at last was upon the Savior.

When those who were there later told it, they said it was at that moment that a massive swarm of red butterflies materialized from nowhere and descended on the House of Power. That the swarm was so humongous they had to fight to see through the chaos of the fluttering wings of crimson-crimson-crimson that suffocated the air and made it hard to breathe. That before the throngs could ask themselves if what they were seeing was indeed what they were seeing, every single one of the red butterflies descended onto the Savior, yes, tholukuthi the Savior who, upon finding

himself thus swarmed, roared and neighed and kicked and lashed at the air. Great were Tuvy's terrible howls as he shrieked for the red butterflies to get off him, as he pleaded for the children of the nation to get the butterflies off him. Tholukuthi no one intervened. Tuvy fought and swung and hollered and cried and begged until his movements grew weaker and weaker, until he doddered like a drunk, until he staggered and fell to the ground like a giant hill of dung, and lay there whizzing. And only then did the red butterflies lift and take off as mysteriously as they'd come.

And so, Tuvius Delight Shasha, better known as Tuvy, son of Zvichapera Shasha and most favorite and most successful son of Buresi Shasha, Ruler of the Nation and Veteran of the Liberation War, the Greatest Leader of Jidada, Enemy of Corruption, Opener for Business, the Dispenser of the New Dispensation, Fixer of the Economy, the Imposer of Order, the Inventor of the Scarf of the Nation, the Most Successful Veteran of the Liberation War, Top Magnate of Jidada, the Genius of Jidada, the Survivor of All Assassination Attempts, Winner of Free, Fair, and Credible Elections, the Main Chief Appointer, Respected World Leader, was loaded in that wretched condition and carted off to join his Comrades at Jidada's most notorious hellhole of horror, the lot of them to serve lengthy sentences for varied crimes, with no possibility of freedom in their miserable lifetimes. Jidada's Seat of Power had fallen at long last.

They said, those who were there, that having apprehended Tuvy, and having heard of the fate of the Crocodile in Lozikeyi, that unlike victorious throngs everywhere, the throngs were silent once more. Now it was the silence of a hurricane that, having unleashed its fury, and having gathered strength, and having come back to devastate a second time, lingered, in case it maybe needed to recross its path. It was when the hurricane was lingering, watchful, that news of the death of the Old Horse spread all across Jidada. Yes, tholukuthi the undying Father of the Nation, him and only him himself, the one who'd kept resurrecting like Jesus but went on

to keep resurrecting and resurrecting and resurrecting, yes, tholukuthi many, many more times, unlike Jesus, who'd only resurrected just once, had finally met his last dawn, and not just finally met his last dawn but met his last dawn in a foreign country, where he'd been receiving treatment because Jidada's decrepit hospitals, he'd said so many times, were so useless an animal went there to die. And for the very first time since they rose like Nehanda's bones on the day that Commander Jambanja and the seven Defenders came for Simiso, the children of the nation, upon learning of the death of the Father of the Nation, broke down and wept.

HEARTBREAK NUMBER TWO

The Father of the Nation, already well on his journey into the land of the dead, was waiting with other new arrivals outside a large brick hall with a flashing yellow neon sign that said "Processing" above the door when he saw his grieving nation right in front of him, tholukuthi as if there were an invisible screen in the air. And when he saw them weep for him like that, his dearly beloved children, unconsoled and inconsolable, tholukuthi the Father of the Nation felt his heart break—which was the second time it was breaking, the first of course being during his lifetime, there, on that day of the coup, when the usurpers removed him and the children celebrated. Only this second time, the heartbreak was intense in comparison so that the Old Horse clutched at his battered heart, convinced by the pain that he was dying again, dying all over, dying anew, dying another death. Tholukuthi he let out the most heartrending wail ever heard in the Processing Center, and the Processing Center heard enough wailing every minute of the day.

But nobody attended him, until at some point, when he was in fact starting to get dizzy from pounding his head on the hard earth, a monkey in a long white robe, an unreadable name tag that matched her lipstick,

approached the Father of the Nation and said, "Pray tell, what seems to be the problem here?" And the Father of the Nation pointed and said, "It's my Jidada, it's my nation. See how they're heartbroken? See how they're in torment? I just can't die death and leave, I have to be repatriated, I have to go back to them." "But why?" the puzzled monkey said. "But why? You mean you can't see even for yourself?" the Old Horse gestured, exasperated. Which was when the monkey, with a face filled with a sympathy that didn't match her voice, said, "Oh sweetheart! Darling! Poor you! Come with me, just come."

HEARTBREAK NUMBER THREE

He followed the monkey through an endless labyrinth; when they did finally emerge he saw they were in a familiar place, and the place was familiar because they were on the streets of the only country he loved best. They didn't walk, him and the monkey, no, tholukuthi they floated, like butterflies, the Father of the Nation so happy to be back in his beloved Jidada with a -da and another -da he actually forgot he was dead and began belting the national anthem, the old revolutionary one. And he was touched to see animals who loved him with their true hearts, who could not deal with the fact of his untimely passing; they recalled between fitting torrents of tears who he was and what he'd meant and stood for and what he'd done for them and the whole of Jidada and even the whole of Africa itself.

But then no sooner had he and his escort begun moving deeper into the throngs than he realized that something was terribly wrong. Because he saw clearly, for the first time, that all the devastation, the weeping, all those torrential tears, the bodies in pain—everything that had broken his poor heart—tholukuthi none of it was for him. He heard the throngs tell foreign journalists that they were only crying for themselves. That they

were devastated for themselves for the things he'd done to them, they announced, for the anguish he'd brought unto their lives, they claimed, for the ruin he'd left Jidada in, they ranted, for the fact that he'd escaped paying for his crimes, dying without ever facing justice for the mass murders, the genocide, they lied, for the disappearances and deaths and torture and illegal arrests throughout his reign, they alleged, for his corruption and rights abuses and so many other ugly things they made up and charged because he was no longer there to speak for himself, things they never brought up when he was ruling and ruling and ruling.

The ugliness of the children of the nation devastated him, their ingratitude wounded him, their contempt angered him. Tholukuthi his heart broke all over again, for the third time. Betrayed, furious, wounded, offended, his heart in shreds, the Father of the Nation, the Liberator, Pan-Africanist, Critic in Chief of the West, Enemy of Sanctions, Enemy of Homosexuals, Opposer of the Opposition, Former Teacher, Education and Economic Empowerment Crusader, yes, him and only him himself, opened his mouth to address the miserable nation only to find that as he was dead, they wouldn't hear him. And so he just seethed inside, hurt inside, bled inside. He regretted being there because he could see he'd made a terrible mistake.

So that when the monkey said, "Have you seen enough, sweetie, are you ready to go?" he nodded. "Just get me away from these ugly children who have no gratitude for all that I did for them, who are liars of the worst order, who have no decency whatsoever to speak ill of the dead, which is downright un-African! Take me to my mother, I want to go to my mother in heaven!" the Father of the Nation cried. And for the first time the monkey looked at him very carefully and said, "Oh sweetheart! Sweetie! Darling! I'm not sure how to tell you this but I'd still hate for you to get there and be surprised. The thing is I can't really take you to your mother coz there's no heaven for tyrants of your kind, you see. What'll happen is you're off to, how do I put it, face your victims, and after you've met every

single one, depending of course on how many there are waiting for you, then, well, from there it's just, Hell, you see, sweetie," the monkey said. "What the hell do you mean, Hell?" the Father of the Nation shrieked, livid and scared all at once. But the monkey had vanished. And he was being whisked away by a mysterious force he couldn't see, couldn't fight. Tholukuthi the last thing the Father of the Nation heard from the only country he'd loved best was an ugly voice that said, "The Devil is dead! He is dead! We're weeping because with the recent events, we can all finally say this is the end of an era and error! Now we can begin again. Breathe again. Dream again. The Devil is dead, Glory Glory Glory he is dead!"

NEW FLAG

And on the very morning following the death of the Father of the Nation, the youngsters of Lozikeyi barged into Golden Maseko's studio without knocking, without a good morning, and, with their little tails wagging, heads bobbing up and down, thrust a crisp white bedsheet at the painter, demanded that he paint them a flag.

"Whoa, wait, on this right here? Where did you steal it?" Golden Maseko said, examining the sheet. He lived in a perpetual fog of devastating sadness since the death of his Destiny, and he now tried to hide his anguish from the little ones.

"But we didn't steal it, Simiso gave it to us," the squad chorused. A few of them carried pens behind their ears.

"Hmmm, Simiso gave this nice sheet to you to play with?" Golden Maseko said.

"Yes! It's not to play with, it's to make a flag. We told her what it's for and she gave it to us," the squad said.

"I see. But I don't know, I mean I've never painted on a sheet before,"

Golden Maseko said. The one face that was also the face of the entire squad fell.

"Very well, then. Tell me what you want on it," the artist said, reaching for his sketchbook.

"Okay okay okay. So you'll start by putting a fire here, right here. And it must look real so when you see it you can feel its warmth in your blood, like an actual, living fire," Gloria said. "And it should also look like it's blooming, like maybe a giant red lotus," Sydney said. "And make it a beautiful fire because a lotus is beautiful, you've never seen an ugly lotus," Nomatter said. "Make sure it shows that it's also the kind of fire to raze the things that no longer serve, so it's a fire that also purifies, that warms without burning, that lights without blinding," said Tha Dope Poet. "And also put butterflies in there somewhere, maybe around the fire, red butterflies," said Cebisani. "But maybe don't put a whole wedding of butterflies so that they're all over the place though," Prince said. "Even just one butterfly will be enough as long as we can look at it and know it's a butterfly, a red butterfly, as Cebisani said," Jealous said. "Remember to put all of a fire's colors in there too, because a fire isn't just one color, the Tyrant told us this at school," Dzikamai said. "You must obviously have the bright red, it's important, for justice," Hardlife said. "Then you'll have the white, for peace, peace is also very important," Pfuluwani said. "The blue will be for compassion," said Brendon. "And orange, for prosperity," said Lele. "And bright yellow, for integrity," Takudzwa said. "And then you make sure that all those colors in there tell whoever is looking that they also represent all different kinds of Jidadans, whoever and whatever they are, that too is important—a Jidada for anyone and everyone no matter the differences, and all are equally the same," Brilliant said. "And then after you put it all in there, you make sure it's a fire that burns all the time," Karabo said. "He means like an eternal fire," Roland said. "What else?" Nyarai said. "I think we should have a tree in there too, trees are

life," S'khonapha said. "The best tree will be the Nehanda tree," Last said. "Yes, the Nehanda tree, and please include Nehanda's bones so we don't forget to rise and free ourselves like Comrade Nevermiss Nzinga, like the adults finally did, and so we don't forget the other deads," Kgosi said. "He means the ancestors, and they are not dead, Sis Destiny told me, and the Duchess agreed," Gloria said. "Make it exactly as we told you, Golden Maseko," Simba said. "Because if you don't make it exactly as we told you we'll sue you, we know our rights," Challenge said. "And then you'll find us a pole like the one they use for flags," Konanani said. "Yes, together with a rope, because we don't want a plaything, we want like a real flag," Kendra said. "A proper flag," Sibusiso said. "Then we'll show you where to put the flag," Nqobile said. "And finish fast, Golden Maseko, because we have things to do," Matha said.

A few days later, tholukuthi a day that would in the future be celebrated as Jidada's new Independence Day, Golden Maseko finished designing the children's flag exactly as he'd been instructed. The process of working on the piece had lifted the heaviness in his heart and filled it with a lightness he hadn't felt since the murder of Destiny. And while his sadness was still there like a faithful shadow, the fog had cleared, and he could see. He hoisted the flag right by the Wall of the Dead, the pole planted just inside Simiso's yard. He was so in love with the beautiful piece he made the children pose with the flag. The painter was getting ready to take the picture when Comrade Nevermiss Nzinga, who, together with her friends, had been sitting with Simiso, having tea, came out of house number 636 to see what the hullabaloo was all about. And when Comrade Nevermiss Nzinga saw the flag she called for her sister friends to come out, and out came the Duchess and Gogo Moyo and Mother of God, the Prayer Warriors, Sis Nomzamo, and a few members of the Sisters of the Disappeared, and Na-Dumi, Mrs. Phiri, Mrs. Fengu, and finally, Simiso.

And from nearby houses out came other neighbors, tholukuthi mothers

who left their pots cooking on stoves, and out came their beautiful little ones, and out came the grandparents of those beautiful little ones, tholukuthi old but glowing with new life, and curious passersby on their way to SPAR Supermarket or visits or errands or wherever it was they were headed, also stopped to see because seeing was free in Lozikeyi, and then out came the birds and the ants and snakes and cockroaches, flies, mice, dung beetles, millipedes, and insects of Lozikeyi, and out came the sun from the deep furrows of clouds where it'd burrowed itself for most of the day, and out came the dead, who were not dead, led by Destiny herself, with Dr. Future Fengu and her grandfather Butholezwe Henry Vulindlela Khumalo on either side, even though no one but the Duchess could see them, and who floated to hold the flag up even as it didn't need holding, and sang praises to the living for having the courage to liberate themselves at long last—tholukuthi with their eyes that could see across time, the dead could already behold the greatness that awaited Jidada now that evil had finally fallen.

It would otherwise have been a better crowd, a bigger crowd, but it was late afternoon and the older, school-going animals were yet to return from schools, and the adults were at the new jobs that'd recently mushroomed and were still mushrooming to finally yank Jidadans off the streets, off their verandas, off their feet, off their behinds, off their despair, off their wagons of poverty, but it didn't matter because still, a short while later, as the pictures and clips of the children of Lozikeyi's flag were going viral on social media, the new workers took breaks from their various occupations and gathered around their gadgets and watched the flag flutter against the brilliant blue sky, yes, tholukuthi watching with hearts whirring for they recognized the new flag they'd been waiting for.

And every one of them—tholukuthi the ones gathered under the children's flag in Lozikeyi, outside Simiso's house, by the Wall of the Dead, and those looking at the flag from gadgets in the different wherevers of

Jidada with a -da and another -da—felt their bodies receive the gift of well-being from the Nehanda tree, whose white fruits reminded them they were also Nehanda's bones she once prophesized would rise. And every one of them felt warmed by the beautiful lotus fire. And every one of them heard the flames of that fire fan and flutter and roar right in their hearts. And every one of them understood that whatever they heard within those hearts was the new national anthem, tholukuthi an anthem that spoke of the kind of glory that burns eternal and glows with living light.

Tholukuthi the End.

ACKNOWLEDGMENTS

I wish to acknowledge, in no particular order:

The Jidadas of the world, clamoring for freedom on many fronts—A luta continua.

My grandmother Elizabeth Moyo and her miserable 💜 son, Noel Robinson Tshele; every storyteller I've known and every storyteller they've known; all my creative writing teachers and their creative writing teachers. How it takes a village, how you all fuel this book, how I'm grateful. Ngiyabonga m'na.

All my readers; tholukuthi we meet again. Your love and support still humble me.

The Zimbabwean sister I met in Francistown, Botswana, in 2018, both of us shopping for groceries. For ingqobe, for reminding me of what storytelling can do, and for trusting in my pen.

I'm thankful to the voices of my compatriots on social media platforms for helping me keep a pulse on some of the book's concerns. A special thanks to the News and Analysis peeps on WhatsApp for letting me be a fly on their brilliant, horizon-expanding wall.

I'm indebted to many inspiring Zimbabweans whose work enriched this project, including Zenzele Ndebele, Sipho Malunga, Alex Magaisa, and Hopewell Chin'ono. I also want to acknowledge admired fellow artists: Peter Godwin,

John Eppel, Christopher Mlalazi, Owen Maseko, Novuyo Tshuma, and of course the inimitable and much-remembered Sis Yvonne Vera, for their silence-breaking work—umkhulu lomsebenzi, much, much love and respect.

Laura Tisdel, Becky Hardie, Nicole Winstanley—my superb book editors. For understanding my vision and making sure I delivered its best version. For your keen and careful reading, for your confidence and unwavering commitment, for your trust, tholukuthi for the absolute joy of working with you. Thank you feels inadequate.

The excellent Kym Surridge, Nicole Wayland, and Jane Cavolina, copy editor and proofreaders, for making *Glory* sing; head bowed. Everyone in Viking production, publicity, sales, and marketing—my sincere gratitude.

Jin Auh, my treasured champion. Because I'm in the bestest of hands.

Alba Ziegler-Bailey, Charles Buchan, and everyone at the Wylie Agency. All my editors and publishers for giving my work loving homes.

Eavan Boland—bath' umuntu ubongw' esefile, dearest Eavan, thank you, lala ngoxolo. Elizabeth Tallent, Christina Ablaza, and former colleagues and students at the Stanford Creative Writing Program.

The Hodder Fellowship at Princeton. The J. M. D. Manyika Fellowship, Professor Henry Louis Gates, and Krishna Lewis at the Hutchins Center for African & African American Research at Harvard University. The Lannan Foundation, and Douglas Humble for taking care of me at Marfa. The Stellenbosch Institute for Advanced Study: Christoff Pauw and Edward K. Kirumira—for the needed start, and for the generosity when it mattered most. The Johannesburg Institute for Advanced Study: Bongani Ngqulunga, Emelia Kamena, Sivuyile Momoza, Reshmi Singh, Vanessa Kennedy, and the JIAS 2019 cohort, including, of course, Chef Malume, who fed me like the relative of the wife.

My countless friends and family, especially those who kept me intact in the recent few years of personal crisis. You know who you are: much gratitude, much love, much respect, and the deepest bow: ngingumuntu ngani, bantu.

Mildred Anti. Dearest baTshele. For riding with me while I was researching

this book: for bringing the magic and the light and the joy, for freeing me, and for the perfect gift of you. Dad'wethu kababa, ende ngikuthanda thandi!

Zazu. Dearest Zazu, Zazu always, and Zazu forever; thank you for all that can never be said.

And last but not least, the ancestors, tholukuthi who are not dead. Angi-hambi ngedwa!